The Bowl of Souls: Book Three

HUNT of the BANDHAM

By: Trevor H. Cooley

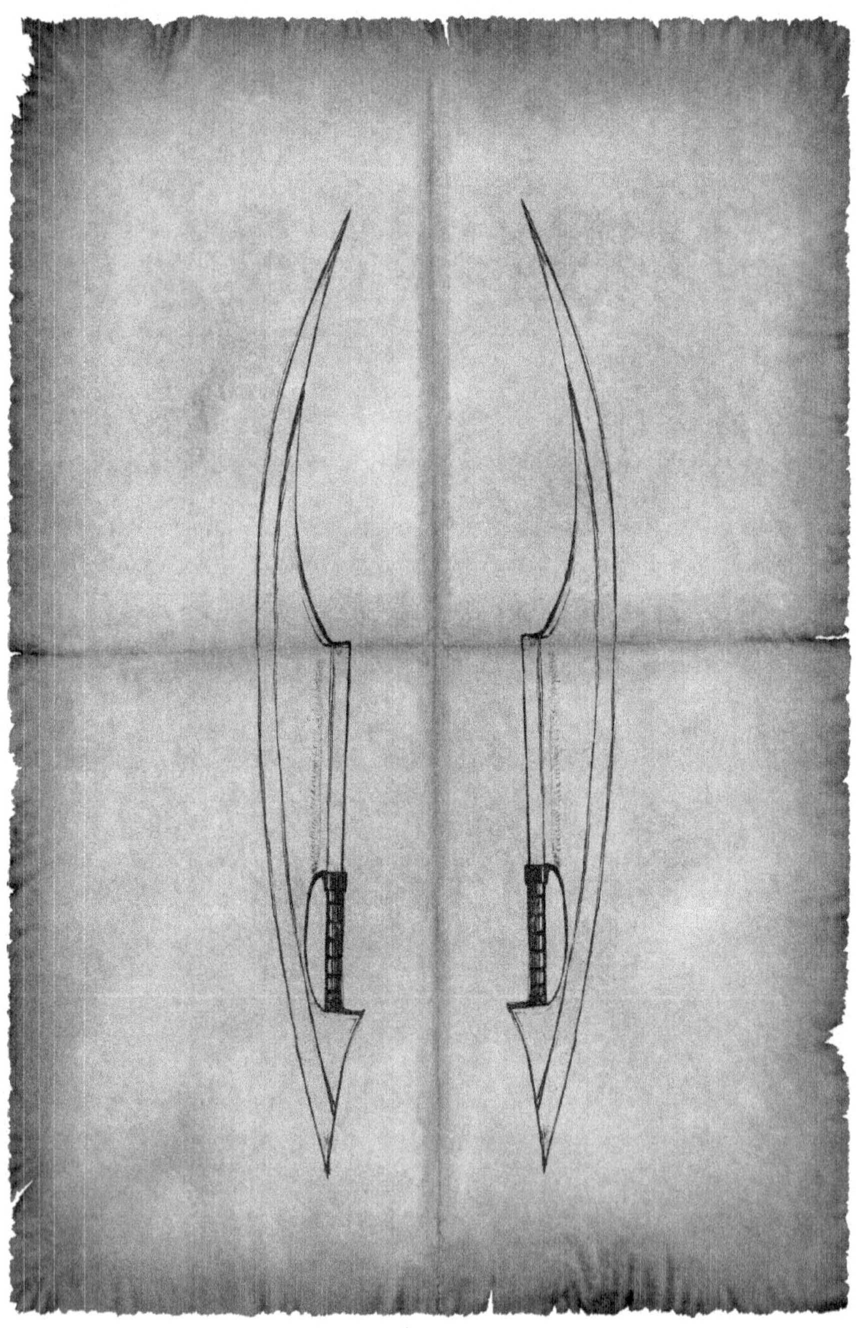

Cover art by: Justin Cooley

Map: Michael Patty

The Bowl of Souls Series:

The Moonrat Saga:

Book One: **EYE of the MOONRAT**

Book 1.5 : **HILT'S PRIDE**

Book Two: **MESSENGER of the DARK PROPHET**

Book Three: **HUNT of the BANDHAM**

Book Four: **The WAR of STARDEON**

Book Five: **MOTHER of the MOONRAT**

The Jharro Grove Saga :

Book One: **Tarah Woodblade**

Book Two: **Protector of the Grove**

Book Three: **The Ogre Apprentice**

Dedication

This book is dedicated to you. Yes, specifically you, the reader who has taken a chance on a relatively unknown author and spent your hard-earned money on my first two books. Here you are, back for the third and . . . I love you.

I tried for years to get my book noticed, but I couldn't find any agents or publishers that were interested. Some friends encouraged me to publish on my own, but I felt like my books wouldn't be a success unless I had a publisher's name on the spines like the fantasy novels I grew up reading. This story and these characters had been living in my mind since I was a teenager. I wanted to give them the chance they deserved, and I worried that by putting them out there on my own I would be cheapening them somehow.

One night in May 2012, I was researching about publishing books on Kindle. I downloaded the instructions and it felt right, so I just did it. It was a whim. I didn't even have a cover at the time. I had no idea what to expect. I told my friends and family about it and downloads started to trickle in. When I put out the second book two months later, that trickle became a stream.

I am blown away every time I think about it. You noticed my book. You read it. Some of you cared enough to tell your friends and write reviews. Those reviews are the lifeblood of an independent book series! Thank you, and please keep doing what you're doing. I'll get going on the next book.

Trevor H. Cooley - 09/04/2012

The Thunder People
Jack's Rest
Trafalgan Mountains
Academy
Reneul
Wobble
Pinewood
Dark Forest
Sampo
Silvertree Elves
Mage School
Tinny Woods
Fandine River
N
W
E
S
Wide River
Malgroo

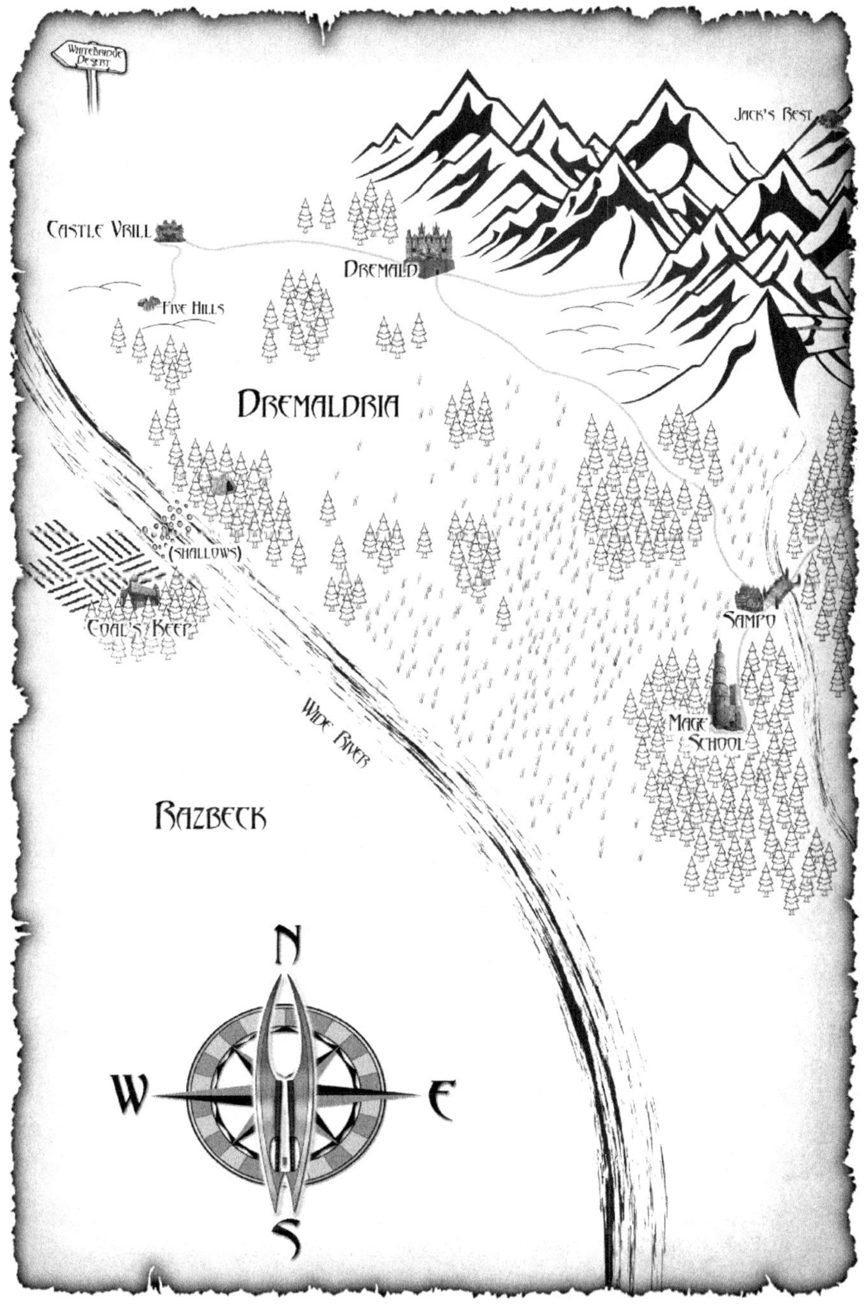

WhiteBridge Desert
Jack's Rest
Castle Vrill
Dremald
Five Hills
Dremaldria
(Shallows)
Coal's Keep
Sampo
Mage School
Wide River
Razbeck
N
W
E
S

Prologue

Deathclaw and Talon darted through the winter-frozen forest. Their lithe, scaled bodies glistened in the beams of sunlight that pierced the boughs of the fir trees. Their claws left behind deep trenches in the snow, but they didn't bother covering their tracks. They didn't fear pursuit. The scent of freedom filled Talon's nostrils, while Deathclaw was simply elated at finding her. They frolicked through the daylight hours, racing each other and putting as much distance between them and the wizard's castle as possible.

Once they had been part of a pack of raptoids, wingless dragon-like creatures that hunted the desert dunes of the Whitebridge Desert. The wizard Ewzad Vriil had come upon their pack looking to create soldiers for his army. The changes caused by the wizard's cruel experiments had killed the others, but Deathclaw escaped and his sister had been taken back to the wizard's castle.

It had taken over a year, but Deathclaw had found the wizard's castle. He fought his way through the mutated monsters that Ewzad Vriil had created and now, despite his wounds that were still healing, Deathclaw felt no pain. He was happy for the first time since the wizard had changed his body. Though he would never again be able to return to his old life as leader of a raptoid pack, the new life ahead of him looked to be full of promise. He wasn't alone any more.

As the sun sank behind the horizon and darkness crept in, they caught the scent of a herd of mountain elk. Deathclaw let forth a throaty chirp and the two transformed raptoids fell back into their old familiar hunting pattern. When they came upon the herd, they stayed downwind so as not to frighten the animals. The elk had stopped for the night in a clearing. The females and young were huddled in the center while the males stayed around the outside for protection.

Deathclaw had his eye on one particularly old buck that would provide more than enough meat for both of them. He was excited. Prey this large stayed away from the dwellings of the humans and he had not eaten a meal larger than a rabbit in weeks.

He chirped a command to Talon, telling her to circle around for support. Then he snuck up as close as possible. When the time was right, he pounced. Deathclaw leapt onto the back of the old buck. The beast reared and thrashed its head back and forth, but Deathclaw nimbly avoided its pointed horns. He tore out the elk's throat from behind with his wicked claws and leapt from its back as it fell dying.

Deathclaw screeched in triumph. But Talon wasn't satisfied with the single kill.

In the brief second of uncertainty caused by the suddenness of Deathclaw's attack, the herd froze. Talon darted into the center of the clearing and began slashing about with her claws, teeth, and tail barb, cutting throats and disemboweling does and young elk. By the time the herd thundered away, four females and three younglings lay dead around her. From the thick trails of blood left behind the fleeing animals, Deathclaw knew that several more would die from their wounds.

Deathclaw watched his sister with his head cocked as she tore at the corpses and screeched with pleasure. What she had done didn't make sense. She had ignored the hunting instincts that raptoids had been born with for centuries. When attacking a herd, it was best to bring down the weak, the old, the infirm. They were easier kills and the survivors would live to grow and breed and produce more food for the hunting pack. Not only had Talon cut down the wrong prey, she had killed far more than the two of them could ever eat.

Deathclaw chirped at Talon questioningly. She ignored him as she continued to rip the bodies apart, destroying the meat as if he weren't even there. He watched her reveling in the blood and chaos. She hadn't killed for food. She had killed for pleasure.

Deathclaw was suddenly wary of his brood mate. The wizard

had done more to her than just alter her body. Like Deathclaw, she was no longer a raptoid, but something different. Something terrible.

Chapter One

Wincing, Justan reached out with one foot and prodded the pile of richly embroidered clothes that remained where Ewzad Vriil had once stood. Part of him expected a hand full of squirming fingers to reach from the pile and grasp his leg. But nothing happened.

It had been nearly an hour since the wizard's apparent death and Justan was the first one to approach the spot. He didn't know if it had been fear that had kept the others away, or just the fact that everyone wanted to move on. Perhaps it was a mixture of both.

Though the wizard's body had disappeared completely, Justan's mage sight showed some trace of magic left in the stain upon the ground. He moved the pile of clothing with his foot to get a better look at the stain and heard a clang of metal.

He carefully moved the pile again to reveal the dark bladed dagger that Princess Elise had plunged into the wizard's arm. Justan crouched down and reached to pick up the dagger, but paused. For some reason, he didn't want to touch it. His mage sight didn't show anything magical about it, but something about the dagger seemed . . . wrong.

Justan shook his head. Yet another mystery to add to the daunting heap that already surrounded him. There were too many questions and not near enough answers.

He ripped a piece of silk from Ewzad's robe and wrapped the dagger in it, careful not to touch the metal. He tucked it into the back of his ragged pants. Perhaps he would ask Qyxal about it later. The elf was much more experienced in magic than him.

Justan stood and looked across the throne room and once again found himself impressed with Captain Demetrius' organizational skills. The captain had taken charge of the chaos immediately after the wizard had disappeared, directing any men that would stop and listen. Things were already moving smoothly and efficiently.

The wounded were lined up in a row against the back wall of the throne room. Qyxal was busy healing the men most severely injured, while any other men with medical skills had been set to work tending those with minor injuries. Ewzad Vriil's serving staff had come to the captain with clean water and bandages and offered their services. None of them looked sad to see their master dead.

This was going to be a long process. The wounded were still piling up as the dungeons emptied. The old keep had belonged in Ewzad Vrill's family for generations and the nobles had never stopped expanding the dungeons. There were prisoners who had been in there for years. Many of them were so close to death that there was very little the elf was able to do.

The captain had commandeered the contractors building the castle and set them to digging holes for the graves of the dead prisoners. He was determined to give them all a proper burial, even the soldiers and guards that had died trying to keep the prisoners from escaping. After all, they had only been following orders.

One person in particular was being given a place of honor. The misshapen remains of Sneaky Pete's body rested under a clean white sheet to the side of the throne room until he could be given the burial he deserved.

The dead goblins and orcs, on the other hand, were to be dragged into a great pile to the side of the castle to be burned. Fist and Gwyrtha were helping dispose of the bodies now. The ogre had torn a large ornate tapestry from the wall and he and Gwyrtha were busy piling the bodies of the beasts on top of it.

Justan was about to join them when he felt a hand on his shoulder.

"Been busy chasin' down that last orc or else I would'a been here to see you sooner. Durn thing was slippery. Chased him fer durn near a mile into the forest."

"Lenny!" Justan enveloped the dwarf in a warm embrace. He almost burst into tears, but forced them down. It would only embarrass his friend.

"Hey now. Hey now." Lenny half-heartedly tried to push him away, but finally patted him on the back. "Calm down, son. No need fer a scene."

Justan pulled back and laughed at the sight of the familiar red handlebar mustache and gap-toothed grin. "Thank you for coming after me."

"Hell, I didn't do nothin'. It looks to me like you had everthin' well in han- . . ." The dwarf's eyes widened. "Wait a gall-durn minute! What's that on yer hand, boy?" The dwarf grabbed Justan's right hand and pulled it closer. His bushy eyebrows rose in surprise and his jaw dropped as he saw the warrior rune. "I'll be dag-gummed."

Justan covered the warrior rune up with his left hand. "Well, I . . . er. I don't understand it myself. It was a bit of a shock."

"Well, tell me all about it, then!" Lenny exclaimed.

Justan looked around and no one seemed to be listening in. He told Lenny about his time at the Mage School; how he had been given the new name Edge and marked as both warrior and wizard; how Gwyrtha had been captured; and how he had been forced to leave the school in order to protect her. The dwarf leaned forward and listened intently, hanging on every word, twirling the end of his handlebar mustache with his forefinger. When Justan showed him the wizard rune on the palm of his left hand, Lenny whistled through his missing tooth.

"The council seemed to think that what happened was impossible." Justan said. He looked down at the runes and shook his head. "They may be right, too. I don't have the skills or powers to go along with this new name, Lenny. I . . . I don't feel worthy of it."

Lenny looked hard at Justan, his lips pursed thoughtfully. "Then maybe you ain't."

"What? Really? You think so?" Justan hadn't expected such a quick agreement. Everyone else seemed to think he was being childish to reject the name.

The dwarf wasn't finished. "But that part ain't up to you is it?

The magic of that bowl ain't like normal magic, son. There's powers behind that thing beyond anythin' you or I ever seen, mark my words on that. One thing's fer blasted sure. There's somethin' special inside you and that bowl done saw it."

"Like what, Lenny?" Justan's frustration over the naming bubbled over. "What's so special about me? I haven't done anything yet! I'm still just a trainee who hasn't gotten into the Battle Academy. I wanted to earn my way, not have it given to me!"

Lenny raised a finger to his lips in warning and Justan saw that people had started to stare. He had grown so agitated that Fist and Gwyrtha had stopped momentarily in their work wondering if he needed help. *It's okay*, he assured them through the bond.

Lenny gave Justan a look that told him a lecture was coming and yanked a thumb toward one of the side doors. The dwarf led Justan out of the throne room into a long hallway. He pushed open the first door they came to and dragged Justan inside what looked to be a guest bedroom. It was lavishly outfitted with rich furs and silks. Justan instantly felt out of place in the rags that were left of his travel clothes.

"Use that thick skull of yers, dag-gum it! People out there are lookin' up to you. You helped save their lives. This ain't the time to be complainin' where folks might hear!" Lenny poked one thick finger painfully into Justan's chest. "Maybe yer not worthy of yer new name yet, who knows? But you got a new name all the same. Who're you to decide when yer worthy, or when you ain't? Yer name's Edge. That's who you gal-durn are whether yer gal-durn worthy of it or not!"

"But it doesn't seem real to me!" Justan retorted. "I mean, in my heart I still see myself as Justan, son of Faldon the Fierce."

"Of course you do." Lenny snorted and partial grin reappeared on his face. "Part of you always will be that angry kid who couldn't fight. Hell, son, part of me's still the wild young dwarf who didn't know a smith's hammer from his own arse. But things change. When I last saw you, you was just startin' to turn into a man, but when I came into the throne room durin' the fight, I almost didn't recognize you. I mean, look at you, dag-blast it!"

The dwarf grabbed Justan's shoulders and turned him to face a full length mirror that was mounted on the wall beside the bed. What he saw surprised him. Standing in that mirror was not the gawky youth that had failed training school. He had grown in the last two years. His frame had filled out. The work Jhonate had put him through along with his obsessive training at the Mage School had turned his weak body into one a warrior would be proud of. The man looking back at him was well toned and imposing. If not for the ragged clothing, the warrior rune would have looked fitting on the back of the hand of this new man.

"I-I . . . I see what you are trying to say Lenny. But I still don't feel worthy and . . ." He shook his head and looked down. Part of him knew that Lenny was right. He shouldn't be ashamed of his new name. But still, he couldn't help but feel awkward about it. "I just don't like having my life changed for me."

Lenny patted his shoulder.

"Sometimes you gotta accept the things you can't control, son. Yer Edge now, like it or not. You can worry about bein' worthy of it later."

Justan nodded his head and looked back at the man standing in the mirror before him. Underneath his ragged shirt, he actually had pecs.

"Well that's enough of that fer now. You could durn well use some better clothes." Lenny began rustling through a wardrobe at the side of the bed. He swore a few times and tossed some fancy apparel aside, but finally pulled out a plain shirt, a fine padded leather jacket, and a pair of long baggy pants that didn't look too frilly. He handed them to Justan and patted him on the back. "C'mon, boy, put 'em on and let's get outta' here. I wanna show you somethin'."

They walked back through the throne room and out the front doors into the bright sun-drenched air. Justan had to put a hand up to shield his sensitive eyes. He hadn't seen the sun in four days. He took in a deep breath and smiled. Despite the bitter cold of the winter breeze, the sunlight felt warm on his body. It was a sensation he had doubted he would ever feel again. He followed Lenny down the long stairway to the courtyard where two familiar warhorses stood calmly chewing the grass.

While Justan scratched Albert and Stanza behind the ears in greeting, Lenny fumbled with a strap to the side of Stanza's saddle and pulled out two sheathed swords.

"These're replacements fer the swords Hilt gave you. Be a bit more careful with these-uns, okay? No breakin' 'em on orcs or nothin'."

"Thank you." Justan unsheathed the swords and stared. He had grown up near the premier warrior school in the known lands and he had rarely seen this level of workmanship. The pommels were etched in silver and the handles wrapped in soft leather for an excellent grip. A goofy grin stretched his lips and he whirled the swords about him, testing their balance. They were excellent.

"Sorry, son, but this was the best I could do at such short notice." Lenny mumbled.

"No, Lenny." Justan shook his head. "You have outdone yourself. These swords are even better than the ones Hilt gave me."

The dwarf shrugged. "They may be, but they still ain't fittin' fer a named warrior. Don't matter how well made they is if they don't sing."

"There's plenty of time for making magical ones later." Justan assured him. An excited gleam came into his eye. "I even have a great idea to put past you. I was doing some research in the Mage School library and I came upon the most fascinating weapon. I have some sketches of it in Gwyrtha's saddlebags."

A shadow passed over Lenny's countenance and he seemed as though about to say something more, but he was distracted by the sight of Fist and Gwyrtha pulling something out of the entrance of the castle. Slowly, the ogre and the rogue horse began backing down the stairs.

Justan looked up to see what the dwarf was looking at and was puzzled until he realized that they were dragging a tapestry loaded down with over a score of dead goblins and orcs. Fist had both gigantic hands wrapped around one corner of the tapestry while Gwyrtha was grasping the other with her razor sharp front teeth.

Justan almost laughed aloud at the strange sight, but a shout pierced the air.

"Hey you! Ogre!"

Fist looked up in puzzlement as a man dressed in worn travel clothes ran down the stairs and stood before him breathing heavily. There was anger and despair etched into the man's face.

"Are you Fist?" Zambon asked.

The ogre nodded, and Justan could sense that Fist wasn't sure why this man would know him. Then again, something about his face seemed somehow familiar. It didn't take long for him to figure out why. The memories Justan had shared with him through the bond came to the forefront of his mind. A grin split Fist's face and he dropped his corner of the tapestry. The bodies of several goblins rolled free and tumbled down the stairs.

Fist clasped one hand on each shoulder of the man and gripped him warmly.

"You are Zambon, son of Tamboor!"

Zambon pulled out of Fist's grip.

"Yes. My family has written me about you," he said. Desperation filled Zambon's dark eyes. "Tell me. Were you there when Jack's Rest was attacked?"

Fist nodded hesitantly, unsure of the man's intentions. This man was Tamboor's son and Justan's friend, therefore part of his adopted tribe, but Fist still did not know him. Was he angry that he had not been able to protect his family? Would he attack? Fist did not want to have to hurt Tamboor's son.

"Hey Zambon," Justan said.

"Tell me what happened to my family!" Zambon demanded.

Fist hesitated. "That is for Tamboor to tell."

"He won't tell me anything!" Zambon shouted, frustration thick in his voice. "When I found him, he was lost in some sort of rage. He was hacking away madly at the body of an orc and screaming. He wouldn't stop! When I finally shook him out of it, he . . . he pulled me to his chest and wouldn't let go. I asked him over and over where they were, but he wouldn't tell me! He wouldn't say anything! He wouldn't even look at me! He just turned and ran down into the dungeon."

"Please, Fist," Zambon pleaded. "If you are truly a friend of my family, tell me. Where is my mother? Where are Cedric and Lina?"

Fist looked down. He felt inadequate with his speaking. He had learned a lot of the human's way of using the common speech from Tamboor's family and since bonding with Justan it seemed a bit easier, but how could he say all the things that Zambon needed to know? He opened his mouth but no sound came out. Justan's voice echoed into his mind, sending soothing thoughts.

It's okay, Fist. He is my friend. I'll tell him.

"Tell me!" Zambon yelled.

Justan arrived at Fist's side. "Zambon."

Zambon whirled to face him. Tears were in the guard's eyes. "Why won't anyone tell me what happened?"

"Zambon, I am sorry, I-"

"No," Fist said, his deep voice rumbling through the air. "I will tell him." The ogre grasped Zambon's shoulders again in his gigantic hands and said, "They are killed."

Zambon looked into the ogre's sad blue eyes and stood still. His lips quivered. "I . . . I thought so."

"Your father and me and Pete, we tried to stop them but the wizard, he . . . froze us. The orcs, they . . . we can not move . . ." Fist searched for the words. His voice trembled and great tears rolled from his eyes. "The orcs did bad things and . . . and Efflina, Cedric, Lina. I-I am sorry. They-they were my tribe and I could not save them."

Fist dropped his gaze in shame. Zambon nodded. The guard's face was pained, his eyes red-rimmed.

Fist's hands fell from Zambon's shoulders. "Your father. Tamboor, he is . . . hurt. His head and heart are . . . broken. The wizard m-made him watch."

Zambon slumped in understanding. "I must go find him." He stepped back from the ogre and walked away from them, ascending the steps towards the castle.

"Zambon!" Justan called out as the guard reached the top of the steps. "It was your father's sword that slew the wizard." Zambon froze for a moment at his words and Justan saw the guard's head nod once before he continued into the castle.

"Poor boy." Lenny shook his head. He squeezed the handle of

his hammer until the leather creaked. “Dag-blast it! I wish there was more orcs around to kill.”

Chapter Two

Justan had hoped to leave the castle right away, but there was too much to be done. By the time the dead were cleared away it was late afternoon. Then he found out that there were still a few men that Qyxal had not finished healing and Captain Demetrius asked them to stay the night.

Captain Demetrius had the castle staff prepare a feast for all of the escapees that still remained. It was the best meal that Justan had eaten since leaving the Mage School and he enjoyed it immensely. Fist ate more than any two men, while Lenny raided Ewzad Vriil's private wine stores.

"All that money and it still ain't as good as my pepperbean wine," the dwarf grumbled after emptying a dusty old bottle and tossing it aside.

After the meal, Captain Demetrius gathered any that would stay. Fist excused himself politely and Justan wanted to leave with him but Lenny's pointed gaze compelled him to remain in his seat. Tamboor still hadn't come out of the dungeons and Zambon had given up the search for his father for the time being. The guard sat at the table quietly, a full wine goblet sitting unnoticed in his hand.

The captain cleared his throat. "Thank you for staying here with me a bit longer. What I wish to discuss could have repercussions for all of us. I am going to have to put together a full report for the king. He and Duke Vriil were close. He won't be happy to hear that his best friend is dead. You need to understand that if he is not satisfied with my explanation, we could all soon have a price on our heads."

Justan winced. He hadn't thought about that.

"Come on. King Muldroomon's got to understand considerin' all that happened here," Lenny said.

"I am confident that under normal circumstances the King would understand," the Captain said. "But from what I hear the King has been, well . . . unstable lately. What I'm saying is when you leave here, stay inconspicuous and keep an ear out for the King's decision. If I am unable to convince him, you will need to stay out of Dremaldria."

There were several murmurs among the group, the loudest among them being Lenny, who openly grumbled about the worth of a king who couldn't see reason. Captain Demetrius cleared his throat and turned to Justan.

"Sir Edge, if you please, I was hoping you might answer a few questions. You see I need to learn as much about what the duke was doing as possible if I am to make a convincing case. Can you add anything?"

Justan told the captain everything he could think of that would help. He told him of the duke's men that were hiding along the roads posing as brigands. He told him about the altered orc he had killed and how he had seen the duke use magic to seduce the princess into going to the castle with him.

"What does the princess say about all this?" Justan asked. "Surely she could convince her brother that Duke Vriil was in the wrong. She did say that he killed her father after all."

"I've asked, but she refuses to speak of it and I'm afraid I can't force her to tell her brother anything. She just wants to go home." Captain Demetrius placed a hand on Justan's shoulder. "You have filled in some of the missing pieces, though. Thank you, Sir Edge. It is indeed fortunate that the duke was destroyed before he could bring whatever he was planning to fruition." He looked into Justan's eyes. "Will you come with me and present this information to the King?"

"Uh, w-well," Justan stammered. He hadn't been expecting such a request. "No. I mean, I am sorry sir, but it is not my place. Um, I have a quest of my own to complete and it really can't wait."

"I see," said the captain, looking disappointed.

Justan thought about it some more. Was he being selfish? He

needed to continue to Master Coal's as commanded by Wizard Valtrek, but could it wait a little longer while he helped the captain?

No, he decided. He thought back to the night they had left the Mage School; how he had fallen too deeply into the bond and what he had almost done to Gwyrtha. Now he was bonded twice and he needed to learn how to control the magic before things got out of control. The wizard's threat was gone and the captain could figure out what to do on his own.

"I think you are ignoring the real danger here," Qyxal said. The elf had remained at the table despite being exhausted from the heavy use of healing magic. "You heard him, didn't you? Ewzad Vriil called himself 'The Messenger of the Dark Prophet'."

There was silence for a while. Of course they had heard what the wizard had said. Everyone in the throne room had heard. In fact they had all been avoiding the subject. If the Dark Prophet were truly back, then a price on their heads would be the least of their worries. Captain Demetrius assured the elf that he would tell King Muldroomon everything and quickly dismissed the meeting.

Captain Demetrius invited Justan to stay in one of the luxurious castle guest rooms. He was certainly tempted by the thought of a warm bed. Lenny and Qyxal had agreed readily enough, but Fist didn't want to spend another night inside the castle and had decided to sleep in the stable with Gwyrtha. So Justan declined the captain's invitation. He took some extra blankets with him instead.

As Justan carried the load of blankets through the courtyard on the way to the stables, thoughts of Ewzad Vriil's true purpose weighed heavily on his mind. What if Qyxal's fears were right? What if the Dark Prophet was back? The prospects were frightening. It had taken decades for the world to recover the last time the Dark Prophet had awakened.

The smells of hay and manure soon filled the air and Justan reached the stable door. He stepped inside and sighed. The stable was only slightly warmer than the courtyard outside. The thought of a soft bed still tugged at his mind.

The stables were dark and quiet. Gwyrtha was already asleep, curled up on her side very un-horselike in the straw. Justan reached down and ran one hand down her side, feeling the patchwork mix of scales and horseflesh beneath his hand. She looked a monster, and fought like a monster, but inside she was the sweetest creature he knew. He had missed her.

Fist was still awake. Justan could sense that the ogre's thoughts were full of indecision.

"You could have stayed for the meeting with us," Justan said.

Fist snorted. "They did not want me. They do not trust an ogre."

"Of course they do," Justan replied unconvincingly. Even though everyone had been cordial to the ogre once the fighting was over, it was obvious that the humans had avoided him when possible. "Well, okay, not everyone is used to having an ogre around." He was still getting used to the idea himself, in fact. Justan changed the subject. "I brought a blanket for you." He set them down and pulled out the largest comforter the servants had been able to find. He handed it to the ogre.

"Thank you," Fist said. The ogre sniffed at it and squeezed the material as if wondering how it was going to keep anything warm.

"Um, you just cover yourself in it. Here." Justan opened the blanket up and draped it over the ogre. It barely covered Fist's large frame.

"Like a fur." Fist said. He sent Justan thoughts of huddling under a pile of furs with the other ogres during cold nights. "But smells . . . nicer."

"Kind of like that." Justan laughed. He sent memories through the bond of warm blankets on cold nights while sleeping in a soft bed in his house at home. The fond memories held a trace of sadness for him. He realized how much he missed his parents.

The ogre had never slept in the kind of comfort he felt in Justan's memories. The smells though . . . they reminded Fist of the smells inside Tamboor's house. He ran one hand along the outside of the comforter. It was so soft. His legs were already starting to feel warm. He liked it.

Justan moved towards Gwyrtha and pulled some straw aside. He draped a sheet over it, before grabbing the other blankets. He started to lay down, then paused guiltily. "I didn't think to bring an extra sheet.

Sorry Fist."

"Why you sleep here?" Fist asked. "The other ones sleep in the big stone house with . . . blankets and beds."

"It didn't feel right," Justan tried to explain. "I . . . couldn't sleep in comfort like that knowing that you were out here in the straw alone."

"She is here," Fist said, pointing to Gwyrtha's sleeping form in the darkness.

"So, uh, have you decided what you are going to do?" Justan said, changing the subject once again. It was okay that Fist did not understand his gesture. He didn't fully understand it either. There was just something about the thought of leaving the ogre out in the stable alone that made him feel as though he was treating Fist like he wasn't as important as everyone else.

It was so dark that Justan couldn't see the ogre shaking his head, but he could sense it through their bond. Fist had not yet decided whether he was going to come with Justan or go back into the mountains, perhaps with Zambon and Tamboor if that is what they wished to do.

"Well, I would be honored if you decided to come with me." Justan said sincerely. The ogre nodded again.

It was quiet for a while and Justan's thoughts wandered back to darker matters. He could sense that Fist was still awake too. "Do you think that Ewzad Vriil was really an agent of the Dark prophet?"

"Don't know," Fist replied.

"Well, let's say he wasn't. What do you think that his armies in the mountains will do once he is dead?"

"They fight each other. Then they go home," Fist said. "The tribes do not like the goblins and slimy ones." There was a snap of hatred in Fist's voice with the mention of the goblins and trolls. Several of the horses, already nervous over the smell of an ogre in the stable, whinnied in fright.

"But what if the wizard was speaking the truth?" Justan whispered.

I do not know, Fist's mind rumbled, speaking through the bond this time for fear of scaring the horses again. *The Barldag sends someone else. Then they attack the little peoples again.*

Somehow, Justan felt that the latter scenario was going to be the correct one. He hoped that his instincts were wrong. It would be better if Ewzad Vriil had been lying. It didn't matter, though. There was nothing he could do about it anyway. His mission was to find Master Coal. Justan closed his eyes and despite his troubled thoughts, he soon fell asleep.

The next morning Fist shook Justan awake with the approach of dawn.

"I will go with you," he rumbled.

Justan wiped the sleep from his eyes. "Are you sure?"

"Yes."

"Zambon and Tamboor might need you." Justan said, though he was truly glad that Fist decided to stay with him.

The ogre shook his head. "They have each other. They are part of my tribe, but they do not see me as part of theirs." He hesitated, not knowing how to express in words what he was feeling. Instead he sent his feeling to Justan through the bond. Fist was concerned that his presence would just remind them of the enemy that killed their family.

"Surely they would not see you that way. They know it wasn't your fault."

"But I do not," Fist said, truthfully. "They need to be alone so they can . . . get better. I would be in the way."

"I am glad you are coming with me," Justan said, impressed with the wisdom coming from this ogre. His grasp of the common tongue was pretty good as well. He was looking forward to getting to know Fist better.

Fist smiled but his eyes were sad. "You should not be. I lose two tribes already. The Thunder People and The Big and Little Peoples are gone now. Maybe it is not good to be with me."

When they left the stable, Justan was surprised to see that it had snowed during the night. A thick blanket of whiteness laid over everything. Justan crossed the courtyard toward the unfinished castle and he saw a group of people gathered in front of the stairs. Zambon and Princess Elise were arguing while Lenny and Captain Demetrius stood to the side, bewildered expressions on their faces.

"I command you not to leave!" Elise shouted.

Zambon put a hand on her shoulder, but she jerked it away. He looked the Princess straight in the eye. "I am sorry, dear Elise. But I must."

"This is an outrage!" The princess' face was beet red and tears began to roll down her cheeks. "You dare leave me in my time of need?"

Zambon looked away.

Elise's voice quieted. "Don't you love me?"

"More than you could ever know." Zambon said. Justan could see that the guard's fists were clenched so tight that his knuckles were white. "But my father needs me. I am all that he has left."

For the first time, Justan noticed Tamboor sitting on the snow-covered steps behind them. He was ignoring the argument and silently polished a long wicked sword. Lying next to Tamboor was a cloth covered bundle strapped to a pair of long poles.

Zambon bent to kiss the princess' hand, but she pulled back and fled up the stairs, crying. With a sigh, Zambon turned to Captain Demetrius. "Captain, please be sure to bring her home safely."

"I will." The Captain promised. "I offered clemency to those of the duke's garrison that were still alive. They have agreed to escort us on our trip back to Dremald. We leave in a few hours. She will be safe back at home by the end of the week."

Tamboor stood and with barely a nod to his son, picked up the end of the poles and began to walk away from the castle, dragging the package behind him, a grim look on his face. Resolute, Zambon bent to pick up a full pack of provisions that lay at his feet and turned to Lenny.

"Good luck be with you, friend. Thank you again for the sword. I have a feeling we might need its magic."

"Sorry 'bout what happened to yer kin, son. Kill a hunnerd of the dag-blasted beasts fer me," the dwarf said. "And give that sword of yers a name. She'll see you through the hard times."

Zambon nodded and trudged through the snow after Tamboor. The veteran warrior hadn't stopped to wait for his son.

Justan ran to catch up to him. "Zambon!"

The guard gave Justan a weary smile but kept walking. "Good luck on your journey, Sir Edge. I guess mine is just beginning."

Justan kept up his friend's pace. "Zambon, I want to thank you."

"No thanks are needed."

"I mean, you didn't have to come after me." Justan said.

"It took me where I needed to be, didn't it? I should be the one thanking you for freeing my father." Zambon patted Justan's back and looked forward to where Tamboor was striding ahead silently. "Perhaps one day, he'll be able to thank you himself."

"When did he show up?"

"Last night after everyone had gone to bed. He had been searching for the weapons storage, I guess. Anyway he found Meredith, his sword. He also brought up Fist's mace. He gave it to him this morning."

"Oh, yeah," Justan said. "Fist has decided to go with me."

"I know. He told us. Father seemed to understand." They entered the edge of the forest that surrounded the castle and Justan stayed with his friend a while longer.

"So, what will you do?" Justan asked.

"Right now I suppose we go back to Jack's Rest and kill any monsters there. Give my family a proper burial."

"Is that why he insisted on bringing Sneaky Pete too?" Justan asked, the contents of the white cloth bundle now obvious to him.

"The man loved Jack's Rest more than anyone. He deserves to be buried there after everything he did for my father. You know, I think it is a good thing. When I saw my father bundling Sneaky Pete to that litter I realized that his mind wasn't completely gone. He is just . . . lost."

Justan looked ahead to Tamboor. "Will this journey be enough for him? Will you be able to come back afterward?"

"I don't know." Zambon shrugged. "I guess we'll be done

whenever Father finds what he is looking for."

"Good luck." Justan couldn't think of anything else to say. He embraced the guard with one arm awkwardly as they walked. "I would help you if I could."

"Even if you didn't already have your own journey ahead, you couldn't help. My father and I have to do this together."

"I understand."

"Actually . . . there is one thing that you could do for me, Sir Edge." The guard stopped and gave Justan a serious look. "Kill as many goblinoids as you can."

Justan nodded solemnly and watched Zambon until his friend disappeared through the snow covered trees. He stood pondering for a moment, then yelped as a clump of snow landed across his shoulders, sending an icy trickle down his back. He looked up in irritation to see a large gray squirrel standing on the branch directly above him.

"Hey, aren't you supposed to be asleep this time of year?" he grumbled, trying to dig the snow out of his collar. "You are lucky I don't have my bow with me or I might spit you on an arrow."

The squirrel cocked its head at him then gave a little hop. More snow plopped onto Justan's upturned face. With a growl, Justan backed out from under the branch. He scooped up a handful of snow and threw it at the squirrel hoping to frighten it off. The creature stepped to the side, avoiding the snowball and chattered angrily, scolding him with one raised fist.

"Squirrel!" came a deep booming voice.

Justan turned to see Fist running up the trail toward him, a wide grin on his chiseled face. He could feel a surge of joy pounding through the bond. The squirrel jumped down from the branch to land on Fist's shoulder and promptly began scurrying all over the ogre as if searching for something.

Fist grasped the little animal and hugged it to his hairy chest, laughing. The squirrel put up with the affection for a moment before scrambling back up onto Fist's shoulder and pointing at Justan, scolding him loudly.

Fist looked back at Justan. "Did you throw something?'

Justan sputtered. "He started it!"

Captain Demetrius had given all of the escaped prisoners leave to take what they needed for their journeys from the duke's stores. This included warm clothes and shoes. He had made the servants unload the vast wardrobe of the Vriil family. Some of it was very valuable. Elise had protested halfheartedly at the sight of a noble family's heirlooms being ransacked by peasants, but soon gave in to the captain's way of thinking. The group of emaciated men walking away from the castle in various mismatching finery was an amusing sight.

As Justan packed away what supplies he could, Qyxal spoke to Captain Demetrius.

"Do you feel at all guilty for letting all those prisoners go free?" the elf asked.

"Why would you wonder that?" the captain asked.

Qyxal shrugged. "Surely some of these men were truly criminals. They can't all have been wrongfully imprisoned."

"It was a judgment call I made in the dungeon and I stand by it. I have no way to sort all of the prisoners out and I needed all of them for my plan to work. So, no, I feel no guilt. Hopefully this experience has reformed them. If not, I'm sure they will be captured again."

"I hope that the king does not kill you." Qyxal shook the man's hand. "We will need men like you if those creatures do come to war."

Lenny already had Stanza saddled up and rigged with his special riding harness when they arrived at the stables. He pulled himself into the saddle and Justan was surprised by how at ease the dwarf looked on the back of the enormous warhorse. "Good, yer finally here. I'm itchin' to be off!"

"You're coming with me?" Justan asked, pleased.

"Well, what'd you think I'd do?" Lenny sounded offended. "Leave you with nothin' but an elf and an ogre to keep you company? 'Sides, I got a feelin' that wherever you'll be is where the action is."

Justan chuckled. “Let’s hope not.”

They left the stable to find Fist standing outside tugging at his new clothes uncomfortably. He was wearing a large woolen coat that they had found in the duke’s stores. It was the biggest one that they could find, but still looked small stretched over his large frame. The ogre didn’t know what to think about his new clothing, though he had been pleased to find a fur-lined pouch for Squirrel to stay in. Justan could see part of its gray tail sticking up out of it.

Lenny looked the ogre up and down. “You know I could let the seams out a bit fer you. Give you a little room to breathe in that thing.”

“You sew?” Qyxal asked in amusement.

“You learn how to do a lot by the time you get my age.” Lenny turned and spat through his missing tooth before mumbling under his breath irritably, “Durn elf.”

Justan ignored them and looked back at the skeletal structure of the unfinished castle. “I can't help but wonder how much good we actually did here.” Qyxal and Lenny exchanged puzzled looks but Justan did not explain further.

“So exactly where are we going?” Qyxal asked Justan.

Justan looked off into the direction Tamboor and Zambon had headed. “On a brighter road than some, I hope.”

Chapter Three

"Why do my rooms have to be so high up?" Locksher muttered to himself, as he trudged up yet another flight of stairs. Though he was glad to be back in the Mage School, the long climb up the Rune Tower to his quarters reminded him why he always enjoyed leaving so much.

His problem with the climb wasn't weakness or age. Locksher was only in his early forties and was quite fit as far as wizards were concerned. He just couldn't stand tedium. He was a man with little patience, which was one of the reasons he made such a good wizard of mysteries. It was also the reason why he took so many trips away from the Mage School. Then again, trips away weren't always full of excitement. His recent journey had been long and though he had learned many things about Justan's mysterious book, most of it had consisted of week after week of monotonous travel.

At last he reached his floor and started down the long hallway that led to his rooms. It would be nice to get back into his daily routine. He wondered if anything interesting had happened during his absence.

As he approached the entrance to his rooms, he saw a young mage pacing back and forth. She had long blond hair and wore a blue robe. Locksher sighed. He wasn't in the mood for a visitor; this one especially. She was so beautiful that it was distracting.

"Can I help you, Vannya?" he asked.

"Oh!" She jumped at the sound of his voice. When she saw who it was, she smiled. Her hazel eyes looked weary, as if she hadn't slept in a long time. "Wizard Locksher! I came up here as soon as I heard you had returned."

"Well it was kind of you to welcome me home, Vannya. Please tell your father that I will speak with him about whatever it is he wants later. I am sure that work is stacked high waiting for me."

Anger flashed in Vannya's eyes. Evidently she did not like his assumption. "That's not what I am here about, sir."

"Good. Surely someone else can help you then."

She stamped her foot in frustration. "No, I have been to everyone else. You are the only one that can help. You are the wizard of mysteries for this school are you not?"

Locksher wasn't in the mood to deal with childish tantrums at the moment.

"I was the last time I checked, young lady. Let us see if your status has changed." He looked her up and down. "Hmm, no rune on your left hand, so you haven't been named. You aren't wearing the collar of a wizard and your double ringed belt tells me that you are still a mage. From the standard white slippers you wear, you are still a student, and from the dark circles under your eyes, a student who has not slept in a long time. All together, this tells me that I far over rank you and should not be spoken to so rudely!" He paused. "Am I wrong?"

"Sorry, Wizard Locksher." Vannya replied, her eyes cast downward.

"Good, then. I am sure that whatever it is can at least wait until I have my rooms in order. I will send for you as soon as I am settled back in." He stepped over the threshold.

"Please wait, sir. I am sorry that I snapped at you. You are right, I-I have not slept in quite a while and I am feeling very stre-." She yawned. "Stressed out. Please hear what I have to say. It's very important."

Locksher slowly turned around. Her persistence was grating,

"Alright then. Make it quick," he said.

"Do you remember a cadet by the name of Piledon?"

"Piledon? Yes. He's quite the sneak, isn't he? I caught him in a few pranks. He got tangled up in that golem mess." One eyebrow raised and a bit of interest entered his eyes.

"Yes, he's the one. Well he came up missing a couple of weeks ago," she said.

"Oh. Well I'll get on it as soon as I can. Thank you for telling me." He started to close the door.

"But Wizard Randolf says he has evidence that the cadet was murdered!"

He stuck his head back out. "Murder? In the Mage School? I would say that's highly unlikely. Wizard Randolf has always been the excitable sort. I will talk to him about it in the council meeting later today."

"No, no! You don't understand," Vannya interrupted, her eyes wild. "He says that Justan killed him!"

"Justan, you say?" His irritation vanished, replaced by concern. "You had better come in then." He stepped out of the way so that she could enter.

Locksher's rooms were a complete mess. The walls were covered in tiny hooks with magical baubles and trinkets hanging on them. The floor was cluttered with stacks of old tomes and strange objects with barely any room to walk between. To make things worse, during the months he had been absent, a thin layer of dust had covered everything.

Vannya eyed the rooms with distaste. She picked up a book off of a nearby stack and blew the dust off of the cover. "Does Vincent know that you have all these books up here?"

"Uh, of course. I told him before I took them. Besides, he has more than one copy of these . . . Well, most of them anyway." In all truth, the librarian would probably faint if he ever walked into this room. But Locksher wasn't worried. The gnome rarely left the library. He took the book that Vannya was holding and put it back on the stack. "Please don't touch anything."

"Would it really matter?" she asked.

"I have a very organized system." He pointed at the floor and showed her a small letter 'f' engraved near the stack. She looked around. Each stack of books had another letter at the base and all the trinkets on the walls had little naming plates. It all made complete sense to

Locksher.

"You know if you returned them to the library you would have a lot more room in here," she said.

Locksher scoffed at the idea. "Then they wouldn't be here when I needed them, would they? I can't go traipsing down to the library every time I need a book. I am far too busy."

"I suppose you are right . . ." She still looked dubious, though.

"Besides," He waived his hand absently. "Too many stairs."

"Why not at least put in some book shelves?"

"Where? The walls are taken up with-." He paused and frowned at her. "What are you prattling on about anyway? Didn't you have something more important to talk to me about? Like . . . say, the reason Justan is being accused of murder?"

"Yes! Sorry, I am just so tired, my mind is all over the place." Her face had turned red in an annoyingly adorable way, making the light scattering of freckles on her face stand out even more. He wondered how Valtrek got anything done when she was a child.

Locksher sighed. "Just sit down, would you? Tell me what is going on."

Vannya looked around for someplace to sit, but there wasn't a chair or anything nearby that wasn't covered with books or boxes or any other assortment of objects. Locksher gestured towards a large desk in the back of the room and after walking around some particularly tall stacks of books, she did see two chairs. He flopped into one chair while she eased into the other and began her story.

"It was a few weeks ago, just after the Apprenticeship Ceremony. Oh, did you know that Justan was raised to the office of Apprentice early?"

Locksher smiled. "Oh, really? Well good for him. In his first year too, how nice indeed."

"Well the next day, he and Piledon both disappeared. No one knew why. Justan's things were all gone while Piledon's things were still a jumbled mess. Some students were saying that Justan had taken Piledon with him, but then why would Piledon leave all of his clothes behind?"

"Interesting. Did the council find out where Justan went?" Locksher asked.

"For the first day everyone was pretty worried, but then my father told the council that he had sent Justan away to study with a different wizard somewhere abroad. That made a lot of the council members pretty angry, especially when he admitted that he had let them take the rogue horse with them-."

"By the gods, girl! Slow down. Let me digest what you say before prattling on." He leaned back and closed his eyes.

"Sorry."

"Alright. Questions then. In order of importance. You said, 'them'. You said, 'let them take the rogue horse with them'. Who else left with Justan? I am assuming that Piledon isn't one of them or we wouldn't be having this conversation."

"Sorry. Again, I haven't got much sleep and . . ." Locksher was twirling one finger to tell her to get on with it. She frowned and cleared her throat. "My father sent Justan, Qyxal and one of the guards named Zambon away from the school that night with the rogue horse and two warhorses."

"Aha!" Locksher grinned. "So, let me see if I follow. Your father took Justan on as his own apprentice, correct?"

"Yeah . . ." Her brow furrowed in confusion. "How did you come to that conclusion?"

"For your father to have the authority to send Justan out of the school without council approval, he would have had to take him on as his personal apprentice. Since everyone knows how much Justan loathes your father, it also makes sense why he would need to send him to learn from someone else."

It took her a moment to follow his round about way of thinking. "Right, that makes sense. You're right, father did take him on as his apprentice and the council signed off on it. That is one of the reasons they are so mad at him. That and the rogue horse situation."

"That would be why Qyxal left with him." Locksher deduced.

"Right," She said, though she looked at him with suspicion. "My father told the council that the rogue horse belonged to the elves and that he had authorized Qyxal to return it to his people-."

"And since the creature is not Mage School property, the council had no say in the matter," Locksher finished. He laughed out loud. "Oh, I am sure that had them hopping mad, having such a prize taken out from under their noses!"

"Why do you take the idea of a rogue horse being here in the school and alive so lightly? All the other wizards are still talking about it."

"Bah, you can't study a rogue horse. They die in captivity, everyone knows that. I mean, I am curious about their origins just like everyone else, I must admit, but I can find that out through other kinds of research. It is best that such a beast remain with the elves. If anyone could keep a rogue horse alive, it would be them." He leaned forward. "So what is your father's explanation for sending Justan away?"

"He won't say. He won't tell the council anything until he is sure that Justan has arrived at his new location safely. He won't even tell me what is going on." Her frustration with that fact was evident on her face.

"Ah, so he is concerned that the council will try to go after Justan once they know. Hmm . . . this does make your father a suspect you know."

"What? How is that possible?"

"If Piledon is really dead, then maybe he overheard where Justan was going and Justan or your father could have killed him to keep it quiet. Or the council might think that Justan killed Piledon and Valtrek sent him away to cover it up. Or Valtrek killed Piledon and sent Justan away to make it look like he did it. The only way your father gets out of this is if he can prove that neither he nor Justan had anything to do with Piledon's death. Then he will simply need to have a really good explanation as to why he isn't telling the council where Justan is."

She stared at him with her mouth open.

"Do they have Piledon's body?" he asked.

"No."

"Well? Tell me what proof Randolph has that makes him so sure Justan killed the cadet."

She gathered her thoughts, "Uh . . . Well, I have been looking into this quite a lot. It's why I have gotten so little sleep. You see, they found blood in the room. A lot of blood. They have witnesses that say Justan promised to kill Piledon if he ever touched his things. They have his leaving to coincide with Piledon's disappearance and I am pretty sure that Wizard Randolph has something else he isn't revealing until the trial."

Locksher nodded quietly, stood and opened one of the many drawers in his desk. He pulled some items out and turned back to her.

"Let's go then," he said, excited for the first time in days.

"Wait, do you think he did it?" she asked.

"Do you?"

"Of course not. Even if he did kill Piledon, he would have had a good reason for doing so. It is not like him to run away."

"Then let's go see what evidence they missed," Locksher said with a grin and made his way past the obstacles and out the door.

Vannya followed after him, shutting the door behind her. He hadn't waited for her and she had to catch up with him in the stairwell.

"So where do we start?" she asked.

"The place where the cadet was killed, of course. The best place to start looking for evidence is the scene of the crime."

They headed down the long stairwell and exited the Rune Tower. They walked over the drawbridge and down one of the pathways that meandered through the manicured Mage School grounds. Several Wizards called out to Locksher as they passed but he shut them down with a polite but curt nod as they strode by. Several of the male students waved to Vannya as well and she shot each one a glowing smile that left a rosy cheek and goofy expression on their faces. Locksher shook his head.

Their path took them away from the center of the school and around the class buildings to the cadet dormitory. The door to Justan and Piledon's room was sealed with a rune. Locksher touched the rune and it glowed briefly. “Locksher, Wizard of Mysteries,” he said and the door opened.

“Blast it!” he swore as they stepped into the room. “They cleaned!”

The place did look like it had been scrubbed down. The floor was spotless and all traces of Piledon’s messiness were gone. The only traces of Justan’s presence left were his elements trophies on the desk in his side of the room.

“Look at that! Clean linens and everything! The rooms weren’t this clean when I was a cadet, I can assure you of that,” Locksher fumed. “They know to leave things alone until I get here. It is almost as if Randolph doesn’t want the truth known.”

“Maybe they wanted to make the room available for the next students,” Vannya said from behind him. “But why leave his trophies here if that was the case?”

“Exactly,” Locksher said. “Luckily I have other ways of finding out what happened. Where did they say the blood was found?”

“On the bed.”

“Hmm . . . so they changed the linens. But did they change the mattress? If I know Professor Beehn, he wouldn’t have let them procure a new one.” He pulled the blankets and linens from the bed and saw that the mattress was clean. He turned the mattress over. “Of course they cleaned it with magic. Vannya, will you hold the mattress up for me please . . . Thank you.”

She held the mattress up while he reached into his robes and pulled out a pipe and a pair of glasses. From another pocket, he retrieved a small box that when opened appeared to be stuffed with little packets of tobacco. Each one was marked with runes.

“What are you doing, sir?” Vannya asked.

“The cleaners here are very efficient. But it is very hard to get rid of blood completely. You see, our souls, the life within us imprints on our blood. No matter how hard you clean, even with magic, there is always a residue of that life force left behind.” He flipped through the packets of tobacco until he found the one he was looking for and stuffed some of its contents into the pipe. He put the glasses on and with a quick spell, lit the pipe.

Acrid smoke belched from the end and Vannya wrinkled her petite nose in distaste. She coughed and sputtered, "How is smok-king g-going to help?"

"Oh, sorry." He fumbled in his robes and brought out another pair of glasses. "Put these on. It should help."

She laid the mattress down and put them on. To Vannya's surprise, her coughing stopped. "Why do these glasses help my breathing?"

"Magic," he said. "Lift the mattress back up please. Now this tobacco is specially treated to bring out the traces of life energy left behind by blood. The glasses will help us see if Piledon really died in this bed."

He took a deep puff, leaned close to the mattress and blew the smoke directly onto it. There was no change.

"That's funny. Put the mattress down, let's try the other side."

"Sir, wait." Vannya said and pointed to the other side of the room.

The bed on Justan's side of the room was glowing with a dim light. Locksher walked over, pulled the blankets off of the bed, and blew smoke directly on the mattress. A silvery glow radiated heavily around the edges of the mattress but the center was dark.

"Was there only blood on the edges?" she asked.

"Evidently he was laying on the bed when it happened and the blood pooled around him." Locksher turned to Vannya. "Didn't you tell me that they found blood on Piledon's bed?"

"Definitely. That is what Wizard Randolph's findings were."

"Then why is the blood in Justan's bed, do you think? Oh, look over there." He pointed to the foot of Piledon's bed. There was a tiny trail of glowing spots leading from the foot of the bed to the door. "So the incident happened on Piledon's bed and the mattresses were switched."

"So that proves that Wizard Randolph is tampering with the evidence!" she said.

"Well, maybe. Or someone else did . . . Or the person cleaning the room was just careless and didn't put the mattress back on the right bed."

"Oh," she said, sounding disappointed.

"At least we know that Piledon was killed in here. Unless . . ." He paused and placed one hand on his chin, his brow furrowed in concern. "Oh I hadn't thought of that before . . . Unless it is Justan that is dead."

"What?"

"Well no one has seen him since that night," he explained. "But then your father would have to be involved because that would mean that he was lying about sending Justan off . . ." He trailed off as he saw the horrified look on Vannya's face. "Sorry, sorry. I don't really think it's likely. I just tend to mull over all the possibilities and when someone is with me I tend to think aloud."

"O-okay," she said. "Besides, I have proof that Justan knew he was leaving so it couldn't be the case. Besides, my father would never-."

"You do? Can I see this evidence? It might tell me something that will help."

Her hand flew to the pocket of her robes. "Oh, I-I would rather not. It is kind of a personal thing and uh . . . I would rather not have anyone read it unless I have to."

"Ah, so he left you a note. That explains why you haven't been able to sleep. More than friends, eh?"

She opened her mouth as if to refute what he was saying, but no words came out.

Locksher chuckled. "Well hopefully we won't need it. But I will warn you that it could be a critical piece of evidence. If that's the case, the whole council will have to read it."

He ignored the look of horror on her face and continued, "So we know that Piledon was killed in this room and his body was taken out through the door . . . Say, did anyone think of the possibility that this could all be an elaborate prank on Piledon's part?" He smiled and shook his head at the idea. "Can't you imagine him doing it? Justan leaves in the night and he takes the opportunity to stage his own death. It would be just like him wouldn't it? He could be hiding in a friend's room somewhere laughing about this right now."

"That's not funny," she said. To his surprise, there was sadness in her eyes.

The smile faded from his face. "You are right."

With her reminder, the thought of Piledon somewhere laughing about the whole thing reminded him of the way the kid seemed to find humor in every situation. He pictured the smile that always seemed to be plastered on the cadet's face and the investigation seemed a bit more personal. Annoying as he was, Piledon had been full of life. This case was about more than just proving Justan innocent.

"Forgive me, Vannya. Sometimes I get carried away." He cleared his throat. "Now where have they searched for the body?"

"The gardens, the storage building, the dormitories . . . Wizard Randolph supposedly even left his body in spirit form and searched around outside of the school."

"Really? How brave of him," Locksher said. Leaving one's body was one of the most risky tricks a wizard could use. It could leave him completely vulnerable to attack. "Alright then, let's conduct a search of our own, don't you think?"

Locksher put the pipe and glasses away and exited the room. He left the cadet dormitories and headed towards the center of the school, Vannya walking beside him.

"So where do we start looking?" she asked.

"Well, we aren't going to start now. I have some sniffing around to do and then I have some announcements to make, then I have that meeting with the council this evening . . . Vannya, why don't you go back to your studies for now. Meet me at my rooms first thing in the morning." He started to walk away, but stopped. "By the way, if you want to tag along with me tomorrow, you had better get some sleep tonight. Go to bed early. I don't care if you have to ask your roommate to cast a sleep spell on you."

"Yes, sir." She looked a bit disappointed.

"Don't worry, Vannya. If my plans work out, we should have this thing cleared up before the council meets again tomorrow night."

Chapter Four

The next morning Vannya was at the wizard's door first thing after breakfast. She had taken his advice and went to bed early the night before. She felt good for the first time since Justan had left. Finally she was doing something instead of standing around and waiting.

Locksher met her at the door. "Good morning. Let's get going, then."

He thrust a small notebook and a small metal rod into her hands and headed towards the stairs. Vannya stared at the rod a bit before she followed. It was smooth and cylindrical with a wooden cap on one end. She ran to catch up to him.

"What is this?" she asked, holding out the rod.

"That, Vannya, is an ink cylinder. They are the new big thing at the gnomish library in Olivera. I brought back a pile of them. That little metal cylinder is filled with ink. What you do is take the wooden cap off and there is a tiny brush coming out of the end that always stays wet with ink. It is an ingenious device. No quills or inkwells or anything. Just make sure you put the cap back on, I ruined a set of robes on the way back just tossing one in my pocket."

She smiled with delight at the little invention. "So why did you give it to me?"

"I want you to take notes. I am a professor after all and since you're a student, we are going to turn this investigation into a learning experience. Pay attention to every detail and we will see if you figure out who the murderer is before I reveal it at the council meeting tonight."

"But what if you aren't sure by then?" she asked.

"Bah, I am pretty sure already. I just have one little test to make sure. The first thing I want you to focus on is finding the body."

"So where are we going now?" Vannya asked as they left the Rune Tower.

"I have a little gathering waiting for us at the center square."

They arrived at the square and Vannya saw fourteen students standing in front of the new water fountain chatting with each other. She knew most of them and waved as they walked up. Her friends Arcon and Pympol were among the crowd. The two of them ran up to her when she arrived.

"Vannya, what is this all about?" Arcon asked.

"Yeah," said Pympol. "A messenger arrived at my room this morning with a summons from the council telling me to be here."

"Locksher is going to explain," she said. Ever since they had been censured for their creation of the golem that destroyed the clock tower, the two were always afraid of being accused of something. Locksher had raised his hands and everybody's eyes were on him. Vannya opened the notebook and took the cap off of the ink cylinder prepared to take notes.

"Yeah, but why?" Arcon asked. "Is this about-?"

"Shhh! Just listen."

"You are probably wondering why you are here," Locksher began. "Many of you may have already suspected this for a while, but yesterday I informed the council that I have verified the murder of Cadet Piledon. I know that this is sad news because we all knew him. This is why I need your help. In order to find out who killed Piledon, we need to find his body."

There were gasps among the students.

"Now I know that this is a difficult thing to ask of you, but that is why I requested you students in particular to lead the search. You were all his friends. Since you cared about him, you will be the most diligent. Now, I have assignment slips for each of you with search areas."

Locksher paired the students up and gave each of them specific instructions. Arcon had been assigned with a mage to search the gardens, while Pympol had been paired with one of the apprentices to search the storage building. Neither of them looked happy that they weren't paired together.

"I expect everyone to meet me back here at noon. Thank you for your assistance." When the students had left for their designated areas, Locksher walked back over to Vannya. "Well, there go our suspects."

"Really?" Vannya was surprised. "But like you just said, they are his friends."

"Exactly. Or, well, his friends and his enemies. He was a prankster remember. I have ruled out everyone else that I was suspicious of except Justan and your father. These are the people that are left."

Vannya took notes as fast as she could. "So why put the killer in a search party? They aren't going to be any help."

"That is why I sent them all to places I knew the body wasn't," he said. "This is the best way to pinpoint who the killer was. Whoever it is will be deathly afraid that I am going to find out it was them and they may tip their hand. Especially when we all meet back here and I announce that I found the body."

"You know where it is?"

"Yes, I verified that last night. I haven't told the council yet, though. Now what I want you to do while the killer is out there scaring himself is see if you can find it."

"O-okay. But why? If you know where the body is and know who the killer is, why go through all of this? Why not just throw him into the dungeon?"

"I never said it was a man. Could even be you, you know."

"I am serious!"

"Vannya, there is a difference between knowing who the killer is and proving who the killer is. We need to tip their hand," he explained. Evidently she didn't look too convinced because a stern look came into his eyes. "I am the professor and you are the student, remember? Learn already."

"Yes sir," she jotted down a quick note. "Where should we start, then?"

"You tell me," he said. "If you were trying to hide a body somewhere on school grounds, where would you put it?"

"You could bury it somewhere." Vannya thought for a moment. "But it would be pretty hard to hide a burial. Disturbed earth is the first thing a search party would look for. Besides, with earth magic, the wizards would be able to probe the place and find a decaying body on the grounds in no time."

"Good. Think of something else."

"You could put it somewhere nobody goes and hope that no one finds it for a very long time," she suggested.

"Like?"

"I don't know, a room somewhere deep in the Rune Tower? Um . . ." A slight smile formed on her mouth. "A corner of the storage building in a cask marked pickled moonrat eyes?"

"Now there is a devious mind at work." Locksher laughed. "Those aren't bad ideas, but the Rune Tower is too risky. Too many wizards walking around day and night to sneak a dead body in. The storage building is a decent spot, but Randolph has searched it already so get a bit more creative with your thinking."

"You could put it in the garden and use earth magic to grow plants over it, but then the students on gardening duty would notice a new pile of plants not to mention the eventual smell."

"Good, good. I like how you are thinking. It's morbid yes, but that is the way a wizard of mysteries needs to think. Put yourself in the place of the person doing the crime," Locksher said.

"Oh! What about a mix of my two earlier ideas? What if you buried the body in a place that no one would ever go? Like in the wall of a new building, like . . ." She turned around and her hands flew to her mouth. "Like the new clock tower!"

"Very good," Locksher said. "Nice choice indeed."

In the months since the golem had destroyed the clock tower, artisans and laborers from all around had been at work rebuilding it. It was a painstaking process because the wizards insisted on magically reinforcing every stone block or piece of wood or batch of mortar that went into the building. They wanted it to last.

At this point, most of the structure was completed. Most of the workers were gone now and there were just enough still around to finish the final reinforcement work that needed to be done before they put the clock on top. The council had announced a plan to place a monument to the six men that were killed in the attack in front of it. A whole ceremony was scheduled. The clock itself had been completed just a week earlier and it stood behind the tower covered with cloth until the unveiling.

"So," Locksher said, staring up at the thirty-foot-tall structure in front of them. "If you were to hide a body in the clock tower where would you put it?"

"Now that I think about it, you couldn't get away with hiding it in the mortar itself. The wizard that reinforced the mortar would detect it as a weakness in the structure. The clock wasn't here yet, so it couldn't be in there either. I guess it would have to be inside the tower itself then."

"Good," Locksher said. "Now first you would have to get the body inside. There is only the one door at the base of the tower."

They walked up to the door and went inside. The interior of the clock tower was empty, but for a single spiral staircase that would lead up to the clock once it was installed up top. For now, the staircase just ended and they could see the blue sky from below.

"Not a lot of places to hide a body, are there?" Vannya observed. "Maybe behind the stairs here at the bottom? The thick walls and foundation might hide it from the wizards sweeping the grounds."

"Why don't you check it out?" he suggested.

Vannya knelt down and rested her hands on the ground. She sent tendrils of earth magic probing through the ground. There was two feet of packed dirt and then solid magically reinforced foundation.

"No body." She stood and dusted off her robes.

"Alright, so one idea shot down. Think on it a bit more. I think you are getting close." Locksher said.

Vannya took out the notebook and stared at it for a moment. She knew it wasn't buried anywhere. Locksher had already ruled out all the places he sent the other students to.

"The only thing left would be to destroy the body," she concluded. At Locksher's slight nod, she went on, "Alright, you could burn it with fire magic, but that leaves traces too. You also run the risk of someone noticing a fire large enough to burn the body . . ."

"Keep going," Locksher said. They stepped back outside and Vannya scribbled a few more notes in the book. It was on the tip of her tongue, she knew it.

"Any way of using magic to destroy the body leaves traces that wizards could find. That leaves more natural means . . ." She turned towards the Rune Tower and her jaw dropped. Vannya looked back at Locksher with a large grin. "The perloi!"

Locksher clapped. "See, I knew you could figure it out."

"But how can you know for sure? If the body was fed to the perloi, there would be no traces left."

"Which is exactly why it is such an ingenious method. However, what most students wouldn't know, is that there are ways to tell what a perloi has been eating. Come on, let me show you."

They walked over to the moat that surrounded the Mage School and Locksher peered over the edge. Vannya leaned over and could see the dark shapes that were the perloi swimming under the water. Locksher looked back at her and smiled.

"You know why the perloi are here, right?"

She nodded. "They are one of the last defenses of the school. If the outer walls were ever breached, everyone would retreat to the Rune Tower and the perloi would be activated."

"Have you ever seen one up close?" he asked.

Vannya shook her head and took a step back. She had seen them fed before though and that was enough. Every once in a while, the mages would throw a goat in. The water would foam up and thrash around and the goat would be gone, devoured bones and all.

"It's okay, watch this," Locksher said. He knelt near the edge and stuck one hand into the water.

She gasped and cried out, "No, wait!"

Locksher leaned in further, plunging his arm deeper into the water, then stiffened and pulled his arm out of the water. He pulled something else out of the water with him. It was about two feet long and looked like a frog except that its head was very large and round. Locksher held it by the waist. It was slumped over limp and its eyes were closed like it was asleep.

"This, dear Vannya, is a perloi. They are really fast swimmers," He lifted up one of its hands and she saw nasty claws on the end of webbed toes. "They were magically designed to be the perfect little feeding machine, too, take a look at its teeth."

He pried its jaw open carefully and Vannya saw wicked curved teeth.

"Now it is asleep right now. All of them are. It's part of the spell on the moat. They swim in their sleep, that is their habit. The only time a perloi becomes awake is when they are fed. It has to be that way or any student that slipped and fell too close to the water would be pounced on and eaten alive in minutes." At the frightened look in her eyes, he added, "Did I mention they can jump out of the water?

"At any rate, they are harmless until they are awakened by the spell that tells them it is time to feed. They are only fed twice a year and for a week afterwards, their eyes turn orange. During times of war, a different spell is used that wakes them fully and they will attack and devour anyone or anything. If they were ever to eat anything human, their eyes turn red for a month." He reached for its eye, then paused. "Uh, you might want to take a step back."

He gently pried back the perloi's eyelid. The eye beneath was red as blood. The moment its eye was opened, it hissed and squirmed in Locksher's grip, snapping and slashing. He stood and tossed it back into the water. Its shadow moved around erratically for a moment and then it rejoined the other shapes swimming in their lazy circle around the Rune Tower.

"So whoever killed Piledon was somehow able to waken the perloi long enough for them to eat the body before putting them back to sleep." Locksher said. "Anyone that spent enough time in the library could find out this information if they looked in the right place. This makes Justan look pretty suspicious. We knew he was preparing a report on weaknesses in the school's defenses. I believe that this is Randolph's crucial bit of evidence he wants to bring up at Justan's trial, if it comes to that."

"Justan told me about that report, but he never finished it before he left," she said. "But wait, Justan couldn't have cast that spell. He had no offensive magic ability."

"I know that and so does Randolph. I don't know how he is going to get around that fact. But he could decide to implicate your father. He could have fed the body to the Perloi after Justan had gone, trying to protect him."

"But you said that you knew who did it," she said.

"I do. I do. At least I think I do. It just never hurts to look at all angles. It's part of the job as Wizard of Mysteries."

"That sounds reassuring," she said, her voice heavy with sarcasm.

They waited until noon, while Vannya jotted down theories under his watchful eye, before walking back to the center square. Each pair of students had returned from their fruitless search. They all looked sad and on edge. A few of them looked rather shaken. Vannya supposed that searching around with the possibility that you might stumble upon the corpse of your friend would be bad on the nerves.

Locksher gathered them all in front of the fountain again. "We are waiting for a few more guests, one moment please."

Vannya was surprised when they were soon joined by a few wizards including several members of the high council. Her father, Wizard Valtrek and Master Latva were there along with Wizard Randolph and Wizard Beehn in his chair on wheels.

Locksher cleared his throat. "I want to thank all of the students that helped in my search today. It is my sad duty to announce that we know the location of Piledon's body." There were several whispers and everyone in the gathering waited anxiously for his next words. He paused for a moment to up the tension.

"We have discovered that he was fed to the perloi."

As he spoke, Vannya took more notes, watching his facial expressions and the way he moved as he manipulated the crowd. There were gasps and astonished glances among the students and the wizards leaned their heads together talking in urgent whispers.

"I would like to thank Mage Vannya for pointing the possibility out for me," he added.

Vannya's face turned a bit red as everyone looked at her. Why was he giving her the credit? How did that help his case?

He continued, "I am also glad to announce that we shall know the identity of the murderer soon. I have had a sample perloi brought up to my study and with some new techniques I have learned, the killer shall be caught. I will announce the results in the council meeting this evening. Please return to your regular class schedules. We will make more announcements after the meeting."

Vannya furiously jot down ideas and questions in the notebook. Who could it be? She went over all the likely culprits in her mind and had it narrowed down to three or four possibilities. All of them were unpleasant.

"Vannya," Locksher said. "If you would wait for me at my study, I have some things to discuss with you. I will rejoin you shortly. It seems I have some tempers to settle." He turned and joined the council members, all of whom looked quite angry.

Vannya went back to his rooms as requested. He took quite a bit longer than expected and that was fine with her because she had a surprise to set up for him.

Three hours later, Locksher arrived in quite an irritable mood, mumbling to himself. He threw the door open and stopped on the threshold, a stunned look on his face.

"What have you done?"

His rooms looked quite different from the condition he had left them in that morning. The piles of books were gone from their haphazard stacks all over the floor and in their place were four free standing bookcases each one eight-feet-high, double-sided and made of fine wood. The entire place had been thoroughly dusted.

"You took so long, I let myself in," Vannya said, clutching her robes in excitement and looking at him expectantly. "Do you like it?"

"My books! My system! How will I know where anything is?" he said in a panic, each hand grabbing a handful of the silver specked hair at his temples.

"Wait, wait! Before you get mad, look." She hurried over to the shelves and pointed to the end of each shelf. They were lettered the same way that the stacks on the floor had been. "Your system hasn't been changed, I took careful accounting of every stack, and each one has its own shelf on the book case with room to grow. Don't worry, they are in the same order you left them in. They have just been taken off the floor. Nothing is out of place, I promise!"

He rushed over to the shelves and ran his hands along the spines of the books, counting them in his head. When he finally looked back at her the anger was gone. A slight grin began to spread across his face. "How did you do this? *When* did you do this?"

"Yesterday after you left, I spoke to a few of the carpenters working on the tower. I paid them a little extra to get the bookcases finished and treated that evening so that they could cure overnight. I asked them to bring them up here while we were gone. I was going to leave the bookcases in the corridor as a surprise, but you took so long to get back . . . Luckily a couple of other mages were sweet enough to help me move them in. I had everything done just ten minutes ago."

"Did you touch anything else? My magic items on the walls, the things in my desk?" He rushed around the rest of the rooms, checking everything.

"No!" she said, quite offended at the suggestion she would rummage through his things. "Just some light dusting is all."

"Vannya, I-I don't know what to say. I suppose the real question is why did you do this?" He walked back to the bookcases and ran a hand along the wood. "This must have cost you a fortune."

"This is thanks for taking the time to help me prove Justan innocent. You were the only one willing to help. And you let me be a part of it. I really needed that. I have been quite tired of everyone treating me like a child." Vannya's voice was heavy with gratitude. "Anyway, don't worry about the money. I made a lot healing at the Battle Academy last year and I never have anything to spend it on. Just, please . . . accept my thanks."

"Thank you very much Vannya," he said sincerely, and seeming a bit uncomfortable, motioned towards the desk. "Can you take a seat, please? We have a lot to discuss."

"What is it?" she said as she sat down.

"The council has instituted a lock down of the school. We don't want to give the killer a chance to escape. Right now whomever it is must be out of their mind with fear. The council wasn't happy with me for flushing them out in this way. Wizard Randolph still insists that it was Justan, but the others are afraid that the killer may strike again in an attempt to escape. I don't think it likely, but . . ." He shrugged. "They could be right about that one. I sure hope not."

"I think I know who it is." Vannya blurted.

"Oh really?" He leaned back and grinned. "Who, pray tell?"

"Well I was thinking about it quite a bit and gathering all the evidence together, I had four possible killers. It was either Justan, my father, Pympol, or Arcon."

He nodded. "Wonderful, though you left out two possibilities."

"Whom?"

"Wizard Randolph for one."

"Really?"

"Sure. For one thing he has been too intense in his attacks on Justan," he explained. "What had the boy ever done while he was here to invite that? He had the time, the capabilities, and the clout to cover it up too. The motive is a bit shaky though. Maybe if Piledon caught him doing some underhanded deals or something . . . Anyway, it wasn't him. Go on. Why those four? "

"But who was the other one I missed?"

"Well, you of course," he explained.

"But it wasn't me."

"I know. Go on with your explanation."

"But if you know it wasn't Wizard Randolph, then why go

through that whole explanation . . . never mind." She shook her head and continued, "The rest of the students were either too inexperienced to understand how to awaken the perloi or just too stricken with sadness over Piledon's death to be the killer. Pympol and Arcon were the only ones to give any hint of fear that they might be suspected."

"Okay, so narrow it down for me," Locksher said.

"Once I had the four main suspects, I eliminated Justan from consideration because of his personality, lack of ability to cast the spell on the perloi, and the . . . letter he left me. Some of the things he said in that letter could not possibly have been written if he had just left because of murdering someone."

"Are you sure that you won't let me read it?" Locksher pleaded.

"No! Next I eliminated my father. You might find my reasons suspect, but first of all, he is my father and though I know him to be capable of many underhanded things, he cares too much for the students in this school to kill one of them. Besides, if he was going to kill someone, he wouldn't have murdered him in his bed with a knife or something. Blood is too easy to trace. He would have talked Piledon into walking with him to the edge of the moat and put a paralyzing spell on him before pushing him in with the perloi."

"My, you do know your father well." Locksher had leaned forward, his elbow on the desk, his head resting on one hand, enthralled with her explanation. "So tell me how you decided that it was one of the other two."

"Well, I feel bad about it, because they are both friends of mine. But Pympol and Arcon along with Piledon were the ones responsible for that golem catastrophe last year. They were always around Piledon and if he knew something about it that he hadn't told the council yet, they might have had reason to kill him. They were also both mages before their demotion and both had the skill to use the spell on the perloi."

"True," he said.

"Both of them were given a lot of extra duties around the school as punishment. That includes helping to feed the perloi, and extra library duty which would have given them the opportunity to study how to awaken them. Now Pympol hates Justan. He never liked him from the moment they met. It got even worse after Justan told the council about his involvement with the golem. That gives him an edge motive wise if he felt that he could frame Justan for the murder.

"Arcon on the other hand, had extra cleaning duty and would have had the opportunity to switch the mattresses in Justan's room to try and cover his tracks."

"Amazing. Well done. Well done indeed. You made good use of the evidence available and puzzled it out. So who do you think did it?"

Their conversation was interrupted by a loud knock at the door. They looked at each other with raised eyebrows. Locksher got up to answer it, but Vannya whispered after him urgently.

"Wait! What if that is the murderer? Right now, since he can't leave the school, the best thing for him to do is make sure that you don't live to reveal him!"

"True," he said. "But I am not defenseless."

He opened the door and Vannya's father barged in.

"It was Arcon!" Valtrek blurted. "I couldn't believe it, but he went missing an hour ago. One of the guards saw him on the wall and he disappeared over the edge. They are out looking for him now. I-." He paused. "It is quite clean in here, Locksher."

"I knew it!" cried Vannya. "That's what I was going to say!"

"I had confirmed it too," Locksher said. "Just before I came up here I spoke with Professor Beehn and confirmed that Arcon was the student on cleaning duty at the cadet dormitory that week."

"Vannya?" Valtrek said. "What are you doing here?"

"She has been helping me with this mystery, Valtrek. And she has done an admirable job too, I might add," Locksher said. Before Valtrek could say anything else, he continued, "I still have some questions for you regarding Justan, though. Why did you send him away? Where did you send him? I have crucial information for the boy regarding that frost rune on his chest."

Valtrek sighed. "I might as well tell you now. I was going to tell everyone at the council meeting tonight anyway. Justan has had plenty of time to arrive at his destination by now."

He told them everything from Justan's unexpected naming at the apprenticeship ceremony, to his bond with Gwyrtha and his journey to find Master Coal. Vannya was stunned, Locksher was ecstatic.

"Of course! By the gods, why didn't I figure it out before? The way the council has been avoiding calling Justan, er, Sir Edge by name and the rogue horse incident . . .What a fool I have been!"

He rushed about the room, gathering items together. Then went in his bedroom and began to pack. His voice echoed out from the room. "Still, a double naming? Fascinating!"

"Locksher, where are you going?" Valtrek asked.

"I might have some crucial information for your apprentice! This could be very big for him. Big for us all, actually. I just need one more trip to make sure. Vannya!" He rushed out of the room and grasped her arm. "If you are willing, I just might have one more way that you can help Sir Edge."

Chapter Five

Arcon trembled in fear as he followed his mistress' children deeper and deeper into the depths of the forest. It had started in such a small way. He had first heard her voice a little over a year prior as the Mage School caravan traveled to the Battle Academy for testing week.

They had been traveling down the protected road through the darkest part of the forest when one of the mages had stepped off the road and been bitten by a snake. While the others tended to the poisoned mage, a moonrat had fallen from above and landed in front of him with a crunch, dead. The light in its eyes had burned a dull green before winking out. As he watched in horror, the eyes had popped out of its head and rolled to his feet.

His first instinct had been to scream out in fright and run, but no sound came out of his open mouth and his feet did not move. After a moment, the fear left him. He grew curious instead and reached towards them. As his fingers neared the eyes, the dull light reappeared, gaining in strength until the green glow was all he could see.

At the time he had not wondered why these eyes were green while all the other moonrats' he had ever seen had eyes that glowed a dirty yellow. It had taken a while for him to understand that the moonrat had been one of his mistress' special children. She had sacrificed it to speak with him.

Now here he was walking through the woods towards his first true meeting with his mistress. The tangle of limbs overhead became so thick that the glow of the moonrats' eyes was his only source of light in the darkness. His fear deepened. He had followed her willingly all of this time. Her promise of power had been so welcome, her promise of love so seductive. Still, he hadn't expected it to go this far.

At first her only needs had been that of companionship. He would hold the eye that was her gift and speak with her for hours. She had been so willing to listen, so concerned about the tiniest problems with his life. Her first requests had been so small, a bit of information here and there. Her requests had seemed insignificant compared to the vast knowledge she had shared with him. At her suggestion, he and Pympol had coerced the elven herbs from Justan. She had also given him the information they needed to complete the golem.

By the time she had demanded Piledon's death, he was hers completely and utterly. He hadn't thought twice. He had enjoyed it even. He had basked in her approval and reveled in the thought of the pleasures that would come with his reward. It hadn't been until later as he used the eye to awaken the perloi and watched them devour his friend's body that he felt guilt and it wasn't until Wizard Locksher had returned to the school that he felt any regret.

When he knew that he had been found out, he had run to the gates of the school, but they had been closed and the wizards were waiting for an escape attempt. Her voice had calmed him and led him up the stairs to the top of the wall. He had been sighted, but before they could get to him, clawed hands grabbed him from out of the darkness and pulled him over the edge. The moonrats had carried him down the wall and into the forest away from the wizards' search. His mistress had rescued him and now he would finally meet her.

The smell of decay had been wafting around for a while already, but as he followed the moonrats deeper into the forest, the smell grew more and more noxious until it stung his nostrils and churned his stomach. The air was warmer and more humid here and the ground began to suck at his boots. He saw more glowing yellow eyes all around him. They were in the trees, on the ground, and even peering up out of the muck.

The moonrats became so many in number that it was no longer dark. It was like he was walking through a tunnel made entirely of yellow orbs. The only darkness was the narrow path at his feet leading to his mistress.

As he got closer, he forgot about the smell. He forgot about the ichor that sucked at his boots as he walked. He didn't even feel the stings on his legs from the teeth of the insects that climbed up his boots. His fear was gone as well, replaced by yearning. He was about to meet his mistress for the first time. She was going to fulfill her promises. Oh how he ached for her.

The tunnel of yellow orbs faded to green as he walked among her special children and then he was before her.

In front of him stood the remains of an ancient tree. At one time it had been magnificent and beautiful, perhaps the largest tree in the forest. Now it was but a husk of its former glory. Its vast trunk was lightning scarred. Most of its branches were bare or broken, and blotches of mold and rot covered what remained.

On either side of the trunk sat a moonrat with orange eyes, his mistress' most prized children. The two precious beasts weren't looking at him, but had their eyes trained on the figure between them. In the middle, rising from between two large roots of the tree was his mistress herself.

Arcon's heart thundered in his chest. She was dark, black as the darkest night and he could not make out her features, but her form was shapely in the glow of her children's adoring gaze and her presence was all at once horrible and irresistible. He wanted to run to her, to leap into her embrace, but instead he fell to his knees in the muck and eagerly awaited her acknowledgement.

It was then that he sensed her anger. She was furious, seething with rage at something that had just transpired far away from here. He was grateful that her wrath was not directed at him. This close to her presence, he was sure that his heart would explode from the power of it. Then her form turned to him and the intensity of her fury dissipated.

"*You finally come to me, dear Arcon,*" she purred, her voice deep and beautiful and terrible.

"I . . . live to . . ." His voice was thick with emotion and the words were so confused that they would not come.

"*Of course you do,*" she said. Her voice dropped lower and carried such a sultry tone that his mouth watered. "*You have served me well and your reward awaits. Come closer to me, my dear.*"

He shuffled forward on his knees in the muck, his mind void of any thought but her promise. As he came closer, her features remained too dark to make out, but the orange glow of the eyes of the children to either side glistened on the edges of her, hinting at a form so perfect and desirable that he faltered and stopped. He was too overcome to move.

She chuckled and the delight in her voice almost killed him. "*Stand, dear Arcon. Come closer. Closer still, that I may touch you.*"

Numb to everything except his devotion, his body followed her commands taking step after step towards her. It did not occur to him to wonder why she did not move towards him. Her smooth black arms reached for him and he tensed every muscle in his body, aching for her touch. Then she grasped him.

Her touch was not as expected. The hands that gripped him were powerful and rough, and as she pulled him closer, her breath was rancid. Her body and countenance were still so black that he could not make out what she looked like. Her presence though, was sultry as ever and he ignored everything else, filled with gratitude for her attention.

"*Oh, my dear Arcon how I have longed for this moment as I know you have*," she breathed and though her body smelled of decay, her voice was filled with such passion that he did not care. "*Now that you are here, I require one more task.*"

"Anything, Mistress," he gasped.

"*I must ask you to go on a journey for me*."

His heart cried out in agony at the thought of leaving. She pulled him closer and whispered in his ear. Her lips touched his earlobe as she spoke, leaving behind something thick and wet.

"*Do not worry. I will give you a piece of me to take with you. After this night, we will never be apart again.*"

"Yes!" he cried, overcome with gratitude.

"*Very well*," She chuckled again and ran one finger down his chest. Where her finger passed, the cloth of his winter robes tore and fell open, exposing his skin. She leaned closer and he shuddered at the chill of her breath on him.

"*Now, you mustn't die. What happens next will be too much for you, but you must live. You can not serve me if you are dead and you can not collect your reward. Do you understand?*"

"Yes!" he cried. "Do it!"

She ran a finger between two of his ribs and his flesh parted underneath. He cried out at the searing pain, but did not move. She then reached out and one of the special moonrats with the orange eyes approached her. She stroked its head lovingly, then squeezed. There was a horrible crunch and a shuddering squeal. Her hand returned holding one glowing eye.

His mistress lifted the orange orb and brought it to his chest. A small clawed appendage sprouted from the bottom of the orb and grasped blindly at the air.

"P-please," he gasped, his eyes filled with terror.

"*Shhhhh . . .*" she whispered gently and reached her black fingers inside of him.

He cried out again as she parted his ribs with her strong fingers and there was a crack of yielding bone. The pain was too much, but he kept his promise and did not die. She pushed the glowing orb inside him, he felt it slipping around his lung to nestle next to his beating heart, which she caressed gently before removing her hand from his chest.

She squeezed the wound shut and with another swipe of a finger knit the wound shut. The healing was far more painful than the wounding had been. He could feel traces of her like decayed leaves remaining inside of him.

"*There Arcon. We shall be connected as long as you live.*"

"Th-thank you, my mistress," he said.

"*Now for the reward I promised you,*" she breathed. The words were throaty and deep with promise. She pulled him in closer and when her arms wrapped around him it was as if she had a thousand arms. She ran a slithering tongue up his neck and along his jaw until her lips finally found his. As his screams echoed through the night, they were indistinguishable from pain or pleasure.

Chapter Six

Ewzad Vriil was dead.

Or at least Ewzad thought he was. He had seen the pommel of Tamboor's sword protruding from his chest. He had felt Elise Muldroomon stab him with the dark dagger. He had seen the swirling blackness and had felt his body being sucked away by the dark power of the knife.

His mind now wandered through nothingness, wracked with pain. Every inch of his nonexistent body was on fire. It seemed to last forever. Was this the afterlife? An empty eternity filled with misery? Perhaps not. The darkness calmed him. The pain began to fade. Ewzad grew sleepy. He let his thoughts slip away. Perhaps there was an end.

The nothingness was penetrated by a voice that jolted Ewzad back into awareness. The voice seared through Ewzad's mind and laid it open, pouring through his thoughts. He knew this voice. Ewzad could hide nothing from the voice of the Dark Prophet.

"**Why do you try to escape, Ewzad Vriil?**" the voice said. "**You are mine. You cannot hide from me.**"

"Leave me alone," Ewzad whimpered. "I am dead. Yes, dead."

"**You are not. Not yet.**"

How could that be? Ewzad wondered. How could he survive that? The voice jolted Ewzad again.

"**Awaken.**"

Ewzad opened his eyes, but he still saw nothing. Wait, he had eyes. Then he could feel his body again. He took a deep breath and gasped in pain. He was lying naked on cold dusty ground. Ewzad reached down and felt the gaping wound in his chest where the sword had pierced him. No, still pierced him. He grasped the sword with squirming fingers and slowly pulled it out of his chest inch by inch until it clattered to the ground. Hot wetness pumped from the wound, pooling underneath him. Ewzad cried out and his mind tried to slip back into nothingness, but the Dark Voice would not let him go.

"**Stay,**" the voice said. Ewzad quivered and squirmed. "**Heal yourself.**"

"I can't! It is impossible!"

"**Use the artifact. It will heal you.**"

"No!" Ewzad yelled. He had used the healing properties of the Rings of Stardeon to heal his servants in the past, but never on himself. He knew that the price to the wielder of the rings would be terrible.

"**It will not be terrible,**" The Dark Voice said. "**It will make you more powerful.**"

"No, their power will weaken!"

"**Their power will not weaken. Your ability to use them will increase. Use the rings. Become one with them. You will have no need to fear weapons again.**"

"I will n-not. N-no I won't. I would rather be dead. Yes, dead!"

"**You will obey me!**" The voice flexed, sending shards of agony through Ewzad's dying mind. "**Twice you have been given to me. Once you gave yourself. Now another gives you. You are mine, Ewzad Vriil. You will do as I say.**"

"Please?"

"**Now!**"

Ewzad did as he was told and for the first time, turned the terrible power of the rings inward. He cleansed the fluids that had been tainted by infection and stitched together the tissues that had been torn apart by the sword. He wanted to stop there, but the magic of the rings had hold of him now. No longer satisfied with merely feeding on his life force, the rings desired to become one with him. Their power surged through his entire body, sending unimaginable pain along his every nerve until it was finished with him.

Moment's later, Ewzad Vriil rose from the floor fully healed and changed forever. He blinked his eyes but still could not see. Ewzad extended one undulating finger and a ball of fire appeared to illuminate his surroundings. He was in a wide square room walled in finely carved stone. The floor of the room was made of marble and covered in a thick layer of dust. Ewzad looked back to the floor where he had awoken and saw many twisted runes carved into the marble under the pool of blood.

"My, my. How did you bring me here?" he asked the voice. When he had first heard the dark voice, it was weak. After being forgotten for two hundred years, the spirit of the Dark Prophet had lost most of its power. Surely it hadn't gained the strength to bring his body away from the castle.

"**Since you have spread the word of my return, the orcs and goblins have begun worshipping me again. My power is growing. When I felt you stabbed by the blood dagger, I pulled you here.**" The dark voice chuckled. "**It was time that you completed your transformation anyway. Look in the mirror. See how you have changed.**"

Ewzad walked to the full-length mirror that stood in the corner of the room. He examined his naked body, clapping his hands in glee. "Oh yes, I have changed. Oooh, it is better, isn't it?"

In the past, when Ewzad wore the rings his body became thin and emaciated, his cheeks sunken, his hair thin and greasy. Now that the rings had become part of him, his body seemed to be in full health. His stomach was taut and muscular. His face red cheeked and healthy. His hair full and lustrous. He could work his plans in the daylight once again.

"Yes, yes. This is better." Ewzad raised one hand to run his fingers through his hair and recoiled in horror. His arm curved up to his hair bonelessly as if it were not an arm at all, but a flesh-colored snake. His other arm hung to his side, undulating back and forth slowly. He had become used to the way his fingers had writhed about when wearing the rings, but this? "This is unacceptable! No-no, not right at all!"

"**It is but a small price to pay for the power you receive.**"

"The power is lesser!" Ewzad cried, and tried to bring his arms under control, to make them bend normally. It was no use. Every movement was more grotesque than the one before. He reached to take the rings off of his fingers but the rings had disappeared, leaving only the gemstones embedded in his flesh.

"**The power is now a part of you forever**."

"No, no. I cannot take them off. I cannot enact my plans with this . . . deformation!"

The voice warmed and soothed Ewzad's thoughts, massaging the fear away. "**I will give you the control you need. You must enter my chamber, Ewzad Vriil.**"

At one end of the room was a wide wooden door with a large brass handle. Ewzad approached as instructed, but his legs quivered. It felt as if they were about to lose their cohesion and writhe as uncontrollably as his arms. Somehow he reached the door and wrapped his fingers around the handle. With some effort, he pulled the door open on squeaky hinges. The ball of flame he had conjured followed.

Ewzad's eyes widened as the ball of flame illuminated the room beyond. He now knew where he was. This was the lair of the Dark Prophet. This was the place where, two hundred years ago, the true prophet and his companions had confronted the Dark Prophet and his minions.

The scars from that battle still remained. The chamber had once been large and ornate with extravagant tapestries and great statues. Now the walls were blackened and the front half of the chamber had been caved in by the violent throes of the Dark Prophet's death. The floor was covered in rubble and scattered with the bones of fallen warriors.

"**Come to me.**" the voice said. "**Find my remains.**"

Ewzad instantly knew which spot was his master's resting place. He stepped carefully around the shards of metal, rock and bone that littered the floor and crept forward to a place where the marble floor was cratered and bubbled. In the center, as if growing out of the floor itself, was a skeleton that had been twisted and elongated by some unknown force. The skull was stretched and curved into an eerie scream while one arm spiraled upward, the hand reaching as if for mercy.

"**Take my dagger.**"

Ewzad dug into the ashes surrounding the bones, ignoring the way his arms swayed as he searched, and found what his master requested. The dagger's sheath had melted to the floor and Ewzad had to twist and pull to wrench the blade free. To his surprise, though the leather on the hilt had burned away, the dagger itself was undamaged.

"**Good.**" The Dark Prophet's approval sent a jolt of pleasure through Ewzad's mind. A sigh escaped the wizard's lips. "**Now follow my instructions.**"

The voice guided Ewzad to the back of the chamber where the Dark Prophet's throne stood. Now broken and twisted, the throne had once been made of the bones of large beasts that were carved with images of torture and mutilations. Ewzad snaked his fingers along the bones, a smile contorting his face.

"Oh such sweet ideas . . ." Ewzad murmured.

The voice told Ewzad to reach around the throne and pull a lever. There was a rumbling sound and the rear wall of the chamber began to open inward. Then a deep shudder issued from beneath Ewzad's feet and the apparatus came to a halt. There wasn't enough room for him to squeeze inside. Evidently the damage to the room was greater than the dark voice knew.

"**You have the power to open it, Ewzad**."

"Yes, yes. Of course I do," Ewzad said with a shake of his head. He approached the opening and sent with the squirm of a finger, another glowing ball of flame inside. The light illuminated an ascending stairwell.

"Hmm, this shall do most nicely, I think." He took a step back and with his two middle fingers vibrating madly, gathered a mighty blast of air. His powers were indeed reduced, but the strength of the blast would still suffice. He raised his waving arms over his head and flung them forward like the strike of a snake, hurtling the focused mass of air towards the jammed doors.

The force of the blast blew the doors into pieces and, too great to be contained in the small passageway beyond, blew Ewzad backwards. He tumbled across the floor along with the ash and dust and shards of metal that littered the floor of the Dark Prophet's throne room. He came to a rest, bruised and battered at the base of the broken throne and moaned.

"Ohh, blast it, too much. Gah! Always too much with me, blast it!"

Ewzad barely noticed that the minor bruises and abrasions he had accumulated during his tumble were already healing. He climbed through the remains of the secret doors, ascended the stairs, and walked through the entrance at the top which opened into a long corridor. Ewzad started down the passage, but paused at a beautiful gold-etched door to his right.

The voice urged him forward, but Ewzad was curious. He placed a hand on the polished golden handle and opened the door into an opulent room. Strangely, this room was free of dust. The room was furnished with beautiful tapestries and silks. An enormous bed piled high with overstuffed pillows filled one corner of the room. The western wall of the room was covered in a polished metal. Glass spheres protruded from the metal in places, but that wasn't what caught the wizard's attention. A large wardrobe along the eastern wall was opened and Ewzad saw a variety of multicolored robes spilling out. He stepped inside hoping to clothe his nakedness, but the voice stopped him with a stab of pain.

"**That can wait.**"

Reluctantly, Ewzad moved on down the corridor to a side stairwell and a final door. It was locked, but Ewzad waved two squirming fingers at it and the knob wilted and fell apart. He pushed the door inward to a brightly lit chamber lined with flameless torches.

The walls of this chamber were more roughly carved than in the rest of the complex. The floor curved downward from all sides like a great bowl with steps leading down to the center of the room. A single red carpet led up the steps to a marble pedestal on top of which sat a large silver bowl filled halfway with water.

"**Approach the bowl and raise the blade.**"

Ewzad stepped into the room. His heart jumped in his chest. He felt feverish. He took a step backward. Something was wrong with this place.

"**Obey me!**" A stab of pain lanced through Ewzad's thoughts and he fell to his knees. Whimpering, he rose to his feet on wavy legs and approached the bowl.

With each step forward his heart beat faster and faster. When he arrived in front of the bowl and raised the dagger, his blood was roaring in his ears. He stabbed the dagger into the bowl and a new voice penetrated his thoughts. This voice chanted in a strange language and to Ewzad's horror, his lungs, tongue, and lips moved of their own volition, echoing these same words from his own mouth.

Suddenly, a bolt of darkness leapt from the waters of the bowl and speared his mind. Ewzad wanted to scream but his voice continued to chant in the unknown language. He frantically tried to resist, to escape, but he had no control. The bolt of darkness was like a lance twisting in his brain. Uncountable images, facts and figures flooded into his mind. Knowledge was crammed into him in a way that seemed a violation. His chanting increased. The knowledge forced into his head combined until a word began to form in his mind. This word became larger until he could no longer contain it.

His chanting stopped. His mouth opened as wide as it could. He coughed and hacked, saliva ran down his chin. The word was too big. It would not come forth. He pushed and pushed until the word ripped free from his throat.

“ENVAKFEER!” Ewzad fell to his knees and looked at his squirming hands in shock. On the palm of his right hand a black rune appeared.

The Dark Voice chuckled. “**Now, my servant, you have been given your real name. But you must keep it safe from the world until you are ready to reveal yourself. Then, Envakfeer, you will let them know that I have returned!**”

“Oh yes. Yes, Master yes!” Ewzad Vriil willed his waving arms under control, and they obeyed, resuming a normal appearance. A giggle of glee burst from the wizard, but it was interrupted by a gasp as he noticed something else new. In his right forearm was set a single shriveled sphere that glowed dully in the dim light. The moonrat eye stared at him unblinkingly.

“**One more thing, Envakfeer. It seems that you have been**

neglecting the servant I gave you to help run my army. This will stop. Like the rings, her treasured gift is now a part of you."

Ewzad's face twisted into a snarl.

"Ah, but Master. She listens! She schemes! She plots behind my back! I cannot have her with me at all times! Besides . . . it is unsightly." A shard of pain stabbed his mind in response and he recoiled. "But I shall do as you wish, Master, yes! It is but a trifle. I can cover it easily!"

"**Have you been listening**?" the dark voice asked. Ewzad opened his mouth, but realized that the dark voice was no longer speaking to him.

"*Yes, my love*," crooned the female voice from Ewzad's forearm.

"**Whom do you obey**?"

"*Envakfeer, of course*," she said, with a hint of irritation.

"**Envakfeer, if she becomes insolent, call her by name. You should know it now**."

"*You told him*?" she hissed in anger. "*Do you not trust my fealty*?"

"**He is Envakfeer now. He has been given the knowledge by the bowl**."

It came suddenly to Ewzad's mind. Oh yes, he knew her name. He knew it indeed. "Yes, yes. You will obey me now. Won't you my dear, Mellinda?"

She hissed again, this time in despair, but answered, "*Yes, my Master. Always*."

Ewzad chuckled and clapped his hands together in glee. Now, he was truly in control. She would obey him and not only did he have power of the rings, he had the knowledge to use it. Thoughts and plans roiled through his mind. Ewzad flexed the muscles in his arms and grinned. He knew just who he would use it on.

* * *

Hamford ducked back into the chamber and shut the door behind him with a sigh of relief before he nearly choked on the smell. In the time since Ewzad's demise, the beasts had continued to decay. It had grown worse every moment. In his brief time outside of the chamber, he had nearly forgotten.

"Well?" Kenn said from within the control room.

"Here." Hamford tossed a bundle of clothes at Kenn's feet. "I had to wait until the princess was gone before I got in line for the clothes with the escapees. Luckily none of them recognized me."

"Good." Kenn busied himself getting dressed. He was eager to put on anything after a day and a half of sitting around in nothing more than a loin cloth. He lifted something gold and lace embroidered. "Hey, what's this? I asked you to get me some pants, what are these? They only go down to the knees!"

"Those are the duke's court pants. You are lucky I didn't bring you a dress. There wasn't much left and I had to hurry before anyone figured out who I was," Hamford snapped. He tossed Kenn some bread. "I got us some food too, though I don't know how I am going to keep it down it stinks so bad in here."

Kenn caught the bread and eagerly stuffed half of it in his mouth before pulling the pants up. "At least it fits. You know our Master would kill me for wearing this stuff."

"Good thing he's dead," Hamford said. "On the bright side, once we get back home you'll be able to sell it for a fortune."

"So when can we leave?" Kenn asked as he tore into the rest of the bread.

"I don't know. I didn't dare get too close, but I overheard the captain saying they were getting ready to depart, so I say we wait until night and take our chances getting out without being seen."

"Why not just lower the ramp leading to the back tunnel again and leave out that way? No one would know. Besides, the dragons have to be long gone by now."

"Do they? What if they aren't, Kenn? We are finally free and you want to get eaten by those things?" Hamford shuddered. "We go out the front. Even if we are captured and taken to Dremald for trial, at least we will still be alive."

“I guess.” Kenn said. “Got anything more?”

“Yeah.” Hamford opened the sack of food he had procured. He took out a hunk of cheese, but as he was handing it to his brother, he froze, letting it drop from his fingers. He clutched at his chest.

“Yes! I knew it!” Kenn laughed. “It’s back! Its weak, but its back! The master isn’t dead!” Then a look of horror spread across his face and he began taking his newly acquired clothes back off.

Hamford fell to his knees, nearly in tears. The seed of power deep inside of him had returned.

Chapter Seven

It was still early morning. The sun had barely peeked over the horizon and the forest was alive with scents and sounds. Two weeks had passed since Justan's party had left Ewzad Vriil's castle and as they traveled further away from the higher elevations in the mountains, the winter became relatively mild. There had been a fresh snowfall during the night, but it had already melted for the most part.

Justan crept forward through the wet leaves carefully, wincing at every sound he made. His prey had very sensitive ears and he didn't want it to notice his presence. Despite the training Qyxal had been giving him, Justan still wasn't very stealthy. He was getting better at tracking though, and he could see that his prey had passed this way recently.

He looked down and examined the tracks again. It was four legged and walked on the balls of its feet. From the depth of the impression, he could see that the beast was heavy. The toes were widely spaced and ended in long claws. This was a dangerous creature. Justan grinned. He was definitely getting better. He was so close and she didn't even know he was following her.

The next thing he knew, there was a loud crash behind him. Justan found himself lying with a mouthful of mud, his face pressed deep into the leaves, a heavy weight on his shoulders.

"Hey!" He protested, spitting out mud and turned his head to see a large reptilian snout full of wickedly curved teeth snap shut right before his face. "Get off me!" The beast pressed him down harder and Justan felt his mind being prodded.

"Okay!" He sighed and said more calmly this time, "Please get off of me, Gwyrtha."

She gave a satisfied snort and the weight was gone. Justan got to his feet and sent Gwyrtha a strong burst of irritation through the bond.

"You cheated. You used the bond to know where I was!" She just snorted again and turned to the side, presenting her flank to him in an invitation to ride. Justan looked at her and frowned. "How did you sneak up on me?"

He had been deliberately ignoring the bond so that he could test his tracking skills. He looked around and his jaw dropped as he figured out what she had done. "You jumped out of that tree?"

Perhaps she had more cat in her than he thought. The bark of the massive oak beside him was torn and chipped from her claws. It was the only tree around large enough to support her weight. The winter wind had left the tree bare of leaves. If he hadn't been so intent on the ground, he would have seen her easily.

Gwyrtha huffed her version of a laugh and Justan could sense her amusement. She nudged him and presented her flank again. *Ride,* she said through the bond and Justan smiled again.

When they had first met, she had been mostly a creature of instinct. The bond had changed them both. Justan had gained stamina and quicker reflexes; she had gained intelligence. They had been bonded for a year and her mind was still evolving. Not only had she started to laugh, she had begun to think in words now and then.

"Fine," Justan said. "You win, we'll go back now. Just don't try so hard to throw me off this time."

He climbed onto her back and held tight to her mane as she started off toward their camp. They both enjoyed their rides. Justan had gotten much better and clinging to her back was almost second nature to him now. Gwyrtha knew that he had become comfortable and liked to make a game out of trying to jostle him loose. She was only occasionally successful, but even when he rode her with perfection, she still found ways to make him sore the next day.

They were only a mile from the camp, but Gwyrtha made the most of it, dodging trees and leaping as high as she could. Justan listened to her movements through the bond as they rode, so he was able to anticipate most of her moves. She even threatened to try a somersault, but Justan pleaded with her not to until she complied.

Qyxal looked up as they rode into camp and smiled, his white teeth bright in the morning light. The elf looked out of place in the wilderness with his hair braided immaculately and his robes unsoiled from the road. “So who found whom?”

“Did you know she could climb trees?” Justan asked as he slid from her back.

“We asked her not to. It’s hard on the trees,” Qyxal replied. “So I take it you lost?”

“She cheated,” Justan remarked. Gwyrtha snorted indignantly and Justan added, “Okay, she outsmarted me. Your lessons are catching on, though. I did better this time. But I think pitting me against Gwyrtha is unfair. She can hear a rabbit's heartbeat in the brush from a hundred yards away and smell whether it's male or female.” He pulled at his travel worn shirt. “I haven't been able to bathe in a week.”

“You would rather track after me for practice?”

“No,” Justan said. He was tired of tracking the elf. Qyxal knew how to disguise his tracks too well and Justan could never quite manage to find him. “At least not for a while. I want to get better before I track you again.”

Qyxal shrugged. “Then go after Fist or Lenny.”

Justan's stomach growled at the mention of the dwarf. “Does Lenny have breakfast ready yet?”

“No. And he isn’t too happy about it either. I’ve had to put up with his grumbling all morning.”

Justan walked over to the fire where the dwarf was going through their supplies and muttering angrily. The dwarf had been getting in a fouler and fouler mood over the last week. Justan frowned. “What’s wrong, Lenny?”

Lenny had become their cook for the journey. When Justan had suggested that everybody take turns cooking, the dwarf had scoffed at the idea. Now the dwarf cooked and cleaned and even repaired any equipment that broke. He had become invaluable as a traveling companion and the food was good, though it had taken some of them a while to get used to the level of spice the dwarf used.

"Whaddya' think's wrong?" The dwarf's red handlebar mustache was pulled down in a scowl. "Where's the gall-durn ogre, boy? He was 'posed to bring the meat. How am I 'posed to cook our dag-blamed breakfast without the meat?"

"Let's see . . ." Justan felt through his bond with the ogre. Fist had left the camp to go hunting before Justan had even awakened that morning. Justan conversed with Fist briefly over the bond and smiled. "Oh, Fist will be here any minute. He's pleased with his catch."

"Well, it'd better be good this time. Remember the-? Hey . . ." Lenny cocked his head and looked Justan up and down. "You look different, son. You've filled out some lately."

"I know." Justan looked down and flexed the muscles in his arms. His forearms bulged quite nicely. His grin grew wider. Right now, his body reminded him of his childhood memories of his father. He even felt taller somehow.

"Hah! Good dwarf cookin' will put meat on anyone's bones," Lenny said, his gap toothed grin beaming with pride.

"It's because of Fist actually," Justan said. "I felt stronger the moment we bonded. I guess my body is just catching up." With the benefits of speed, stamina and strength he received from his bonds with Fist and Gwyrtha, Justan was now in the shape he had always wished to be. He wondered if he would continue to get stronger.

"Dag-nab it, son, you have all the luck," Lenny said with a bemused shake of his head..

"Here he comes," Justan said. He could hear the ogre's deep rumbling voice coming through the trees.

Soon Fist came into view. He was weighed down with something large and furry that he had half slung over his shoulders. Whatever it was, it was big enough that its hind legs dragged on the ground behind him. His face was animated as he talked with the gray rock squirrel that was perched on top of his kill, calmly chewing a nut. Justan could see that the bond had changed the ogre too.

Fist didn't walk quite as hunched over as he used to and he didn't look at all uncomfortable in his new traveling clothes anymore. At first, the pants and button down shirt had looked ridiculous stretched over the ogre's bulging muscles, but Lenny had let out the seams a little and they fit him much better. Fist had even done some alterations to the pants himself. Lenny had been teaching the ogre to sew, something that Qyxal found endlessly amusing.

" . . . and then, Squirrel, we have our own territory again," the ogre was saying as he approached the fire.

He dropped his kill at Lenny's feet, then stretched, reaching out his long, thick arms and rose to his full height of over eight feet. His back popped with several loud cracks and he sighed in relief. The moment that Lenny got a good look at the kill, he went into a fury.

"A bear?" The dwarf jumped up and down, shaking his fists at the ogre. "What the garl-friggin' hell am I 'posed to do with a bear, you big dumb varmint?"

"It is good meat. This bear will feed us many days," Fist said, scratching his head in puzzlement. Squirrel shook one tiny fist and chattered at Lenny angrily.

The bond had affected the ogre in other ways as well. He had always been intelligent for an ogre, but his range of thoughts had expanded over the last two weeks. The rest of the companions had been working with him and his pronunciation of the common tongue had improved greatly.

"Good meat? Thing'll be tougher than a horse's hind hoof! I shoulda' gone huntin' myself."

"You could have, if you weren't so busy sleeping off your firewater," Justan said. Gwyrtha ambled over to Fist and nuzzled his side. The ogre absently scratched behind her horselike ears.

"Don't go takin' his side, boy," Lenny said. "In the last two weeks since we left the duke's castle he's brung us a wolf, a couple polecats and a big damn snake! I wanna eat somethin' normal fer once!" He scowled at Fist. "Why couldn't you just kill a deer?"

The ogre shrugged. He had grown used to the dwarf's tantrums. "They are too damn fast."

"You are a bad influence on him, Lenny," Justan said to the dwarf.

Qyxal strode up to see what the commotion was about. "A black bear? Good job, Fist. I haven't had bear meat in a long time."

Lenny fixed the elf with a glower. The elf smiled sweetly in response. Justan was pretty sure that Qyxal had taken Fist's side just to needle the dwarf.

"The pelt will fetch us a good price the next time we come to a town if we prepare it right." Justan said, trying to smooth it over. "We are running low on funds, you know. Besides Lenny, I have faith in your cooking. If you can make a snake taste like chicken, you can make anything taste good."

"It's gonna take us all mornin' to clean the durn thing and wrap it all up, much less prepare the blasted pelt! We're not gonna find yer Master Coal 'till spring if we don't get a move on." The dwarf was still complaining, but he had lost the argument and he knew it. "Alright, Fist. Well, yer gonna have to help me clean it this time."

They dragged the carcass away from the camp and began dressing it. Fist was actually pretty handy with a knife. Justan turned to Qyxal.

"Have you ever really eaten bear?"

"Once when I was little. One of the other children in my hunting party accidentally killed a bear cub and our teachers made us eat it." The elf shivered. "It was awful."

"You can't help yourself can you?" Justan shook his head in exasperation. "What's your problem with Lenny anyway?"

"Oh, don't worry about him," the elf said. "He's just upset because he woke up this morning and discovered that Gwyrtha had buried him again."

Justan looked at Gwyrtha with a frown. The rogue horse just huffed silently in amusement. Justan still hadn't quite figured out why Gwyrtha didn't like dwarves. She had grown quite fond of Lenny after a fashion, but she continued to take her anxieties out on him with her little pranks. It had something to do with her past and every time Justan pressed her about it, she shrugged him off. She was too frightened of those old memories to relive them through the bond.

"Well both of you need to treat him better," Justan said. "The only reason he is journeying with us is out of friendship for me. He cooks your food every day and if we were ever in a battle, he wouldn't hesitate to save your life."

"He doesn't hesitate to complain about me either," Qyxal muttered in irritation. "Especially lately."

"I know what you are saying, but still . . . that's just Lenny being Lenny. You two should know better."

The elf's face stiffened at the rebuke.

"But of course, Sir Edge." Qyxal bowed and strode away. Gwyrtha ignored Justan and calmly chewed on a tuft of dead grass.

Justan winced at Qyxal's parting remark. He had stung his friend's pride, but the things he told the elf had needed to be said. Justan had a feeling that the journey was going to get dangerous before they reached Master Coal and he wanted his group to be as together as possible. They didn't need any turmoil that could tear them apart when times got tough.

He looked down at the new fingerless gloves on his hands and resisted the urge to take them off and stare at the runes. He felt that compulsion a lot lately. He needed to understand why the bowl had chosen to mark him. Since he wasn't the perfect warrior or wizard that the runes marked him as, what did the runes really represent? He hoped that Master Coal could give him some answers.

Until he felt worthy of his new name, he had again asked all of his friends to continue to call him Justan. Lenny and Qyxal weren't comfortable with the idea. They thought it a sign of disrespect to the bowl itself. Justan had given them the excuse that he didn't want to advertise his named warrior status to anyone who might overhear. It was a legitimate concern. There were many rogues and bandits that would love to be able to say they had defeated a named warrior in battle. Though Justan's skill had greatly improved along with his physique, he was still far from being ready to take on challengers.

Justan walked over to his saddlebags and rooted through them. He felt a tinge of unease as his hand brushed against the silken bundle that contained the dagger he had found in Ewzad Vriil's remains. He had showed it to Qyxal and the elf did not seem to like the look of it, but he didn't feel the same sense of menace that Justan did. Maybe Master Coal would know what it was about.

He moved the bundle to the side and pulled out the map that Professor Valtrek had given him. Justan had looked at it so many times since leaving the Mage School that he practically had it memorized by now. Still, he gazed at it. Looking at the map helped order his thoughts.

They had left Ewzad Vriil's castle in a westerly direction. For the first few days they had traveled as quickly as possible in case the king ordered any retaliation over the duke's death. Maintaining a fast pace was difficult because, even though they had two stout warhorses and Gwyrtha with them, Fist had to walk. He was far too big for either horse to handle for long. It wasn't until after they had put a comfortable distance between themselves and the castle that they could slow down to a comfortable pace.

As far as Justan could tell, they should now be very close to the Wide River. The river served as the border between Dremaldria and the neighboring Kingdom of Razbeck. Valtrek had told Justan that Master Coal lived just over the border somewhere in Razbeck, but the wizard was not quite sure where. There were several places in Razbeck that they could go to look for information on Master Coal's whereabouts and Lenny had some contacts that could help, but that wasn't Justan's first concern. Their first obstacle would be crossing the river.

The Wide River was accurately named. There were points along the river where you couldn't see the other side. Valtrek's map wasn't very detailed where the width of the river was concerned. Justan couldn't tell where crossing would be easiest, especially since he wasn't completely sure of their position on the map. The best places to cross were the bridges or ferries along the major roads, but Justan didn't want to cross someplace where they might be seen.

Their party was lacking a good guide. Justan and Qyxal had never been this far away from their homes and Fist had lived in the mountains his whole life. Lenny was the only one with experience traveling this part of the land, but he had always kept to the main roads and he had only crossed the Wide River at the main crossings, or at least that's what he said. The closer to the border they got, the more Justan sensed that the dwarf was holding something back.

With that thought in mind, Justan walked back to the fire with the map in hand. Lenny and Fist already had the bear skinned and gutted. Gwyrtha was tearing into a few of the organs that Lenny didn't want to use for food. Justan shook his head. She never looked less horselike than when she was eating meat. Lenny was lowering thick slices of bear into a hot pan on the fire.

The dwarf looked up as he approached. "Hey son, that went quicker than I thought. Ends up the ogre's purty good at skinnin' a bear. Still gots to scrape the hide clean, though."

"Do not make it hot this time!" Fist said, eying the meat in the pan.

"Dag-nab it, Fist. You ain't never had food this good before you met me."

"Is good food, yes. But it burns my mouth and hurts me inside."

"It's called yer belly," Lenny replied as he went back to chopping away at the bear. "And that's just 'cause you still needs toughenin' up."

Fist had a harder time than anyone getting used to Lenny's cooking. He loved experiencing the new flavors, but he had never eaten seasoned food before. He had spent the first few days with burning in his chest and stomach cramps. The worst part had been a few nights previous when Qyxal and the dwarf had talked him into trying Lenny's firewater.

Fist had taken three large gulps, before leaping up and grabbing at his throat in pain. It had not been a pleasant evening after that. The alcohol affected Fist differently than Justan had seen it affect anyone before. His skin had flushed red and he became enraged. Justan had tried to soothe him through the bond, but the ogre went on a rampage.

He had enough control over himself to flee the camp to avoid hurting them, but then he ran through the woods, ripping down the branches of large trees and pushing over smaller ones. It had lasted for several hours before he had collapsed and fallen asleep. The next day, Fist's head had hurt so bad that Justan's own head had throbbed.

"He's right Lenny," Justan said. "Fist and I weren't raised on the spices you use. Besides, aren't you afraid you're going to run out before we get to Master Coal's?"

"Nah, we ain't too far from a town that's got a decent supply store."

"You know where we are now?" Justan asked. "I thought that you never went off of the road when you traveled this way."

"Oh, well uhh . . ." Lenny tossed a handful of spices on top of the meat and flipped them over in the pan. "You see, I just done recognized where we was this mornin'."

"Good," Justan said, now more sure than ever that there was something the dwarf was holding back. He looked at the map again. "But Lenny, I don't see any towns on the map. Are you sure that you know where we are?"

Justan held the map out, but Lenny raised his hands to show that they were covered in blood and spices. With a sigh, Justan moved next to him and held it open. He pointed to a spot. "This is where I think we are."

"Son, that map of yers must've been made more than twenty years ago. I came this way 'bout four months back and there's a fine little town down by the road a bit south of here . . ." The dwarf trailed off, deep in thought. After a second or two, he shook his head and continued, "Tell you what, after we're finished with the dag-blamed bear and eat our breakfast, we can head down south a ways and then you and me'll go to town."

They needed to keep their group unseen while they traveled. The sight of Gwyrtha would scare anyone and it would not be easy for them to explain an ogre in their party, no matter how well he was dressed. Even Qyxal stood out too much since it was rare to see elves away from their homelands. The plan they settled on was for Justan and Lenny to go into the towns to find information and leave Fist, Qyxal, and Gwyrtha in hiding.

"Okay, good," Justan said, but he wondered why the dwarf was acting so strange. "Do you think they might be interested in taking a bear skin this fresh in trade?"

"Don't rightly know. Can't hurt to ask, though."

They finished butchering Fist's kill, ate quickly, and set off to the south. The bear meat was tough and a bit gamey, but edible and they definitely had enough to last them for a while. They scraped the hide out and set it to dry over Stanza's back as they walked. As long as they stayed upwind of it, the smell wasn't too bad.

By mid afternoon, they spotted smoke trails in the distance and knew they were nearing the town. They left Fist and Qyxal to set up camp, then Justan and Lenny took the two warhorses and started towards the town. Lenny was silent as they rode, acting very unlike his usual boisterous self. It wasn't long before Justan had to say something.

"Lenny, what's been bothering you lately? The closer we get to the Razbeck border, the stranger you act."

Lenny was startled by the question and took a moment to think before responding. "Well son, you see I got some unfinished business to attend to round these parts and I been tryin' to figure out what to do about it."

"What kind of business?"

"Well, it's the kind that might take me away from you fer a while. Not too long, maybe a few days till I get it sorted out, then I can meet right back up with you along the trail."

"But . . . oh wait." Justan grinned. "Is this . . . girl business?"

"Girl business?" Lenny burst out in a deep guffaw that had the dwarf shaking so hard that Justan became worried he was going to fall out of the saddle. It went on for long enough that Justan had no choice but to join in.

"What's so funny about that question?" Justan asked once the dwarf's laughter had finally trailed off. "You've been acting so mysterious that I figured that maybe you had a lady friend nearby you wanted to visit or something."

"Lady friend? Hooo boy," the dwarf gasped, wiping tears from his eyes. "Lemme tell you somethin'. Girls'r trouble, that's fer shure. But I'd rather have that kind of trouble any day than this. Hmm . . . havin' a girl to curl up with would be purty nice about right now, though."

"Then what could it be? I mean, I guess it's none of my business really, I'm just grateful to have you along with me. But if there is any way I could help? I want to get to Master Coal's as soon as possible, but a few days delay isn't that big of a deal."

"It ain't that easy, son." Lenny was silent for a moment, staring at the ground while stroking his handlebar mustache. "This is somethin' that could get you killed."

Chapter Eight

The horses stepped out of the trees and onto a well traveled road. Lenny turned Stanza to the west and Justan followed, bringing Albert up beside the dwarf. He could smell smoke from stoves and fireplaces. They were getting close to the town.

"What? Are you going somewhere that you are afraid people might see Fist or Gwyrtha and attack us?" Justan asked. "Don't you think we can handle ourselves?"

"Just a dag-blasted minute, boy," the dwarf started, but held his tongue. They heard raucous voices and soon a group of men heavily armed and with a swagger that could only come from drunkenness came around the bend. They paid no mind to Justan and Lenny, but continued on their way laughing and pushing each other around.

The last few weeks of being alone with his friends had been so involving, that Justan found the sight of a group of strangers on the road jarring. He stared as they passed and turned his head to watch them continue on their way, but Lenny slapped him on the shoulder.

"Hey, keep yer eyes forward. Drunkards don't like people starin' and we don't need no trouble here. Them boys probly fell asleep in the saloon last night and just now woke up."

The outskirts of town came into view. They passed a few modest cabins with a winter-barren garden or two before coming to the center of the town. It wasn't a large town, maybe eight buildings in all were lined up along either side of the main road, but it didn't consist of the kind of businesses Justan expected to see in such a small place. They rode past two inns, a brothel, and a tavern before coming to the supply store.

“What kind of town is this?” Justan asked. “I mean, why would people choose to stay here out in the middle of nowhere?”

“It’s a border town, son. These kinds of places come and go when there’s a lot of travel on a road. This here’s the road to the main river crossin’ a few miles down. Lots of good folks been leavin’ Dremaldria lately to get away from the troubles, while at the same time, lots of bad folks’r comin’ in to be a part of the troubles. The place’s grown some since the last time I was here, though. Somethin’ else must be bringin’ folks in.”

They dismounted the horses and walked to the front door of the store. It was a large but modest looking store from the outside. Large wooden letters on the face of the building read, “SUPPLY”. When they walked in, Justan saw what Lenny had meant when he said that the place was decent.

Every inch of the store seemed to be taken up with goods. There was a large center aisle, but aside from that, there was barely room to walk between the shelves upon shelves of all the things a traveler might need. There were rows of pots and pans and cups and utensils. Barrels of different kinds of horse feed, bags, harnesses, replacement stirrups, knives, daggers, low quality weapons and more.

“Hugo! I brought you some business!” the dwarf bellowed as they entered the store. The owner, a middle-aged balding man wearing a long sleeved red shirt and a dirty apron looked up from behind the front counter and grinned.

“Why Lenui Firegobbler! Never thought I’d see you again after that last time.”

“Yeah, well I got some business to attend to round these parts.” The dwarf leaned on the counter. “I got me a high grade bear pelt this mornin’ if yer interested.”

Hugo shrugged. “I suppose I can take it in trade if the quality’s good. I do get some decent merchant traffic nowadays and someone will take it off my hands, but I don’t know how much I’ll be able to give you for it. I got lots of pelts coming in lately with all the monster hunters in town. We’re famous now since the rock giant took out that duke’s men.”

“Sure, I’ll bring it in then.”

As the dwarf left the store, Justan walked up to the front counter. He noticed that the man had a brace of throwing daggers around each upper arm. No doubt running a store in a place like this, he needed to know how to use them.

"Excuse me, Lenny and I are looking for a man named Coal. He's supposed to live just over the border and I was hoping -," Justan paused because the moment he had mentioned the name Coal, the man's face had split into a wide grin.

"Looking for Coal, eh? A nicer man you'll never meet. Why he's the type of man that'd help a fellow out even if he barely knew ya." The grin faded a little and a wary look came into the man's eye. "What are you looking for a man like him for?"

"Uh, actually I am hoping to learn from him," Justan explained. "I needed a teacher and a wizard at the Mage School sent me out to find him."

"Oh, well that's alright then." The grin reappeared on the man's face. "Hell of a man, Coal. Normally, I wouldn't direct passer's by his way, though. Twouldn't be nice to the man since he already helps so many and all. But since you're with Lenui, I guess I can make an exception. He's not too far on the other side of the border. If you can get around the rock giant's territory, you can probably cross the river at the shallows and be there in a day's time. Just head straight west past all the farms just in the woods there."

"Hey Lenny," Justan said. The dwarf had reappeared and dropped the pelt on the counter. "This man knows Master Coal."

"That's good news, son." Lenny patted Justan on the back and wandered over to the corner of the store where the spices were kept. "Hugo, why don't you point it out fer the boy on his map."

Justan got out his map and Hugo pointed the spot out. "Once you get there, ask anyone. Everybody knows the man. You couldn't miss him."

"Thank you so much," Justan said. "So you know Lenny pretty well?"

"Sure, he comes through from time to time. Shared some ale with him the last time he came through. He near cried on my shoulder the night after the rock-."

"Hugo, don't you go tellin' no stories now," Lenny growled.

"What don't you want the boy to know?" Hugo looked back to Justan "It's a funny story."

"He don't need to hear yer gall-durn stories! We're just here fer some trade, that's all," the dwarf snapped. He began looking through the spice barrels.

"Now I have to hear it, Lenny," Justan said with a chuckle. "You have got to tell me what would make this tough old dwarf cry."

"I weren't cryin' dag-blast it!" Lenny slammed his fist on the closest shelf, knocking pouches of ingredients all over the floor.

"I said 'near'," Hugo protested. "Alright, alright. I'll look at your pelt, then." Lenny bent over to pick up the pouches. While Hugo was inspecting the pelt, he motioned to Justan and winked. Justan leaned over the counter and the man whispered, "He's just upset because our rock giant beat him up and took his hammer."

"What?" Justan's mouth fell open. Now he started to understand. "Lenny, is that what all this is about? A giant stole Buster? I wondered why you didn't have him with you."

There was a muffled thud and a plume of brown powder came up from the corner of the store.

"Son of a-," Lenny came roaring up the aisle, half of his face covered in powdered chili. "Hugo, you dirt eatin' son of a dog! What'd I tell you? I outta' peel yer hide and sell it to yer competition!"

"Just a minute!" Justan yelled, interrupting the dwarf's tirade. "You think that the five of us together couldn't handle one giant?"

"W-well. It ain't that simple!"

"It isn't? Explain it to me then!"

The half of Lenny's face not covered in spices was red and his jaw worked as if trying to decide what to say. Before it came to him, more customers came into the store. The dwarf shut his mouth and sighed. He dusted off his face and tried to knock the spice out of his mustache.

"Later, son. I'll tell you on the way back," he finally said.

Hugo seemed a bit embarrassed about the scene and gave them a more than fair amount for the pelt. The more Justan thought about it, the more upset he became about the dwarf's lack of trust in his abilities. He fumed in silence as they picked up the miscellaneous items they needed for their travels and paid Hugo the difference. When they were finished, they loaded up the horses and headed back up the road. They left the town in silence. They were a ways into the woods before either one of them said anything.

"Look, son, it's a story I aint proud of-." Lenny hesitated. Justan said nothing, just looked at the dwarf expectantly. "Some blasted bastard stole a magicked sword I made. The idjit got himself killed by this rock giant and when I went to get it back, the garl-friggin thing took Buster and booted me out of his territory. I dun tried lots of times to get him back, but it kept beatin' me 'till I gave up."

"Is this why you won't talk to me about the new swords I want you to make?" Justan asked. He had asked the dwarf to look at the drawings with him several times during the journey, but Lenny kept making excuses.

"Well, I can't make anything magic with any other hammer. It just wouldn't . . . be right." Lenny scowled. "Dog-gone it, can't you see this is a private thing? If one of you was killed 'cause I was stupid enough to get my Buster stolen, I would . . ."

"If one of us needed help, would you want us to leave you out of it?"

"Why hell no, but-!"

"Lenny, we look out for each other. We would all put our lives on the line. That's what friends do," Justan said. "Am I wrong?"

"Look, son," the dwarf said, frustration mounting in his voice again. "This ain't just any rock giant or I woulda killed it myself a while ago. It's fast and smart and killed lots of men just fer the fun of it."

"And we have a mage and an ogre on our side. With your strength, Gwyrtha's speed, and my Jharro Bow, what chance would the giant have?" Justan asked.

"Well . . . I guess you got yerself a point there." The dwarf shook his head and finally sputtered in surrender, "Fine then. If ever'body's willin', y'all can help me get Buster back."

"Good." Justan reached into the bond and sent a message to Fist explaining what they needed to do. He laughed at the ogre's response. "Fist is excited. He says he hates giants."

"Another thing I've been meanin' to tell you, son," Lenny said. "When you got a weapon that sings as sweet as that bow of yers, you can't just call it 'my Jharro Bow'. You got's to give her a name. That there bow's a lady, and you can't treat a lady like any other piece of equipment."

"Yeah?" Justan took the bow off of his shoulder. "I guess I never thought of it that way."

He ran his fingers across the warm gray wood and felt the bow's magic flow up his arm as if asking what he needed of it. In a sense this bow was bonded to him every bit as much as Gwyrtha or Fist. It was the most precious gift he had ever been given. Lenny was right about another thing, it was definitely a she. But what to name her? After a moment's thought a smile crossed his face.

"I think I'll call her . . . Ma'am," Justan said.

"That's a right nice name," Lenny agreed.

Chapter Nine

Talon was broken. Deathclaw was sure of that. He just didn't know what to do about it. The last two weeks had been miserable for him. His initial joy at finding his sister had turned to disgust at what she had become.

Deathclaw lived by the laws of the hunter; they were as much a part of him as his own blood and claws. Talon understood those laws just as well as he did. They had hunted together for almost sixty years. But she had cast them aside.

At first, it hadn't been so bad. Having no particular goal in mind, they moved at Talon's whim. This had bothered Deathclaw in the beginning because as leader of the pack, he should be the one deciding the direction they traveled. But the changes the wizard had made in both of them were vast and the old pack hierarchy no longer applied. Just as he began to make peace with this fact, her behavior had become more and more peculiar.

A hunter must always look out for the other members of their pack, but Talon began treating him oddly. At times, she would coo and rub her body up against him in new and troubling ways. She would continue this behavior until his heart began to beat fast in his chest, then without warning, she would bite or claw him. When he hissed and struck back at her in anger, she would dart away, gurgling with a strangely human sounding laughter. The wounds she left healed, but the maliciousness of her game disturbed him deeply.

He began avoiding her touch, even at night while they slept. But the more he resisted her, the more persistent she became. Whenever he gave in to her attentions, she would attack him and run off again. It had finally got to the point where he would not let her touch him at all. Whenever she tried, he slashed at her until eventually, Talon tired of the game and turned her attentions elsewhere.

She began hunting down any creature whose trail they came across. It didn't matter whether the creature was large or small or insignificant. Sometimes she would eat it, but most of the time, she would abandon its body after toying with it for hours, torturing the creature until it died from the pain or she finally took its life on a whim. She did this not for food, but for pleasure and Deathclaw could not comprehend her reasoning. Hunting was for survival.

In an attempt to make her actions more sensible, Deathclaw tried to eat her kills, but sometimes she killed things inedible or poisonous. Often she would kill so many things, that there was no way he could eat it all. He tried to stop her, but no amount of commands or coercion changed her mind. If she caught the scent of something alive, she was determined to kill it.

If there was nothing to hunt, she became destructive, taking pleasure in ripping apart anything in her path. She would rip plants out of the ground, tear the bark off of trees, throw rocks. One day she spent an entire morning destroying a fir tree, gnawing off branches and ripping it apart until the forest around her was riddled with pine needles and the tree was torn and bare. She had hurt herself, broken a tooth in the process, but that extra pain seemed to thrill her even more.

Deathclaw kept his distance from her when she was in these moods because she was just as likely to attack him as anything else. He sat back and watched her behavior, analyzing it, trying to figure out why she did the things she did. Stealth was a hunter's best ally. Wanton destruction chased your prey away and drew unwanted attention.

He finally came to the painful realization that the beast she had turned into no longer resembled the raptoid he used to hunt with. She no longer acted like a member of the pack, she wasn't even like him, she was . . . wrong.

Deathclaw hid in the top of the trees and pondered what to do as he watched the creature that used to be his sister hunt a large mountain cat. Talon stealthily tracked her prey down, but when she came upon the beast, she stopped using any tactics at all. The creature outweighed her by at least three times, but she just ran at the cat head on, hissing with glee.

The cat was powerful and quick, but Talon fought it claw to claw. It did not desire the fight and tried to flee several times, but each time, she pursued it and leapt onto its back, tearing and stabbing at it until it had no choice but to strike back. In the end, she got what she wanted. The cat fought for its life and the battle was as fierce as any Deathclaw had seen.

By the time it was over, the cat was nearly unrecognizable. It had one eye left, its skin was in shreds, and it could no longer move its rear legs. The cat had to know that it was dying, but it pulled itself toward Talon with its front claws, dragging its entrails behind it through the blood drenched snow. Talon stood bent over and exhausted, dripping blood. She watched the beast, but made no attempt to move. The cat died just before it reached her.

Talon was victorious, but her wounds were grievous as well. She was bloodied and torn and the cat had bitten her several times, leaving gaping puncture wounds. She rested only a moment before leaping onto the dead creature and flaying it apart, hissing in rage and glee.

Deathclaw saw that her wounds had already stopped bleeding. Her frenzied movements didn't even tear them back open. The wizard's magic had increased her regenerative abilities far beyond Deathclaw's own.

It was then that Deathclaw decided what to do. He needed to put her down.

Sometimes in a raptoid pack, one member of the group would be injured in such a way that it could no longer take care of itself. When this occurred, the only choice the pack had was to kill it. This was done both out of respect for the damaged raptoid and for the good of the pack.

Talon was now in such a state. Her very existence was an affront to the raptoid she used to be.

He watched her roll about in the cat's remains and tried to decide how best to do it. Should he try to tell her why he needed to destroy her? No, she would not understand. She would find it a game. That was a dangerous path to take. In some ways she was stronger than him. If he took her on directly, it was likely that they would both die.

Perhaps he should wait until she slept and tear out her throat. He would have to time it perfectly. If he missed the opportunity, she would never let him try again.

Talon had tired of rolling in the gore by that time and began to decorate the forest with her kill, hanging the entrails of the cat in the trees and slinging pieces of it all around. She was limping. Some of her wounds had not completely healed yet. The best time to destroy her was now.

Deathclaw crept forward along a thick branch and timed his attack. He landed on top of her, using his greater weight to drive her into the ground. While she was stunned, he grabbed her head in an attempt to break her neck and end it quickly. But she was too slick with blood and he couldn't get a good grip. She squirmed out from under him and attacked back.

She bit and slashed and stabbed with her tail. As he had done while fighting her in the wizard's dungeon, Deathclaw used his precise body control to move defensively, avoiding crippling wounds. This time however, his return strikes were meant to kill. He slashed at her throat and sent his tail spike at her in an attempt to pierce vital organs.

Talon sensed his intent and hissed in fury, moving just fast enough to avoid the fatal blows. She laughed in delight at first, then after his repeated attacks, she screeched and chirped, demanding that he stop. Deathclaw would not. Her existence needed to end.

The battle went on for several minutes and Deathclaw realized that they were too evenly matched. He began to doubt his ability to defeat her. A strategy developed in his mind. The one move that he could think of would leave him vulnerable, but if he had to die in order to erase her existence, it would be worth it. They would both die together. Somehow that seemed fitting.

He leapt into her, taking a painful tailbarb strike to the leg. He wrapped his arms around her, bringing her in for an embrace, then sank his teeth deep into her throat. He bit down and tensed, waiting for her to use her rear legs to rip out his unprotected belly, but she did not. Instead, she returned his embrace and gurgled lovingly through her damaged throat. He could feel the vibrations in his teeth.

She ran her hands gently up his back and cupped his head, welcoming death. Deathclaw closed his eyes and gurgled back, thankful that she was accepting her rightful end. Then, just before he ripped her throat out, Talon made her escape.

She pierced through his cheeks with the claws on her thumbs and tore downward, severing his jaw muscles. His grip on her throat loosened and she twisted with both hands, dislocating his jaw. Talon pulled her throat free and kicked out of his embrace. Deathclaw stumbled back a few steps in amazement as she ran away.

He chased after her, but his leg was wounded from her tail barb and she was faster than him. After a few moments of the futile pursuit, he stopped and reached up to pop his jaw back into place. The pain was excruciating, but the jaw would heal. His only concern was how to destroy her.

Deathclaw thought for awhile and came to an unsettling conclusion. He could not defeat her on his own. With a pained hiss, he turned and headed back the way they had come. He needed help and he knew where to find it.

He ran toward the wizard's castle.

* * *

Hamford tied the sack onto his belt before opening the heavy door to the fifth level dungeon. He stepped into Ewzad's playroom. The chamber stank even worse now than it had just a few weeks before.

He entered the control room and released the lock on the door, then crossed the main chamber. He made sure to walk down the very center of the corridor, not wanting to get too close to any of the doors. Ewzad had wasted no time in creating new beasts to play with. He called them works in progress, but Hamford had seen enough of them to know that they were already deadly. He could hear their movements behind the doors and the smells coming from their cells were horrific. But none were as bad as the smells emanating from the cell he was headed to;

Talon's old cell.

He stopped before the door and retched before raising one shaking hand to the handle.

"Kenn," he whispered. "Kenn, I brought you some food." Hamford creaked open the door and gazed down upon his brother.

"Can I come out now?" Kenn whimpered.

After reappearing in the throne room in his new glorious body, Ewzad had been furious and as the dungeon keeper, Kenn had taken the brunt of his anger. First Ewzad had swelled Kenn's feet until they were so large that he couldn't run. Then he had scolded him with the long list of the things that had gone wrong, sending bursts of horrible pain through Kenn's body to punctuate every point.

Hamford's sole punishment had been the command to drag his brother down to the dungeon and shackle him in the cell with the remains of Ewzad's prized creations. He had been wracked with guilt about it ever since.

"Oh, Kenn." Tears welled up in Hamford's eyes once more upon seeing his brother's state. "I am so sorry. This is all my fault. I shouldn't have brought you into this."

"It is your fault," Kenn gasped in agreement. "Why haven't you come sooner?"

Ewzad had ordered Hamford to leave Kenn alone in the cell. Any request to see to his brother had earned Hamford a stiff glare and a series of agonizing abdominal pains. It had taken several days before the wizard was distracted enough for Hamford to chance bringing him food. How he wished he had not waited, Ewzad's wrath be damned.

Kenn was in horrible shape. He had always been thin, but now he was just skin and bones. It appeared he had caught some kind of disease from the corpses. His body was covered in red sores and a thick yellow liquid oozed from the corners of his eyes.

"Didn't they feed you when they came to feed the other beasts?" Hamford asked.

"They drop it in the slot, but I can't reach." He pointed to a pile of meat crawling with maggots just inside the door. With his arms shackled, Kenn's reach stopped a foot short of the food, and with his feet still swollen so large, he couldn't move his legs far enough to bring it closer.

"Food!" Ken demanded weakly. "Now, Hamford. Can't you see I'm dying!"

Hamford untied the bag at his waist and handed Kenn a flask of water. He guzzled it eagerly, but cried out in pain with stomach cramps. He motioned for more anyway and Hamford gave him some bread and cheese which he devoured along with a couple sausages. This hurt him as well, but Kenn didn't seem to care.

"Please, Hamford. Tell Master that I have learned my lesson. Tell him that I remain his faithful servant."

"I-I will try Kenn, but I don't think that he will listen, I-."

"Oh won't I?"

Hamford turned to see Ewzad standing there looking handsome and resplendent in his new silver inlaid robes. Hamford found his master's new appearance, even more frightening than the old one.

Ewzad had been furious when he found out that his family's priceless heirlooms had been given out to his prisoners as parting gifts. Fortunately, he had brought a new wardrobe back to the castle with him from whatever dark place he had come from. This fact, however, didn't stop the wizard from taking particular pleasure in recapturing and torturing any of the escaped prisoners that tried to sell his family's things. His spies among the merchants were on the lookout for any suspicious sales.

"I am sorry, Master," Hamford said. "But they had not been feeding him, and-and I did not want him to die . . ."

"No, no. Of course you didn't. Dear Hamford. Family is family, yes?" Ewzad brushed by the guard to stand in the doorway. "Oh my, Kenn. No-no. What a sad state you are in now, don't you think?"

"I have learned my lesson, Master. Truly I have," Kenn sobbed. "I will do whatever you ask. I will never fail you again, I promise."

The wizard squatted down beside Kenn and reached out. Hamford's eyes widened as for a moment he swore he saw Ewzad's entire arm undulate bonelessly. Ewzad caressed Kenn's face and whispered, "So, my dear Kenn, you have been in Talon's cell for long enough. Do you have her scent yet, do you think?"

Kenn didn't look like he understood, but he nodded. "Oh yes, Master."

"Good," Ewzad said and gestured. With the writhe of one finger, the shackles fell off and clattered to the floor. "Stand up then, Kenn. I have work for you. Oh yes, much much work."

"Thank you, Master! Thank you!" Kenn cried and he tried to move, but he was too weak. "Master, I'm sorry . . . I am sick."

"You will not obey me?" Ewzad snapped. Then he paused as if listening to someone. "Oh, so he has the death fever, does he? Boo hoo. Did I ask for your opinion in the matter? Did I?"

"I am sorry Master?" Hamford said. "I didn't say anything."

"I wasn't talking to you," Ewzad said, waving at Hamford absently. Then his face twisted in anger and he pulled his sleeve back, exposing a wrinkled white orb embedded into his forearm. He shot a writhing finger at the orb as he shouted, "Be silent, blast you! Do I need to order you by name in front of my servants? Hmm?"

He pointed at Hamford and this time the guard was sure that he saw the wizard's arm move in serpentine fashion. "Help Kenn up, will you? He will live until I have him where I need him. That's good enough, isn't it? Now follow me. I have much, so much to do."

The wizard stormed away and Hamford tried to help Kenn up, but his brother was simply too weak to move. He ended up carrying him on his back. He was surprisingly light, despite the weight of his enlarged feet.

"Did he say death fever?" Kenn asked.

"Yes," Hamford sobbed. Tears were rolling down Hamford's cheeks again as he began mourning for the brother that he knew would soon be dead.

"It will be okay, Hamford," Kenn said. "Master will heal me, you'll see. I will have his promise of power."

Hamford knew better. He had been around Ewzad long enough

to understand that the wizard's promise of power meant power for himself only. Ewzad Vriil did not share power.

They followed Ewzad up the stairwell and into the throne room. Every trace of the battle was gone now. The tapestries had been replaced and the wizard had forced the servants to scrub all traces of blood or ash from the floor. The faint smell of smoke still lingering in the air was the only subtle reminder of what had occurred just a few short weeks ago.

The wizard led them down a series of hallways until they came to his personal quarters. The room used to be blazing hot from the heat emanating from Ewzad's precious bandham egg, but whatever had kept the egg warm had stopped working while the wizard was gone, yet another thing Ewzad had been furious to learn upon his return.

"Here, Kenn. Please-please sit, won't you?" The wizard said and gestured towards an empty chair by his bed. Hamford took his brother to the chair and gently laid him into it.

Ewzad extended his arm. His fingers writhed and the bandham egg rolled away from the corner of the room until it came to rest at Kenn's feet. The egg was about two feet long from end to end. Whatever had laid it was a large beast indeed.

"Ah, but I still mourn for the loss of my sweet-sweet bandham. She was to be the jewel of my collection, you see. Her magic was even more precious than that of dear Talon. Alas, she died while I was delayed in my return. So sad. However, I have thought of a way that the power she carried could still be of use to me even in a reduced capacity. That is nice. Don't you think?"

Kenn didn't realize that his master wasn't expecting a response. "Oh yes, that is nice," he replied thickly.

"Oh, nice is it?" Ewzad snarled. "Nice indeed? Well, dear Kenn perhaps you don't want to share in that diminished power. Is that what you are saying?"

"No, Master, no! I want to share. I do! Please let me share." Kenn pleaded, though he was so weak that he could barely stay upright in the chair.

The anger left the wizard's eyes and he smiled. "Of course, of course dear Kenn. You shall share. You shall take the remnants of the bandham's power and run an errand for me, oh yes you shall."

The wizard stuck out both arms, one aimed at the egg, the other at Kenn. His fingers writhed. Kenn stiffened and gasped. Ewzad made a slight gesture. The bandham egg cracked open. A tiny red-scaled hand fell from the shell and touched Kenn's leg.

Hamford watched in horror as the side of Kenn's leg opened up like the jaws of some ravenous beast and clamped down on the tiny hand. With a sucking noise, the corpse of the beast was pulled from the depths of the egg into the hungry hole in Kenn's leg. Hamford caught a glimpse of tiny black horns and wings before it disappeared. Kenn's leg bulged weirdly and he screamed as the bulge moved up his leg and into his abdomen.

"Yes, yes. That's right." Sweat popped out on Ewzad's brow and this time there was no mistaking it, the wizard's arms undulated along with his fingers. "Come, come Kenn. Accept the power! I'm trying to give it to you, aren't I?"

Kenn's face was contorted with pain, but he cried out, "Yes, I accept! Give it to me!"

The wizard laughed and there was a popping sound within Kenn's body. Starting at his navel, his skin turned a bright red. The red spot grew, overtaking his weakened body. The open sores from the disease that ravaged him were replaced by glistening scales. They multiplied. Soon his entire body was covered. His emaciated frame swelled outward and took on muscle. His legs and arms bulged, his feet returned to their normal size.

"Aaaaand . . . there!" Ewzad said. His arms stopped their undulating. He looked Kenn up and down. "Stand Kenn, won't you?"

Kenn stood and opened his eyes which were now a fiery yellow. He stretched and extended a large set of black wings that had sprouted from his back. "Thank you, Master. I feel it! Oh the power."

Hamford's jaw dropped in surprise. That was Kenn's voice and those were Kenn's features, but the red skin, the scales, the eyes. What had his brother become?

"You see, Hamford?" Kenn said. "I told you that our Master would deliver on his promise and look!" He raised a hand whose fingers were now tipped in black claws and made a fist. The muscles on his arm bulged and Hamford felt a wave of heat come off of Kenn's skin.

"Ooh! Yes, Yes." Ewzad giggled, clapping in excitement. "Kenn you are adorable! Yes you are. Are you ready to do my bidding?"

"Anything, Master."

"Good, good. You go and fetch my Talon. Bring her back to me. You have her scent still, yes?" Kenn nodded and Ewzad giggled again. He glanced at Hamford's confused face and added, "You see, Hamford, bandhams are the only creatures known to kill and eat dragons. Dragonhunters, they are called in some lands."

"Dragonhunters . . . I like that." Kenn smiled and heat rolled from his body again.

"Yes-yes! Sweet Talon can't escape you now, Kenn. Hurt her if you must but do not kill her! I have been calling her ever since my return and I can sense that she hears, but she is rebellious. That is not acceptable. She must be brought back so that I can remind her who her master is, don't you agree?"

"I go now, Master." Kenn said and grinned at Hamford as he left. The floor slightly shook at the weight of his steps.

The guard shivered at the sight of his brother's teeth.

"Now, Hamford. I have work for you too. So much work. Send a letter off to Elise in Dremaldria. Tell her that her Duke plans to pay her a visit soon. We have much to discuss and I have so much to show her!"

It took Hamford a moment to focus in on what the wizard was saying, but he nodded. "Of course, Master."

"Andre did what?" Ewzad snapped, his eyes wide.

"I didn't-," Hamford began, but Ewzad waived him off again, staring at the orb imbedded in his arm.

"No! Unfair! I am still Duke! No-no. You toy with me, don't you, Mellinda? He would not dare, would he? He knows the results of such a betrayal does he not?"

Ewzad stopped again as if listening and Hamford felt like he was hearing one side of a two way conversation. Whatever had happened to cure the wizard's looks had not cured him of his eccentricities. If anything they were worse.

"Unacceptable!" Ewzad fumed. "Hamford, you send that letter to Elise. Tell her that I am coming and tell her that I bring gifts!"

Hamford nodded and fled the room. As he left, he could still hear the wizard muttering.

"Oh, dear Andre, my friend. You have made quite a mess of things haven't you? But all that will pass. It shall. Your power will wane and there will be a new heir. Oh, yes!"

* * *

Talon's whims had kept the two raptoids from putting too much distance between them and the castle. It took Deathclaw only a few days of hard travel before the spires of the wizard's castle came into view.

Work on the castle had resumed in their absence and the wizard's smell hung thick in the air all around. Humans milled about in greater numbers than before and they had been joined by other creatures. Green and yellow skinned ones of various sizes stayed together in large groups in the woods around the castle.

Deathclaw had to move very carefully in order to avoid being seen. He skirted several camps of these new beasts, following some of his familiar trails until he crossed the stream and came to the place he was looking for: the small grassy clearing where he had defeated the red-haired human.

A group of five large creatures now occupied the clearing. They had started a fire and were eating one of the smaller yellow skinned beasts that Deathclaw had seen earlier. He kept out of sight and waited until dark. The large beasts stayed awake for a while shouting strange words at each other before they finally laid down and slept.

Deathclaw crept around their camp and approached a dead tree on the far side of the clearing. Slowly, in order to make as little noise as possible, he pulled aside some thick pieces of bark and reached his hand into the hollow space he had found there less than a month ago.

He grasped hold of what he had been searching for and pulled out a sheathed sword. It was the weapon that the man with the red hair had wielded against him in battle. He recalled how the wound the sword made had burned him and how long it had taken the wound to heal. This was the help he was looking for.

Deathclaw slung the sword and sheath over his shoulder in the way that he had seen the red haired man wear it. It fit nicely on his back and would not hamper his movements. He gritted his teeth in determination. The muscles in his jaw had healed nicely.

Deathclaw set off to hunt down his sister.

Chapter Ten

The border of the rock giant's territory wasn't that far away from the town. Justan had told the rest of them about Lenny's plight as soon as they arrived back at the camp. Fist and Gwyrtha found the situation endlessly funny, but were eager to help. Qyxal had been the only member of the group hesitant to take the giant on.

"What is so special about this hammer again?" Qyxal asked as they walked.

"Buster's a magic hammer, you durn elf!" Lenny said. "Every hit with Buster does double the smashin'. That's a hard magic to come by. My great granddaddy made him and he's been passed down from Firegobbler to Firegobbler ever since." The dwarf paused for a moment. "'Sides, I might wanna pass it down to a little varmint of my own some day."

"You have plans for 'little varmints'?" Qyxal laughed.

"He is also the only hammer Lenny will make weapons with," Justan remarked.

Lenny ignored the elf. "I can work harder stuff with Buster than with a reg'lar hammer and I don't gots to keep the metal as hot."

"Alright, fine," Qyxal said, repressing his mirth. "This I can understand. As long as it's not about revenge, I am willing to help."

"Dag-blast it! You don't have to help if'n you don't want to! I can do it myself. The only reason I'm lettin' y'all help is 'cause the boy's makin' me."

"Lenny, we are all going to do this together," Justan said.

Fist snorted. "Giants not too hard to fight. They is slow."

"'Are' slow, Fist," Justan reminded. "You say, Giant's 'are' not too hard to fight. They 'are' slow. When there are more than one, you use 'are'. When there is only one, you use 'is'."

"Oh." Fist nodded. "I forgot. Giants 'are' slow . . . A giant 'is' slow."

"Good. You got it." Justan said.

"Now listen here, dag-nab it!" Lenny said. "Y'all are actin' like this is going to be some easy fight, but it ain't. This giant ain't slow! It's more'n a foot taller than Fist and he's faster too!"

"Alright, Lenny, we get it," Justan said.

"Giants are slow," Fist said again.

"We are taking this seriously," Justan said. "We just need to have a plan. Tell us everything you know about the giant and we'll figure out what to do."

"First of all you gotta know that it ain't called a rock giant just fer nothin'. The durn thing's skin is covered with rock. Yer swords ain't gonna cut the thing and I don't know what Gwyrtha'll be able to do."

"Okay," Justan said. "That means that our best weapons are going to be Bertha, Fist's mace, and Ma'am."

"What was that?" Qyxal asked.

"Oh!" Justan grinned. "I didn't tell you. That's the new name of my Jharro Bow. Ma'am."

The elf laughed. "I like it!"

"I know!" Justan said. "It fits, doesn't it?"

"What is Ma'am mean?" Fist asked.

"What 'does' Ma'am mean," Justan corrected. "When you are speaking in the past tense-."

"Dag-blast it!" Lenny snapped. "We gotta stay on target, here! Look, we're at the edge of its territory right now. See this here?" The dwarf pointed to the tree in front of them. There was a large "x" cut into its bark. All of the trees in the vicinity had a similar mark. "The locals done the same thing to all the trees along the border."

"How is the giant's territory so well defined?" Justan asked. "I mean, there's no fence or anything. Why are we safe if we stay on this side of the trees? What's to keep it from just coming out and ransacking the town?"

"Don't know, son," Lenny said. "All's I know is that they say it stays inside its territory."

"I don't know," Qyxal said. "The more I hear, the more there is something familiar about this thing. I just can't place it . . ."

"Lenny, is this thing completely made of rock?" Justan asked. "I mean, can it be broken?"

"It ain't all rock, I know that much. When I hit him with Buster, his skin cracked open and he started bleedin'." He paused for a moment. "It healed up real quick, though."

"Alright, so at least we know it can be hurt. We'll just have to play it by ear," Justan said. "But first, let me talk to it. If I can get it to listen to reason, maybe we can work out a deal to get Buster back."

Lenny snorted. "Don't think so, son. I tried when I come back the last time. I brought gold and other weapons to trade and all the dag-burned dirt-farmer wanted to do was fight fer it. At least he let me go after he beat my arse."

"Nevertheless, let me talk to him before we do anything, okay?" Justan asked. There were grunts of agreement all around. "Let's go in, then."

They decided to leave Albert and Stanza tethered at the edge of the forest. The forest area was thick and if they had to leave in a hurry, there were places the large horses wouldn't be able to navigate through. Besides, Lenny explained to them, the giant liked horse meat.

As they walked through the trees, Justan saw the first signs of the giant's presence. There were sets of deep footprints set into the damp leaves and every so often there were skeletons lying about. Either the giant looted his victims or someone was taking advantage of its thirst for battle, because every skeleton was stripped clean.

"Bloodthirsty, isn't he?" Qyxal remarked.

As they continued to walk deeper into the giant's territory, the footprints became more common and so did the dead enemies. Soon, sounds of battle reached their ears. It started with shouts and curses. Then they heard the giant's laughter. It was deep and throaty, a not altogether unpleasant sound if it hadn't been accompanied by screams. Justan motioned for silence and they approached the sounds carefully.

The woods ended abruptly into a wide open space several hundred feet wide. The ground was littered with rocks of all shapes and sizes from pebbles to ten-foot-tall boulders. At one end of the huge clearing was a rocky hill with a wide-mouthed cave piercing its side. A battle was taking place about a hundred feet from where they stood.

The giant looked every bit as formidable as Lenny had described. At least nine-feet-tall and bulging with muscles, its skin looked to be made entirely of granite. Despite its large size, it moved at the speed of a regular man, which was something Justan found hard to wrap his mind around. For clothing it wore only a bedraggled pair of cut-off leather breeches.

From the looks of things there had been five men fighting the giant to start out with. Three of them were now motionless forms on the ground. One man, an archer, stood a ways back from the giant futilely shooting arrows that bounced off its rocky skin. The other remaining combatant had an axe and as they watched, he took a chop at the giant's knee. The blade sparked as it bounced off of the rocky skin.

The giant countered with a kick that knocked the weapon out of the man's grip and most likely broke his arm. He then bent and grabbed the man by the leg. With a laugh, the giant pulled the man up off the ground, dangling him upside down and laughed in his face. Justan watched in astonishment as the giant spun a few times, swinging the man around by his leg. He picked up speed, gathering momentum as he went and with a mighty heave, released. The man screamed as he cart-wheeled through the air, clearing the top of the first tree before crashing into the forest beyond.

"He can't have survived that," Qyxal observed.

"You aren't getting away that easily!" the giant shouted at the archer who was now running for the trees.

The giant picked up a boulder about the size of a man's head and hurled it. The archer made it just past the treeline when the boulder struck. They couldn't see the impact, but by the way the giant raised his arms in the air and shouted in triumph, it was evident that he had struck his target.

"This giant is not slow." Fist said. No one bothered to congratulate him on getting it right.

"They must'a done somethin' to make him angry," Lenny explained. "He usually let's you run away. That way you can tell yer tale and get more folks to come fight him."

"Okay, this is what we are going to do . . ." Justan had to stop for a moment and gather his thoughts. His heart was beating madly in his chest and he wasn't sure if it was from fear or excitement. "Lenny and I are going to go out and try to talk to him. Fist, Gwyrtha and Qyxal stay in the trees unless we need you."

"Are you sure that's wise?" Qyxal asked.

"No," Justan admitted. "But I'm afraid that if we all step out together, he will be too distracted to listen. So wait here. But if he charges us, don't wait for me to call you. Just come out and help, alright?"

There were nods all around. Fist whistled and Squirrel jumped from his shoulder to the nearest tree, scampering up to watch.

Justan slipped Ma'am off of his shoulder and held an arrow at the ready. "Okay, Lenny. Let's go."

He and the dwarf stepped out from the cover of the trees and approached the giant. It was looking at the three men laying on the ground. Though they looked to be mangled pretty badly, two of them were still breathing. It nudged one of them with its foot. The man cried out in pain.

Justan cleared his throat and the giant turned in surprise.

"Oh, so there are more of you! I was just trying to decide whether to put your friends out of their misery." The giant sounded remarkably intelligent. Justan was encouraged that they might be able to reason with it.

"We ain't with them," Lenny said.

The giant's eyes widened in recognition and he pointed at the dwarf.

"Hey, I know you . . . You're that dwarf that keeps coming back for his hammer! I remember you because of the mustache." The giant laughed. "You brought a friend to help this time? Hah! That's just great. I love a new challenge."

"We don't want to fight you if we don't have to," Justan said.

The giant looked at Justan as if for the first time. He frowned. "So the human speaks for you now, dwarf?"

"He wants to try talkin' with you first," Lenny said.

"May I introduce myself?" Justan pressed.

"Don't bother telling me your name," the giant said. "I'll just forget it once I've beaten you."

Justan realized that getting the giant to listen wasn't going to be easy after all. With a sigh, he slid the glove off of his right hand. He made a fist and raised it so that the Giant could see the rune.

"My name is Edge."

"A named warrior, eh?" A sparkle came into the giant's eye. He laughed again and bowed. "A pleasure to meet you, Sir Edge. You will not be the first named warrior I have beaten."

"And I have beaten things bigger than you," Justan replied. It was true to a certain extent. The Golem had been about twelve feet tall and he had delivered the killing blow. "I hope it doesn't have to come to that, though. Can I have your name?"

"Huh, persistent aren't you? Fine, my name is Charz."

"Nice to meet you, Charz," Justan said. "All we want is to negotiate for the hammer. Can we make some kind of a deal?"

"A deal? What are you going to do, pay me? I don't need your money. I've got nowhere to spend it. Besides, if I wanted anything you have, I could just take it off of your corpses. I've got all the trinkets I need back in my cave."

"I wasn't talking about a trade of goods, but if you have everything you need, why is it so important to keep that particular hammer?"

"Hmph, a shrewd one. The thing is, I like my trophies and by keeping it, I have been able to beat the dwarf twice. Now he brings even more fun with him."

"Surely there is something else that you need," Justan said. As long as the giant was willing to keep talking, there was a chance that they could get out without fighting. "Is there anything that we could do to help you in exchange for the hammer?"

The giant looked taken aback by this suggestion. He thought for a moment, then shook his head and laughed.

"Nah, you can't help me. There's only one person who can help me and he ain't coming. Nope, there is only one deal that we can make and it is the same deal I give everyone. If you beat me, you can take anything you want from my cave. I've been collecting trophies for nearly a century now and there's some pretty nice things in there."

"As you wish, Charz," Justan said and sent a message to Fist and Gwyrtha through the bond. They immediately left the treeline and approached with Qyxal a few steps behind them.

"What's this?" The giant's grin grew even larger. "An ogre and an elf and a . . . what is that, a lizard mount? No, wait. It's a rogue horse! What do you know? I ain't seen one of those in years! What an interesting group this is. How exciting!"

"Again," Justan said. "Is there any wa-."

"No! Let's get going, we've talked enough." He clapped his hands together. "Time for action."

"Very well," Qyxal said, and cast the sleeping spell he had been preparing.

The giant's eyelids drooped a bit, but then he shook it off and laughed. With his mage sight, Justan could see the spell fall apart as if it had been cut by unseen scissors.

"En elf mage, eh? Haven't met one of those before. Sorry, magic doesn't work on me here, but just in case . . ." The giant bent and picked up a boulder. "I have a cure for wizards right here!"

"Wait!" Justan shouted. He had the bowstring pulled back until the power was humming in his ear. Ma'am was eager to strike. "You start throwing boulders and I end this right now with a hole in your head."

"With what? Arrows can't hurt-."

Justan released his shot. With a flash, the boulder in Charz's hand exploded into powder and tiny shards.

"Ow!" Charz said, shaking his rocky hand. His eyes narrowed in anger and he studied the bow. "Okay, we add a rule. No boulders, but you can't use that bow either."

"Agreed," Justan said and handed Ma'am to the elf. "Qyxal, it looks like you are going to have to stay out of this one."

"But that's our most powerful weapon," Qyxal protested.

"We don't have much choice. Charz! Can I make one more request before our mage leaves?"

"Another request? What?" The giant frowned.

"What're you doin, boy?" Lenny asked. He had Bertha unwrapped and ready to go.

"Can he heal the two men over here that are still alive?" Justan had hoped to try and help them after the fight, but now he didn't know how long it was going to take. He held up his hands. "Now I don't want them to try and help, I just want to get them out of the way."

Charz looked at Justan like he was a strange puzzle. "I don't know, they jumped me while I was taking a nap . . . Fine, whatever, just make it quick. I'm ready for this fight to start."

Qyxal walked over to the two men and knelt down. He ran his hands over the first man, a rotund balding man with a large beard. After a moment, the man gasped and sat up. He saw the giant and the rest of Justan's party and leapt to his feet, then stumbled and fell back down again.

"Careful, man. You had some bad injuries. It will be a while before you can just run away," Qyxal said. He began examining the other man, a shirtless muscle-bound individual covered in tattoos. He closed his eyes and concentrated. Justan could see Qyxal's woven elements enter the man. The elf's spells were always heavily blackened with earth magic. "Your friend, on the other hand, won't be walking out of here by himself. I have . . . one second here . . . there! I stopped the bleeding inside him, but I can't heal him completely. Sorry, I'm just not that good of a healer. You will need to drag him away yourself and find some help for him. Maybe a healer back in the town? Got it?"

The rotund man nodded and slowly got back to his feet again. He was sweating profusely. He tried to pull the man away, but looked as if he might pass out.

"Hey!" the giant said. "I'm not waiting any longer. Let's go already!"

"Qyxal, go ahead and help the man get his friend to the forest. Just stay ready in case we need you when this is over." Justan drew his swords and nodded. "Okay. Lenny, here's the plan. You-,"

The dwarf was already running at the giant, his hammer Bertha swung back at the ready. Gwyrtha ran with him. Justan and Fist had to catch up. Justan knew that this was not a good start.

Charz took a step towards the dwarf and kicked, but Lenny dodged to the side. At the same time, Gwyrtha leapt, digging her claws into the giant's rocky skin and sending him stumbling to the side under her weight. Charz laughed the way a man would if his dog jumped up on him when he got home. Gwyrtha snapped at his face. He grabbed her by the throat and shook a finger at her.

"Uh-uh. Bad horse!"

Justan arrived, but couldn't find a way to get in close to the giant without being in the way of the others. Fist ran around the other side of the giant while Lenny swung Bertha into the giant's leg. The blow sent chips of rock flying and Bertha's magic superheated the strike. A gout of flame erupted from the wound, causing Charz to yelp in surprise.

The giant released Gwyrtha's throat and grabbed her two front legs, prying them away from his chest. Fist slammed his mace into the giant's lower back and Lenny hit his leg again. Charz yelped again with the impacts. "Hey!" He twisted and swung Gwyrtha by her front legs. Her heavy body sent Lenny flailing into the nearest boulder before the giant released her into Fist. The two heavy beasts fell to the ground in a tangle of limbs as the giant laughed.

Justan saw a bleeding spiderweb of cracks in the giant's back where Fist's mace had struck the giant. Remembering the battle with

Rudfen in Ewzad's dungeon, he darted forward and thrust his right sword into the wound. The blade only sank in two inches before binding in the rock. As the giant growled in pain, Justan could see the cracks knitting back together. The wound was rapidly healing.

"Don't think I forgot about you, Sir Edge," Charz said and reached back for him.

Justan tugged quickly, but the sword wouldn't come out. He was forced to let go and leap out of the way. He watched in horror as the giant's hand gripped the blade and twisted. With a crack, Justan's brand new sword snapped in two.

"That was a gift!" Justan swung his remaining sword at the giant's knee with all his might. In a testament to the quality of the workmanship, the blade did not break, but chipped a chunk of rock free.

Charz's left hand darted in so quickly that Justan did not have time to dodge. The giant caught him by the arm. Justan felt a surge of anger through the bond and saw Gwyrtha leap at the giant's back. Using her momentum against her, the giant reached up with his right arm, grabbed her by the mane and threw her over his shoulder.

At the same time, Lenny swung his hammer again, this time aiming for the shard of sword still protruding from the giant's now mostly healed back. Charz swung around and the blow just missed. Charz's foot didn't. It caught Lenny in the stomach. The dwarf soared several feet through the air. The giant's movement wrenched Justan's arm and he felt something pop in his shoulder. He cried out in pain as Fist roared in, mace raised high.

Charz saw the ogre coming in and twisted around, grabbing the weapon as Fist brought it down. He ripped it free of the ogre's grasp and followed that up with a vicious backhand that caught Fist across the jaw, sending him sprawling. Gwyrtha was back on her feet and coming in again, but Charz dangled Justan in front of her, causing her to lurch to a halt. He took the opportunity to raise his foot and stomped on Fist's mace, breaking the head free and sending it rolling across the ground.

By this time, Justan was sure that his arm was dislocated at the shoulder. Every movement the giant made sent pain shooting down his arm. The giant lifted Justan up to his eye level and laughed.

"Hah! Great named warrior, eh? Are you sure that rune isn't just painted o-hnchk!"

Charz's speech was cut short as Justan thrust his remaining sword into the giant's open mouth. The blade lodged in the back of his jaw, tearing tender flesh before stopping against rocky bone. The giant bit down on the blade and tossed Justan aside in frustration. Justan landed on his shoulder with a scream of agony. Charz grimaced and yanked the blade free from his mouth, before gripping the end with his other hand, and bringing it down over his knee. The fine steel sword broke in half.

"Close one, that," Charz said, blood flowing down his chin. He hacked and spat more blood onto the ground. "An inch further and you might have done some real damage. Maybe your name isn't fake, Sir E-"

Lenny's hammer struck the small of the giant's back, again just missing the blade piece. The giant hissed in pain and turned on the dwarf, Lenny tried to run, but the giant was too fast.

Justan struggled to stand and watched the giant knock Lenny down and grab his legs. Fist was back on his feet, but before he could help, Charz began to swing Lenny around.

"Stop!" Justan shouted.

"Or what?" the giant laughed and spun. "Ready dwarf? This time I'm going for distance!"

Lenny shouted an unintelligible string of curses as the giant spun and picked up speed. Then, with a large step, the giant leaned forward and released his momentum in a powerful throw that sent Lenny hurtling through the air. The arc of his flight was much higher than the man they had seen the giant throw earlier.

"Lenny!" Justan couldn't comprehend what had just happened. He was in such a state of disbelief that he barely felt Gwyrtha's teeth grip his collar. She pulled him away from the giant as fast as she could while limping on one hurt leg. Fist caught up to them and threw Justan over his shoulder, before running for the woods.

"Hah! Run away, then! No one beats me!" the giant shouted, blood still running from his mouth. They could hear his victory yells echoing after them long after they fled into the trees.

Chapter Eleven

It didn't take Qyxal long to catch up to them. Fist and Gwyrtha had stopped as soon as it was evident that the giant wasn't going to bother chasing them. They lay on the cold wet forest floor gasping. Squirrel, who had been riding on the elf's shoulder, leapt onto Fist and ran all over him, chattering in concern. Fist groaned in response, holding one hand to his jaw.

Qyxal ran to Justan first. "I can't believe what I just saw. For a second there I thought one of you was going to get killed for sure. I'm going to need some help with that shoulder. Fist, can you come over here?"

While the elf continued to talk, giving Fist instructions, Justan lay there stunned, going over the fight again and again in his mind. What could they have done differently to win? Did the giant even have a weakness?

His thoughts were interrupted as Fist grabbed his injured shoulder. The ogre had to try a few different times under the elf's guidance before it popped back in. Justan nearly passed out.

Sorry, Fist said to him through the bond. The ogre was in a lot of pain as well.

"It's okay, Fist. Thank you for helping. Qyxal, help Fist. I think his jaw is broken."

"I know. Give me a second. He's next."

The elf grasped Justan's arm. As he felt the healing energies entering his body, he closed his eyes and looked inward with his mage sight. Justan could see the black threads circling his shoulder. He watched as the elf sent out tiny threads of the other three elements, reattaching each torn ligament and repairing each damaged blood vessel. The elf's low levels of strength in the other elements made the work a bit crude, but it was effective. The magic then flowed further down his arm, repairing a sprained wrist that Justan hadn't even known was there.

When the elf was finished, he moved on to the ogre. Out of curiosity Justan closed his eyes and sent his senses through the bond, focusing on Fist's energy this time. His vision shifted to the inside of Fist's body and he watched what Qyxal was doing with his mage sight.

Fist's jaw was indeed broken, in several places in fact. As he watched Qyxal knitting the bones back together, Justan once again cursed his lack of offensive magic. If only he could use his magic to heal, he would at least be useful.

He left Fist and sent his senses into Gwyrtha. Once he could see within her, Justan was startled by the intensity of the magic that made up her body. There were traces of every element scattered through each individual cell. The way she was made up seemed so unstable, he couldn't understand how she stayed together. No wonder the wizards were all so eager to study her.

Hello? She seemed to want to know what he was doing.

Just checking you out, sweetheart. Making sure you are okay, he replied.

"Qyxal, Gwyrtha is bruised up, but her main issue is in her right hind leg. There is a . . . I can't tell . . . something, torn in one of her joints."

"You can see that?" Qyxal said. From the sound of his voice, he must have finished with Fist and was moving over to her. "You aren't even looking at her."

"I can see it through the bond," Justan explained, but he kept his eyes closed.

Something interesting was going on. Her body was responding to his presence. Some of the magic within her was reaching out towards his own. Justan realized that whatever part of him was looking within her was a bundle of magic itself. He opened his eyes and for a brief moment he was sure that he saw a trail of energy linking his body to hers. It wasn't the color of any of the elements, though. It was white. Just as quickly as he had seen it, the link dissipated. The trail was gone.

"Lenny!" The sudden realization hit him. How could he have been so preoccupied? "Qyxal, did you see where Lenny fell?"

"To the south of here," Qyxal said, pointing. "But I don't know what we'll find. He fell pretty far."

"Let's go, then!" Justan got to his feet and started to walk, then paused. Qyxal was still working on Gwyrtha's leg. "Sorry, Qyxal . . . thank you. Thanks for taking care of us."

"That's my job on this trip, right? Resident healer?" The elf grinned and stood. "Let's go find what's left of that dwarf, then."

It turned out that Lenny wasn't too hard to find. They could hear him hollering from a distance. Smoke wafted through the trees and they soon saw the dwarf stuck up in a fir tree with needles burning all around him. Somehow he had managed to hold on to Bertha during his flight.

Lenny cursed and beat at the flames with his free hand until his mustache started smoldering. He dropped Bertha and patted frantically the mustache trying to limit the damage. As they watched, he lost his footing and fell out of the tree, landing on his back with a thud. Bertha lay on the forest floor beside him. Her potent magic had set fire to the wet leaves around her as she landed.

Qyxal rushed over and placed his hands on the dwarf's chest.

"Leggo, dag-gum it! Yer healin' won't work on me," the dwarf said as he tried to sit up.

"Hold still!" Qyxal shoved him back down and concentrated. The elf frowned and sweat beaded on his brow as he tried to pour magic into the dwarf. Finally, he let go and stood back, breathing heavily. He shook his head. "Sorry. It is just too hard trying to heal a dwarf. You are so resistant to magic that it makes things . . . fuzzy."

"I done tried to tell you," Lenny groaned as he stood up. "'Sides, I got my healin' right here." He pulled out his waterskin and took a swig. From the sound of his sigh afterwards, Justan knew it wasn't water in there.

"He is okay?" Fist asked.

Qyxal laughed. "Dwarves are pretty tough as a whole, but Lenny is tougher than most. He's bruised up pretty bad, but as far as I could tell, he didn't break any bones."

"I'm just glad we're not diggin' any dag-gum graves," the dwarf said. He picked up Bertha and stomped out the small fire around her. "Now y'all get the hell outta' here. I'll catch up when I'm done with that corn-jigger."

"What are you talking about, Lenny?" Qyxal said. "You can't take that thing on alone. We should all get as far away from that thing as possible before it decides to come after us."

Gwyrtha agreed with the elf. She nudged Justan. *Ride*.

"Just a minute, Gwyrtha," Justan said, and addressed everyone else. "Listen, I think-."

"I will stay with Lenny and fight," Fist announced. "The giant hurts peoples for fun."

"No, dag-blast it! Y'all go! I can handle this myself! I never shoulda' drug you guys into this in the first place!"

"Fist, Lenny is right," Qyxal said. "No one needs to get killed over one stupid hammer."

"Buster ain't stupid!" the dwarf snapped. "But he ain't worth any of you dyin' over."

"I want to fight," Fist repeated. Squirrel chattered in agreement, shaking his tiny fists at everyone.

Ride, Gwyrtha pressed, nudging Justan.

"But-." Justan said.

"Yer goin!" Lenny barked.

"Listen to me, damn it!" Justan shouted. They stopped their arguing and looked at Justan in surprise. "We are not just giving up!"

"He said 'damn'," Qyxal pointed out. "He must be serious."

"Look, this failure was my fault," Justan explained. "I underestimated the giant and brought us in without a valid plan. We leapt in there unprepared and that's why he was able to beat us."

"We can win," Fist said in agreement.

"Then what're you wantin' to do different?" Lenny asked.

"Let's think things through," Justan said. "Qyxal, I caught a glimpse of Charz with my mage sight back there and there is a thick cord of earth magic leading from him to the cave."

"Yeah, I saw that too."

"Well, earth magic is your specialty. Couldn't you use that against him, like use it to cast your earthquake spell on him or something?"

"Maybe . . ." The elf's eyes widened. "I could possibly tie a spell into the magic that is already there. If I could create enough dissonance, it could shake him apart. The force of that much earth magic would have to kill him!"

"Do you have enough magic left to work that spell?" Justan asked.

The elf's grin faltered. "Yes but to use a spell like that would take all the rest of the energy I have. If I try it and the spell fails, I wouldn't be of any use to anyone for awhile."

Justan sighed. "Alright, we'll have to abandon that idea for now, but hold on to it. Save your magic. We may need you to use that spell as a last resort if everything else fails."

"Then what?" Lenny grumbled. "How are we 'posed to beat the dag-blasted thing?"

"We can," Fist said again. Justan could feel his frustration again through the bond. He was having a hard time explaining himself. "But there are too many of us."

"You don't make a lick of sense sometimes, durn ogre."

"Yes he does," Justan said as he grasped Fist's thoughts through the bond. "Fist, you make perfect sense. Thank you! He means that our problem was that there were too many of us attacking at the same time and we had no battle plan. We were getting in each other's way out there!"

"So what're you sayin'? We take turns?"

"No, here is what we do different. Fist, Gwyrtha, and I will attack the giant. Lenny and Qyxal, you two head straight for the cave.

We will delay him while you two find Buster."

"Dag-blast it, son! Can't you get in yer dull thick head? This is my fight! Buster's my hammer."

"I know that Lenny, but the three of us can coordinate our attacks a lot better through the bond without having to worry about an extra person. We need you in the cave looking for Buster. Just think of it as . . . payment in advance for the weapons you are going to make us to replace the ones the giant broke."

"What do we fight with?" Fist asked.

"That's another thing, Lenny." Justan took a deep breath. "Fist is going to need to borrow Bertha for the fight."

"Dag-!"

"She's the only weapon we had last time that really seemed to hurt him, and with Fist's extra strength, it might be enough."

"But Justan," Qyxal said. "Wouldn't I be of better use with you in case we need to use that spell?"

"No, I am going to be using my bow this time and I don't need him throwing rocks at you. Besides, we don't know how big the cave is or how hard the hammer will be to find. Buster's magic will stand out to your mage sight. If Charz does somehow get past us and confronts you in the cave, you use that spell and kill him."

The elf nodded.

"I still don't like it," Lenny said. "Yer takin' all the risk here."

"It is the only plan that makes sense. Look, we have two choices. We either follow this plan, or we abandon the idea and everyone leaves together. So what do you say? Are you with me on this?" He knew that Fist was ready. Gwyrtha didn't understand why it was so important, but she was willing to go along with him. It was up to Lenny and Qyxal now.

"Justan, you always seem to have the right luck with you. I'll do what you want to do," Qyxal said.

Lenny swore under his breath for a moment, but finally walked over to Fist and held the hammer out. "Now remember, she will burn anything she touches. Yer so durn hairy yer liable to go up like a haystack. So careful, okay?"

Fist nodded. "I will burn him with your hammer. You like cooked giant?"

"Them's the only good kind." Lenny replied.

"Oh . . . one more thing," Justan smiled as the idea came to him. "Lenny, I need your firewater."

"What fer?"

He forced the smile down and turned to the ogre. "Fist, I need you to drink it."

"Drink? No," Fist rumbled and took a step backwards. He remembered what it had been like the last time he had drank the fire. All of his rage, his expulsion from the tribe, the killing of Tamboor's family, it had all come to the surface. He could have hurt his new tribe. "I don't want it."

"Remember how strong you were the last time?" As he spoke, Justan explained his idea further through the bond. "All that anger you felt? We need you to use it on the giant."

"Dag-nab it, son. You are one wily varmint," Lenny said with a chuckle and handed the skin to the ogre. "Take yer medicine, Fist."

"Don't want it," Fist said again and Justan pressed him through the bond. *Please, Fist. I know it burns, but it may give us the edge we need. You won't hurt us. Just focus on the giant.* The ogre resisted for a moment longer, but finally took the skin from Lenny. He whimpered in anticipation of the burning, then lifted it up and sucked it dry.

Chapter Twelve

Moments later Justan, Fist, and Gwyrtha were standing at the forest's edge watching Charz curse as he contorted, reaching around behind his back, trying to grasp hold of the shard of metal still imbedded in his rocky flesh. Lenny and Qyxal were sneaking further down through the trees to get closer to the cave entrance before the fight started.

Okay, our goal is to delay Charz until Lenny and Qyxal get out of the cave with Buster, Justan said through the bond. *Fist, you take Charz head on. Just try and keep him from grabbing you. Okay?*

Fist nodded. *It hurts!*

He was sweating profusely and his mouth was still ablaze from the firewater. His skin was flushed red and his rage was beginning to build. Justan felt horrible about what Fist was going through and wondered if he had done the right thing. Was the firewater really necessary? Was he just torturing his friend in order to get a slight advantage?

Justan stopped that line of thinking. He couldn't afford to doubt now. He could regret all he wanted later. Now was the time to focus.

Gwyrtha, I know that you will want to rush him right away, but what I need you to do is stay behind the giant and don't attack unless it will help Fist. Do you understand? He sent mental images of what he wanted, but he could tell that she understood her role already. The growth of her intelligence was truly impressive.

They waited a minute for Lenny and Qyxal to get closer to the cave, but Fist's rage was building. His self control would not last much longer. Justan notched an arrow on his bow and nodded. *Let's go.* They stepped out from the cover of the trees.

"Charz!" Justan shouted.

Charz turned and a wide grin split his rocky face. Justan noticed that his mouth was no longer bleeding.

"Hah! You're back already? Oh right, you had the elf mage with you. I should keep one of those around. I love round twos."

"This time we are changing the rules," Justan said and raised his bow. "Throw all the rocks you want."

"Okay." Charz frowned and picked up a boulder. Justan pulled back on the string and a sparkle came into the giant's eye. "So where is the dwarf? Did I kill him? Or . . . are you cheating? Hah!" He turned and threw the boulder so quickly that Justan didn't have time to get a shot off before it left the giant's hand.

Justan's arrow blasted into Charz's shoulder, sending out chunks of rock and a spray of blood.

"Ow! Whoa, no fair!" The giant screeched as he stumbled with the impact and Fist roared forward, Bertha hot and ready in his hands.

Justan watched the arc of the boulder as it flew towards the edge of the forest near the cave. He heard a faint curse and saw Lenny dive out of the trees just before the boulder struck the shadows where he had been hiding.

The boulder hit a tree two feet from where Qyxal was standing, peppering him with splinters of wood. He darted forward, helped the dwarf to his feet and ran. There was still a hundred feet of wide open space between them and the cave's entrance. Lenny hobbled after him.

"Come on, Lenny!" Qyxal shouted. "You have to go faster than that!"

"I'm still sore, you dag-gum tree-licker!" Lenny yelled.

They could hear Fist's roar and the sounds of battle behind them, but neither one dared look back until they reached the cave's entrance. The cave's interior was large and open. The ceiling was twice as high as the top of the giant's head in the center of the cave and large boulders crowded the floor, some of them nearly reaching the ceiling. It was too dark to see the rear of the cave, so Qyxal switched to his mage sight, hoping to see Buster's glow.

"Oh my . . ." The cave was flooded with the brilliance of elemental magic. The ceiling was reinforced with fire and earth and the rear wall of the cave shone forth with intense amounts of air and water. The black cord of earth magic connecting the giant to this cave originated from the center of that wall.

"Gall-durn it, can't see a dag-gum thing in here!" Lenny spat.

Qyxal placed his hand on the cave wall and sent tendrils of earth magic along the surface of the rock, altering the tiny molds and fungi that clung there to produce a luminescent glow. Soon the cave was flooded with a soft green light and it was evident that their search was not going to be as easy as they thought.

The giant wasn't lying about his trophies. Pieces of broken weapons were scattered about the cave along with packs and bags, boots, saddles, anything that the people he defeated might have been carrying. There was a pile of gold and random coins in one corner and the bones of multiple different animals, mainly horses were lying everywhere.

"Dag-blast it! We don't have time fer this. Findin' Buster's gonna be harder than tryin' to find a tater in a turd storm!" Lenny rooted around through the giant's loot cursing, while Qyxal moved toward the rear of the cave. What he saw there stunned him.

"Lenny! It would have to be back here!" Qyxal shouted. The rear wall of the cave was scarred and chipped all around the spot where the earth magic originated. At the base of the wall, the ground was littered with broken pieces of what must have been dozens of magical weapons that glittered brightly in his mage sight. "That is, if it is still in one piece."

"Cheaters! Ow, Hey!" Charz roared as Fist knocked him backward with a tremendous blow to the chest. Flames and rock flew from the impact.

Justan held another arrow to his ear and waited for the right opening. He couldn't afford to hit Fist accidentally. A shot from this range could kill him.

The ogre's fury was frightening in its intensity. Fueled by his reaction to the dwarf's liquor, Fist's speed was greater than that of the giant. He rained blow after blow on him and Charz hadn't been able to get in a counter attack.

Charz was covered in cracks and burn marks. Every fierce strike of the hammer left a wound glowing with heat. The magic that healed the giant was having a hard time keeping up, but it seemed to have speeded up in response to the magnitude of the damage. The wound from Justan's first arrow strike had nearly closed.

Fist readied another swing, and Charz kicked out, catching the ogre in the chest. The kick knocked Fist onto his back and the giant turned to run towards the cave. Justan shot another arrow, this one aimed behind the giant's left knee. The blast took out the joint just as Gwyrtha dove at the giant's legs from the front. Charz tumbled over her and crashed to the ground, yelling in pain and frustration.

"Take out his limbs!" Justan shouted.

Fist was already there. Despite several broken ribs that Justan could feel through the bond, the ogre swung the hammer with crushing force at the side of the giant's knee and the impact bent the leg at an odd angle. Gwyrtha leapt onto the giant's back, using her weight to hold him down.

"Cheaters! It hurts!" Charz howled. Justan walked up and drew another arrow.

"Do you yield?"

"I would never yield to cheaters!" Charz snarled and began to push himself up with his arms despite Gwyrtha's weight.

Justan shot the same shoulder he had started the battle with. The giant collapsed back to the ground. Justan drew another arrow and blasted out the other one. The giant lay helpless. "Fist, watch him and make sure these wounds do not heal. As soon as they get back, we'll leave."

The ogre nodded grimly and held the hammer at the ready.

"Cheaters! Aaaagh!" the giant cried.

"Shut up Charz, you lost." Justan said.

"I never lose! I will hunt you down and eat you alive, every one of you!" the giant snarled.

"No, I don't think you will," Justan said. "I think that you are somehow imprisoned in this place. A monster like you . . ." Justan paused while Fist bashed one of the giant's knees again, causing another cry of pain to escape Charz's lips. "You wouldn't be satisfied with staying in a cave. You would be roaming the countryside challenging the biggest and the best warriors out there."

"I can leave whenever I want!" Charz snarled.

"I can see the magic binding you to this place, you know," Justan said. "It is a cruel spell, whatever's keeping you here. I am just glad it's there so I don't have to kill you. Though I wonder if the magic can heal your brain . . ." He pulled another arrow back, aiming between the giant's eyes.

"You sound mean," Fist said, an impressed tone in his voice.

"I know," Justan responded. "I can't help myself. He deserves it."

"Why they take so long?" Fist asked in concern, looking towards the cave.

"Why 'do' they take so long," Justan reminded him. "I don't know. Maybe they are having a hard time finding Buster."

"Shut up, you two. I'm in pain, here- argh!" Charz growled as Fist bashed the other wounded leg for good measure.

They come, Gwyrtha said.

Justan turned and saw Lenny and Qyxal running towards them. They were both weighed down with bulging sacks slung over their shoulders. Lenny still managed to hold out Buster triumphantly. It didn't take them long to arrive, though Lenny was hobbling quite a bit.

"You beat him!" Qyxal said as they came up next to them. He winced at the state the giant was in. "You two are vicious."

"Yes," said Fist as he moved forward and bashed Charz's shoulder which had stopped bleeding.

"Aaagh! You . . . Hey, dwarf!" Charz said. "You taking my stuff?"

"'Spoils of battle.' Ain't that what you called it?" Lenny said with a grin.

"Well you dwarves live a long time." The giant snarled. "One day I'm going to escape from here and track you down. I'll kill you and your friends an-!"

Lenny dropped the sack and ended the giant's threat with a two-handed blow to its head so heavy Justan felt it in his feet. The giant's head cracked down the middle and he stopped moving. The dwarf lifted the hammer and kissed it, getting dust all over his handlebar mustache.

"Buster's still singin'!" Lenny said proudly.

"What did you two find in there?" Justan asked.

"Later. We need to get goin! That ain't gonna keep him out fer long." Lenny said. Sure enough, Justan saw that the wound was closing fast.

"You aren't going to kill him?" Qyxal asked the dwarf in disbelief.

"Nah, we got more than we needed out of him. This should teach that durn rock-biter a lesson," Lenny said. "'Sides, who knows if we even could?"

"Right. Let's go, then," Justan said.

Fist bashed the giant's leg one more time for good measure and they ran.

Chapter Thirteen

They didn't make it very far into the forest before they heard Charz yelling. Boulders began crashing into the trees behind them. The voice didn't fade as they made their way through the dense leaves. It was evident that he was coming after them.

"How did he get up and moving so fast?" Justan asked.

"I don't know how his magic works," Qyxal replied. "Maybe he can control how fast he heals. Who knows? We just need to keep moving."

They were at a disadvantage with both Lenny and Fist injured. The sacks that the elf and dwarf had brought out of the giant's cave were extremely heavy. Justan put Lenny on Gwyrtha's back despite both of their protests, but there was nothing he could do for Fist besides ask that he bear with the pain of his broken ribs as they ran. Qyxal simply could not heal him on the move and they didn't dare stop. Running as quickly as they were able, the group headed for the spot where they had tethered the horses on the edge of the giant's territory.

When they finally reached the forest's edge and the horses that awaited them, they tied the dwarf's sacks of loot to the saddles. Qyxal put his hands on Fist's chest. The ogre's breathing was ragged and his face was still red from his reaction to the liquor. He was no longer enraged but Justan knew that he felt quite ill.

"That's strange," Qyxal said as he released his hands. "His body's not reacting to the healing as well as he should. His ribs aren't broken anymore, but I couldn't get rid of all the bruising. I'll try again once we get to safety. Sorry, Fist."

The ogre just grunted in response.

The shouts of the giant were still too faint to make out what he was yelling, but he was getting closer. They mounted the horses and Justan turned to the ogre. "Fist, are you sure you don't want to try riding Stanza for a little while? Lenny could ride with me for now."

Gwyrtha snorted in dismay, glad to have gotten rid of the dwarf.

"I will run," Fist said.

They rode towards the shallows that the supply store owner had promised they would find where the giant's territory and the Wide River met. Charz's shouts faded in the distance and Justan breathed a little easier.

As they rode, Justan kept a concerned eye on the ogre that ran alongside them. Fist's steps were uneven and his breathing got more labored as they went. Justan, keeping his body at one with Gwyrtha's movements, closed his eyes and sent his mage sight into the ogre through the bond.

His worries grew. Despite the chill air, Fist's temperature was running hot. His blood vessels seemed swollen and his heartbeat did not sound regular. He had a pounding headache and his skin, still flushed and red, was now covered in welts that Justan had not previously seen because of the clothing the ogre wore.

Fist, you are sick, he sent.

I am good, the ogre replied. *We are almost there.*

Justan opened his eyes. He was right. They were nearly at the river. They came to the top of a hill and as the ground sloped downward, Justan could see its expanse in front of them. The river was so wide that he could barely make out the shoreline on the far side. The shallows stretched out before them. Rocks and boulders were visible sticking up from the water leaving it white and frothy.

The forest ended a short distance from the river's edge and once they reached the shore, Justan called a halt. Fist swayed on his feet as they stopped. Justan ran over and made him sit down. Squirrel darted about on the ogre from shoulder to shoulder, chattering in concern before finally curling up around Fist's neck.

Fist held his head in his hands and mumbled, "It is ok, Squirrel. Just need rest."

"Qyxal," Justan called. "Fist isn't doing well. I think he had a bad reaction to the firewater. His chest is broken out in welts."

The elf dismounted and put his hands on the ogre. Justan could see the magic pouring from his fingers. Qyxal concentrated and a frown pulled down the corners of his mouth.

"You are right Justan. Unfortunately, I-I can't just . . . heal that. The alcohol is in his blood and whatever is affecting him has spread throughout his entire body. Broken bones are one thing but this is beyond my skills. If I had something specific to treat . . ." The elf looked into the ogre's eyes. "Fist, what is bothering you the most?"

"Head hurts. Skin itches."

"I can help with the headache at least." Qyxal reached into Fist's head with his magic and soothed the swollen vessels, reducing the pain. "It will last only so long though. The reaction will subside on its own eventually, but until your system purges your blood of the alcohol, the headache will just come back again. I'll see if I can get your liver working faster . . ."

"There's somethin' else son," Lenny remarked. He pointed out over the river. "Looks like the shallows extend all the way to the other side as far as I can see, but it's gonna be rough goin'. You see them rocks, in the water there? There's a crossable path between the boulders, but the currents're gonna be strong and the water could still be purty deep in spots."

"Do we need to find another place to cross?" Justan asked, eyeing the water with concern.

"Nah, the horses'll get us across I think. But it won't be easy on 'em."

"It's not just the horses we need to worry about," Qyxal reminded. "The water is going to be freezing cold and with Fist being ill, I don't know if we can afford to cross it right now."

"Then we should wait until he feels better," Justan said. "That should give us the time to figure out how best to cross anyway. Qyxal, would it help if-?"

They were interrupted by a crash in the forest not too far away. Justan turned and saw a tree move at the top of the incline. The giant's voice cried out in triumph. He must have found their trail at his territory's edge. Justan's stomach dropped.

"Aw hell! Dag-burned dirt-eater's determined to make us kill him," Lenny growled.

"Saddle up!" Justan said. "Sorry Fist, we need to keep going. Can you stand?"

The ogre rose to his feet on shaky legs. "I can fight."

"What do we do?" Qyxal asked. "I don't have enough magic left in me to cast that spell we spoke about and we are too tired to fight. We could retreat and come back later, but he could just sit out here on the shoreline waiting for us and we might never get across."

"We have few choices." Justan said. "We could go downstream out of his range and come back to fight him later, or go even further down and try to find a place to cross elsewhere, or-."

"Ha! Thought you could get away did you?" Charz boomed. He was making his way down the incline and Justan knew that he would be upon them soon.

Was it really a good idea to come back later and fight him again? The giant knew their tactics now and Justan couldn't give Fist any more firewater. Qyxal's spell could possibly kill the giant, but what if it didn't work? If they traveled downstream further would they find another crossing as good as this one? He didn't know.

"We start across now." Justan decided. He pointed at the markings on the trees at the edge of the forest. "His territory ends here! He shouldn't be able to follow us into the river."

They galloped down the bank and into the water. Lenny and Qyxal took the lead followed by Fist. Justan and Gwyrtha came behind him. Justan wanted to make sure the ogre didn't falter and get swept away. Lenny kept them on the best possible path he could find through the shallows, weaving through the boulders and never letting the water get more than a couple feet deep, but the rocks were slippery and the water swift, making the footing treacherous. If one of the horses broke a leg, they were in deep trouble.

The water was so cold that there were still pieces of ice floating in it from the colder weather upstream. Fist and Gwyrtha were both miserable. The ogre was shivering already and the water hadn't reached his knees yet. Justan was just beginning to think he had made the worst possible decision when the first boulder fell.

Charz had found them. The giant stood on the shoreline taunting them and picking up more rocks. His wounds were still fairly grievous. The giant was limping and one shoulder still had a gaping wound from Ma'am's last arrow strike. He must have somehow forced the magic to heal his legs just enough to get him mobile before he came after them. Why he wasn't healed completely by now, Justan had no idea.

They had only made it a quarter of the way across the river and there was no way to hide or dodge the incoming rocks. They were fortunate that the giant's accuracy was affected by his injuries and none of his throws had hit their marks. They continued to make their way as quickly as they could through the water with boulders splashing all around them.

One of Charz's boulders landed not a foot from Fist. The ogre slipped and fell forward and the swift current nearly pulled him into the deeper water. He was able to struggle back to his feet, but his already bruised and battered body expended a lot of energy to do so. Both he and Squirrel were now soaked with the icy water. Squirrel was quite indignant about it too, chattering up a storm.

Justan told Gwyrtha to stop and turn to face the shore. He pulled Ma'am from his shoulder and cocked back an arrow just as Charz released another boulder. From the arc of the shot, Justan could tell that Lenny and Qyxal were in serious danger. He let his thoughts and emotions go, focused on the target, and released. The boulder disappeared into a cloud of rock and dust mid-flight.

The time for mercy had passed. The giant would have to die. Justan pulled back another arrow and aimed between Charz' eyes. The look on Charz's face stopped him. He no longer looked triumphant or cocky. He seemed so desperate, so afraid to lose that Justan felt a sense of pity twang within him. Suddenly it felt wrong to kill him. Justan changed his target at the last second.

The elbow on the giant's throwing arm exploded in a shower of flesh and rock. The boulder he was about to throw fell to the ground and his forearm now dangled uselessly at his side. Charz's scream of agony echoed across the water, causing the rest of the party to look behind them.

"Yeah! Got the dag-blasted rock-biter!" Lenny cried.

Justan didn't feel so triumphant. Charz fell to the ground, cradling his ruined arm. The giant was weeping in pain and failure. Justan felt sorry for him. What a miserable existence the giant lived. Justan turned Gwyrtha around and moved to catch up with the others. Had he done the right thing? Perhaps it would have been better if he had killed him after all.

He didn't have the luxury of dwelling on the giant for long. They reached half way across the river and the water had gotten deeper. Lenny scanned for a safer path to follow, but Fist was fading fast. Justan had to do something. He gripped Gwyrtha's mane tightly, leaned in close, and asked her to be careful with her movements. He closed his eyes and left his body behind, focusing all his attention on Fist through the bond.

What he saw frightened him. Fist's clothes were soaked and his temperature was no longer high, but alarmingly low. Whatever Qyxal had done was working. His body had removed much of the alcohol from his blood and the rash was nearly gone, but the positive effects had faded as well. His energy was down and his heartbeat had slowed. Fist's thoughts were a jumble and it was a struggle for him to put one foot in front of the other.

Justan tried to speak with him, but Fist was in such a trancelike state, that communication was impossible. Instead, Justan headed further into the ogre's consciousness, pushing the cold and the weariness from his mind and replacing them with feelings of warmth and comfort. He convinced Fist that it was a hot, sunny day and the water wasn't cold; it was refreshing. On the other side of the river was a picnic. The ogre didn't understand that concept, but he understood that there would be food and a place to take a nap.

Fist's steps picked up. A grin crossed his face. He was in a dreaming state now and Justan's thoughts kept him moving.

He continued to feed these thoughts and emotions to the ogre, but Fist's body was starting to shut down. The ogre was shivering. Despite the increased movement, his circulation had slowed.

Justan hid these facts from Fist, keeping him moving, but he didn't know how long the ogre would be able to keep it up. In desperation, Justan reached back through the bond and grasped all the energy he could muster from within his own body. He struggled to bring it back with him through the bond and to his relief, he was able to pull it through.

He began feeding his own energy to the ogre's failing systems, focusing first on Fist's heart, getting it pumping faster, then his limbs, feeding his muscles with the energy they needed to keep moving. Fist's steps picked up and his temperature rose. Justan was encouraged by the development and pushed harder.

Fist suddenly awoke from the trance Justan had placed him in. Justan heard him cry out in alarm both aloud and through the bond, "*Justan!*"

I'm here, he responded. He felt quite tired himself now. He had given a lot of energy to Fist, but that was okay. They could rest on the other side. *It's okay. Just keep moving. We will be there soon. I am sorry about . . .*

Justan couldn't continue the thought. What had he been saying again? His mind was muddled. Something was pulling at him. He felt his thoughts being dragged back into his own body.

"*Justan!*" This time Gwyrtha's voice had joined in with Fist's.

He opened his eyes to darkness. It was cold. He started to gasp in alarm, but realized his mouth was filled with water. He must have slipped from Gwyrtha's back. He felt rock and mud under his hands and knew he wasn't too deep, but the current was dragging him away. He wanted to stand, but he was too weak.

There was splashing all around him, but Justan barely registered what was going on. He felt strong hands grasping him and there was a blur of sounds and noises until he slept.

Chapter Fourteen

He was warm. That was Justan's first thought. He was warm and covered in blankets in his bed. Though his eyes were closed, he could see the brightness of the morning through his eyelids and considered whether he should get up. His mother would have breakfast ready most likely. His stomach growled at the thought, but the bed felt so good. Surely he could sleep a little longer. He hadn't slept in a bed in such a long time. Fist was so missing out . . . Fist?

Justan sat up with a start. He was indeed in a bed, though the room was not familiar. It was a small tidy room with a window in one corner. There was a small desk and washbasin in the opposite corner. A chair stood beside the bed and Justan saw that his clothes were folded neatly on top. He pulled the covers aside to find that he was naked.

He wondered who had undressed him. He hoped it had been Lenny or Qyxal. He didn't need some stranger knowing about the frost rune on his chest or his naming runes. He reached inside his mind to feel the bond. Fist and Gwyrtha were there and both seemed content. Gwyrtha was sleeping and Fist was eating. The ogre noticed his presence and called out to him.

Justan, you are awake!

Fist, are you alright? he asked. *I am so sorry about what happened. I should never have made you drink that stuff.*

It is okay. I am feeling good. Come, eat with us. The food is good.

Justan caught the sense of a table piled with food and people talking. The scent of bacon and freshly baked bread hung heavy in the ogre's nostrils and his mouth was full of what could only be warm gravy. Justan's mouth watered. Wherever they were, they were in a much better position than before. Perhaps a farmer had taken them in. Maybe the people here would know how to find Master Coal.

He pulled his clothes off of the chair and as he started to put them on, noticed that they had been cleaned and repaired. Justan dressed quickly. He donned his gloves and felt sad as he looked at the empty sword sheathes. He left them there and threw his bow and quiver over his shoulder. Perhaps they could find some replacement swords soon.

When Justan opened the door, he could hear people talking. Outside of the room was a hallway lined with doors on either side. A few of them were open and Justan saw neatly made beds. In the room across from his, a sleepy-eyed man was sitting up having just awoken. When he saw Justan looking, he nodded and yawned. Justan nodded back and walked towards the stairs at the end of the hallway. The smell of food and sound of voices echoed from below.

What kind of place was this, he wondered. Were they at an inn? If so it was a pretty nice one. All the rooms were clean and everything looked well cared for. Where did Lenny get the money to pay for it?

At the bottom of the stairs was a large room with a long table in the center that was loaded with a breakfast feast. Many men and women were gathered around the table laughing and talking. Lenny, Qyxal, and Fist were sitting on the far end speaking with a middle aged man. To Justan's surprise, no one seemed to be giving the ogre more than a second glance.

Lenny and Qyxal called out to him and Justan walked over to join his friends. He sat down in an empty spot next to Fist. The smell of the food overwhelmed his senses.

"The ogre said you was awake," Lenny said. "Good to see you up and movin', again."

Fist placed a large hand on his back and rumbled through a mouthful of bacon, "Justan, how you feel?"

"It's how 'do' you feel," he reminded with a smile. The ogre chuckled and Justan continued, "I am actually feeling very good, thank you. But I am a bit confused . . . where are we?"

"We have arrived at our destination," Qyxal said. He gestured at the man they had been talking to when Justan came in. "Sir Edge, this is Master Coal."

Justan's jaw dropped in surprise. The wizard didn't look as Justan had expected. He wore simple farmer's garb instead of mage robes and he didn't look that old, maybe in his late fifties to early sixties. His brown hair was graying at his temples and his skin was a bit weathered, but he had a kind face and most of his wrinkles were laugh lines. His eyes sparkled with a youth and vigor that reminded Justan somewhat of Master Latva's. His eyes dropped to the man's left hand and though he held a piece of bread, Justan saw the edges of a naming rune.

"Uhh . . ." He had so many questions for this man, had so many things planned to say, but he couldn't get anything to come out.

"He can talk to me later. Let him eat first," Coal said to the elf. His voice had a good natured quality to it. He gestured at the food "Go on, Sir Edge. Take all you want. Sleep isn't all your body needed."

"Th-thank you, Master Coal." Justan's mouth was watering so heavily that he had to swallow to keep from drooling. He loaded his plate with bread and bacon and eggs, then covered it all with a heaping ladle of gravy. "Lenny, how exactly did we get here? How long have I been asleep?"

The dwarf explained as Justan ate, "Well son, I'm not rightly sure how you fell. We was almost at the shore when I heard Fist holler. I just turned around and you was in the dag-gum water. Fist threw you up on his shoulder and carried you out. By the time we got up the bank and started a fire, you was both out. We did our best to keep you warm. Hell, Gwyrtha kept tryin' to lay on top of you like you was an egg."

"Both of you were in shock from the cold," Qyxal put in.

"Yeah, well Fist slept durn near twelve hours and you still wasn't awake yet. I wanted to strap you down to Gwyrtha's back, but the elf didn't like the idear."

"I was concerned that it would jostle you too much," Qyxal clarified. A wry grin came upon his face. "Fist ended up carrying you like a baby. It was kind of sweet actually."

"Can you let me tell the gall-durn story?" Lenny grumbled. "Anyways so we come up over the rise and just past the trees, there's acres of farmland stretched out far as the eye can see. I was worried 'cause it's so wide open, there's nowhere to hide. Sure enough some farmer sees us and starts a hootin' and hollerin'. Next thing you know-."

"Well, our visitor is finally awake! Glad to see it." A handsome woman maybe a few years older than Coal walked up to the head of the table. She kissed the wizard on the cheek. "Morning, love. Did you enjoy your meal?"

"Delicious as always." Master Coal put an arm around her and looked at Justan. "I tell the workers that the reason I work them so hard is to keep them from getting fat on her cooking. Sir Edge, this is my wife, Becca."

Justan stood and bowed, remembering his manners. "Nice to meet you, ma'am."

"Come now, sit down. You must keep eating," Becca said, though she seemed pleased with his observance of the proper decorum. "You have been asleep in that bed upstairs for two days for goodness sake. We could barely get you awake enough to pour water down you."

Justan looked down at his empty plate with surprise. He had been so intent on Lenny's story that he hadn't realized that he had finished the food.

"Thank you, ma'am," he said and began to reload his plate.

"Sir Edge, if I might make a suggestion," Master Coal said. He passed over a platter of a strange vegetable, yellow in color that looked like a combination of tomato and squash. It had been seasoned with herbs and roasted until it was blackened on the edges. "Try some of this. It's called honstule. It was developed by one of my bonded years ago. Great for energy."

Justan added some to his plate and took a bite. It had a pleasant peppery flavor. "Mmm . . . hey, Lenny."

"I know it, son. It'd go great in my pepperbean stew, doncha' think?" Justan saw that the dwarf's plate was already piled high with it. "I already done asked Master Coal here if I could take some seeds with me to plant back home some day."

"Bah! And I'm sure that he was more than happy to oblige you that request," Becca said. "Coal here won't be satisfied until he has old Honstule's vegetable on every plate in the known lands. Will you, love?"

"Of course not, dear. It is the best way to honor his memory, after all."

Coal smiled at her and Justan was struck once more by the complete oddness of the situation. Was he still dreaming? Surely this couldn't be the master wizard that Valtrek had sent him to find. The thought that he was still dreaming was reinforced by Justan's realization that he had emptied his plate again. There was no way he had that much room in his stomach.

"Full," Fist groaned, leaning back clutching his belly. The ogre smiled contentedly.

"As well you should be with all that food you stuffed down," Becca said. "Come, Fist. You promised to help me with the dishes this morning."

"Uh, yes Becca," the ogre replied and gave a somewhat apologetic look to Justan. He followed Coal's wife into the kitchens, having to hunch over to get through the doorway. Justan could hear him rumble, "What do we do now?"

"Qyxal, my friend," Coal said and he stood. "Would you like to come along with me as I show Sir Edge around? If he is finished, that is."

"Yes, of course. I'm ready." Justan said, eager to learn what Master Coal could teach him. Qyxal nodded and accepted the invitation.

"I'll tag along too, if'n you don't mind," Lenny said to Master Coal. "I'm interested to hear more about this operation you have here."

"Please do," Master Coal said and he led them out the door into the sunlight. "This is my wizard's keep, though it is a keep in the very loosest sense of the word. We are just inside the forest on the edge of the farmlands."

As he looked around, Justan resolved to stop being surprised when it came to Master Coal. The place didn't look like a keep at all. The outer walls were perhaps twelve feet tall and made of thick logs erected vertically. The space inside was wide and open. A small town could have fit inside.

One side of the enclosure was taken up by a stable and corral with over a dozen horses inside. Justan could see Stanza and Albert among them. The rest of the space was taken up by several buildings and houses. Justan heard the sounds of a smithy in the back.

Master Coal explained as they walked, "I have a working farm just outside of the forest about a half mile from here. The men and women you saw in the lodge this morning work it for me. We also provide metal and leather work for the rest of the farmers in the area in exchange for food and services. Our little farming community provides a large part of the produce and meat for the Kingdom of Razbeck."

"So what's yer angle then?" Lenny asked. "I'm a businessman myself and I 'magine you could make a decent livin' with yer crops and all, but yer a master wizard. What's keepin' you here when you got the whole world open to you?"

Justan was worried that the dwarf's frankness might irritate the master, but Coal just looked back at Lenny with a smile.

"Ah, but there is more to life than profits or power. I imagine that even a businessman such as yourself might understand that. After all, look at the company you're keeping. I wonder what profit there is for you in staying with Sir Edge, here."

Lenny laughed. "Well, I reckon you got yerself a point there, Coal. Ain't no mistakin' it."

"I have been wondering ever since we arrived," Qyxal said. "With the quiet lifestyle you lead here, why do you need the walls?"

"These walls have been needed a time or two in the past. Especially in the beginning. When we first arrived, this was a much wilder place." His brow furrowed a bit as he remembered darker times, but the mood passed quickly and the wizard smiled again. "Those times are over, though. The King of Razbeck has the major roads patrolled and it is much more peaceful now. Problems are rare and my bonded and I provide protection for the community if any is needed."

As they continued down the center street, Justan realized that he had been so caught up in everything happening around him that he had not thought to thank the wizard. "Master Coal, I must thank you for taking us in and feeding everyone. You didn't have to do that."

"Oh, yes. About that. I understand that you wish me to teach you about bonding magic?" Coal asked.

"Uh, yes. I brought a letter of introduction from Wizard Valtrek, but I don't have it with me right now."

"Yes I know. Qyxal was nice enough to give it to me when you arrived. In fact I received another letter much like it from Valtrek a few weeks ago, telling me that you were coming. Frankly, I was not pleased to receive the news. This is a farm. I do not run a rural branch of the Mage School here. I left that life behind me years ago." He frowned. "This is exactly the kind of thing that Valtrek likes to do. Get's in everyone's business. Don't misunderstand me, he is a good man at heart, but I never could stand his tactics."

"I know what you mean," Justan said.

"Yes, Qyxal told me how he manipulated you into going to the Mage School in the first place." Coal shook his head in distaste. "It was a deplorable thing he did."

"So does this mean that you won't teach me?" Justan asked. It hadn't occurred to him that the master might refuse.

"No, I can't possibly refuse you now that you are here. Valtrek knew that when he sent you. You need the knowledge I can give you. The thing is, Sir Edge, I am a very busy man. I have many people that depend on me here and in order to teach you and Qyxal as Valtrek has requested, I will have to take a lot of time away from my other duties. If that is going to happen, I have several requirements."

"Yes, sir. Of course." Justan was relieved. The thought of going back empty handed after everything they had gone through was unthinkable.

"You should hear me out first. This does not concern just you. Every member of your group that stays with us will have to follow by the rules of my house. This means that I expect you and Qyxal to work in exchange for the lessons and the food and lodging. As for your bonded and Lenui," He nodded to the dwarf. "They will be treated like all of the visitors here. I will expect a full day's work from them and in return, I will provide their food and lodging and pay them a fair wage."

Justan had heard enough. "I don't have a problem with any of your terms, but I can only speak for myself. Let me check with Fist and Gwyrtha." He closed his eyes and discussed it with them. After a minute or two, he had their answers. He smiled. "Sorry, it took so long. I had to calm Fist down. He didn't understand why washing the dishes made his fingers all wrinkly." Lenny and Qyxal laughed. "Gwyrtha is quite happy to help and Fist doesn't mind at all. He is very interested in farming."

He turned to the dwarf. "Lenny, I don't know how I could ask you to stay. If you want to leave and go to your new shop in Wobble, I'll understand."

"Don't worry yerself, son. Master Coal's goin' about this the right way. A little hard work never hurt nobody. When I was just a kid, I started my smithin' career hoofin' horses and fixin' wagon axles. No reason I can't do that here fer a while. I'll stay at least 'till I get the weapons made that I promised you."

"Thank you, Lenny. Qyxal?" Justan asked, turning to the elf.

"If you need someone to work with the horses, I will be more than willing to give this a try, Master Coal," Qyxal said.

The wizard nodded. "Then I suppose it's time to introduce Sir Edge to my bonded. Samson is on his way here now, but Bettie is complaining that I am taking her away from her work for something so trivial."

"You have two bonded?" Justan asked.

"Three actually, but Willum is away training at the Battle Academy."

"Willum . . .?" Justan's hand went to his forehead. "I think I know him! He uses a scythe, right?" The master nodded. "I can't believe it! He was accepted into the academy at the end of my first year in Training School. Nice guy, Willum. Great fighter. Everyone said he had potential."

Master Coal laughed. "He would be pleased to know that a named warrior thinks so highly of him. I shall have to tell him about that later tonight. It is difficult to reach him. He is so far away that I have to concentrate very hard just to get through. Night time is my only chance to catch up with him."

"You can really communicate with him when he's that far away?" Justan asked.

"I have had a lot of practice." Master Coal explained. "Oh, here comes Samson now."

Justan looked towards the gates at the front of the keep and saw Gwyrtha come in, followed by an enormous man riding a horse. At least that is what Justan thought he saw, but there was something odd about the man. Gwyrtha was frolicking about him, getting in the way and Justan couldn't get a good look at him. He was laughing and talking to her. The man had short brown hair and a neatly-trimmed beard. He must have just gotten back from working the fields because he had a shovel over one shoulder.

Then it hit Justan. The man wasn't riding a horse; he was part of the horse. His torso rose from the place where the horse's neck was supposed to be. "Samson is a centaur? I thought that they were just myths!"

"No. He isn't a centaur," Master Coal said. "Well . . . he is, but he isn't. He's a centaur of sorts, but not a centaur like in the myths. There is no real race of centaurs. At least I don't think there is. There is not proof that they exist anyway."

Samson arrived with Gwyrtha at his side. He was taller than Fist, his waist starting at Justan's shoulder. He scratched Gwyrtha behind the ears fondly. Justan could feel her happiness through the bond. Somehow it felt as if she had known the man for a long time.

"Justan, this is Samson," Master Coal said formally. "He is a rogue horse."

Justan stared stupidly up at Samson for a moment before remembering to extend his hand in greeting. "Uh, good to meet you."

"It is good to meet you, Sir Edge. Gwyrtha is very happy with you, I see," Samson said, his voice a proud baritone. He bent to grasp Justan's hand, but paused and cleared his throat. "Coal?"

"Sorry," Master Coal said.

To Justan's further surprise, Samson began to shrink. His lower body went from the size of a large quarter horse to that of a small pony. He shook Justan's hand and smiled, now only a foot or so taller than

Justan.

Master Coal sighed. “As for your meeting Bettie, she has refused to leave the forge. It looks like we will have to go and meet her there.” The wizard headed towards the rear of the keep.

Justan followed him, but glanced back over at Samson once again. He was having difficulty processing this particular development. He wasn’t sure why. After all, he had seen some amazing things over the past year. Perhaps it had something to do with the odd way his day had started out.

“I know how you feel, son,” Lenny whispered. “Samson and Bettie were the ones that approached us when the farmer’s started hollerin’. When I first saw Samson there I nearly lost my drawers. But wait till you meet Bettie. She’s a right fine filly that one. A bit strange maybe, but built like a . . . well she’s a real woman I’ll say that much.”

The dwarf had a twinkle in his eye, but Justan wasn’t sure what was causing it. Lenny had called her a filly. Was she a rogue horse too? They arrived at the forge just as she came out. Bettie wore a heavy blackened leather apron and large thick gloves that she was taking off as she muttered to herself.

“Fine, Coal. Fine. I’ll come meet this new student of yours. Don’t matter how much work I . . . oh.” She saw them standing in front of her and stuck out her hand. Justan shook it despite being afraid she might crush his hand in hers. She forced a cursory smile. “Hello then. I’m Bettie.”

Bettie was the most muscular woman Justan had ever seen. She was tall. About his same height, and the way her arms bulged out reminded him of Fist’s. She had a full head of curly black hair that was pulled back into a pony tail to keep it from the stray sparks generated by the forge. Her eyes were a light yellow color and her skin had a greenish tint to it. It took Justan a moment to realize why. Then he noticed the way her teeth were slightly pointed. He was sure of it. She was a half-orc.

“I am Ju- Edge. Nice to meet you,” he said and gave a short bow as was proper when meeting a lady for the first time.

“Hey, he actually bowed.” Bettie laughed. She slapped Justan on the arm. “Lenny, he’s just like you said. I like this one. Even got some meat on him.”

She released Justan’s hand and reached out to grab Lenny’s shirt sleeve. “C’mere dwarf. I could use your help with an order I got to fill.”

“That’s our Bettie,” Coal said with a chuckle. He peered through the entrance of the forge and turned back to Justan. “Why don’t you come on in? There is one more person I would like you to meet. He was out working by the time you got up this morning or I would have introduced you sooner.”

As Justan followed Master Coal inside, the wizard called out, “Son?”

A large man working at a table in the back of the forge turned towards them with a grin. When he saw Justan walking towards him, his cheeks went red and the smile faded.

Justan stopped in disbelief. The day couldn’t possibly get stranger. He immediately went back to the theory that this was all a dream.

“Sir Edge, this is my son, Benjo. I- . . . Wait, do you two already know each other?”

Chapter Fifteen

Master Coal's question hung in the air and Justan could see the panicked and pleading look in Benjo's eyes. He took that to mean Master Coal didn't know everything that Benjo had done in Training School. Justan wasn't sure what to say. He didn't really care if Benjo got in trouble, but he didn't know how Master Coal would react to hearing the horrible things his son had done. Besides, the last thing he needed while he was there was to have an enemy plotting against him at every turn.

"Wow, y-yes I knew him at the Training School!" Justan said. He walked forward and shook Benjo's hand very tightly, careful to make sure that Master Coal couldn't see his facial expression. "Benjo, so good to see you! I didn't know that Master Coal was your father."

"Justan!" Benjo said, swallowing quickly. "You didn't know? Benjo, son of Coal, remember?"

"Oh! Right!" Justan slapped his forehead. He had gone by the name of Benjo Plunk back at the Training School. "Don't know why I didn't put that together. We definitely have some catching up to do," Justan said, conveying as much menace as possible with his eyes without showing it in his voice.

"So what are you doing here?" Benjo asked, blanching at Justan's look.

"Benjo, he isn't Justan anymore. He was named a short time ago. This is the 'Sir Edge' we have been talking about."

Benjo's face went even paler and he said only, "Congratulations."

"What a nice surprise, you two knowing each other. I can't wait to tell your mother!" Coal said, clapping the two of them on the back. "Well, we'll let you get back to work, son. Sir Edge and I have a lot to discuss." Coal gestured towards the doorway.

"Benjo, I'll come by and see you later. We'll talk." Justan said with a cheerful tone in his voice. But he shot him a parting glare just before they left the forge. The large man gulped.

Master Coal walked up to Qyxal, who was still talking with Samson just outside of the forge. "Samson, would you please take Qyxal up to the stables and show him what responsibilities we will need him to take on?" When they had left, the wizard turned back to Justan. "As for you, Sir Edge-."

"Master Coal, may I make a request?" Justan interrupted.

"Of course."

"Could you just call me . . . Edge?" Justan had wanted to bring this up all morning. He would rather that the wizard call him Justan, but it seemed inappropriate to ask him to do so. "I feel awkward with you calling me 'Sir Edge' all the time."

"As you wish." Coal smiled and nodded. "Now that we have that out of the way, follow me. We need to talk about your teaching."

"But shouldn't Qyxal come with us? He is going to study with you too."

"Qyxal doesn't need to learn about bonding. Besides, he is a mage. He is at the point in his learning where he needs to decide the direction of his own studies. I will help him as I can, but that is a discussion that he and I can have later. You, on the other hand, have very specific needs."

He led Justan back along the center street past a row of houses. Each one was built with smooth timbers and painted a different color. They weren't large, but looked comfortable.

Justan had to ask, "Whose houses are those?"

"The first house is Bettie's and the second one is Samson's. Willum's house is just behind them and my home is the one next to the lodge."

Justan tried to imagine Samson living in a house. The picture seemed a bit odd. He looked at the second house again. There was no front porch and the doorway was taller than the others. Before he said anything, Coal answered his question.

"Yes, Samson uses his house. He doesn't sleep indoors unless it is raining, but everyone needs a place of their own to get away to from time to time."

Justan followed the wizard between his and Samson's house, past Willum's and behind the lodge where there was a garden full of the vegetable that Coal had called honstule. The plants had large waxy green leaves and each vegetable was tipped with a gorgeous purple flower. Justan couldn't imagine what farmer wouldn't want to have that plant in his own garden, if only just for their beauty.

A stone-lined path ran down the center of the garden and ended at a building that was twice the size of any of the other houses. Unlike the others, this one was made of red brick and mortar and a well-kept flower bed ran around the outside of it. Master Coal opened the door and beckoned Justan inside.

"This, Edge, is my study."

Justan walked inside to find that the building consisted of one large room well lit with glowing orbs and lined with bookshelves. The ceiling was high and arched and the floor was covered with a fine burgundy carpet. There was a large, highly polished wooden desk towards the back under a wide window, a comfortable looking couch and a few padded leather chairs with small tables beside them. Justan walked over to the books and scanned the titles while Master Coal spoke.

"This is the one place in my keep where I can sit and feel like a wizard. It is my little piece of the Mage School, so to speak and this is where we will have most of your lessons." He gestured to a chair. "Please, Edge, have a seat."

"Thank you, Master Coal," Justan said and sat in the chair the wizard offered. "It feels nice to be in a library again. I miss the one in the Rune Tower very much."

"So do I," Master Coal said and for a moment, Justan could see sadness on his face. "Now, before we start, let me quickly thank you for your kindness to Benjo back there."

"Kindness, sir?"

"When you said that you didn't realize he was my son, the look on his face told me everything."

"It did?" Justan asked. How much had Benjo told him?

"Don't worry about it. I completely understand why he didn't use my name when he lived at the Training School," Coal said. "I am not his birth father after all. His real father died when he was young and I married Becca while he was still a teenager. I truly do consider him my son, but it has not been easy for him to accept me." The wizard sighed and eased into the leather cushioned chair opposite Justan.

"Besides, despite the fact that he is seven years older, Benjo has always looked up to Willum and that boy wouldn't use my name either. He is so headstrong. Willum just wants to accomplish everything on his own, without his father's name propping him up."

"I understand that feeling," Justan said, thinking of his relationship with his own famous father. "Wait, so you are Willum's father too?"

Coal smiled. "Well, not exactly. You see, I bonded with Willum when he was only four. I happened to be in Dremald on business that day and his parents were to be executed in the public square. They had two men standing there each one grabbing an arm, forcing him to watch. It was a horrible spectacle and I wouldn't have stayed, except for the pitiful sight of that single child screaming for his parents while the rest of the crowd was yelling and throwing things at them . . ." Master Coal shuddered.

"The moment the headman's axe came down the second time, ending his mother's life, I felt the pain of the bond hit me. The little fellow was in so much agony that I couldn't bear it. I bound the two men guarding him with air, scooped him up, and carried him off and never looked back. Not many people know that we are bonded. As far as the rest of the world is concerned, Willum is just an orphan child that I adopted."

The more Justan found out about who Master Coal was, the more he liked the man. "I see. I cannot imagine what it must have been like being bonded to a traumatized child. It is difficult enough being bonded to an adult."

"Well, as you know, Edge, when it comes to bonding, there is not much choice in the matter. So!" Master Coal leaned forward in his chair. "That is enough about my life for now. We still have important matters to discuss. I need to know some things about you so that I can know the best place to start with your teaching."

"Of course," Justan replied, ready to share anything that would be of help.

"First of all, what are your elemental strengths? What have you learned to do so far?" he asked.

"Professor Locksher told me that I had strong talent in air and water magic, but very low levels in earth and fire."

"So you have the makings of a frost wizard in you. That's rare. Very interesting indeed," Master Coal said.

"However, I have no offensive magic to speak of. I can only do defensive spells."

"You have learned no offensive spells at all?" the wizard asked in surprise.

"Well, not exactly. I can't perform offensive spells, but I have tried to learn all I can about them. I figure that I need to understand how offensive magic is done if I am ever going to be able to defend against it."

"Ah, smart. That's good. Hopefully this means that we won't have to start from the very beginning. You see, you are quite wrong when you say that you cannot do offensive magic," Master Coal said.

"I am?" Justan replied, stunned. He smiled in excitement. "So you can teach me?"

"You have been using it already. Bonding magic is by its nature an offensive type of magic," the wizard explained. "The act of bonding itself is an offensive spell."

"I never thought of it like that," Justan said. It made sense though. Bonding was his mind linking itself with another. "If only the bond would allow me to perform other kinds of magic."

"Oh it can, but we'll get to that later," the wizard said, a thoughtful gleam in his eye. "For now, tell me what you know about bonding magic."

"I know that it's rare. Valtrek said that there were only three known bonding wizards alive."

"Well, that's not quite true. There just happens to be only three bonding wizards that Valtrek knows about. Though it is true that bonding wizards are rare, it is a large world that we live in. I have met four others myself and that was before I met you."

"But why then, if there are so many bonding wizards out there, do you never hear of them? And why was Valtrek the only wizard at the Mage School that was able to figure out that I had bonding magic?" Justan asked.

The master nodded approvingly. "Astute questions. The answers are complicated though. For one thing, bonding magic cannot be seen with normal mage sight, so the Mage School cannot find people with this ability using any of their usual techniques. Also, we bonding wizards tend to be secretive. We end up bonded to other beings that most people would shy away from, so we become adept at hiding ourselves." The master looked like he was about to say more, but sighed. "There are other reasons as well, but we will not discuss them today. There are a lot of other things you need to learn first."

"I see," Justan said, wondering what made Master Coal hesitant. "I do have a question though. Why is it that bonding magic cant be seen with mage sight?"

"I see we must start at the beginning," Master Coal said. "There are two kinds of magic: Elemental magic, which is the magic that is taught at the Mage School, and spirit magic."

"Spirit magic?" The term sounded familiar. It took him a second to place where he had heard about it. "You mean like the magic the Bowl of Souls uses?"

"Exactly right. So you have been doing some research of your own then. That's good." Coal smiled. "The Bowl of Souls uses spirit magic to probe the souls of those that approach it to see if they are worthy to be named. Bonding, on the other hand, uses spirit magic to form a link between two souls. That is why it cannot be seen with regular mage sight. Only those with spirit magic can see it."

"I still don't understand why this is not taught at the Mage School." Justan said.

"Quite simply because the wizards haven't been able to figure out how it works and though they wouldn't admit it, they are always wary of the things they don't understand. The Mage School doesn't like to acknowledge spirit magic's existence."

"But doesn't that go against their very principals? I would think that the Mage School would be doing all they could to learn about it," Justan said.

"Hundreds of years of frustration have curbed their appetite for this particular knowledge, I'm afraid," Master Coal explained. "So . . . Now that you know what bonding magic is, let's talk about what it can do. What have you learned so far?"

"Well, I can communicate with my bonded. More recently I have discovered that I can see inside of them much in the same way that I can use my mage sight to see inside myself," Justan said. "And the other day I was able to send my own energy through the bond to help Fist."

"Oh . . . so that is what happened on the river? My, that was a very dangerous thing to attempt," the wizard said. "You are lucky that you didn't kill yourself."

"Why is that?"

"Did you give any thought to the fact that Fist is two to three times your size? You were trying to use the energy contained in your-." He looked Justan up and down. "Say . . . two-hundred-and-twenty pound body to power a seven-hundred pound ogre? Magic does not change the laws of reality, Edge. You need to use common sense too."

"B-but I had no choice. Fist was close to collapse in the middle of the river. He could have died!" Justan said.

"A little bit of energy just to keep him going may have been okay, but you could have done something much more effective if you had thought it through," Master Coal chastised. "Gwyrtha weighs at least as much as Fist does and, being a rogue horse, she has vast amounts of energy. You could have pulled the energy from her to help keep the ogre going with little or no effect on her. As a bonding wizard, you can use your own mind and body as a channel in which to transfer thoughts, emotions, and energy from one bonded to another."

"I can do that?" The possibilities started tumbling through Justan's mind.

"Yes. You could have brought Gwyrtha's energy into your body and passed it on through the bond to the ogre. That technique is a bit tricky because if you try to hold too much of that energy inside of your body, you could hurt yourself, but after a bit of practice, you will find that it comes naturally."

"But . . . wouldn't it be . . . wrong to just take it from her like that?" Justan tried to imagine what it would be like if someone just started siphoning energy off of him.

"It could be. It would especially feel that way if she did not want to give it. Hopefully if you explained to her that it was for Fist, she would give it to you willingly."

"She would," Justan said with confidence. "She loves Fist dearly."

"Good. This is one of the most important things in a bonded relationship. They should understand that they are a part of you now and you are a part of them, but it is also important that they realize that through you, they are now a part of each other. It is crucial that all of you spend as much time together as possible. Hopefully they will learn to be as close to each other as they are to you. It is unfortunate, but that is not always the case. I have had bonded in the past that truly disliked each other."

"That would be hard to deal with," Justan mused.

"There may be times that come up when you need something from your bonded, and it might make them uncomfortable or even cause them pain. If their relationship with you and each other is strong, then they will give of themselves anyway and willingly in fact. But here is where the danger lies." Coal leaned forward and looked Justan directly in the eyes. His tone was deadly serious. "What if they don't? What if you or another of your bonded needs something from them and they refuse to give it? In times like that, you will need to make a choice. Do you respect that or do you take what is theirs against their will?"

"No!" Justan said, aghast at the idea. "That would be . . ."

"The damage to your relationship could very well be irreparable." Master Coal concluded. "There is a fine line between treating your bonded like the closest of family and treating them like mere cattle for you to feed off of when you feel the need. It is something that you need to be very aware of. It is easy, especially if you are very involved in something important to you, to forget that.

"Over the years, I have found that it is best to set a policy to never take their energy unless you really need it. And always ask first. That is very important. Any time that you enter their body or mind for anything, you should ask permission first. Think of it as a knock before entering, as if you were sharing a house with them. Your mind is your most intimate place, and it is horribly rude for someone to just come barging in. There are things in your mind that you don't want to share even with your bonded and you shouldn't have to.

"This is one of the first things that I will be teaching you as we start your training. You must learn how to keep thoughts to yourself and how to avoid listening in to your bonded's thoughts when they don't want you to."

Justan's mind was buzzing. There was so much that he hadn't thought about. The bond suddenly felt like it carried a great amount of responsibility with it. "Thank you so much for your help, Master Coal. There is so much I need to know."

"It is good that you are willing to learn." Master Coal said, pleased with his sincerity. "Now, it is almost time for lunch. Let's talk about your schedule. Do you have any particular daily needs?"

"Well, I want to have time for exercise and time for my warrior training. But I can fit that around whatever schedule you set for me."

"It shouldn't be a problem. You will get plenty of exercise working the farm in the mornings. And along the lines of what we have been discussing, I have made sure that you will be working together with your bonded during those hours. Make the most of that time together. Teach them what we learn in our lessons. It will keep your mind off the strain of the work and it is good information for them to know as well.

"From the noon meal until dinner, you will work on your studies.

Sometimes I will be with you, sometimes I will have assignments for you to work on. After dinner, the time will be yours to spend as you wish. This is probably a good time for you to do any additional training you want."

"Thank you, Master Coal. That sounds very reasonable."

Master Coal stood. "Let's go eat, then."

Justan left Coal's study looking forward to learning much more from the master.

Chapter Sixteen

That evening as everyone was getting ready for bed, Justan went to Benjo's house. It was the first building in the enclosure, just in front of the stables. It was situated away from the other houses and he wondered if Benjo had chosen the place for just that reason. Justan knocked. The door opened right away and the large man invited him in

The house was small, just two rooms. There was a small table and a cabinet in the main room, along with a couch to sit on. Justan could see a bed and dresser in the next room through the doorway in the back. To his surprise, it was all kept quite neatly. He had always seen Benjo as kind of a slob.

"I-I was expecting you to come," Benjo said and gestured to the couch. "Uh, would you like to sit, Justa- . . . er, Sir Edge?"

"No, I think we need to get to the point," Justan responded. "I am going to be staying here and learning from Master Coal for a while, I don't know how long actually, and I don't need you creeping around in the shadows trying to think of ways to stab me in the back."

"Oh, no no no, I-I wouldn't. I mean, well what happened back at . . ." Benjo stopped for a moment, gathering his thoughts. "I know how much you must hate me for what I did. I have been trying to think of what I was going to say to you ever since I saw you earlier. Maybe it is best if I start at the beginning?"

"I just need an answer. Are you going to be a problem?"

"N-no, of course I won't. But please, will you let me explain my side of the story?" Benjo looked so desperate, that Justan couldn't say no to the man.

"If you must."

"Well, I left this place to go to the Training School after Willum entered the academy. Coal was so . . . proud of him that I just wanted to accomplish something too. I-I didn't want to be a farmer all my life. And I was pretty good. I had sparred around a lot with Willum and he's much better than me and all, but he taught me a lot of stuff. I figured that if I put my mind to it, I could do it and you know, be an academy graduate some day. Coal didn't want me to go, though. Said I had responsibilities here. I know now that he was right, but I was tired of him telling me what to do and I went anyway."

Justan found himself understanding how Benjo must have felt and he didn't like it. Part of Justan wanted to punch the man in the face just for making him sympathize with him.

"When I got there, I ran into Kenn. I hadn't seen him since we were kids back before Coal married my mom. He showed me around and stuff and helped me out. He talked me up, you know? Had me feeling big and tough, like I could really make it in the academy.

"When he got mad at you after the strategy test and asked me if I would help him get back at you, I thought he just wanted to scare you at first, you know, teach you a lesson. The situation kind of got out of hand though and got . . . rougher than we planned."

"Speaking of Kenn, I saw him just a few weeks ago," Justan remarked. "You want to know what he was up to? The weasel was a dungeon keeper in charge of torturing people. Frankly, at the time I expected you to still be with him."

"But I'm not like him, I'm . . ." Benjo turned his head away in shame. "I-I guess I can see why you'd think that of me after everything that happened. Anyways, after we woke up after that . . . lady knocked us out, I was done. I had learned my lesson right there. I just wanted to go through Training School and get on with my life, but Kenn wouldn't let it go. Getting even with you was all he could talk about. I-I wouldn't have anything to do with it all year. I even talked him out of a few things he had planned, I swear. I was able to scare him off of it by telling him that the . . . lady would protect you."

He watched Justan for a reaction to what he was saying, but

Justan did not let his emotions show. He refused to give in to the man's story. He waited with his arms folded, not saying anything until Benjo continued.

"Well, uh. Then testing week came and the day before the stamina test, Kenn told me what you had told Mad Jon about me and I got so mad that I-."

"He told you what?" Justan interrupted.

"About how you told Mad Jon I had sneaked out of archery class to meet my girl. I got pulled before the council and they almost kicked me out for it." Benjo misunderstood the dumbfounded look on Justan's face for something else. "Oh, it's okay. I mean, I don't blame you. You had every right to be mad at me after what we did to you in the alley."

"Benjo, I have no idea what you are talking about. I couldn't have cared less what you did. I was too focused on my own training." Justan said. He had a pretty good idea what had really happened though. If Benjo wasn't going to follow Kenn's little schemes, it would be just like the little man to tell on his friend so that he could blame Justan.

"But, Kenn said-. He . . . that son of a dog." Benjo laughed then. It was a self-mocking laugh and Justan lost grip on some of the anger he had been holding onto so tightly. "Oh, Coal was right about me. He said that I wasn't ready to go out on my own yet."

"So that's why you pushed me in the stamina test?" Justan said, subconsciously fingering the frost rune through his shirt. How strange that his encounter with the Scralag wouldn't have happened if not for a lie that Kenn had told Benjo.

"Yeah, I was really mad. I mean not only did I nearly get kicked out of the Training School for skipping class, but the council told my girl's father about it and he forbade her to ever see me again." He shook his head. "It all seems so childish now. But anyway, after the race, when you chose not to tell the council that I was the one that pushed you, I was so confused. Kenn wanted me to help him jump you in the night but I wouldn't do it."

Justan remembered that night. The next day, he had awakened late because Kenn had covered his windows. He had almost missed the archery exam.

Benjo went on, "Then the next day after the archery test, Kenn was so humiliated after what that . . . lady did to him, that-"

"Please stop calling her 'that lady'. Just call her . . ." Justan wasn't sure what he wanted to tell Benjo to call her actually. He didn't deserve to know her real name. Even hearing the man call her Ma'am seemed like it would be an insult. "Just refer to her as my trainer."

"O-okay. So Kenn wants revenge so bad and this guy in a white robe shows up and offers to sell us a sleeping potion. I said no way and got out of there. I told Kenn that I was through with him. Then that night, he snuck out of the barracks and headed towards your place. I followed him, trying to talk him out of it and up comes Swift Kendyl. He was waiting for us. No one would believe that I was trying to talk Kenn out of using the potion. They expelled both of us that night.

"I didn't know what to do. I had nowhere to stay. I didn't want to go home. Kenn found this old storeroom for us to sleep in and I just laid there on the floor for an entire day, trying to figure out what to do. Then Kenn came in that night and said that the old man had given him another bottle of the sleeping potion. He wanted me to go with him and . . . I really don't have a good excuse as to why I went that time. I was so lost at that point that I just followed him. He told me that the plan was to dose you with the sleeping potion and then take you out of town so that by the time you woke up and got back to the Training Grounds, you would miss the test.

"But that- er, your trainer . . . she showed up and Kenn splashed her with the potion. After that, things got way out of hand real quick. Kenn started acting crazy, ranting and stomping around. I nearly ran out of there a couple times, but the way he kept eyeing her, I was afraid of what Kenn might do to her if I left him alone. I-I just . . .

"Anyways, you know the rest. After you got there and Kenn tried to . . . I took off. I didn't look back. I just headed out of town. I knew they would be looking for me and I didn't want Kenn to find me either. I couldn't believe that I had let that little man ruin my life.

"But Willum found me. He showed up as I was heading into the hills and stopped me, demanding to know what I had done. I-I told him what happened and . . . I'll never forget the look of disgust and pity on his face. He said a lot of things, but in the end, he told me that he wasn't going to say anything to Coal about it. H-he said that he would leave that to me." Benjo finished his story and sat down on the couch with his head in his hands.

Justan looked at the man, saw the agony on his face, and imagined the guilt that must have been plaguing him ever since. The last bit of anger that Justan had been holding onto slipped away.

"If it helps at all, Benjo, the last time I saw Kenn, I left him on one of his own torture tables to be found by the other escaped prisoners. I never did hear what became of him after that."

"It doesn't matter." Benjo said. "I don't care what happened to Kenn. I wish I'd never met him in the first place. I just want to forget that part of my life ever happened. I still haven't spoken to Coal about it. When I got back, I couldn't bear to admit what had happened. I just told them that I failed the tests.

"Coal was so understanding and I felt so guilty about lying to him about it. He wanted me to go back to farming and I was ready to do what ever he wanted. But then Bettie pulled me aside and started teaching me the forge. I am okay at it too, but leatherwork . . ." Benjo looked down and stared at his hands. "I love it. I really do."

"Benjo, you should have listened to Willum. Trying to forget it ever happened is not going to work. You are never going to be able to put this past you until you go talk to your father about it," Justan said. "You know him far better than I do, but if what I know about Master Coal holds up, he would understand. I won't be as nice about this as Willum though. If you won't talk to him about it, I will."

Benjo looked at him with terror in his eyes. His bottom lip quivered for a moment and then he grit his teeth. A look of resignation entered his haggard eyes.

"Y-yes. You are right. I will speak with him about it."

"Good," Justan turned to leave, but stopped before he reached the door. "Benjo, I want you to know that I forgive you for your part in what happened." He really had no reason to hold a grudge. In a way, his life had turned out for the better in part because of the things Benjo and Kenn had done.

"Thank you," Benjo said. He looked down at the floor and Justan decided to go.

"Sir Edge," Benjo said.

Justan paused in the doorway.

"I could have made it in, you know. I was at the top of our training class in both hand-to-hand and armed combat by the time the year was over." Benjo sighed. "If only I hadn't been so stupid."

Justan thought of all his wasted years training alone and shutting everyone out. How close had he come to losing it all himself? "We are all stupid sometimes, Benjo. It's what we do after we realize how stupid we are that counts."

Justan left Benjo's house and headed back towards the lodge house to get ready for bed. He had wanted to say something profound to Benjo as he left, but what had come out of his mouth had sounded so ridiculous. He chuckled at himself. Oh well, giving speeches wasn't one of his strong points.

Benjo however, laid awake thinking about what Justan had said late into the night. Finally, despite the hour, he walked over to his father's house and knocked on the door.

Chapter Seventeen

"Ewzad Vrill, how dare you enter these chambers? You shouldn't even be in the castle! Your noble rank has been revo-!"

The wizard silenced the man, freezing everyone in the room with one wave of his snakelike arm. "My-my, councilor. How rude of you to interrupt me before I even begin speaking. That won't do, no-no it won't. I am the only one who will be talking tonight."

He had caught all ten councilors in his spell. Just by looking at their faces, Ewzad could tell who his true enemies in the room were. It wasn't the men who were half out of their chairs, faces frozen in anger. These were the men who knew nothing of Ewzad's true power. The truly dangerous ones were paralyzed with a look of pure fear. One of them had gotten halfway to the rear door before being stopped in place.

The Dremaldrian Council Room was opulently furnished. Silken tapestries lined the walls and a nine-tiered crystal chandelier hung from the ceiling. Each piece of furniture was a unique work of art carved from a single tree. Each councilman's overly padded chair had its own lush rug for their feet to rest on and three separate fireplaces were always kept blazing to keep their old bones warm on the coldest of winter nights.

The council table was the centerpiece of the room. Enormous and polished to a mirror-like shine, it was lined in gold and carved in the shape of a crescent moon so that all the men could gaze on the throne in the center of the room. The throne itself was quite plain in comparison. Though it was also highly polished, it had a plain wooden seat and a high back contoured to keep the king in an upright position. King Andre had often complained to Ewzad that its true purpose was to be just uncomfortable enough to keep the king awake while the councilors droned on.

For generations, the Muldroomon family had sat in that throne and decided the direction of the kingdom based largely in part on what these old noblemen had to say. Their influence had only taken one brief recess. When Andre had first become king, he had caused quite an uproar among the noble class by replacing the old councilors with his own friends. Ewzad had been one of them.

How delicious that time had been. Andre had ended his banishment and placed him right near the seat of power. But it had also been constricting. There was only so much that Ewzad could do to further his plans while under the scrutiny of the nobility of Dremald. Once Ewzad had convinced Andre to name him duke and moved back to his family keep, he had the freedom he needed. Unfortunately, in his absence Andre had succumbed to pressure from the nobility and reinstated the gray-haired councilors.

"I hate this room, you know." Ewzad stepped up and sat in the throne. It was as uncomfortable as Andre had described it. "I always have. Yes, even when I myself sat at the table I hated it. It always stank of old men. Revolting, yes?"

He swallowed his disgust and began the speech he had prepared beforehand.

"Gentlemen, oh esteemed councilors, I must thank you so much for your allowing me to speak in your illustrious presence. Yes, you see, I traveled here from my nearly completed castle because I was made aware of several terrible, nasty rumors about me that were being spread about the kingdom, especially in the noble circles. People were saying that I, Duke Ewzad Vrill, was a madman and torturer. Me! And that I consorted with goblinoids and monsters. Horrible! Scandalous rumors to be sure, I know!

"Then I heard that you great, wise men had advised my friend, the king to revoke my dukedom. I am afraid that I was horrified by this news and came as soon as I could to discuss the matter. Yes-yes, I must set the record straight! Well, actually, I am embarrassed to admit that I cannot disprove those rumors. They are in fact true for the most part. Yes, I am not here today to refute those rumors, no. Instead, you see, I have come before you today to kill you all."

He waited for a moment, leering at them and then frowned in disappointment that there was no reaction.

"*They can't move*," Mellinda said.

He ignored her remark. Of course, they couldn't move. He knew that. He had frozen them himself after all, but as he had prepared his remarks, he had always imagined gasps and whimpers of terror. Oh well, things couldn't always be as one dreamt, now could they?

"*This freezing of victims is too quiet for my tastes. You know that they cannot harm you. Why miss out on all the running around and screaming?*" Mellinda asked.

"Oh my!" Ewzad laughed. He knew that he was the only one that heard her, but he didn't care what his servants thought. Let them think he was crazy. That would add to their fear and fear was useful. "Dear Mellinda, your way is so unnecessarily messy. This is much more tidy and keeps me from having to kill every servant or guard within hearing distance that comes to their aid. My way is much better. Yes, much-much better, don't you think?"

"*As you like, Master*," she grumbled.

"Now be silent. You are disrupting my fun." He cleared his throat and resumed his speech.

"Yes, I know what you are thinking, dear councilors. 'Kill us? He wouldn't dare! Why, there would be a cry of outrage if anything happened to us.' Oh yes, I know your thoughts. I know you all so well." Ewzad cackled with glee, "How pompous those thoughts of yours, don't you think? What you should be thinking is, 'We are frozen! Why can't we move? How did he do that? Where are the guards? Please, don't kill us, Duke Vriil!' Well it is much too late for that! Don't you think so, Arcon?"

The mage stood by the throne and nodded slowly, his face betraying no emotion. Ewzad's gaze narrowed on the man for a moment. Surely that statement had deserved a laugh. The man had appeared at Ewzad's keep two weeks ago and announced himself as a gift from Mellinda. She had promised Ewzad that having a mage at his side to help with the magical burden would be of great help to him. Ewzad had been skeptical then, but with Kenn still gone on his errand, this gift of Mellinda's had indeed proven useful. Still, he didn't trust him. Any gift from Mellinda was suspect.

"*Why do you still think him suspect, Master*?" Mellinda crooned. "*Has he not been all that I promised*?"

"Have I not commanded you to stay silent?" Ewzad snapped, inwardly cursing the moonrat eye imbedded in his arm. She was always listening to his thoughts now. Always, always listening. "Yes, yes I have! So shut it, you horrible beast!"

"*Of course, Master*," she replied meekly, but Ewzad knew that she would interrupt later anyway.

He looked back on the paralyzed councilors and his scowl turned to a giggle. Even thoughts of Mellinda's treacherous ways couldn't dampen his spirits tonight. In fact, they had given him an idea.

"Oh, Hamford! Come to me, please. Bring my dagger." The large man came from the doorway and held out a dark bladed dagger with a jeweled hilt.

Ewzad had found it along with several other very interesting trinkets within the wardrobes of the Dark Prophet's chambers. It was quite similar to the dagger that Elise had stabbed him with that day in his throne room. He was glad that he had brought this new dagger back with him. He never had been able to find his old one. He was still upset about it too. Such memories he had made with that dagger.

"Thank you, dear Hamford," Ewzad said and took the blade from the man. He could feel the hum of its connection to his master as he held it in his hand. "Arcon, would you be so kind as to take this dagger and kill these men? Yes-yes, please do."

Ewzad kept a keen eye on Arcon's reaction. The mage's eyes widened at the command, but he did not refuse. Arcon merely cocked his head for a second as if listening to someone before nodding slightly and walking forward to take the dagger. With only the slightest bit of hesitation, he walked up to the nearest councilor.

"*Why test Arcon this way?*" Mellinda asked. "*These are not his close friends. This won't seal him.*"

"No, but he will sense it, won't he? Yes, Mellinda, each sacrifice will give him a feel for what the Dark Prophet offers. A good taste of what's to come, yes?" Ewzad whispered, though the way Arcon stiffened, it was obvious that the mage heard him.

"*Yes, of course,*" Mellinda agreed.

Arcon raised his blade to the first old man's throat. His hand shook.

The rear door to the chamber flew open and King Andre Muldroomon strode in. At his rear were the two guards that he kept at his side at all times. Their excellent academy training was evident in the way they immediately grasped the situation and moved to protect the king.

"Gentlemen, you must leave the-." Andre stumbled and his hand went to his mouth in shock at the scene before him.

Ewzad imagined what his friend must be seeing. The council members were frozen in place as if in a painting. A strange painting where his old friend Ewzad Vriil was young and handsome and sitting on his throne. The thought brought the wizard great pleasure.

The two guards stepped in front of the king, their swords drawn and at the ready. They began backing him towards the door.

Ewzad's arm shot forth and with a squirm of his finger, the door slammed shut behind them, blocking their escape. Ewzad stepped down from the throne. "Oh my, how rude of me, Andre. I am in your seat, aren't I? No-no, I apologize. Truly I do."

"E-Ewzad!" Andre stammered. One of the guards tried to open the door. It wouldn't move. The king's face went from a look of shock to one of rage. He opened his mouth to call for more guards.

That was as far as he got before Ewzad's spell froze them. The wizard shook his head as he approached the king. "Oh, dear Andre, how you have changed! Were we not friends? I brought you this power, killed your father for you and how do you thank me? By declaring me a monster and taking away my family lands? Unacceptable, yes? Of course it is!"

Ewzad stood in front of the king's guards and placed one hand on each of their helmets. His arms undulated as he wove a heat spell. The helmets burned a bright red as he boiled the water in their skulls. Steam rose with a sickening aroma and he released their paralyzation, letting their bodies fall to the ground. He approached the king.

"Now if you will excuse me, dear, dear Andre, I need to make a visit to your sister. Perhaps she will decide your fate, hmmm?" Ewzad turned his head and shouted back to his servant, "Oh, Hamford, please take good King Andre and carry him over to his rightful place on his throne, would you? Yes, I think he should spend some time contemplating the final advice of his councilors until I return. "

Ewzad giggled in amusement at his own dark joke.

"Arcon!" The mage was still standing in front of the first councilor, staring at the dark blade in his hands stupidly. "Continue on! I will expect them all dead by the time I get back, yes?"

Ewzad grinned as he strode from the room. The mage would be sickened by his own actions at first but it would get easier. The dagger would help him along. With each kill, the mage would feel the pull of the Dark Prophet's power on his soul and by the time the last man was dead, he would probably enjoy it. Oh yes he would.

"My-my, what a delightful evening this is turning out to be!"

"***He comes***."

Elise Muldroomon curled into a ball in the middle of her lush oversized bed and pulled the blankets over her head. She had been plagued with bad dreams as a child and since it was unbecoming for a princess to awaken screaming in fear, her loving father had brought in a wizard to create an enchantment to end her nightmares. Her father told her that her blankets were now magic and that no ghosts or monsters could harm her when she was under them. All she had to do was hide under her covers and she would always be safe. It had worked. The bad dreams left. Unfortunately, her blankets didn't bring her the comfort now that they had back then.

Since returning from Ewzad's castle Elise stayed in her bed most of the time. Everyone thought that she was traumatized from the events that happened while she stayed with the duke. She heard the servants whisper about it outside her door. There were even rumors that she was with child now. The mere thought of it still made her skin crawl. She had rushed out into the hallway and beaten the servant woman that uttered that bit of scandal. How dare they think such a thing? She shuddered at the idea of Ewzad's squirming fingers reaching for her.

"***He is here.***"

She held her hands over her ears, but it was no use. The voice did not come from outside the bed. Her blankets could not protect her. It came from within her own head.

She heard a muffled sound at the door. Elise released her ears and sat up. There was a light knock. She pulled the covers off of her head. It was still dark. The thick velvet curtains on her canopied bed shut out the light of the fireplace that she demanded was kept lit at all times.

"I do not wish to be disturbed!" she shouted.

"Oh, but sweet dear Elise, surely you wouldn't keep out an old friend?"

Elise gasped. It was true. He was still alive! It frightened her that he was standing outside her room, but even more frightening was the small part of her that was glad. Why hadn't the guard at her door stopped him? "Go away, Ewzad!"

She heard her door open, the door that had three separate locks, the door with an iron bolt engaged that sealed it to the floor. How dare he overcome her precautions and stroll right into her private quarters? A few short weeks ago, she would have stormed out of bed and slapped him for such insolence. That was before she had seen what he could do. She pulled the covers back over her head and curled back into a ball. The blankets would protect her as they used to. Her father had promised.

"Elise? Dear sweet Elise, come out and talk to me, won't you? Oh yes, you must."

He was standing just outside the curtains, she was sure of it. What would he do to her? She had stabbed him the last time she saw him. How angry was he? Was that one large vein pulsating on his forehead at that moment?

"Go away, Ewzad! G-get out of my room this instant. H-how dare y-you . . . I . . . I-I wasn't trying to kill you, I promise," she whimpered.

"Oh, my-my. Dearest Elise, of course you weren't." She heard the curtains open and the faint glow of the fireplace penetrated her blankets. She felt her bed move as he sat down. “Yes, my love. It is alright, yes-yes it is. Come out and see. I am quite alive. I couldn’t very well be speaking with you if I were dead, could I? No-no, of course not!”

A light laugh came from his throat and the sound of it reminded her of the old Ewzad. The Ewzad that was her friend. The Ewzad that helped her plot her power plays. In fact, now that she thought about it, his voice sounded like the old Ewzad as well.

“Y-you are not mad?” she asked.

He laughed again, and she felt his hand on her hip through the safety of the blanket. “Angry? At you? Why no-no sweet Elise. You did me a service. Come out from under there. Look upon me, you will see.”

A warmth spread through her body from the place where his hand rested on her. Her heart beat faster in her chest and she felt an odd kind of hunger. She had to swallow back the saliva that filled her mouth. Part of her wanted to resist, but despite the cries of terror that echoed from the back of her mind, Elise found herself reaching up and pulling the blankets down. The firelight revealed his face.

“E-Ewzad . . . you are beautiful,” she said. And it was true. Gone were the sallow cheeks and sunken eyes. His skin shone with health and his eyes were vibrant and filled with life. His black hair, no longer thin and greasy, was full and flowing. She wanted to touch him.

“Yes, Elise. This is why I cannot be mad at you. No-no, what you did, I understand. It was all a misunderstanding. Yes, a misunderstanding is all it was, yes?” He grinned, showing perfect white teeth.

“B-but my father. You killed him.” Elise remembered the anger and sadness that had poured through her as she had plunged the dagger into his arm. She shook her head and it felt as if a fog was clearing from her mind. She withdrew from him, pulling her hip out from under his hand.

“Me? Oh, my dear Elise, never. It was not I, not I that killed your father. Though he disliked me, I would never have wished him dead, no.”

“Stop it Ewzad.” She didn’t believe him. Ewzad lied. That was his specialty. “Get out of my room. Get out or I will scream for the guards!"

The grin faded from Ewzad's handsome face and anger flashed in his eyes. "No-no, dear Elise. I will stay, yes. You cannot order me about. No longer. You must obey me now. The Dark Voice commands it. Yes."

"No. N- . . ." She withdrew to the far corner of the bed, her blankets pulled up to her chin.

"Yes, you know the Dark Voice, don't you? He speaks within your head, doesn't he? Yes, impossible to shut him out, isn't it? Oh, I know that voice too, sweet Elise."

"Th-that voice. It isn't real. It is just my imagination."

"Oh, it is real, sweet Elise. It is the voice of the Dark Prophet and you belong to him now. You gave yourself to him."

"No!" she gasped. Ewzad reached for her face, his fingers writhing and she recoiled, realizing that she was sitting right next to him again. When had she moved?

"Tsk-tsk, sweet Elise. Don't you see? You gave yourself to him when you sacrificed your oldest dearest friend to him with his ceremonial dagger. It would have killed me too if I hadn't belonged to him already. You see I first heard his voice when I sacrificed my own dear friend. Remember Blem, Elise? He was my first gift to the Dark Prophet." She shook her head and began to pull away again. Ewzad pressed, "Think back Elise. Think! What were the first words the Dark Voice said to you, hmm?"

She did remember. The moment the dagger had pierced Ewzad's arm, she had heard it.

"Elise Muldroomon, you are mine," she whispered.

Ewzad smiled and the Dark Voice spoke again to her.

"***Go with him***."

"You see Elise, you have no choice, do you? No-no you don't." Ewzad rose and stuck out his hand. She pushed her blankets aside and stepped out of bed, clad only in her nightgown. "Now get dressed. We have an errand, don't we?"

Elise felt his eyes on her as she changed into a proper dress.

Then they stepped over the unmoving guard in front of the door and left the room. As they walked through the castle, he ran his hand down, then up her back and across her neck. She ignored the way his fingers slithered through her hair and forced a smile on her face. Maybe this would be okay. Perhaps she could live with his presence now that he had changed. He was handsome now. He even smelled nice. They came to the council room and Ewzad giggled.

He opened the door to a grotesque tableau. Elise's heart froze in her chest as she saw the councilors dead on their feet, like statues with their lifeblood pooled on the crescent moon table in front of them. The table was completely covered and reflected the scene around it like a scarlet mirror.

She had never liked the old men and the way they had looked down on her, but this? She didn't run away though. She wasn't sure why. At this point, she wasn't even sure that she still moved her own feet.

Soon she looked up upon her brother who stood in front of the throne. He stared out over the council as if presiding over the macabre event. His face was frozen with an enraged expression, almost like he had been the one ordering their executions. Two men stood beside her brother. One unfamiliar fair-faced man in mage robes looked straight ahead with an expressionless gaze. The other, a large man she had met in Ewzad's castle, gave her a brief look of pity before turning his gaze to the floor.

Ewzad placed something in her hand and she felt the promise of the Dark Prophet's power surge into her. She looked down to see a dagger much like the one she had stabbed Ewzad with. The blade was covered in a fresh coat of blood.

"Wh-what . . .?"

"Dearest Elise, this is the moment. Yes, the moment that we have planned for since we were children. You will be the queen. Yes, the highest power in the land. Queen Elise Muldroomon. Sounds wonderful, doesn't it?"

"No, not like this." Elise tried to step back, but her feet wouldn't move. She willed her hand to drop the blade, but her fingers would not open.

"Oh, so sorry Elise. Truly I am. But it is the only way, yes. It was the way that your brother came to rule as well. You see it was he, not I that struck your father down."

"You lie," Elise said, though her voice was weak.

"No-no. No, my love. You see, I told poor Andre that I didn't want to kill your father. I refused for your sake. Yes I did." Ewzad's face was pursed with sorrow. "Andre took it upon himself I'm afraid. I knew it when he gave me your father's ring. 'I did it, Ewzad. The kingdom is ours now.' Yes, that is what he told me."

Elise gazed upon the angry face of her brother and there wasn't the slightest twitch, not the smallest movement in denial. She knew what her brother was capable of and would not have believed it before. But standing in front of Andre now, what Ewzad said rang true to her. At least in the part of her mind that wasn't sobbing in horror. How could he have done it? How could Andre have killed their father?

"***Do it***."

"Do it, dearest Elise," Ewzad whispered. His hand rested on her lower back and she once again felt that odd throbbing hunger awaken within her. "You will be queen and I will be, at first, your loyal protector and advisor, then your husband. My army will protect our people. We will rid our kingdom of a few pesky nuisances and then our power will be complete. The Dark Prophet has promised this to me. When he rises to power, our kingdom will be-!"

Ewzad stopped abruptly as Elise stepped back from her brother, leaving the handle of the blade protruding from his chest. A dark swirl leached from the hilt and entered Andre Muldroomon's body. She imagined that she saw it pull something out of him, before the dark swirl dissipated altogether.

"***It is sealed***," said the Dark Voice. "***You are queen***."

Ewzad ended the paralyzation spell on the room and all of the bodies collapsed. A squeal of joy pierced his lips and as he cavorted and danced about the corpses, Elise stared down at her brother's face. Andre was no longer angry. His eyes stared forward blankly as if he had lost something. She wondered how she should feel at that moment. Why wasn't she crying? Where was the regret? Where was the sorrow? Ewzad stepped over Andre's body and sat on the throne.

"Yes-yes-yes! Elise, our union will be the height of Dremaldria's power. We will rule! Yes! We will conquer. And there will be an heir," Ewzad promised. His squirming fingers reached for her and she didn't pull away this time. Elise Muldroomon stepped up to the throne and fell into his snakelike embrace. "Oh yes . . . that I am most sure of."

Chapter Eighteen

Faldon the Fierce moved down the corridor with quick strides, grumbling to himself. The news that the Battle Academy Council had received that morning was greatly disruptive to his plans.

He was so preoccupied that he didn't register that he was being followed until he had nearly reached his classroom. Then the scuff of a boot pricked his ear and his old habits kicked in. His well-trained mind processed the information. Two people were walking behind him, and by the sound of their footsteps, one was quite a bit lighter than the other. He glanced over his shoulder. When he saw who it was, a grin widened his face.

"Why Locksher, my friend! I haven't seen you in years. Not since that trouble with the vampire in Razbeck."

"Yes, that was a nasty business wasn't it? Good to see you, Faldon." The wizard smiled and shook his hand. He had aged very little since the last time Faldon had seen him, though the graying hair at his temples had widened a bit. His companion, though . . . Locksher noticed Faldon's gaze shift to the stunningly beautiful woman at his side. "Oh, Faldon the Fierce, this is my assistant, Mage Vannya. She is one of your son's friends from the Mage School."

"A pleasure, miss," Faldon said, giving a slight bow. She was quite striking. Long blond hair, full lips, fair skin . . . he was impressed with his son's taste in friends. "I am leaving on a mission first thing in the morning, but both of you should come to the house for dinner this evening. Darlan will want to hear all about what Justan's been up to. We rarely hear from him."

"That would be wonderful," Vannya said, beaming. "I would

love to meet her."

The mage's smile was arresting and her voice had a pleasant alto tone that spoke of vocal training. Faldon was sure that in his younger days, he would have had been quite smitten. He turned back to the wizard.

"So, it looks like the two of you have just arrived," Faldon said, gesturing at their traveler's robes still dusty from the road. "What brings you to the academy?"

"I am actually here on an errand on your son's behalf," Locksher explained. We are investigating his encounter with the Scralag. I need to inspect the area in which he met the creature. The problem is that the hills have been declared off limits. The guards quite rudely refused to allow us in without council permission. We have been trying to see someone since we arrived this morning, but the council has been in session all day."

"I see. Sorry to keep you waiting. We've been busy discussing what to do about the current disaster in Dremald," Faldon explained. "I am glad that you're here, though. That issue with the Scralag has bothered me ever since it happened. I will make sure you get the permissions you need. Unfortunately, I'm on my way to another meeting and I'm already running late as it is. It will have to wait until afterwards."

"Ugh," Vannya grumbled. "We have been waiting so long already."

"I hate to ask you to wait around here. Why don't you go and see to your lodging? By the time you get back, I should be ready to help you."

"One moment, Faldon," Locksher said. The wizard had one eyebrow raised, and Faldon remembered that look to mean that the wizard was curious about something. "You mentioned something about a disaster in Dremald? I am afraid that we have been on the road for over two weeks trying to get here. We haven't heard anything about it."

"Really? I'm surprised. I would think the streets would be crazy with gossip by now. You always seem to know everything before anyone else." Faldon hesitated. His students were waiting for him. An idea came to him and he gave Locksher a thoughtful look. "It's quite complicated . . . I'll tell you what, come along with me. I need to pass the news along to my students anyway. No need to explain it twice. Besides, you might have some insight that could be of help to our mission."

"Of course." Locksher bowed. "Happy to be of assistance, my friend."

"Follow me then. It's just around the corner," Faldon said and he took them to the classroom.

Battle Academy classrooms looked much like most of the classrooms at the Mage School. The walls were plainly adorned except for charts here or there. Rows of chairs and tables crowded the floor, and students were lounging and talking while waiting for the teacher to arrive. That was where the similarities ended though.

Unlike Mage School students, the moment Faldon entered the room, these students stood at attention. They were also armed to the teeth. Faldon walked past them and stood behind his desk at the front of the classroom.

"Go on, sit." Faldon said and waited for the students to settle back into their seats. Even after they did so, the students didn't relax, but remained straight backed and focused. He gestured at Locksher and Vannya, noting that the male students had already taken notice of the mage. "This is Locksher, the Wizard of Mysteries from the Mage School, and this is his assistant, the mage Vannya. I have authorized them to sit in on this meeting."

He turned his focus to the visitors.

"You two may have noticed that this is a small class. These are my advanced graduate students. They are the most skilled students in the academy and they would all have moved on a long time ago if they had not agreed to be part of this special class."

He introduced his four prize students to them.

"Starting on your left, this is Jobar da Org, Qenzic, son of Sabre Vlad, Poz, son of Weld, and as for the woman on the end, you may refer to her as Daughter of Xedrion until she tells you differently." Faldon always hated introducing Jhonate. Her customs made the ritual so complicated. Half the time, he ended up having to explain everything to the people. To his relief, Locksher and Vannya took it in stride, simply nodding politely. “You two may sit down in the empty seats if you like.”

There were plenty of empty seats left for them to choose from. They took seats on the second row just behind the four students. To their credit, Qenzic and Poz kept facing their instructor even while following the mage as far as they could with their eyes. Jobar, though, half turned in his seat to watch with a stupid grin stuck on his face. Jhonate elbowed him in the ribs to get his attention back to their commander.

Faldon shook his head and walked around to the front of his desk. He leaned back against it, his arms folded across his chest. “I am sorry about the delay first of all. The council received some horrible news this morning and we have been in meetings ever since. I must announce the sad tidings that King Andre Muldroomon and all ten of his councilors were assassinated two days ago.”

Stunned silence gripped the room. Locksher was the first to speak.

“This has been confirmed?” The wizard’s eyebrow was raised again.

Faldon nodded. “Proud Harold, the Dremald representative on the Academy Council, confirmed it this morning.”

“What do we know about what happened, sir?” Jhonate asked.

“Only what Dremald is saying. The official position is that somehow assassins snuck in to the castle and slaughtered everyone in the council room while they were in session with the king. No alert was raised until after the assassins were gone. There’s only one eyewitness and he says that he saw three foreigners wearing red cloaks.”

“Foreigners?” Locksher said. “How did he know they were foreigners?”

“That’s a good question. Tad the Cunning asked the same thing and Proud Harold did not know the answer,” Faldon said. “Do you know of any assassin group that uses red cloaks? I asked the other members of the council and even Hugh the Shadow didn’t know any.”

“No. Assassin organizations prefer dark or drab colors. Red stands out too much,” Locksher said. “Now, several military organizations use red, but I can’t think of any that would have a reason to incite war. Dremald Castle is in the center of the city. Whoever did this would have had to travel through throngs of people to get there. Surely they would have been noticed. But then again, I very much doubt that they would have donned their red cloaks until they were ready to attack. What time did this take place?"

"In the evening. Proud Harold said that the king liked to meet with his councilors just after dark. Evidently he knew the old men would keep it short so that they could get to bed."

"There has to be other witnesses. Dremald Castle is still full of people at that time of night. What about guards or servants?"

"No one."

"What are those fools doing in Dremald? The king dies and so little is known about it? Such shoddy investigative work . . ." Locksher's lips were pursed, his brow furrowed in thought.

The two men had been the only ones talking. Everyone else in the room was too focused on the conversation. The students weren't even facing forward in their seats anymore. They were all watching Locksher think. Faldon smiled a bit. He had reacted the same way the first time he had met the wizard.

"You wish you were there right now, don't you Locksher?" Faldon remarked, his smile widening. He looked to Vannya. "Can't let a mystery go by, can he?"

Her eyes were focused on the wizard too. "No he can't. In fact, we would have been here a few days ago, but he had to stay in Wobble to help the dwarves figure out -."

"Could you please be quiet, Vannya? I am thinking here . . ." Locksher said. "Faldon, could you tell me more about this witness?"

"Yes, and I think that you will find this bit of information interesting, Locksher. The witness is none other than Ewzad Vriil. Remember him?"

"Of course I do. King John banished him after we uncovered his involvement with that vampire." Locksher frowned in concern. "I had heard he was back in favor after King Andre was crowned."

"That was true up to a couple weeks ago. The word was that the king was furious with him and revoked his title and lands. Now he is being hailed as the big hero coming out of this event. They are saying that he saved the life of Princess Elise. Supposedly, he happened to be walking by and saw the assassins killing the guard outside of the princess' door. He fought them off and escorted the princess to the throne room where they found the bodies of the king, the councilors and the king's two guards."

"Weren't the king's guards academy-trained, sir?" asked Poz, son of Weld.

"Of course," Faldon said "I knew those men. Sanger and Lupold. They were ex-students of mine and very skilled. To be selected as the king's personal guard, you have to be. Those assassins must have been good."

"How were they killed?" Vannya asked.

"The report is that they all had their throats slit, except for the king who was killed with a knife wound to the heart," Faldon responded.

"Throats slit? Academy-trained guards would not have been killed so easily," Jhonate said. "They would have fought to the death to protect the king."

"True. There is a lot wrong with this," Locksher observed. "Were there any other wounds on the bodies?"

"I really don't know. Harold only had so many details he could give us," Faldon said. "Perhaps after you leave us here, you could go help them with the investigation."

"There has to be something that is being covered up by the nobility," Vannya remarked.

"Yes. Most likely," Locksher said. "The more I hear about this, the less I think they would want my help. They know more about what happened than they are telling the populace. They have to . . ." The wizard shook his head as if clearing his mind and glanced up to see everyone's eyes on him. He looked apologetically to Faldon. "Forgive me for taking over your meeting. I know that you have more to discuss with your students. Vannya and I can make our plans afterwards. Please go on."

"Right." Faldon had been so interested in what Locksher was

going to say that he had almost forgotten what the purpose of the meeting was. He cleared his throat. "Unfortunately, the result of these events is that the plans for our mission tomorrow have been altered. Proud Harold announced to the council that Elise Muldroomon was coronated Queen of Dremaldria yesterday."

"That quickly, sir?" Qenzic asked. Any coronation without weeks of pomp and pageantry was unheard of. Such events were the lifeblood of the nobility.

"Yes, and Ewzad Vrill was given the status of Lord Protector to the Queen. Her first official act was to recall all Dremaldrian troops to Dremald."

"All troops, sir?" Jobar said.

"What about the border?" Poz put in.

"All troops, Jobar. Even Proud Harold is being recalled to the capitol. The Queen is convinced that these 'foreigners' may attack again and in force next time. She is fortifying the city," Faldon said. "We have filed an official complaint for Harold to take back to Dremald with him, but to answer your question, Poz, the academy will be patrolling the border on our own until someone can talk some sense into the queen. This morning, the council decided to pull our remaining troops together and take strategic positions. The patrols will warn the villages on the border and advise them to withdraw as well.

"Our forces will be stretched so thin that we are lucky our mission is still on at all. It wasn't easy to convince the rest of the council to let us continue with our operation. The end result is that we will have no Dremald support troops, so it will just be the five of us. This means that we must do this quietly. We are not to attack any enemy forces, no matter how tempting the target. This is a reconnaissance mission only."

Locksher was unable to hold his tongue any longer. His eyebrow was raised so far, it had to be giving the man a cramp. "Faldon, pardon me for interrupting, but I must ask, where are you taking this mission where there would be enemy forces? Is there a war going on somewhere?"

Faldon told Locksher about the army of trolls and ogres and goblinoids that had been massing at the border and how it had suddenly disappeared into the mountains. When he told Locksher about the moonrats they found among the army, the wizard's excitement was palpable.

"Moonrats controlling trolls? Fascinating. How strange to see them so far from the Tinny Woods."

"The last one we cornered had some kind of mental powers. Some strange voice tried to take our minds over as well," Poz said.

"The moonrats were behaving strangely when we came through the woods on our way here too," Vannya remarked. "In the darkest part of the woods, they were so thick in the trees around the road, that it seemed they were testing the barrier."

"True," Locksher said. "I cannot say that I have ever seen so many of those creatures gathered around the path before. The road was littered with the corpses of moonrats that had come too close to the barrier and when we neared the end, I had to kill two of the beasts that had entered the path from the far side. It was quite eerie actually."

"Our mission has several purposes," Faldon explained. "We received reports in the fall that the town of Jack's Rest was attacked by the enemy army. This is a town well-known for the number of retired academy warriors living there. We usually have a lot of correspondence coming back and forth between the academy and the town, but we haven't heard from any of those retirees since the attack. There were rumors that the invading army was using the town as a base. Then two days ago, we received reports of fighting going on in Jack's Rest again.

"Our first priority is to search for survivors in the town and if there are any, see what we can do to offer assistance. Our secondary mission is to scout out the opposing army, see if they are still infesting the area, and look for clues as to who is controlling this army. This is all the more important with the recent events in Dremald. If this army was to regroup and attack the border again while Dremald has called their troops away, we would be in serious trouble."

"Faldon," Locksher said. "We would like to come with you if we may. I can't help but think that this situation with Dremald is somehow related to this army you are speaking of and if the moonrats are somehow involved, then this could be linked to something much worse."

"But what about Sir Edge's book and the Scralag?" Vannya asked.

"That will have to wait until we get back I'm afraid. This is much more important."

"You mentioned the Scralag." Jhonate said. "You are here to investigate it?"

"Yes," Vannya said. "We are here about the book the Scralag left with Sir Edge after placing the frost rune on his chest . . ." Vannya stopped as she noticed Faldon and Jhonate's open mouthed stares. "What?"

"Vannya, I don't think that your father has told them about Justan's naming," Locksher explained. Now everyone was staring.

"Justan's naming?" Faldon asked.

"Ah yes," Locksher said, looking uncomfortable. "I apologize. We had assumed that you would have known by now. It probably isn't my place to be the one telling you this, but you see, when your son went into the ceremony to receive the office of Apprentice in the Mage School, things didn't go as expected. The Bowl of Souls took over and named him instead."

"Twice," Vannya added, to the further astonishment of all in the room.

"No, once," Locksher corrected. "He was named once, but as both warrior and wizard. He has uh . . . ." He held up both hands, the left palm and back of his right hand facing out. "Two runes to prove it. His name is now Edge."

"Justan named?" Jhonate said, twisting the ring on her finger. "That can not be right, can it?"

"But the Bowl of Souls is never wrong, Jhonate. The Bowl of Souls is never wrong!" Faldon said with glee. "My son, Sir Edge. What amazing news!"

"Sir Edge . . ." Qenzic grinned at Jobar. "Does it still sting that he beat you, Jobar three-lobe?"

"Shut up. He didn't beat me." Jobar frowned, fingering the ear where Justan had ripped out his earring. The mages had repaired it, but

Jobar had never worn an earring in that ear again. "It was a tie."

"No, my battle with him was a tie," Qenzic said, laughing. "You were beaten. At least you can now say that the only man to beat you in hand-to-hand was a named warrior."

"I cannot wait to tell Darlan!" Faldon said.

Locksher looked perturbed that the conversation had gone off track. "So Faldon my friend, will you have us on this mission of yours?"

"Of course," Faldon said, still giddy over the news. "At the very least, I'll have two capable healers at my side. My only concern is whether you two have the capacity to travel quietly."

"I do," Locksher replied. "And as far as Vannya, I have some magic that can help her with that."

"Very well, then." Faldon shook his hand. "We will leave in the morning. My earlier offer still applies. You are welcome to dinner this evening. In fact, I insist that you stay at my house tonight. Darlan will have so many questions for you."

"I will requisition another tent and extra supplies for the journey," Poz said.

"Okay, but wait. Uh . . . we do not wish to share a tent," Locksher said.

The male students looked at each other, relieved that Vannya was available. Jobar got a stupid grin on his face and Faldon was sure that the student was about to make his own suggestion as to where the mage could sleep.

"Jobar," Faldon said in warning, just as the student was opening his mouth.

"She will be tenting with me," Jhonate announced, giving the men a glare that told them in no uncertain terms that she would not tolerate bad behavior. The grin on Jobar's face faltered.

"Thank you," Vannya said. She walked over to Jhonate and gave her an appraising look. "So you must be Sir Edge's mysterious trainer, then? This will be fun, sharing a tent with you. We girls need to stick together, right?"

"As is proper," Jhonate said, though by the way she eyed the mage, it didn't look like she had done so out of any sense of camaraderie.

"We have much to talk about. We can both tell stories about our time with Sir Edge. Why, he told me so much about you . . ." Vannya remarked. A frown darkened her features for a moment, but she quickly turned that frown into her prettiest smile. It was evident to Faldon's experienced eyes that the smile wasn't completely genuine. "I must say that with all the time we spent together, I am surprised that he never mentioned how beautiful you were."

Faldon winced at the double meaning in those words and he saw Locksher's eyes widen as well. Jhonate's features tightened and it was obvious that she didn't take Vannya's remark as a compliment.

"As I should expect from my pupil," Jhonate said and forced a smile of her own that almost mirrored Vannya's in its brilliance. "I do find it odd, however, that despite your beauty, in all his letters home, he did not mention you at all."

Vannya's face went red as her smile faded.

Faldon saw the death grip Jhonate had on the ring Justan gave her and gulped. He could tell that this was going to be a long journey.

Chapter Nineteen

The hunt took much longer than Deathclaw expected. The trail Talon left behind showed him that after he left her, she had stopped her meandering ways and took a direct route to the west. She still left death in her wake. He found the remains of her victims along the way, but she no longer wasted her time in trivial actions of destruction. She seemed to be moving with a purpose.

Her tracks headed straight in a westerly direction and she was stopping only to eat and sleep. Then whatever focus she had found must have faltered, because she found something to distract her. She had come across an isolated human dwelling inhabited by a male, a female, and three children. From the age of the tracks, Deathclaw could tell that she had stayed in the area around the small house for several days just watching the movements of the humans. Then she began their torment.

She started by killing some of their livestock. From the scent of blood around the home, it looked like she had strewn their remains about to terrify the humans. Then Talon had taken the smallest child, a female, from the home and brought it into the forest with her.

There Deathclaw found the remnants of a battle between Talon and a mysterious beast. The beast must have attacked before Talon had finished her twisted game, because the girl child somehow survived the ordeal and though injured, had escaped and made it back to the family's home. By the time Deathclaw arrived, the humans had abandoned their dwelling. The small house was empty, their animals and wagon were gone, and their tracks showed that they had fled to the east.

Deathclaw crouched down and looked at an enormous five toed footprint in the wet leaves of the forest floor. Some of the leaves were charred as if whatever left the print was extremely hot. He leaned in closer and inhaled, filling his senses with the creature's essence. The scent was both foreign and familiar, but he couldn't grasp why.

The damage to the forest around him told of the battle that had taken place. Trees were broken and blackened, while the ground was scarred with rips in the earth and there were even more footprints like the one he was examining. The blood of both Talon and this creature was scattered around the battle site.

One set of tracks seemed out of place and Deathclaw stopped to examine it carefully. This set of tracks looked and smelled much the same as those of the large beast's, but were much smaller. They must have belonged to a creature more similar to Talon in size. These tracks were present at the start of the battle, but vanished part way through and did not return. He wondered where the smaller creature had disappeared to.

It was unclear who had won the battle. Neither combatant had died, or at least there was no corpse. The tracks of the two strange beasts had simply disappeared, but Talon had escaped and fled to the west.

A grim toothy smile showed on Deathclaw's scaly face as he examined the freshest tracks. He was now just three days behind her. Soon he would catch up to her and he could finally end her horrible existence.

Now that he knew that his prey was close, he began taking time to try and figure out how to use the magical sword that the red-haired man had called "Star". When he had followed the human Hamford out of the desert a year earlier, Deathclaw often watched the man practice his sword work. One time, when Hamford was working on a farm for a few weeks, he had met with another man every evening to swing swords at each other. At first Deathclaw had thought the men were trying to kill one another, but over time he came to understand that they were practicing to improve their skills.

It had been a foreign concept to him. Raptoids did not practice individual fighting skills; they fought from instinct and experience. But now that his self awareness had increased and he was alone without a pack, Deathclaw understood that such training could be useful.

He found that the long claws on his fingers made it hard to grip the hilt like he had seen the humans do. He was forced to adjust his grip, angling his claws up over his palms with most of his gripping strength focused on his thumb and forefinger. The end result was that his grip wasn't very strong, causing the muscles in his hand and forearms to grow tired and sore quickly. Deathclaw continued on, swinging his sword around whenever he had a spare moment, knowing that his body would adjust if he kept at it.

Talon's trail became more difficult to follow. She was running as if afraid that this beast was going to follow her. She rarely stopped to kill any more and when she did, she ate it quickly without bothering to torture it.

Deathclaw soon decided that her fears were well founded. He began finding traces of the other beast every once in a while along her trail. This creature could fly. That was the only explanation for the way its scent came and went. It also explained why Talon's movements had become so bizarre. She was hugging the trees as she traveled, avoiding any open spaces and when sleeping, buried herself in the snow and leaves, keeping herself unnoticeable from the air.

Deathclaw wasn't sure of the reason for the creature's dogged pursuit, but the sheer determination such a chase required told him that whatever it was, this creature was intelligent. No normal beast would have kept up a hunt for so long. Its ability to use fire combined with its intelligence convinced him of only one possibility. It was a dragon, and one of a type that was unfamiliar to him.

What was this dragon doing so far from the desert and why was it so determined? Had she killed its children or a mate? The odd familiarity of its smell had Deathclaw wondering if she had angered the creature when he was still with her. He had stayed with her most of the time after they left the wizard's castle and didn't recall coming across anything like it. He would have remembered if Talon had killed a dragon youngling.

The set of smaller tracks he had found at the scene of her battle with the beast tickled his mind. Perhaps she had injured a youngling after all. But he hadn't found a body. Deathclaw couldn't see why a dragon would pursue Talon if its child had flown away.

Regardless of the creature's intensions, he hoped that he would find evidence that it had caught and killed her. Then at least his mission would be accomplished. Then he could . . . but Deathclaw did not know what he would do next. The thought and the indecision that came along with it brought up an anxiety that he did not want to face. Whenever the question came up in his mind, he pushed it away. He needed to focus on his current goal. The rest would take care of itself.

Then Talon stopped running for a while. She had so well disguised her presence that it took him awhile to figure out why. She had found a good hiding spot in the hollow of an old tree, and by the age of her tracks had waited there for well over a day. At first, Deathclaw did not understand why she would do such a thing. He circled the hiding spot and found the tracks and scent of the creature that was pursuing her all around the area. It had come close, but hadn't found her.

Out of curiosity, Deathclaw climbed into her hiding place and the answer became quite clear. From within the hollow of the tree, she had dug holes into the wood from which she could see out in any direction. She had been watching the dragon's movements and learning its methods.

After leaving her hiding spot, Talon had spent her time meandering around as if searching for something. Soon Deathclaw understood what she was up to. It was the same thing he would have done. She had been looking for a good place to ambush the creature. She was determined to stop being the hunted one. Now both she and this mysterious beast were hunting each other.

A short time later, Deathclaw found her ambush spot and came upon the site of a second battle between Talon and the creature. Talon had hid in the top of a tall tree and waited until the dragon flew by. Then she had pounced.

Deathclaw examined the damage to the area, gathering in the sights and smells until a picture of the battle was formed in his mind. She had attacked the beast in mid-air, slashing and tearing at its wings until they crashed to the ground in a heap. The creature fought back, scorching the earth and trees around it.

Talon would have enjoyed the challenge. Her speed, agility, and healing ability versus the dragon's sheer size, strength, and fire. The battle had gone on for a long while. In places, the damage overlapped itself on the battlefield, making it hard to make out the particulars.

It looked like Talon won the fight, because the beast had limped away trailing blood after it, but for some reason she hadn't stayed around to finish the creature. Instead, she left and headed to the west again, this time with more confidence, as if she no longer feared pursuit.

Deathclaw tried to decide whether to follow the beast's trail, if only to satisfy his curiosity about its identity. It was a tempting diversion, but in the end he followed Talon. Destroying her was his sole reason for existence now and he was now only a few hours behind her.

After following her trail a few miles more, Deathclaw came to the top of a ridge and stopped in his tracks. Before him raged an enormous river swollen with melted winter snow from upstream. The water stretched as far as his eyes could see.

Deathclaw's heart beat fiercely in his chest. His fear of water had been crippling when he had first entered this wet land from the comfort of the desert, but he had learned to control his fear and now even used streams and creeks to his advantage. This river though . . .

He had been forced to cross it once before, during the summer when the water level was much lower. After following the human Hamford for the larger part of a year, the man had arrived at this very body of water. The man traveled along the river until he found a shallow area to wade across. Deathclaw's fear had grown to the point where he nearly gave up his obsession with the man. But Hamford was his only link to the wizard that had changed him and he couldn't just let him go. Deathclaw had gathered his courage and followed behind him during the night. It was the most horrifying night of his life. The sounds of the water surrounding him and overwhelming his senses, while the horrible cold wetness at times came up to his chest. The memory caused him to shudder even now. He had vowed never to cross it again.

Deathclaw continued in Talon's wake, following her tracks hesitantly now, hoping that she had been too scared to cross.

To his dismay, Talon's trail ended at the water's edge. She hadn't hesitated, but dove straight in. He paced back and forth, overwhelmed with anxiety. This was no shallows. The water was swift moving, deep, and ice cold. He would not be able to wade across this time. He would have to swim or die.

His mind searched for alternatives. Perhaps Talon was dead. Perhaps she had been pulled under and drowned or swept away and crushed against the rocks. But then again, it was also possible that the wizard had given her the ability to swim or even to breathe underwater. The only way he would ever know was by following her.

He continued pacing for an hour, battling with his fears. Finally, he hissed in defiance and threw himself into the water. Deathclaw struggled to make forward progress, ignoring the panic screaming within him. The current pulled him down stream. He struggled to move towards the far bank while keeping his head above the churning water.

The water's icy grip sucked the warmth from him and his body struggled to adjust to the new temperature. The magic of his body's natural adapting capabilities, increased by the wizard's changes, produced intense amounts of heat to combat the water's chill, but that only helped for so long. His body had adapted to the chill of the winter over time, but this cold was on another level; it was immediate, invasive, and persistent. Not long after he started across the river, his energy began to fade and the heat his body generated could no longer keep the chill at bay.

His temperature plummeted and his movements grew sluggish. Keeping his head above water became more and more of a struggle until just as he was about give up and sink into the depths of the river, a large log floated by. Deathclaw latched onto it desperately, digging his claws into the wood and pulling himself on top. He lay there, gasping and shivering. The water quickly rolled from his scaled skin, but the sun stayed behind clouds and the bitter chill of the winter air didn't help to warm him.

After a time, he looked up to see that the log was floating towards a small island in the middle of the river. It was little more than a pile of rocks and a few pine trees, but to Deathclaw it might as well have been the shoreline itself. It soon became evident that the current was going to carry the log near the edge of the island. Deathclaw had only a second to decide whether to stay with the log or try and swim for the tiny piece of land. The decision was made without conscious thought. He found himself immersed in the water again, struggling to pull himself towards the island.

He barely made it, latching onto the rocky outcroppings and pulling himself up to the foot of the trees. It took the last bit of energy he had in him, but he was able to climb up into a tree and grasp hold of the trunk, taking advantage of the thick pine boughs to shield him from the harsh wind. There he slept while his body struggled to heal.

He awoke many hours later, his muscles stiff and sore and a fiery hunger burning within him that he couldn't possibly begin to feed. The tiny island had no source of food for him. There were a few birds nests, but they had been empty since the fall. Though the magic within him caused his body to recover quickly, it had been overworking his body's capacity for too long. He required a large amount of fuel to repair the damage his crossing of the river had done and he had little in the way of fat stores. The way his muscles ached, he knew that the magic was beginning to break them down in order to survive.

Deathclaw looked out over the expanse of water and saw that he had made it well over half way across during his struggles. He had no choice but to continue on to the shore to find food and he needed to go soon, before he became too weak and lost the ability to get there altogether.

Deathclaw crept to the edge of the rocks and stood staring at the flowing stream of life-stealing water for several minutes in trepidation before plunging in again. To his relief, the current on this side of the island was slower and the water not nearly as deep. The last quarter of his journey, he was able to walk through waist deep water to reach the shore. He dragged himself to the forest's edge and collapsed atop the wet leaves and pine needles until he had the energy to stand and hunt.

It wasn't until after he had killed and eaten a plump rabbit, that he realized what a bad position he was in. The river had carried him a number of miles downstream from his starting point and he did not know where Talon had reached the shore. Her trail was completely lost, and he had no idea how far behind her he was.

Deathclaw gripped the hilt of the sword over his shoulder. To his relief, it had stayed sheathed throughout his crossing. He pondered what to do. Finally, he headed up stream and searched for her trail once again.

Deathclaw didn't see the pair of reptilian eyes watching from the trees behind him. He didn't sense the mind churning behind those eyes in indecision. He did not notice her turn and run in the opposite direction.

Talon was bored of confrontations. All she wanted now was some entertainment.

Chapter Twenty

The farmers worked their fields early in Razbeck. The winter was mild and the growing season long. In a few short weeks, it would be spring and those who did not get their fields ready for planting now would find themselves behind with the first harvests of the year.

Justan and his bonded had been assigned to help a local farming family whose father was recently killed. The widow, Miss Nala, had three boys and two girls. The farm was too large for them to handle by themselves until the children were older. Master Coal had offered to help with the farm work in exchange for the widow's skill in making and mending clothing for his workers.

At first, Justan and his bonded had been given minor chores, like chopping wood and repairing some of the fences, but the work got harder as spring approached. They had spent the last few days taking compost made from the manure gathered by the family throughout the winter and spreading it across the frozen acreage. Now came the equally unpleasant work of mixing it into the soil.

Master Coal had come down in the morning and thawed the frozen earth with his magic by pulling the warmth up from the ground far below. Qyxal came with him to observe the process and soon they left to do the same for the other farms in the area.

Justan looked at the warm ground steaming in the cold winter air and wrinkled his nose. The smell of the dung and compost that they were to mix in with the soil wafted through the air unpleasantly and Justan had to force himself not to sulk. The morning farm work was his least favorite part of learning from Master Coal. It wasn't that he had a problem with hard labor. It was good training for his body after all, but

Justan felt out of his element working on a farm. Growing up in the city of Reneul by the Battle Academy had allowed him to avoid this kind of work in the past.

Justan reminded himself that the labor itself was only part of what he was supposed to accomplish in the fields. Master Coal had instructed him to use the time spent laboring to practice the new techniques he learned during his lessons. As he dug and turned the soil over, Justan kept in constant communication with Fist and Gwyrtha.

Recently he had learned how to open a direct link between Fist and Gwyrtha so that they could speak mentally to each other without Justan having to relay the message. He couldn't keep the extra connection open all the time, but it was an exciting development, even if it did have the unfortunate side effect of causing throbbing headaches. Master Coal said that they were normal and would go away as he trained his mind to handle the burden. Justan hoped so. The headaches always put him in a bad mood.

Justan, don't feel bad. It is a bright morning and good! Fist sent. The ogre smiled, attacking the earth with gusto.

Good! Gwyrtha agreed.

To Justan's annoyance, Fist thoroughly enjoyed farming. Tamboor and his family had let him help with their garden and had taught the ogre to work a small one of his own, but something about the enormity of the vast fields ready for plowing had the ogre energized. Each day, as soon as the other farm hands showed them what to do, Fist threw himself into the work, all the while humming and grunting to himself.

The ogre had picked up a tune or two from some of Master Coal's farmhands that played instruments in the evenings. The lodge house was often filled with songs and laughter. The human's songs were quite different from the grunting chants of the thunder people, but even though his pitch was a bit off at times, he was a fast learner.

This morning the ogre belted, "Oh! The lady wakes up and makes the bread. She makes the bread. She makes the bread! The laaaaady wakes up and makes the breaaaaad! Early in the morning!" His voice was deep and rumbling but exuberant and the workers burst out laughing.

It was hard to ignore Fist's cheerful mood. Despite the headache that was already building, Justan's grumpiness melted away until he was working beside the ogre with a grin on his face. Sometimes he even sang along. The two of them weren't exactly wonderful to listen to, but the other workers didn't seem to mind.

Fist's interest in music made Justan hope he would get the opportunity to show the ogre what it was really about one day. He wanted to take him to Reneul and let Fist experience the music of his childhood. He would show the ogre everything from the places where full bands and orchestra played, to the marketplaces where bards and musicians sang for change on every corner, to the sweet song of his mother by the fireplace at night while his father played his wood flute. Fist would enjoy that.

There was so much that Justan wanted to share with the ogre. Fist was fascinated by the culture of the humanoid races and wanted to learn everything. Lately Justan, Qyxal, and even Coal's wife Becca had taken turns trying to teach the ogre to read and write. The concepts were foreign to Fist, but he was an enthusiastic student and picked things up quickly.

Gwyrtha on the other hand was simply happy doing any kind of work. She enjoyed pulling the plow and carrying heavy loads almost as much as she liked to have Justan ride. As Master Coal had instructed, Justan spent a lot of time practicing the transfer of energy through the bond. He made sure to ask permission first and sometimes Fist was a bit put off by it, but Gwyrtha was always pleased to let him take energy from her.

In fact, she was so amenable to nearly everything Justan asked of her when it came to the bond, that he became a bit concerned by it. When she was so willful about everything else, why would she react so positively to such personal requests? Once he had asked her why she didn't mind his constant intrusion and she would only say "*I like.*" He had spoken with Master Coal about it and the wizard had put him off, saying that they would speak about the behavior of rogue horses when he was further along in his lessons.

Whenever Justan was away from her during the day, Gwyrtha liked to spend time with Samson. The two rogue horses had a long history together and though Gwyrtha would not speak of the past, Justan got the impression that they were like brother and sister. As busy as Samson often was, he never seemed bothered by her company. Instead, he would immediately put her to work, which helped to keep her happy.

Time passed quickly. Before he knew it, noon had come. Justan bid good day to the family, but Fist stayed behind to eat lunch with them. This had become a regular practice for the ogre lately. He enjoyed being around the children.

Before he rode away, Justan had one last thing he wanted to practice. *Fist, do you mind if I try to pass on some energy to you through the bond? Since you are tired from the plowing, now would be a good time to see if I can make it work.*

Will it hurt this time? Fist asked pointedly.

I don't think so, Justan replied with a wince. *At least I hope not.*

On the three previous occasions that he had tried to pass energy from Gwyrtha to Fist through the bond, he had not been successful. The first time, he had tried to tap into Gwyrtha's boundless energy and somehow pulled the energy directly from one of her limbs. She had been carrying some heavy rocks at the time and her leg had buckled scattering her cargo all over the road. Justan had since learned that she had a central reservoir of energy to tap into.

On his second attempt, he pulled the energy from the right place, but had pulled in more than his body could handle. The overload caused a burning sensation throughout his nerves. It had been so painful that he couldn't focus well enough to give the energy back to Gwyrtha or pass it on to Fist. He had sprinted for several miles before the energy levels were reduced enough that he didn't feel like he was going to explode. He had spent the rest of the day unable to stay still for a moment.

The last time he had tried the transfer had been only a few short days ago. He was able to pull a manageable amount through the bond and accomplished the feat of moving the energy from his body to Fist's. He had attempted to ease the ogre's tired limbs as he had the day he collapsed in the river, but instead he had put too much energy into Fist's legs. The ogre had hopped around and yelled for quite a while before Justan was able to drain some of the energy off. Again, Master Coal had to remind him to transfer energy to the central reservoir of his bonded.

If it burns, can I punch you? Fist asked. He understood how important it was that Justan learn how to control this power, but the ogre was only partially kidding.

If I burn you again, I will deserve it, Justan replied and Fist reluctantly agreed to let him proceed.

With Gwyrtha's permission, Justan reached through the bond and tapped into her central reservoir. Instead of pulling and storing the energy within himself first and then passing it along, Justan reached through to Fist's central reservoir and simply channeled the energy through his body without letting it pool within him. He paid close attention to the reactions of Fist's body and stopped the flow of energy as soon as he sensed that the ogre's energy levels were full. It didn't take long. Within a few seconds, Fist felt revitalized and no one was hurt.

So do I get punched? He asked.

Not this time. "I could plow two more fields!" Fist laughed and Justan realized how much more human the ogre sounded every day.

After the short ride back to Master Coal's keep, Justan left Gwyrtha at the stables and ate lunch at the lodge. It was a hearty potato stew with chunks of beef and honstule, served with a thick crusty bread. He probably ate more than he should have, but he found that when he ate a meal with honstule in it, he didn't feel tired afterwards. Next on his schedule was his lesson with Master Coal.

Lenny ran up while Justan was leaving the lodge. The dwarf had been spending most of his time down at the forge with Bettie. The two of them were a lot alike. He was a master weapons maker and she was a master of agricultural smithing. They were both good at heart, but at the same time ornery and quick with a curse. As a result, they hollered and swore at each other all day. You couldn't walk anywhere near the forge without hearing the two of them arguing.

They were learning a lot from each other. Lenny had been working with metals for more years than he would admit, but even though he was several decades her senior, she had fine-tuned areas of smith work that he had never focused on. Lenny had never seemed happier.

The dwarf wore a wide grin under his red mustache and was nearly hopping from foot to foot in excitement as he met Justan at the door to the lodge. "Hold 'er up there, son. I got somethin' to show you!"

"You do?" Justan said, returning his smile. "What has you so excited?"

"C'mon, follow me down to the forge so's I can show you," the dwarf answered. "I got somethin' in this mornin' that'll have you wettin' yer britches!"

"Sorry, Lenny. I can't go with you right now. I need to meet Master Coal at his study." Justan was quite curious about what had the dwarf so excited this morning, but the thought of making his teacher wait around for him didn't sit well. "I'll come straight over to the forge when my lessons are over."

"Awright fine, dag-gum it." The dwarf grumbled. "I guess it can wait 'till then. But when you come, bring them sword drawin's of yers."

"My sword drawings? You're finally ready to look at them?" Now Justan really wanted to know what the dwarf was up to.

"That's part of what I'm wantin' to show you," Lenny said, satisfied that he had gotten Justan's curiosity piqued.

Justan had been trying to get Lenny to look at those drawings ever since leaving Ewzad Vriil's castle. Even with Buster back, Lenny wasn't ready to start on Justan's swords. He kept saying he was waiting for something else. Maybe his mysterious excitement meant that he was finally ready. Justan was relieved. He had felt naked without any swords.

Justan continued on to the master's study. The wizard bade him come in and Justan put thoughts of Lenny's surprise to the back of his mind. It was time to focus on his studies. The time between noon and dinner was his favorite part of the day. He found Master Coal's lessons enthralling. Everything Justan could learn about his abilities was crucial to the survival of both him and his bonded.

As had become their usual routine, Master Coal first asked Justan to report back on what he had tried and succeeded at with the bond since the previous day. So far, the wizard had been impressed by his progress. Justan told him about his successful energy transfer with Fist earlier in the day.

"Fantastic, Edge! Once you can transfer the energy from one bonded to another without pain, you are ready for the next step," Coal said. "First things first, though. Do you have any questions for me?"

Master Coal asked that question every day. At first, Justan asked plenty of questions, but he hadn't been able to come up with anything that the wizard would answer. Master Coal was unwilling to tell him about things that would get him thinking ahead of his lessons, explaining that he didn't want Justan to go off and try something he wasn't ready for. He found the master's insistence on waiting quite frustrating and lately his answer to the question had simply been no.

This afternoon however, Justan did have something pricking his mind. He almost didn't ask, but Coal was leaning forward with an open expression, waiting for a response. He hoped that the master would not refuse this time.

"I do have a question. You have said that the only people that can see spirit magic are those that can also use it. Is this something that I can learn?"

"Yes, in fact you can. But that isn't something that comes easily. Most bonding wizards only learn to see it after they have mastered many other aspects of bonding."

"I see," Justan said, a little disappointed. "But there have been a few times when I was withdrawing through the bond that I have seen some kind of white . . . trail connecting me to Gwyrtha. Was that spirit magic?"

"Really? You have seen it already?" The master looked rather impressed. "Wonderful, then. This shouldn't be too difficult to explain. Yes, spirit sight is much like mage sight except that you can only use it while enveloped in the bond."

"Enveloped? You mean like when I send my mind into the bond to communicate with Fist or Gwyrtha?" Justan asked.

"Not quite so enveloped," the wizard explained. "If you tried while you were completely immersed in the bond, you wouldn't be able to open your eyes and see anything. At least, not at first. Remember how you created a link between your bonded? How did you go about doing that?"

"Uh, I . . . kind of envisioned taking the bond and stretching a piece of it between them and they were able to communicate with each other."

"Alright, this is similar. Except that what you are doing is taking a thin piece of the bond and pulling it up and over your head like a hood or a mask. Once you have done so, you can switch to your spirit sight and see spirit magic."

Justan tried to grasp the concept. "Do you mind if I try right now?"

"Go ahead," Master Coal replied and leaned back in his chair with his arms folded. "I am doing something with spirit magic right now. Can you tell me what it is?"

Justan envisioned what Master Coal had said. He reached inward with his mind and grasped the bond. He tried, but couldn't pull it over his head like a hood as the master had suggested. Instead, he pulled a piece of the bond away and wrapped it around his eyes.

"I have the bond wrapped around my eyes, but I don't see anything. I switched to mage sight and still nothing."

"Mage sight and spirit sight are two different things," Master Coal explained. "It may take you a whi-."

"Wait! I think I saw something just there. Uh, you were making a circle with the spirit magic? I see something hovering above your hands." He was trying so hard to focus on it, his eyes hurt.

"Yes that is correct. Very good, but don't strain yourself, Edge. Once you have grasped how to do it, using spirit sight is just as easy as using mage sight." The master smiled and reached for a cup of tea on the small table beside him. Once he had taken a sip, he continued, "Keep practicing throughout the day. Spirit magic is all around us. Everything living has a bit of it, so you may be surprised at what you see."

"Like ghosts?" Justan asked eagerly.

Master Coal laughed. "No, I doubt you would see ghosts. That would be extremely rare. When someone dies, you might see something briefly, but most souls soon pass beyond the realm of mere spirit sight. You would be able to see the soul of a wizard that had left his body to scout around if one were that foolhardy, but that is about it as far as that goes."

"Then what were you suggesting? What am I going to be surprised about?"

"If I told you, would you still be surprised? No, there is one thing in particular that I have noticed, something quite interesting in fact. But I think that you should find it out for yourself. We can discuss it afterwards. I will tell you however, that I have been quite amazed at how active your bonding magic is."

"Active?"

"Yes, yours is the most dynamic bonding magic I have seen. All bonding wizards send out feelers with their magic when they meet someone new, testing for a bonding match. But you . . ." The master shook his head. "Everywhere you go, you send out tendrils of spirit energy that go about touching every living thing. Sometimes there are so many waving around you that it can be quite confusing visually. I suppose that explains the high number of bonds that you have."

Justan, still trying to process the idea of tendrils of spirit energy, took a second to realize what Master Coal had just said. He gave the wizard an odd look, "But I only have two bonded, sir."

"Well, you have the bonds to Fist and Gwyrtha, that is true. But you also have a bond with that bow of yours. Ma'am, I think you call it?"

"You can see that?" Justan had never thought of the possibility of his link to his bow being a true spiritual bond. "I didn't think that would count."

"I am not sure why, but the wood that your bow is made of positively glows with spirit magic. You may not think about it all the time, but it is constantly monitoring you. It was built with a desire to please and wants to do as you command it. Its intelligence level is just too low for it to truly speak with you."

"That makes sense, actually," Justan said. Whenever he grasped the bow, he could feel its eagerness. He leaned back in his chair, deep in thought.

"Oh, and there are two more," the Wizard added.

"Two more? How?"

Master Coal took another sip of his tea, taking delight in dragging out Justan's suspense. "Well, first there is your rune dagger."

Justan pulled the ceremonial dagger from the sheath at his waist and looked at its dual blades with wonder, trying to switch to spirit sight so that he could see the bond Master Coal spoke of.

"Or . . . rune daggers in your case, I suppose," Coal clarified, noting the individual runes on each blade. "Every named warrior or wizard has a bond to their rune weapon. Consider it a gift from the Bowl of Souls if you will."

"But what good does that bond do? I mean, what is it for?"

"You do know that rune weapons are indestructible as long as the wielder is alive, correct?" He waited for Justan's nod before continuing. "For one, you can never lose it because your bond will tell you where it is. In addition, a rune weapon can be used as a channel for offensive magic. Not much of a help to named warriors that don't have elemental magic I know, but to a wizard it can be quite useful. Imagine what you could do if every strike of your blade delivered a blast of fire or paralyzed your opponent."

"But can't you do the same thing without a blade?" Justan asked. "And from farther away?"

"Don't be so unimaginative, Edge." Master Coal looked perturbed. "How far have you seen a spiritual bond stretch? With a dagger connected to you by spirit magic, you don't have to be close to it. You could be two days ride from here and I could still attack you with a spell if you touched my dagger."

"Why hasn't anyone told me of this?" Justan asked in frustration.

"It isn't something that the Mage School tells students about. They have enough people clamoring to get in to the Bowl of Souls as it is. They don't need extra incentive. Besides, it gives us an advantage in tight situations if our enemies don't know we have that particular trick available," the wizard explained. "As for you, I think that your naming caught everyone off guard and you left so quickly that no one had the chance to tell you about it."

"I see . . . but wait, you said there is one more. What is the other bond I have?"

"Well, I would have mentioned it to you days ago, but I had been waiting for you to bring it up. It has to do with that rune on your chest," the wizard said pointing in a slightly accusing manner.

Justan's hand went up to the mysterious scar on his chest that after over a year was still encrusted in frost. He could feel the coldness of it through the fabric of his shirt. "Really?"

"Sorry to bring it up that way," Coal said, looking a bit embarrassed. "I saw it while I was healing you when they first brought you here. I ask you every day if you have any questions for me hoping that you would bring it up, but you never mention it. Since you have been so secretive, I figured that it is something quite private to you. I understand if you don't wish to speak of it and if you wish, I will not bring it up again, but I must admit I am quite curious."

"Oh . . . I haven't been avoiding talking to you about it. It's just that I have Professor Locksher at the Mage School looking into it for me and I . . . guess that I didn't think you could help." In actuality, he had thought to bring it up on occasion. But there had always been something more pressing on his mind. "Besides, the frost rune is just . . . there. It does nothing. Sometimes I don't think about it for weeks at a time."

"It does nothing?" The wizard seemed quite surprised. "Surely . . . Tell me, Edge. How did you get this rune?"

Justan relayed the story of his encounter with the Scralag. The creature's frightening appearance still gave him shivers. He couldn't forget its beady eyes and mouthful of sharp curving teeth . . . "The symbol has been there ever since. No one can tell me what it is for."

"And this creature that you met, the Scralag? Did you ever find out what it is?"

"Well, Professor Locksher called it a frost elemental. Supposedly the book it gave me might help decipher what the rune is supposed to mean. He was off in another country looking into it for me the last I heard. I wonder if he found anything . . ."

"Edge, you don't understand. The bond tying you to that rune isn't like the bond to your bow or your dagger. It's hard to explain but this bond is every bit as solid and strong as your bonds with Fist and Gwyrtha, which means that what ever is hidden within that rune is alive. If it's just a marking or a message or a spell, it is unlike anything I have ever seen."

"You mean . . ." Justan's mind reeled. "You mean, the Scralag put some . . . living thing inside me?"

Chapter Twenty One

Justan withdrew his fingers from the frosted rune on his chest. The idea that the hideous creature had bonded something to his magic was frightening. How could he have been living with something like this so long, sleeping with it even, and not known it was there?

"Whatever is inside the scar is a living thing to be sure," Master Coal replied. "It's also your first true bonded I'm afraid."

"My first bonded?" Justan frowned. He didn't like the Scralag taking that position. The status of first bonded had always belonged to Gwyrtha in his heart.

He tried to feel at the scar through the bond, but it was like nothing was there. "How could that be? It does not feel like a . . . being. The scar doesn't communicate with me. It just . . . sits there."

"And yet the bond is real," Master Coal said with certainty.

"But it didn't feel like a bonding when it touched me. I didn't feel the pain in my head. It was just like a scary dream," Justan pressed.

"Awakenings are sometimes that way, Edge."

"Well this-. Wait. Awakening?" Justan asked, struggling to keep track of all the new information. As sometimes happened with Master Coal, the knowledge came fast and it was easy to feel overwhelmed. He needed to start taking notes.

"When a wizard first begins to show his power, he can't control it. Since he doesn't know what is or isn't possible, strange things can happen. That is what we call an 'awakening'," Master Coal explained. "Some set their houses on fire. Some heal people and don't know how they did it. Some do incredible things that can't be explained or replicated. Myself for instance . . . my awakening was quite strange.

"When I was twelve, I stole a pie from my neighbor's windowsill. I had quite the child's crush on her back then. Polla, her name was. She was very lovely and made the most delicious desserts. The children in our town used to be able to smell her cookies from a mile away. Delicious, oh even thinking about them still makes my mouth water." Coal smiled and leaned back in his chair as he spoke, the memory fresh in his mind.

"This particular pie smelled heavenly. It was a tartberry pie, which unbeknownst to me was her husband's favorite recipe. I remember how hot it was in my hands, almost uncomfortably so. Her husband saw me sneaking off with it and started yelling. He was a large, strong man and the look in his eyes was frightening. I dropped the pie and ran as quickly as I could. The pie was ruined and that made him even more furious. He chased after me and I could hear him gaining. He was fast and I was a gawky twelve-year-old. There was no way I could escape.

"At one point I remember his fingers brushing my back and at that moment I wanted more than anything to be able to fly away. The next thing I knew, I was on the roof of my house, with no idea how I had gotten there. Did I create a portal? Did I fly? I still don't know. I have never been able to replicate it with any magical spell. It drives me mad just thinking about it sometimes, but there you have it. My neighbor told the local authorities what I had done and a week later Mage School representatives were on my doorstep."

"Awakening . . ." Justan sat back in amazement. Another lingering mystery was solved in his mind. "That may explain how I was able to pull energy from the crowd during the tests at the Battle Academy. But . . . how could I have done what I did even with bonding magic? And Valtrek saw it. He said he could see me pulling energy from the crowd. He can't see spirit magic so I had to have been using a mix of elemental magic and spirit magic at the same time. Is that even possible?"

"Yes, of course it is. I have never seen it done the way you describe, but we mix the two magics together all the time. You did it yourself with Fist, using spirit magic as a tunnel to bring your elemental magic through the bond. In fact, that is how I am going to teach you to use your magic to heal your bonded," Master Coal said with a twinkle in his eye. He stood from his chair. "And that brings us to what your lesson will be on today. Come, take a walk with me, Edge."

It took Justan a moment to catch up to what Master Coal had said. He stood and followed the wizard half way to the door before the grin hit his face. He stopped in his tracks.

"Really? You can teach me to heal them?"

"Yes. Don't dawdle now. We are a bit late as it is. Qyxal is probably already waiting for us." The master headed out the door.

Justan caught up to him on the garden path. "Where are we going?"

"The infirmary. With your offensive limitations, you cannot do the ideal thing, which is practice on outsiders first. You are simply going to have to watch as Qyxal and I heal. Pay close attention to the ways in which we use magic to effect different changes upon the body."

"Of course, sir," Justan said, eager to learn. Lately he had been feeling like the benefits of the bond were weighted too heavily in his favor. Now there was a way that he could be truly useful to his bonded.

The infirmary was on the far side of the lodge against the wall of the keep. It was a many-windowed long wooden structure that had been painted a bright white. With as many laborers as Master Coal employed, there were bound to be injuries from time to time. He took care of any ill or wounded people from the farms in the area, so the place always had a few patients in it.

Qyxal was waiting outside the building when they arrived.

"Why is it that every infirmary I see is painted white?" Justan asked the elf as they approached the building.

Master Coal laughed. "It looks cleaner that way, Edge. Patients feel better in a clean environment."

Qyxal added, "Besides, it's easier for us to know when it's clean. Any dirt or blood stands out."

They entered the infirmary and Master Coal started by explaining how each magic element interacted with different parts of the body's chemistry. Justan had learned all of this in his classes at the Mage

School, but hearing it again with the new perspective he had with the bond was quite interesting.

There were three men that had been injured in the fields that day waiting for treatment and another man that had been ill for some time. Coal had Justan watch with his mage sight as he and Qyxal healed the men, paying close attention to the intricate movements of the elements.

The three wounded men were ready to leave in short order and would be back at work the next morning. The sick man was a different story. He was a laborer from a farm on the edge of the community who had eaten some contaminated food and contracted parasites. Master Coal used a form of the magnifying technique that Master Latva had shown Justan his first day at the Mage School and created a floating image above the man to show Justan the little creatures in the man's digestive system. They were like tiny worms latched on to the insides of his intestines by their teeth. Master Coal was waiting for an herbal medicine to come in for the man that would help flush them out of his system.

"Why can't you just go in with your mage sight and use small amounts of fire to kill each one individually?" Justan asked.

"They are too small, Edge," Qyxal explained. "Tiny injuries can be repaired if you stimulate the tissues in the general area, but to kill individual parasites, you would have to be able to see them much more clearly than is possible by using regular healing magic. If you tried to do it anyway, there is a large risk that you could miss or overdo it and burn the inside of the patient."

"But when I am looking into Fist or Gwyrtha through the bond, I can see even the tiniest things very clearly," Justan said.

"That is an advantage of the bond," Master Coal explained. "If Samson or Bettie had these parasites, there are any number of techniques I could use to get rid of them. But while examining a patient from the outside you cannot get as clear a picture. Now there are several healers at the Mage School much more talented than Qyxal and I that could do it, but in this case, we have to use more traditional methods."

Justan thought back to the floating vision that Master Coal had given him when showing the parasites. "I could see them quite clearly with the technique you just used."

"It takes a lot of concentration to bring up that image," Master Coal said. "It would not be possible for me to do that and use healing techniques at the same time."

"So what if you brought the vision up for Qyxal and had him use it to pinpoint the parasites precisely with his magic?" Justan asked. Qyxal and Master Coal looked at each other and the wizard shook his head in astonishment. Justan saw the look and figured they must be getting frustrated at his questions. "Sorry, I am just trying to learn and I tend to think out loud at times like these."

"No, Edge, it isn't that," Master Coal said with a chuckle. "You are asking a very apt question. Honestly, I don't know why we hadn't thought of trying that."

"It could work," Qyxal added, giving Justan an approving nod. "But it would take some time."

"I suppose that I have been so used to healing people on my own, that I am out of practice when it comes to teamwork," Coal said with a smile. "By all means, let's give it a try."

The patient, having listened to the whole conversation, was now quite nervous about being experimented on. Master Coal assured him that all would be fine and Qyxal put the man to sleep with a quick spell. The two healers worked out a plan for coordinating their magic and were bent over the patient about to start, when Justan had another idea.

"What if you . . . oh, never mind. Sorry to interrupt."

Master Coal stopped and looked back up at him. "No, don't worry about it. Go on."

"Would it maybe be faster if instead of using the magnifying technique, you just had Qyxal go through with fire, killing all the parasites he could and you just followed behind him, healing whatever damage he caused to the patient as it happened?"

"In theory, perhaps," Qyxal said. "The only difficulty is that burn damage doesn't heal as easily as cuts or tears. We can stimulate the body to replace the dead tissue, but the newly healed tissue would be very sensitive. He would be in pain for days."

"Oh," Justan said, filing that knowledge away.

"Good thinking though, Edge," Master Coal said. "If there was an emergency and you needed to work fast, that might be your best alternative. You have the ability to think around your problems. That trait will serve you well with your bonded."

They bent back to their task. It was slow and painstaking work, but the procedure went quite well. Justan tried his best to focus, but after an hour, his mind began to wander. Master Coal noticed his distraction.

"Qyxal, let's pause a moment," the wizard said. "Edge, we may be at this for another hour or so and I doubt that you will learn much more by continuing to watch us. Why don't you spend the rest of your class time studying the physiology of your bonded with your mage sight?"

"But they're not hurt."

"In order for you to heal them when they are injured, it is best to know what their bodies are supposed to be like when healthy," the master said. "While you are at it, practice bringing your elemental magic through the bond with you. But, don't try any healing yet. It is very possible to hurt your bonded if you don't know what you're doing. You will require a lot of practice before you are ready.

"For now, you can try some defensive magic from within them, preparational spells, nothing too fancy. That will at least give you some experience using your magic through the bond. Tomorrow I want you to bring Gwyrtha to my study with you and we will try a few things together. With her permission, of course."

"Yes sir. Thank you. Good luck with the rest of the procedure." Justan walked towards the door of the infirmary, but stopped before opening the door. He ran his hand over the rune on his chest and turned back. "Master Coal. What should I do about . . . this?"

Coal knew what he was referring to. "Now that you know you are bonded to it, whatever is residing in that scar is part of your responsibility as the bonding wizard. Maybe it is time you tried in earnest to communicate with it. There is a path to it somewhere within the bond. You'll find it eventually. You just need to work at it."

"I will. Thank you again sir, for all your help," Justan said and walked out the door.

He went to his room in the lodge and laid down on his bed before reaching out to his bonded. Fist was helping the widow Nala fold laundry. She was repairing some pants for Master Coal's laborers and telling him stories about her youth. Justan decided not to bother the ogre and went to Gwyrtha.

She was helping Samson pull bales of hay from one of the farms up to the stables. She didn't mind at all if he examined her. He sent his mage sight through the bond into her body and was once again amazed by the way her every cell was imbued with traces of elements so unstable that she should by all rights simply fall apart.

He had asked Master Coal about it and had once again been told that what he wanted to know would be part of another lesson on another day. He struggled for a while trying to figure out how to bring his elemental magic through the bond with him. He was just able to do so successfully when he became distracted by the smell of food. He withdrew into his body and sat up, realizing that people were already eating dinner in the lodge below him.

He had almost forgotten about his meeting with Lenny. Justan gathered his sword drawings and headed to the forge.

Chapter Twenty Two

Justan could hear the two of them from quite a distance away.

"It won't work, I tell you!" the half-orc was yelling.

"Dag-blast it, Bettie! I was doin' this fer decades before you was even born. It'll work I say!"

Justan stopped in the doorway to the forge and waited a moment to let his eyes adjust to the dimmer light. The tall and fearsome Bettie was glaring at Lenny and shaking a fist at him with such force that it caused the muscles in her sculpted arms to flex quite impressively. Her slightly green-tinted skin gleamed in the forgelight.

"Not like that it won't, you goblin brain you!" she shouted. "You'll blow the damn horse up!"

"It'll work!" Lenny stood a few feet away with his feet planted and arms crossed in firm defiance. A very uncomfortable looking Benjo stood between them holding a beautifully constructed saddle.

Justan cleared his throat and both combatants turned their glares on him. Ignoring their glares, he walked up to Benjo and examined the saddle, his presence diffusing the argument for the moment. It wasn't hard to pretend to ignore the tension in the air. The saddle was exquisitely crafted.

"This leatherwork is fantastic," Justan said.

"I made it, Sir Edge," Benjo said with pride.

"Really?" Justan said. "I am truly impressed."

Justan was impressed by a lot of what Benjo had done lately. Master Coal had told him that Benjo had confessed what really happened during his time at the Training School. Since then, Benjo acted like a completely different person. No longer carrying the burden of his guilt, the man was quick with a smile and a laugh. He had started sparring with Justan in the evenings and he was really good. It was a shame that he had been kept out of the academy because of Kenn.

"The man's a natural with the leather, son," Lenny added. "And he's a durn quick worker too. All the dag-gum farmers in the area are runnin' around with harnesses and tool belts that'd fetch a fine price at any decent shop in Dremald."

"Thank you, sir," Benjo said, smiling at the praise.

"Ehh! He's okay," Bettie said. "Maybe in a few years he could even catch up and be almost as good as me. He's already more creative with the trim."

"Oh I could never, Bettie." Benjo was blushing now. "You are a master."

"So if this is Benjo's work, what were the two of you arguing about then?" Justan asked.

"Dwarf's in to killing horses," Bettie replied.

"Yeah, and the half-orc's as ignorant as a full-orc!" Lenny snapped, then said to Justan, "I want to improve on her magic saddles by workin' some rune metal in, but she don't think it'll work."

"It won't!" she barked.

"She makes magic saddles?"

Lenny sighed. "Yeah, she's stubborner than a mule, but son, the lady makes saddles that can sing."

"Darn right," she agreed.

"But how?"

"Yer Master Coal magics-up the leather fer her and she can use runes to shape the magic, kind of like I do with steel. Now, the magic ain't as strong as with metal, but she can make a saddle that'll make yer horse run faster or last longer, or even make yer arse warm in the winter time."

"I can make one that'll do all three," she said.

"Can you make a leather coat or vest to do the same for a

person?" Justan asked, thinking of the possibilities.

"Can and have," she said and pointed to her leather apron. Justan switched to mage sight and saw that the apron glowed with a faint green hue. "This piece here helps protect me from the forges heat."

"Not that she needs it," Benjo said. "It'd take more than a forge to melt Bettie."

"Darn right!" she agreed.

"Woman won't tell me who taught her to use the runes this way, but I aim to figure it out," Lenny murmured. The dwarf looked lost in thought "It's got to be a dwarven technique from some other family . . ."

Bettie laughed in response to the dwarf's confusion, and started back to work. She pulled two hot metal bars out of the forge and brought them over to an anvil, then started working the glowing metal with a familiar hammer.

"Lenny, you let her use Buster?" Justan asked in surprise. He couldn't imagine the dwarf allowing another smith to touch his family heirloom. He must really like the woman.

"Huh?" The dwarf looked back at Bettie and shrugged. "It's part of our deal."

"If you don't hold up your end, I'm keeping him!" she promised.

"No you ain't!" He sighed. "I promised her I'd make her another one like him. Well, maybe not exactly the same, my grandpappy was the best, but somethin' close."

Justan looked at him, both eyebrows raised. "You can do that?"

"Yeah. I can with the new-." The dwarf paused and excitement ripped the contemplative look from his face. "Hell, son! That's what I called you in here for anyways! C'mere!"

Lenny ran over to the corner of the forge and opened the door to Bettie's storage area. He dragged two enormous bulging sacks from inside. Justan recognized them as the sacks that Lenny and Qyxal had pilfered from the giant's cave. The dwarf stood there grinning. "Well, son? You ready to see what's inside?"

"Uh, sure!" He had almost forgotten about the dwarf's loot. He didn't have the time to wonder about it during the escape from Charz's territory and his mind had been occupied with other things since waking up at Master Coal's.

The dwarf opened the sacks and Justan leaned over to look inside. They were full of shards and chunks of metal and it took him a moment to realize that they were actually pieces of broken weapons. He cocked his head and furrowed his brow in puzzlement.

"Lenny . . . I think these might be the wrong sacks."

"Naw. Look at 'em with yer wizard's eyes," Lenny said. Justan switched to his mage sight again and his jaw dropped. The dwarf saw his expression and chuckled. "That there cave was loaded with decent loot. But these are dag-gum priceless!"

"Is this possible?" Each piece of metal shone with elemental energy. "I thought magical weapons could not be broken."

"Nothin's completely unbreakable, son," Lenny explained. "'Specially when a garl-friggin' rock giant is beatin' a magicked wall with 'em. Qyxal reckons the beast'd been collectin' magic weapons from the folks it beat and was tryin' to bust up the wall so's it could break whatever magic's been holdin' it there. Buster was the only one it hadn't broke yet."

"But . . . what can you do with a couple bags of broken magical weapons? They can't be reforged, can they?"

"Nope!" Bettie yelled. She was dipping the two, now flattened, metal rods into a quench bucket. Plumes of steam rose as the water hissed around the hot metal. "Dwarf's got less brains than a cow's left cheek, he does! Won't listen to me!"

Lenny chuckled. "She's right about one thing. They can't be reforged. Once a magicked weapon's been finished, it won't melt down, least not without a fire hotter than hell's blaze itself. Even if'n you could get it hot enough, it'd break the magic and they'd blow up in yer face.

"But what the lady don't know is I got a way around that." The dwarf held up a palm-sized leather pouch. "Just came in today. I figgered we'd be here a while so I sent a courier out the day after we got here."

"So that's what you've been so blasted happy about all day," Bettie grumbled. She put the hammer down and walked over with her hand outstretched. "Lemme see that."

Lenny ignored her.

"With one tiny scoop of this, I can melt even magicked metal down to its basic state and start from scratch. The best thing is, son, these weapons are pure and clean magicked steel. I'd have to refine three wagonloads of ore to get this much pure metal. Why I could make ten Busters with what's in them two sacks."

"Lemme see it, Lenny," Bettie demanded.

"Just a gall-durn minute, woman! You'll see it soon enough," the dwarf snapped. He tucked the pouch inside his shirt pocket before turning back to Justan, the grin still on his face. "My grandpappy called it 'the kiln dust of the gods'. Stuff's rare. Blasted expensive too. Cost nearly four hunnerd gold fer this one little bag."

"Where did you come up with that kind of money?" Justan wondered. "We were down to selling fresh bear skins not that long ago."

"Oh . . . Well, that stupid rock-biter also kept a right neat little pile of jewels in his cave. More than I could stuff in my pockets. Still, it took over half of it just to buy this."

"So that's how you are going to make my swords."

"Swords that sing, Edge. Swords that sing," the dwarf said. "So, you got them drawin's?"

Justan handed the parchment over and Lenny backed into the better light by the workbenches to examine it. The dwarf's eyes narrowed. Pictured were two long curving weapons the length of regular swords, but the entire front face was a blade, extending even down past the hilt to end in a point just past the pommel. There was a gap between the blade and the hilt just big enough for his fingers to slide through. The back sides of the swords were dull starting just above the hilt, extending halfway up the blade before curving out towards the tip. Lenny shook his head and whistled through his missing tooth.

"Son, you sure are ambitious." He walked over to one of the workbenches and moved some things out of the way to lay the paper down. "Benjo, boy! Wouldja' get me some ink to write with?"

"Yes, Master Smith Lenui, sir!" the man said and brought the dwarf a quill and ink.

"Finally someone gets my durn name right," he mumbled, before looking back at Justan. "Hold out yer arms, son."

Justan did so and Lenny made some notes in the margins of the parchment. His brow furrowed as he studied the drawings. "Where'd you see this design again? More like an axe blade than a sword blade. Looks like they was pulled off the end of a bardiche or somthin'."

"Bardiche? I saw it being wielded by a warrior on an old tapestry in the library of the Mage School. The weapon that the warrior carried was much larger and made to be carried two-handed, so I modified it to better fit my style. See, with the flattened piece along the back side, I could flip my grip around and rest it against my forearm for close fighting."

"Oh yeah, I can see the possibilities . . . They'd be heavier than regular swords though."

"Good thing the bond with Fist has made me stronger. Also there is one other thing," Justan said. He unsheathed his rune dagger and held it out to the dwarf. "I want you to find a way to take the blades out of my rune dagger and inset them into the swords."

"But . . . that's yer rune weapon." He scratched the stubble under his chin. "I dunno what would happen if I tried."

"I have been thinking about it ever since I saw the runes on the two blades. I'm not only a magic user. A rune dagger doesn't do me any good. It feels to me like this dagger was designed purposefully just to hold my runes until the right swords came along. Lenny, what I am trying to say is, I'm asking you to turn these two swords into my naming weapons."

The dwarf's eyes widened. "Well I . . ."

"Can you do it?" Justan pressed.

Lenny took the dagger and gave Justan his gap-toothed grin. "I always did love me a challenge."

"I have faith in you, Lenny."

"Yeah. I did some beautiful work on this dagger though. Hate to take it apart like that . . . Oh, one more thing, son. When the courier came in this mornin', he also had some letters." Lenny walked to the coat rack and pulled some sealed letters out of the pocket of his winter jacket. He handed them to Justan. "They was forwarded to you from the Mage School, I think."

"Thanks Lenny," Justan said. He saw his mother's handwriting on the outside of the first one. A lump rose in his throat. He hadn't realized how much he missed her. "I-I'll see you around later. You are planning on sparring with us tonight?"

"Sure, son," the dwarf said.

"You too Benjo?"

"I'll be there!" the man replied with enthusiasm.

Justan made it half way to the doorway with the letters clutched in his hands, before he stopped.

"Benjo?" Justan said. "How much would you charge to make a saddle for me?"

"Wh-what?" Benjo looked startled by the question. "For you? Why . . . I couldn't possibly charge you, Sir Edge."

"No. I'm paying you," Justan said. "I am asking for custom work. Gwyrtha won't be an easy horse to fit. Lenny, what do you think a fair price would be for work of his caliber? Say, if you were selling it in your shop?"

"Lemme think here . . ." The dwarf stroked his thick red handlebar mustache as he thought. "Well, you done been ridin' her bareback and getting used to a reg'lar saddle'd be tough. He'd have to modify it so's you could lay forward when she was runnin' hard. There'd be special leathers involved and he'd have to spend time with Gwyrtha, measurin' and maybe even ridin' her to get it right. . . I'd say about eight golds when you consider how good he is."

"Magic leather too," Justan added with a smile. "I don't need my rear end cold in the winter months."

"Oh, thirty then, easy."

"Thirty!" Benjo blurted. "N-no way I could accept it after all I have done."

"That's forgiven," Justan said, then turned to the dwarf. "Sounds a fair price to me, Lenny. Pay the man."

“What? Me? But-.”

“Lenny, you have plenty of money left,” Justan reminded.

“Yeah, but thirty?” The dwarf balked. “I’m not fer payin’ my own prices.”

“In return for our help recovering Buster, you have already agreed to make two swords for me and a mace for Fist. Consider this saddle your gift to Gwyrtha. In comparison to the value of the weapons you are making for Fist and I, the cost of the saddle is a paltry sum.”

The dwarf laughed. “Fine! Yer right, there. I’ll do it. But Benjo, you gotta’ let me oversee the work. I got some idears fer what’d be perfect fer her.”

Benjo looked pale at the thought of being paid thirty gold for one of his saddles. “O-of course, Master Smith Lenui, sir. I would be honored.”

“You ain’t blowing up his rogue horse!” Bettie yelled, back to work hammering the hot metal.

Before the argument leapt into full swing, Justan reminded the dwarf, “Don’t forget about Qyxal. You owe him too.”

“I ain’t forgot nothin’!” The dwarf grumbled. “I don’t forget my debts.”

As Justan left, he heard Lenny bellow, “Bettie! I’m gonna’ need yer help with this one!”

Chapter Twenty Three

Justan headed to the lodge and snatched a chunk of bread and cheese to eat in his room, eager to read the letters. There were seven in all. Three were from his mother, two from his father, and there were two others whose handwriting on the front he did not recognize. He set those aside for the moment and started with the letters from his parents.

His father's letters were difficult to read because of the sloppy handwriting. As usual, they contained very little news about what Faldon was up to, but were full of praise for the improvements Justan was making at the Mage School. Evidently Valtrek had been writing them with updates. To Justan's disappointment, he found that his father had not been told about his naming. That was one subject he very much wanted to hear Faldon's opinion on. It was the only thing that Justan had done that his father hadn't been able to do. Justan laid the letters down and pushed his disappointment away. Until he felt worthy of his new name, he had no right to expect Faldon's approval.

He picked up his mother's letters. Darlan's familiar flowery handwriting made him smile. Her words were a slice of home and that was just what he needed. She spoke of the local gossip and her day to day doings, while mentioning how tired she was of worrying about his father when he would leave for weeks at a time on secret missions with his graduate students. She ended each letter expressing her love for him in the way that only mothers can. By the time he finished, there were tears in his eyes.

Fist's voice popped into his mind with concern, *Justan, are you okay? Why are you sad?*

Justan explained as best he could and assured the ogre that he was okay. Gwyrtha nudged him mentally as well and it was a few moments before he was able to get to the remaining letters.

The next letter he opened was from Professor Valtrek.

Edge,

If my calculations are correct, you should be receiving this letter under the care of Master Coal. As of this writing, I have not as of yet received word that he has agreed to teach you, but knowing him as I do, he won't turn you away. Take heed of his word, Edge. He possesses great intelligence and wisdom. It was quite a blow to the Mage School when he took leave of us to lapse in obscurity. In addition, I believe that you two will get along quite well. He was always a very stubborn and moral man and you share many of the same tendencies.

There is one unfortunate event that occurred right after you left the school, that I feel I must tell you about. It is about your old roommate, Piledon . . .

Justan read with horror as Valtrek described the discovery of Piledon's death and the accusations brought against him. A pang of guilt struck him as he remembered Piledon's request for help on the night he left the school. The cadet had seemed quite frightened, but he had been so preoccupied that he had brushed his pleas aside.

Valtrek then explained that Locksher had discovered the true identity of the killer. Justan was shocked that Arcon was capable of such a thing, but as he thought about it, the pieces began to come together. The mage had always been a bit shifty, just not enough to raise his suspicions. The wizard went on:

We still have not been able to locate Arcon, but his name has been stricken from the rolls of the school and he has been labeled as a rogue wizard and outlaw in missives sent to every major city in Dremaldria and the surrounding kingdoms. I have no doubt that with our substantial resources, he will be captured eventually to stand trial for Piledon's death.

Once you were cleared of any wrongdoing, I informed the rest of the council about your bonding magic and our agreement. My announcement ruffled a few feathers, but in the end they were forced to admit that I had done the correct thing in sending you to Master Coal. You do not need to worry about the school searching for you.

As you can tell from the other letters I forwarded to you, I have not yet told your parents about your naming. The council believes that it should remain a secret until they reach a consensus on what to say about it. Wizard Randolf with the support of a few other council members has undertaken an investigation into your dual naming.

As for me, I think that he is acting foolishly. There is no reason to doubt the legitimacy of your naming. I will leave it up to you to decide when to tell your parents about it. I will back your decision, whatever that may be. Since you are my apprentice, they will have to accept my decision. In regards to the way you represent yourself to the rest of the world though, my suggestion as your master would be to keep it to yourself if you can. Being named may help you in some situations, but it may also bring you trouble. With your youth, some may not believe your naming to be real. I have come across enough ruffians with false runes tattooed on the back of their hand in my time to understand that sentiment.

If you feel you must let your status be known, you are good enough with your swords to convince people that you are legitimate as a named warrior. However, I strongly recommend that you keep your wizard rune hidden at least. Proving your authenticity as a wizard would be more difficult.

I have asked Master Coal to write me with updates as to your progress. I do not expect you to write me a response. If you have any questions, Master Coal should be able to answer them as well as I. When we next meet, I hope that things will have settled down here at the school and you will be prepared to make a decision in regards to your next area of training. I do hope that you will decide to complete your training at the Mage School before you continue to the Battle Academy.

In regards,

Your master, the Wizard Valtrek

"Of course you hope I will decide to stay at the Mage School," Justan grumbled. He still couldn't entirely forgive the man, but he did have to admit that having Valtrek on his side was a lot more convenient than having him as an enemy. He pondered the wizard's words as he picked up the final unread letter. This one was sealed with wax, but also tied crisscrossed with a green ribbon.

Perhaps Valtrek was right. Wizards continued to study all their lives even after being named, but he did not know how the academy would feel about taking a named warrior in as a student. Then again, it could all be a moot point after his bonding to Fist. How would the academy react to a student that came with an ogre at his side?

He turned the last letter over in his hands, still mulling over what Valtrek had said, when the significance of the green ribbon struck him. His heart skipped in his chest. He ran his fingers along the ribbon. There was no mistaking it, the letter had to be from Jhonate. It was the same kind of green ribbon that she kept in her hair.

Justan lifted the letter to his face, but stopped himself from smelling it. He laughed. What was he expecting? It couldn't possibly smell like her after traveling so far. Besides, what was he hoping for? The most common smell that came with his memories of her were of the dirt of the training grounds mixed with his own sweat after hours of training while she stood over him and scolded him over some clumsy attempt at an attack.

Justan knew he was lying to himself, though. There was one scent he longed for. It was the one that always accompanied her in his dreams . . .

He shook the thoughts from his mind and carefully untied the ribbons from the parchment. He paused before breaking the wax seal on the back. Why was she writing him? He didn't know what to expect.

His feelings for her had evolved over their time together and in the time since leaving Reneul, he had come to realize that he truly cared for her, or maybe even . . . Justan stopped that train of thought. He knew that he couldn't expect Jhonate to feel the same way. But what if the letter showed that she felt nothing for him? Could he handle that?

Justan's hands trembled as he unsealed the letter and opened it. A slight smile reached his face. The handwriting fit her personality so well. The lettering was perfectly formed and legible and the tone was quite formal.

To Justan, son of Faldon the Fierce,

I am unaccustomed to writing former pupils of mine, but your father has suggested that I write you with words of encouragement to help you during your time at the Mage School. He has told me of your letters home and the things he has heard from your teachers there.

I understand that you are progressing quickly, which is to be expected. I approve of your achieving the rank of apprentice so early and urge you to use the remaining year of your contract attaining the rank of mage. That should be sufficient for your short stay there.

I have also been told of the exercise regimen that you have been helping the professors implement for the students. This is commendable and speaks highly of your dedication to the principles I taught you in the Training School.

Justan's excitement dimmed as he read. His father had suggested she write him? So far, the letter sounded like Ma'am, the trainer, the woman that saw him as a project to be completed. His hope that her feelings for him were similar began to fade. He read on, desperate to find something that sounded like Jhonate, his mentor and friend, the woman that he had grown so close to in the final days before he left.

I would be remiss, however, if I did not warn you of some possible distractions during your stay at the Mage School. I have overheard several of my fellow academy students quite crudely speaking of the allure of certain female mages at the school. You should beware of the possible disruption to your studies these female students could cause you. In my past experience, I have noticed a tendency among young female magic users to pursue ways of using their magic to get what they want from the men around them. Do not fall victim to their wiles.

Remember, you are there to study and gain control of your

abilities. This will require the same amount of focus and dedication I demanded of you at the Training School. When your two years at the school are over, you still have years of study at the Battle Academy ahead of you. There will not be time for the pursuit of females until after you have graduated.

Your father told me that you have asked of my status and suggested that I speak of that as well. I will let you know that I have extended my contract with the Battle Academy for two more years in order to further my training in the more advanced warrior tactics. So I shall be here when you return.

I want you to know that I am pleased with your growth. Every time I look at the parting gift you gave me, I am reminded of the way you advanced during your last year at Training School. I hope in return that when you use your Jharro Bow, you will remember the lessons that you learned under my tutelage.

Be steadfast. Be focused. Return with the desire to continue to increase your abilities. I look forward to greeting you at the gates of the Battle Academy when that time comes.

Your former trainer and current friend,

Jhonate Bin Leeths

He laid the letter down for a moment, unsure of the feelings he was reading into her parting words. On the positive side, she still had his ring and she had called him friend. Perhaps all wasn't lost. She had tried to warn him off of the girls at the school, but he knew her well enough to realize that was probably just Jhonate being Jhonate. In reality, she hadn't given him any true indication that her feelings were more than that of friendship, so maybe he was fooling himself.

He picked up the green ribbon that had been tied about the letter and twined it about his fingers. He lifted them to his eyes to examine them closer and fancied he caught a faint trace of the scent he had been chiding himself for looking for earlier. He brought them under his nose, inhaling deeply to make sure he hadn't imagined it. The scent filled his nostrils. It was really there.

It was something that Justan had only smelled three times before.

The first had been when Jhonate had held tightly to him after he helped free her from Kenn, the second when he had embraced her following his final battle against Qenzic, and the last time he smelled it was when she had leaned in to kiss his cheek as he left her in Reneul on his way to the Mage School.

It was the smell of Jhonate's hair, an earthy smell, like the smell of the forest after a rain, not flowery or sweet, but clean and pleasant. He crushed the ribbon to his cheek, knowing at once that the only way it could smell this way was if she had taken it out of her own hair to tie the letter. Jhonate would not remove her ribbons lightly and most certainly wouldn't have used them to wrap a letter to a mere acquaintance.

He smiled at the realization and his heartbeat quickened again. He sat and held the ribbon under his nose, keeping her scent fresh in his mind as he read the letter over and over again, this time sure that her words meant more. Justan did not leave the room until it was time to spar with his friends, and even then he kept the ribbon and the letter in his jacket pocket.

Chapter Twenty Four

Fist's back ached as he walked up the road from Miss Nala's farm to Master Coal's keep. He tried to stretch and a sharp jab of pain shot up his spine. Fist winced. The long days of work combined with playing with Miss Nala's children were taking their toll. Perhaps he would have Qyxal take a look at him when he got back, but he wasn't planning on making any changes. It was worth the pain to be able to play with children again.

When he had first seen the children, he had found it difficult to even be around them. The horrible last memories of Cedric and Lina kept creeping into his mind. But the boys had finally come right up and asked him to play and he had not been able to say no. Fist found it irresistible how innocent and open human children were. They didn't fear him because of his size or strength like many of the adults did. Not that the humans in this community treated him unkindly, they were always polite. But they tended to avoid being in his presence if they could.

Miss Nala was different from the others. When she had seen him playing with her children, she had come out and invited him to eat with them. She readily accepted his help with the family chores, and it became a regular habit for him to stay behind with the family after the morning work was done.

He would put the children up on his wide shoulders and give them rides all around the outside of their home, or sometimes he would pretend to be the giant that they got to defeat with their imaginary swords. His favorite game though, was one created by the smallest children who were three and four years old. They called it simply "Fist, save us" and it involved the older children pretending to be robbers or monsters and the smaller ones would run to Fist for protection.

Ogre children would not have understood such games. They may have pretended to hunt or defend the tribe, but for the most part, their play ended up devolving into a brawl with each other. The fighting could go on for hours and the adults would allow it to go on, even if one of them were hurt.

Humans treated their little ones so differently. Miss Nala for instance, was so warm and loving to her children, finding ways to make sure that each one of them felt like they were important to her. She was protective, warning them when their play became too rough, but she also knew when to let them figure things out. Since their father had died, her role had become even more important.

Fist had decided early on after spending time with Tamboor's family that the reason humans were so much more advanced than ogres was the way that their parents raised them. Especially human mothers.

Earlier that night when Justan had shared the memories of his own mother, Fist understood why her letters had made him so homesick. Fist wished that he had a mother like Miss Nala, or Justan's mom, or Tamboor's wife Efflina. He didn't even know which ogre female had birthed him.

In ogre culture, once the children were weaned, the female stopped seeing the child as hers and left them to be raised by the older females in the community. This way the females of child bearing age could return to the mating area and become pregnant with the next child. Ogre males on the other hand, sometimes took interest in the male children that they sired. Fist had been lucky enough to grow large and strong, so that his father had decided to take pride in him, but for the most part, ogre children did not have real parental figures.

Lately, since spending so much time with these children who had lost their father, Fist's dreams had been full of old childhood memories. Most of them were of fighting with the other children or the times when his father Crag would stop by and push him around or beat him to teach him toughness. But there was one dream he had nearly every night. This dream was of an old lost memory. A memory of a time when he had experienced something somewhat like the relationship humans had with their parents.

It was still foggy in his mind, but in the dream there was a human man. Fist could make out his face, the kind eyes, the easy laugh. The particular thing that he remembered the man doing was holding him close and saying comforting words. He didn't remember why he had been so distraught in the first place, or how long he spent with the man, but it was the only time in his life before meeting Squirrel that Fist could remember feeling loved.

As Fist continued towards the keep, Squirrel scampered up to sit in his usual place on the ogre's shoulder. The creature was content, having found a nice hollow in a tree near the farm house to stash some seeds. Squirrel did that quite often. It was his main occupation actually. He had little stashes near every location that Fist spent time in.

Squirrel usually stayed in the fur-lined leather bag that Fist carried around with him everywhere he went, but if the ogre was ever about to do anything strenuous, he would leave and go to the nearest tree to start searching for food. The children loved the little animal, but Fist had to do a lot of coaxing to get Squirrel to allow them to pet him. Squirrel wasn't used to attention from people. He liked Gwyrtha and Qyxal, but stayed clear of Lenny and just barely tolerated Justan.

"You need to like Justan, Squirrel," Fist chided for the hundredth time. He knew that the animal was jealous of Justan's connection with him. "He is our tribe now. He is the leader of the Big and Little People. He needs . . . your respect."

Fist smiled in pride. Respect was his new word that day and he could already spell it. Not that he hadn't known the concept of respect. It was very much demanded in ogre culture, though in their minds it was more of a demand for an understanding of ones place in the tribe. But the human word "respect" meant more than that. In human culture, at least among Justan's people, it meant consideration to others no matter a person's status. It was a concept that Fist had always believed in. Now it was something he had a word for.

Squirrel gave a little snort and folded his arms in defiance. It was going to take more than Fist's fancy new words to change his mind on the subject of Justan. But Fist wasn't worried. His friend would come around sooner or later. He knew Justan's character well enough to believe that Squirrel wouldn't be able to dislike him for long.

As the road entered the forest that surrounded Master Coal's keep, they came upon Samson who was heading the opposite direction on his way down to the farms.

"Good evening, Fist," the centaur called out with a cheerful wave. He gave the ogre an appraising look. "Is that a new shirt you are wearing?"

"Yes! Miss Nala gave it to me today," Fist said, lifting his enormous arms so that the centaur could get a better view of the long-sleeved shirt. In fact, Miss Nala had given Fist two shirts and three pairs of pants that afternoon and he was carrying them in a cloth sack over one shoulder. "It is warm. She makes good human clothes."

"Good for you," Samson replied. "She has made many nice shirts for me in the past as well."

Fist had learned to prefer this human clothing over the heavier and bulkier furs that he used to wear. They allowed more freedom of movement and did not constantly itch. The only problem was his propensity to sweat through them, and the human's insistence that they be washed often. With the new clothes he brought back with him tonight, he now had a different shirt for every day of the week.

"Are you still working tonight, Samson? You look big," Fist remarked. The centaur was always much bigger when he was going to help with field work and much smaller when at the keep. He did not understand how Samson changed, but had decided to take it as a point of fact that it was something he could do and leave it at that.

"Yes, the men have been clearing some land at the edge of Coal's property and there are still a few stumps that need to be pulled out. Would you like to join me?"

"Not tonight," Fist said. "I am fight- . . . sparring tonight." Sparring was one of the first new words Justan had taught him in the days after they bonded.

"Very well," Samson said. "Good night then."

"Good night." Fist said with a smile. He enjoyed the human tradition of exchanging pleasantries. It was another way to show respect.

Squirrel felt that Fist was taking on too many human traits and was afraid that the ogre would start shrinking too. If it weren't for all the extra food to be found around the humans, he would have taken more opportunities to scold Fist about it.

"I will not shrink," Fist assured the squirrel as they approached the open gates of the keep. Justan had told him so. But part of him wished that he could.

If he could have the ability to shrink like Samson and grow back to ogre size only when going into battle, his life among the humans would be so much easier. He could go into regular towns with Justan without fear of attack from the people. He could ride a horse without hurting it. He could even sleep in a regular bed like the ones that Justan and Lenny slept in and be comfortable instead of sleeping on a pile of blankets and straw on the floor.

Fist entered the front door of the lodge and saw that there were only a few people still sitting at the long center table. Dinner was long over and it would be a few hours before everyone came back in for the night. Most of the rooms in the lodge were too small for his large frame, so an old storeroom had been converted into his quarters. He walked around the table and through the door at the far side of the dining hall that led to the kitchens. He headed past the sinks and ovens, but before he reached the door to his room, Coal's wife Becca called to him from the doorway.

"Fist, dear. You are a bit late, but I . . . did set aside some food for you." Becca was out of breath, as if she had run to get there.

"Thank you, Miss Becca, but I ate at Miss Nala's house before I leaved-, uh . . . left. We had hot bread and tuber soup."

He continued towards his door, but she hurried around and stood in front of him, blocking his path. "And where do you think you are going?"

"To my room. I need to change clothes and Squirrel wants to put some seeds away," he explained, unsure why she was acting so strange. "Miss Nala made some new shirts and pants for me."

"Mmm hmm. And have you bathed today?"

Fist winced. Miss Becca had a very strict bathing rule. All

workers that stayed in the lodge at night had to bathe at least every other day. A bath house had been built out behind the lodge against the keep wall next to the infirmary. Large wooden tubs and showerheads filled the building and a wooden wall separated the women from the men. The water was pumped up from the ground below and was collected in a huge tank heated by a wood-burning stove.

The stove did an adequate job, but when many people were using the bathing area at once, the water was barely warmed at all. Sometimes Master Coal would heat up the tank with magic to give the stove some help, but that was only when he or Becca were about to bathe themselves. Most of the time, the temperature of the water depended on luck and timing.

"No," Fist admitted. "But I can't right now. I will be sparring with Just- Edge tonight. I would just get dirty again."

"Alright then. Go ahead and spar in what you have on. No sense in you getting another shirt soaked," Becca said, sticking her hand out. "You go ahead and give those new clothes to me and I'll put them away for you. But when you are finished, I expect you to go down and bathe before coming in to sleep."

"But the water will be coldest then," he complained.

"Are you going to make me go in there and scrub you down myself?" she asked.

"No!" Fist said and handed the clothes to her. "I will do it."

Her threat was not an idle one. She had nearly done so the first time he had refused her request that he bathe. He had been afraid that if the hot water made his fingers wrinkled when washing dishes, it might do the same to the rest of his body. He had unknowingly let her drag him to the men's bathing room, but when she came at him with soap and a scrub brush, he had called out through the bond in a panic. Luckily Justan had arrived in time to intervene.

Fist had to admit that it felt nice to be clean and to smell good, but the act of bathing oneself was the one human custom so far that he didn't like. Squirrel found the subject endlessly funny and often chattered in squirrelish laughter when the subject came up, but when Fist replied that it would be very easy for him to give Squirrel a bath of his own, that usually shut the creature up.

Before coming to Master Coal's, Fist had never bathed in the way that humans did and hadn't known what to do. Ogres occasionally played in shallow mountain streams, but cleaning one's body was just for the women and the wounded. Justan had to show him how to use the soap with the hot water to lather up and how to rinse it out of his thick hair.

Fist thanked Becca and was about to leave when he realized something. "I will need clothes to change into when I am done."

She wordlessly reached into the bag and handed him a shirt and a pair of pants.

Humans had another tradition that Fist hadn't been aware of called modesty. The first time he went to the bath house by himself, he had not brought a change of clothes. When he had felt himself to be sufficiently clean, he had tucked the dirty ones under one arm and left the building intending to run back to the lodge quickly through the chill air. He had walked right into a group of women that were heading to the bathing area themselves. Fist had always been proud of his body. The women of his tribe always enjoyed watching him walk by, but the human women had a very different reaction. Their screams had chased him all the way back to the lodge.

After that embarrassing incident, Justan had explained the concept of modesty to him. It was not proper to be unclothed in front of females, because humans associated nakedness with mating. Fist thought the idea ridiculous, but after experiencing their response, he could not argue the point. Modesty was his new word the following day. Now Fist avoided bathing in front of anyone except his friends if he could. He found that the sight of his nakedness also made the other men uncomfortable.

The ogre, now in a foul mood at the thought of the bath that awaited him, strode towards the training area at the rear of the keep behind Master Coal's study. The dirt dueling circle and training closet, along with accompanying archery range, had been built for Willum's benefit as he prepared himself to enter Training School. After he left, it had remained in a state of misuse until Justan came along.

Since Justan's arrival, weeds had been cleared, new training weapons built, and a few benches added for resting between matches. Justan, Fist, Lenny, and Benjo had been the only participants at first. Then Bettie and Samson began to join in from time to time. Soon the word had spread and people started to come and watch. Now there were ten strong men among Coal's workers that participated in the sparring and training every evening until it became too dark to see.

Several people were there already when Fist arrived. He called out in greeting and the men waved back. Squirrel leapt from his shoulder and retreated to his customary seat in the tree next to the dueling circle. There he was able to watch Fist fight and stay out of danger while eating the food he had stashed high in the tree.

"Fist, are you ready for defeat?"

He turned to see Benjo walking over from the forge on the other side of the keep's center road.

"I will try not to break your arm this time," Fist promised. He had accidentally done so the week prior and as a result, Master Coal had asked Qyxal to begin attending the sparring just in case such an event transpired again. Fist thought it was wonderful to have such a convenient way to heal injuries.

"How nice of you." Benjo laughed. "That was my fault. This time I won't let you get me into such a tight hold."

"We will see." Fist was glad that Justan had gotten over whatever had occurred between the two humans in the past. Benjo was a good man and Fist liked him.

"Where is Sir Edge? He is usually the first one here," Benjo said.

"I will find out." Fist reached to Justan through the bond. He hadn't bothered Justan since speaking with him about his parents earlier and the man's current feelings surprised him. Justan was reading a different letter than before and was no longer sad, but this new emotion filled with hope and yearning was one that Fist was not familiar with.

Justan, what has happened? he asked. *Your feelings are . . . confusing.*

He sensed Justan's laughter.

Yes they are, Justan agreed. *I am fine, though.*

We are waiting for you.

I am on my way.

"He will be here soon." Fist said, "Do you need to wait for Qyxal to get here before we start?"

Benjo snorted. "I think I will be okay, thank you."

While the two men currently sparring finished their match, Fist and Benjo went to the training closet and selected their weapons. Both of them chose practice spears. Fist had always been proud of his skill with the spear, but Benjo was brilliant with the weapon.

Before meeting the man, Fist had only considered using the spear as a stabbing or throwing weapon. Benjo on the other hand, almost never threw his spear. He wielded it more like a quarter staff, only using it to pierce the enemy when he had a good opening. His technique had taught Fist a new way to look at the weapon and as always, the ogre enjoyed the opportunity to learn.

They walked to the center of the circle and bowed to each other. This was a human tradition Benjo had picked up at Training School that Fist liked. It showed respect to the opposing warrior as well as a lack of fear. Fist felt a slight twinge in his back as he bowed, but he ignored it. A little back pain wouldn't stop him from defeating the man.

Benjo was quicker and more polished in his spear skills, but Fist was stronger and had superior reach. He also had one other thing that Benjo didn't and that was years of practical battle experience. Fist decided upon a plan of attack and roared as he came at the man.

Benjo leapt out of the way of the first strike, but Fist wasn't about to give him time to counter attack. He kept the man at a distance with long sweeping slashes of his spear, waiting for him to lose patience and try to rush in. It didn't take long.

Benjo timed his move perfectly, waiting for the instant the wooden weapon flashed by before darting forward and extending his own spear towards the ogre's unprotected ribs. But Fist was waiting for it. The moment Benjo made his move, Fist let go of his spear with his right hand and reached out to grasp the man's spear below the head, halting it mere inches from his chest.

He twisted his torso to jerk the weapon from Benjo's grasp, and felt a slight pop in his back. A sharp stab of pain arced through his body and Fist let go of the spear.

Benjo didn't hesitate. He reversed the weapon and swung the butt end around in a powerful swipe that caught the stunned ogre in the jaw. Fist crashed to the ground and yelled in agony, but the ache in his jaw was an afterthought. He arched his back and his legs twitched as he tried to find a position that did not aggravate the injury.

"Sorry! That strike was a bit harder than I intended," Benjo said, his face lined with concern.

"It is okay, Benjo," Fist grunted and laid still on the ground, his muscles spasming around the wounded area. "It was not you."

Squirrel leapt down from the tree and ran over to scamper around on Fist's chest, chattering in concern. Fist wasn't supposed to get hurt.

"It is okay Squirrel."

"Fist, are you alright?" Justan had arrived just as Fist hit the ground and was now kneeling beside him.

"Yes," Fist said with a grimace. Squirrel ran up to his shoulder and he rolled over and got to his knees in an attempt to stand. He got his legs underneath him, but his back cried out in protest and Fist hobbled hunched over to sit on one of the benches. "My back."

"Sorry, Justan," Benjo said. "It's my fault."

"It was not you, Benjo," Fist said again through clenched teeth.

"*Can I look at it?*" Justan asked, both aloud and through the bond.

"Yes," Fist said. He opened his mind to allow entrance and felt the now familiar sensation of Justan's magic searching around in his body.

You have a bulging disc, Justan said. Fist had no idea what that meant and Justan added, *I see the hurt place in your spine. Master Coal has been teaching me how to use my magic to heal, but I shouldn't try it yet. I could hurt you more.* He was silent for a moment, then said, *Gwyrtha is bringing Qyxal. I will try to numb it a little for you until he gets here.*

Fist felt a sensation of coolness in the tender tissues around his spine and the sharp twitching pain subsided. He sighed in relief. “Thank you, Justan.”

Qyxal soon arrived and Fist felt Justan watching closely from within him as the elf used his magic to correct the problem. Once Qyxal was finished, Fist thanked him and stood, raising his arms and arching his back in a mighty stretch. There was a slight crack and he let his arms fall, sighing in relief. Squirrel stepped up close to nuzzle his ear and Fist patted his friend’s little head.

“If it bothers you again, come see Master Coal or I,” Qyxal said. “We don’t want this to become a reoccurring condition. Alright?”

“Yes, Qyxal. It feels good now.” Fist felt Justan withdrawing through the bond and was surprised when his friend cried out.

“Fist!” Justan’s eyes were wide and he was pointing at Squirrel with one hand while his other was pulled up to his mouth in surprise. “What is that?”

“What?” Fist turned his head and looked at Squirrel in concern. The creature was busy opening a nut, only slightly irritated at Justan’s pointing. “It is Squirrel.”

Qyxal recognized that Justan had to be seeing something to do with magic and cleared his throat to get Justan’s attention.

“But! . . . oh.” Justan looked around and let his hands fall, realizing that everyone was staring. He grinned to the crowd and forced out a laugh. “Sorry, for a second I thought it was something else.”

Fist, come with me! Justan sent as he came closer, the fake grin still frozen on his face. He put his arm around the ogre and turned him away from the workers, then walked Fist away from the training area a ways before continuing. “Fist, um . . . I’m going to try and show you something, okay?”

Fist felt a distant sensation as if something fine and delicate had been wrapped around his head. Then he sensed Justan reaching into his mind through the bond and there was an odd sensation of pressure in his head, like Justan had planted a finger firmly right between his eyes. Fist’s vision shifted.

Justan now glowed softly as if filled with a strange shimmering light. Fist could see multiple tendrils of cloudy white light reaching from the man in every direction, pausing every once in a while to brush against someone nearby as if feeling them out before moving on. One of them practically danced around Qyxal, examining the elf several times as he looked around, trying to see what Fist was staring at. One thicker cord of light arced from Justan directly into Fist's chest, and he realized that what he was seeing was the spirit magic that Justan talked so often about.

I see the bond! Fist thought and a smile stretched his face.

Good! Now look at Squirrel! Justan demanded.

Fist turned his head the other way and saw another thick cord of white light arcing from himself to the creature sitting on his shoulder.

When did that happen? Justan asked.

"What?" Fist said aloud. "Did you do that?"

"No!" Justan whispered loudly, then sent through the bond, *That magic isn't coming from me. It is coming from you, Fist. You are bonded to Squirrel!*

"You bonded just can't say things aloud, can you?" Qyxal grumbled, having been trying to follow along in the conversation from their expressions alone. Neither of them registered the elf's complaint.

Fist was still trying to digest what Justan had said. He stared again at the cord of light tying Squirrel to him and reached for it with his forefinger extended, almost expecting it to have a tangible substance. But his fingers passed right through it without disturbing the light at all. So he was bonded with Squirrel and the magic was coming from him? Fist smiled, finding the knowledge pleasing. "Oh . . . how?"

"I don't know!" Justan's intense curiosity was oozing through the bond and it was beginning to make Fist nervous. The ogre's smile faded. Was there something wrong with being bonded to Squirrel?

Justan sensed Fist's confusion and paused a moment to calm himself before continuing. "Can you hear Squirrel's thoughts?"

"No. Well . . ." Now that Justan put it that way, Fist realized that he had been able to understand Squirrel's thoughts for some time. "Yes. I know what he wants."

"So you are bonded to Squirrel?" Qyxal said, suddenly understanding what was going on. "Good for you, Fist! How did you not know until now, Edge?"

"How long have you been able to do that?" Justan asked Fist, ignoring the elf.

"I am not sure. It started a little bit and then got so I could understand more."

"So it came gradually?" Justan noted Fist's confusion and added. "Gradual. It means something that starts one way and changes over time. That can be your new word tomorrow. 'Gradually'."

"Yes! It came gradually." Fist wondered how to spell this new word . . .

"Okay, we can get to that later," Justan said. "Just think back to when this bond with Squirrel could have happened."

"Right," Fist said. "I will show you."

He closed his eyes and thought back to the first time he had met Squirrel and allowed Justan to share in the memories. Fist started with their meeting at the stunted mountain tree the morning after he had fled his tribe's territory, his head throbbing from the beating his father had given him the night before. From the beginning Squirrel was persistent, unwilling to leave the ogre's side, but Fist hadn't been able to understand why it followed him. As they got to the part of the story where Fist and Squirrel were reunited outside of the duke's castle, they were interrupted by Lenny's loud voice.

"Edge!" The dwarf ran up to them. He was sweating and a worried look was stuck on his face. "I got bad news, son!"

"What? Don't tell me your magic powder isn't working." Justan said, preparing for disappointment.

"That ain't it, son," Lenny said. "The king's dead."

"Dremaldria's King? King Andre?" Justan asked and the dwarf nodded in response. "But how? He isn't that old, maybe in his thirties."

"They're sayin' it was assassins from some other country."

The other men in the training area caught part of the conversation and were coming closer to listen. Most of them were from the Kingdom of Razbeck, but being this close to the border, the goings on in Dremaldria affected them as well.

"Where did you hear this, Lenny?" Qyxal asked.

"When the courier came in this mornin' he also had a letter from my brother Chugk in Wobble. I was just so excited 'bout my other shipment, that I didn't read it 'till just now."

"That's too bad," Justan said.

Fist could tell that there was some sense of guilt within Justan that he wasn't more upset by the news. Justan felt that a Dremaldrian was supposed to love their king. The attachment humans felt for far off leaders they had never met was something that the ogre didn't understand.

"At least we don't have to worry about the king sending men after us anymore," Qyxal said.

"You ain't heard the bad part yet," Lenny said. He looked at the ogre. "Fist, I hate to tell you this, but yer pal, the wizard duke with the wiggle fingers ain't dead."

Chapter Twenty Five

"What?" Fist said numbly, caught off guard by the dwarf's statement. "But he is dead. I saw him . . . melt."

"I can't 'splain it," Lenny said with a shrug. "But that's what Chugk's letter says. Zambon's girl, Elise, is the Queen of Dremaldria now and Ewzad Vriil got raised to the rank of Lord Protector to the Queen."

"If he's still alive, then he must have used some kind of spell to take him out of the throne room at the last moment," Qyxal said. "That was some clever illusion work."

"I saw Tamboor's sword go right through him. I don't think that was an illusion," Justan said. "When I searched the pile of clothes after he was gone, the sword wasn't there."

"Then when he left he must have taken it with him," the elf replied. "I don't know how he survived. Someone must have been waiting to heal him, wherever he went."

"This is bad," Justan said. "If he's alive, then . . ."

"But he is dead," Fist insisted. Why was everyone ignoring that fact? His anger was building.

"We need to go talk to Master Coal," Justan said. He turned to the workers that were gathered around, listening. "Sorry guys. You will have to spar without us tonight."

Justan led the four of them away from the training area, but didn't go straight to the lodge where Master Coal liked to spend his evenings. Instead, he headed towards the stables. Fist followed, his heart in turmoil. If the wizard wasn't dead, then Tamboor's family was not avenged.

Justan stopped just outside of the stables and a concerned Gwyrtha came up to join them. Justan put an arm around her and stroked her head for a moment before turning to face the others. His eyes were wide with the worry that Fist could feel emanating from him through the bond.

"We need to decide what to do before we talk to Master Coal," Justan said. "If what Chuck says is true, we could be endangering everybody around us just by being here. Not only did we tear up his castle and try to kill him, but we know what Ewzad Vriil really is. What if he decides to come after us?"

"Maybe, but he don't know who we is," Lenny said. "How's he gonna' know to look fer us?"

"He knows who I am," Justan said. "Kenn knew me as Justan, son of Faldon the Fierce. I never thought to check if he made it out of the dungeons alive. And I named myself as Edge right in front of the wizard. I showed him both of my runes."

"Don't even consider leaving until we talk with Master Coal," Qyxal said, seeing the frightened look in Justan's eyes. "And if you go, we will all go. Right Lenny?"

"Yer darn tootin'," the dwarf said, though he looked dismayed at the thought.

Justan nodded, but Fist knew that he was still considering leaving on his own to keep everyone else safe. *They would find us anyway,* Fist told him. Justan frowned in response and Fist added, *You could not hide from Qyxal.*

"How is the rest of the kingdom reacting?" Qyxal asked Lenny.

"It's hard to say. Chugk don't know much. The queen called the whole dag-gum army back to the capitol, sayin' she was worried about attack from some other country and now they dun got Dremald locked up tighter'n an elf maiden's skirt. Er, sorry Qyxal."

"The Barldag's army!" Fist said, a new realization hitting him.

"What was that, Fist?" Justan asked. Everyone turned to face him.

"That wizard with the snake fingers led the Barldag's army. If he is alive, the army is still in the mountains waiting to crush all the small peoples."

"Ah, there you are!" Master Coal said. The wizard approached with Bettie and Samson at his side. "I was down visiting Bettie in the forge and some of my men said you were looking for me?"

Everyone looked at Justan, who somewhat reluctantly stepped forward. He told the master all that they had been discussing. The wizard listened, only stopping Justan a few times to ask him brief questions. When he had finished, Master Coal wasn't panicked, just thoughtful. He leaned back against Samson's sturdy shoulder and stroked his chin with one hand as he considered their options.

"No one leaves until we know for sure that the farmlands are in danger," he said finally.

"But how would you know?" Justan asked. "There could be soldiers on the way here now. I learned your whereabouts from a shopkeeper. If they were able to track us to him, they could know where we were headed."

"I know the shopkeeper you speak of. Hugo is an old friend of mine. When you first arrived I sent someone to instruct him not to tell anyone of your whereabouts. Believe me, I have loyal people in the lands all around. I would know quite quickly if a force was on its way here."

"We can take care of ourselves, Edge," Bettie added. "Don't think we ain't been through our own share of troubles."

"I don't think they would dare attack this place anyway," Samson added. "We are in the Kingdom of Razbeck. If Dremaldrian soldiers attacked the largest source of food for the kingdom, it would be an act of war."

"He wouldn't send Dremaldrian soldiers," Justan said. *He has monsters*, was the unspoken thought that only Fist could hear.

"I will stand firm on this, Edge." The wizard's tone left no doubt as to his resolve. "I believe that you are quite safe here. There are other more pressing things you should be worrying about. How big is this army, Fist?"

Fist was startled that the question was directed at him. "Uh, I do not know. They were gathering all the ogre tribes and the goblin peoples and the trolls in the mountains. After they took us from Jack's Rest, we were brought through many armies and many camps."

The memory of the journey to the wizard's castle was still fresh in his mind. The three of them had been taken in open cages atop a wagon, being pelted with rocks and filth from the howling army. Fist remembered the time with shame as well as horror. Tamboor and Petyr killed anything that got too close to the cage, but he had been immobilized with grief and despair, having lost his second tribe and not knowing that Squirrel had survived. He spent the journey curled up and weeping, unable to attempt even the minor acts of revenge that Tamboor and Petyr carried out.

"Hundreds of hundreds of soldiers, all wanting to kill little peoples for glory and for the Barldag," Fist said.

"Barldag? . . . that ain't good," Bettie said, looking quite shaken. "That Barldag stuff is . . ."

"It'll be okay, Bettie." Lenny put a comforting arm around her waist. "Dag-blast it, we don't know that any of that stuff's true. Gall-durn wizard's a liar."

Master Coal gave the dwarf a sideways glance, but agreed. "The Dark Prophet was defeated a long time ago. If he had truly found a way to come back, there would be a lot more signs of his power. The most likely explanation is that Ewzad Vriil has simply been using the traditions of the mountain tribes to bring them together."

"I don't believe in the Barldag," Fist said.

"The academy!" A sudden jolt of fear went through Justan, causing Fist's heart to beat faster in response. "If Ewzad Vriil wants to take over Dremaldria, he would first have to destroy the Battle Academy. What if that's why he has been building the army?"

"Don't forget the Mage School," Qyxal added. "As soon as they find out that Ewzad Vriil is a dark wizard, they will hunt him down and destroy him. Using magic to gain power over the kingdoms is not allowed. Otherwise there would be wizards ruling all the known lands."

"You are both right," Master Coal said. "But the academy is where he would strike first. With Dremaldria's forces withdrawn, the academy is weakened. If they were defeated, the Mage School would be easier to strike."

"We have to warn them," Justan said, his mind churning. "If I left with Gwyrtha now and didn't stop, I could make it to Reneul in two weeks."

"Don't be a goblin brain!" Bettie snapped. "We got Willum!"

"Calm down everyone," Master Coal said. "She is right, Edge. Write a letter to your father describing exactly what has happened. Tonight, I will contact Willum and dictate the letter to him. He can take it to your Father. With your word and mine together, they have to listen. I will also send an urgent letter to the Mage School so that they can prepare."

"Can you get a message to my people for me?" Qyxal asked.

"Of course, but realize that until we know more, I expect you two to keep to your studies. There is nothing more that you can do. Understood?" There were nods all around.

"Yer a good man, Coal," Lenny said. He had not moved his arm from around Bettie's waist and she wasn't making him. "I reckon I should warn my stupid brother too. Wobble's too dag-gum close to the academy."

Darkness had fallen and the temperature dropped with it. Everyone scattered to write letters to send off. Fist took a moment to scratch Gwyrtha behind the ears and headed towards the lodge, heavy thoughts weighing his mind.

When he arrived at the kitchens, Becca was waiting for him.

"Well?" she said, tapping one foot and looking him up and down. Fist slumped.

"I forgot." The last thing he wanted at that moment was to go take a bath. "But I did not spar much. Look, no sweating!"

"Okay, Fist. I will overlook it tonight," Becca sighed, then put on a stern look and shook her finger at him. "But you are not getting out of that bath tomorrow. Am I clear?"

"Yes, Miss Becca," Fist said and gave her a large hug in gratitude. Hugs were another of Fist's favorite human traditions.

"Oh!" She patted his back, but made a show of wrinkling her nose as he pulled away. "Now go on before I change my mind."

Happily, Fist headed to his room and unlatched the door. As the room opened before him, he froze in stunned astonishment. Gone were the dust and cobwebs, gone were the crates and barrels of supplies, and gone was the pile of straw and blankets that he had been sleeping on. The room now had a clean floor with a thick rug in the center. Along one wall, there were two rows of shelving, one filled with books and the other with his clothes. A small table with paper and ink sat in one corner. But the thing that caught his eye most of all, was the enormous bed with an ogre-sized mattress that took up a large part of the room.

"Miss Becca . . ." Fist turned and looked at her, tears in his eyes. "For me?"

"Yes, for you!" Becca said, clapping her hands together in joy at his reaction. "And don't forget Squirrel."

Mounted on the wall next to Fist's bed was a large red birdhouse that had been converted to fit Squirrel's size. Fist walked forward and held out his arm so that Squirrel could run down and jump to his new house. At first, Squirrel was irritated that his old stash of nuts between the two barrels of pickles had been cleaned out, but when Fist explained to him that the humans had built the place just for him, the creature was satisfied. Inside, there were several clean rags and scraps of cloth for him to nest in along with a large area to store his food.

"He likes it!" Fist said and turned to embrace Becca again. "Why did you do this for me?"

"Well, we all felt quite bad that you were sleeping on the floor in the corner like a family pet. You deserve a room just as good as anyone else's. So some of the girls and I cleaned out the room while you were gone this morning. We decided to store those things in Old Honstule's house for now. The reason I wouldn't let you in earlier was that we hadn't brought the mattress in yet."

"It is wonderful." Fist walked over and laid down on the bed. He closed his eyes and sighed with pleasure. "This bed . . . It's just like the one in Justan's memories. Like laying on the clouds."

"Miss Nala and I worked on it together. A while ago, we got

some of the men started on making your bed frame. We ordered the fabric and she made the sheets and the blankets, while I made the mattress with a mix of cotton and down. But wait! I'll be back in just a moment."

Fist didn't mind waiting. The bed felt so nice. He reached out with his mind and felt for the bond. His link with Justan was there, thick and tangible as always, but where was the bond he was supposed to have with Squirrel? He listened for Squirrel's thoughts. The creature was still in his new little home, arranging the bits of fabric into his own comfortable nest of a bed. Fist followed the creatures thoughts in his mind searching for their source. Then it was there, the link he searched for.

Squirrel, can you hear me? The creature's thoughts twitched in puzzlement. *I can talk to you without talking now.* Squirrel shook his head, trying to dislodge the voice from his mind. The ogre laughed. *It is me, Fist. We are bonded, you and I, like Justan is bonded to me. Is that not great?*

There was no surprise, just slight irritation at Fist's intrusion. Squirrel had known of their bond. Even though his thoughts were too small for Fist to hear at first, Squirrel had heard the ogre all along. The bond is how he had tracked Fist all the way through the mountains to the wizard's castle, even though he hadn't dared get too close to the monstrous army.

The door to the room opened.

"Fist, I'm ba-, oh . . ." Becca lowered her voice to a whisper. "Are you asleep?"

Fist opened his eyes. "No. I am still awake."

"Good." She walked over to the bed and pulled something from behind her back. It was a thick pillow in a soft cotton cover with the name Fist sewn into the fabric. "I made you this. It is stuffed with flowers from the honstule plant. They are the most amazing thing. When the flowers wilt they don't degrade, but turn into the softest, most fluffy material. And they smell wonderful forever."

"My name is on it." Fist sat up and reached out. The pillow was light, as if it weighed nothing and she was right about the smell. He pulled it in and crushed the softness to his face. The scent was sweet, but not overwhelmingly so. Just nice, like a freshly cut melon. "Thank you, Miss Becca. You have done so much. I . . . I will work extra hard for both of you from now on."

She laughed. "Fist you are already the hardest worker we have. If you promise to bathe every other day like I have asked you, I will be satisfied."

"I will!" The thought of bathing didn't seem so much of a punishment at the moment.

Becca leaned forward and kissed him on the forehead. "Good night then, Fist."

Fist laid back down and placed the pillow under his head. He felt so comfortable, that his body did not want to move, but he was too excited to sleep. He called out to Justan and made him come down so that he could show him everything. Justan was genuinely happy for him and even tried out the bed and pillow, saying that they were much nicer than the ones in his room.

After Justan left, Fist undressed and pulled the blankets over himself, enjoying the way the fresh blankets felt against his bare skin. He blew out the lantern that lit his room and communed with Squirrel through the bond until they both fell asleep. It wasn't long before Fist dreamt.

He was floating peacefully on a bed made of cloud, unafraid of being so high in the sky above the earth below. Fist was content just feeling the hot sun on his body. Life was perfect, but his peace was interrupted by a thudding noise. He sat up and turned his head to see his father Crag running at him, his feet obliterating the clouds beneath him with every step. Following closely behind Crag was an army of winged beasts, dark and terrible.

Crag yelled at him to stand up and fight, but Fist didn't want to. He laid back on the cloud and closed his eyes, focusing on the warmth of the sun, willing the darkness to go away. But they didn't. The sounds of his father's footsteps and the approaching army grew louder until Fist opened his eyes and his father stood over him, blood running down his body from several open wounds, his face pummeled and swollen as it had been when Fist had beaten him on the night he had left the Thunder People forever.

"Toompa!" his father yelled and swung his arm down in a mighty punch that knocked Fist through the cloud.

Fist watched his father's disappointed face get smaller and smaller as he fell unprotected through the sky towards the earth below. The dark army roared and dove through the air after him, but it didn't matter, he was going to die anyway. He closed his eyes and grit his teeth waiting for the impact, but he didn't hit the hard earth. His body plunged into the icy depths of a deep river, the shock of the cold blasting the air from his lungs. He struggled to swim to the surface but the current dragged him down and down deeper and deeper until he knew he was going to die. As he was about to open his mouth and suck in the deadly water, a hand closed over his mouth.

Suddenly he wasn't cold anymore. The hand moved away and he could breathe easily. Fist turned to see brown hair framing a face with familiar kind eyes and a short trimmed beard. The man pulled him in for an embrace and Fist was as small as a child again.

"It's okay, Fist. You will be fine, someone is coming for you," the man said.

"But why must I go, Big John?" he asked. "Can't I just stay here with you?"

The man held him close again and patted his head. "I wish you could stay, but you do not belong here with me. You have too much work to do. Do not worry, we will see each other again."

The man's voice faded away and Fist was in the icy depths of the river again. He wasn't panicked anymore. He kicked upwards and as his face cleared the water, he saw Justan standing on some rocks not too far away. The river brought them closer together and Justan reached out his hand to pull Fist from the river. As they grabbed each other by the wrist, the dream changed.

Fist was sitting naked in a tub of soapy water. But he wasn't in the washing area. Somehow he had forgotten and started to bathe in the main room of the lodge. It was dinner time. Everyone was sitting around the table laughing and feasting. He was petrified. What if they saw him? He slowly rose from the water. If he could only make it to the kitchen door before someone noticed. But as soon as he stood, one of the women screamed and pointed at his-.

Fist was startled awake by a loud knock on his door.

"What?" he said, his thick rumbling voice even thicker from sleep.

The door opened and in came Miss Nala's second oldest boy, Jerrold, followed by Master Coal. The wizard was carrying a lamp and from the state of his rumpled bedclothes, looked as though he had just been roused from sleep himself.

"Sorry to wake you Fist, but Jerrold refused to tell me what was going on without speaking with you first," the wizard said.

He sat up, and the young teen threw himself into Fist's arms, shaking in fear. The ogre was startled, but pulled the boy in close, patting him on the back awkwardly. "What is it, Jerrold? What is wrong?"

"Bindy is dead!" the boy cried out.

"Your goat?" The family kept many animals, but Bindy was their milking goat and the children's favorite. She was quite old and had provided milk for all of the children since they were infants.

"Yes! All our animals are dead! But Bindy . . ." He buried his head into Fist's hairy chest and sobbed.

"All of them?" Fist looked to Master Coal for an explanation, but the wizard shook his head.

"What about your brothers and sisters?" Master Coal said. "Is your mother alright?"

The boy nodded and raised his head. "They are okay, but mom sent me to get help. Steffen wouldn't go with me though. He stayed behind to protect everyone else."

"A good brother," Fist said and put the boy gently to the side, before pulling on clothes as fast as he could. At his suggestion, Squirrel came out of his house and ran over to the boy, curling up in his lap and offering a nut. "I will go now. Stay here with Squirrel. He will watch over you until I get back."

"Samson is coming with you, Fist," Master Coal said. "He is waiting outside. I will follow with others shortly. Tell Justan."

Fist ran for the door, not bothering with shoes as they would take him too long to put on. When he ran out the lodge door, the cold air hit him like a slap in the face, but he ignored it. Samson was waiting and he had grown big. He held two steel-tipped spears and tossed one of them to Fist. The ogre caught it with a nod of thanks.

"Get on. There is no time for you to run."

The centaur knelt down and Fist swung his leg over the saddle. He barely had time to get his toes in the stirrups before Samson was up and running. Fist was not used to riding a horse, but Samson was the first one he had ever ridden that was large enough to carry him without being overburdened. The centaur understood that he was inexperienced and gave him as smooth a ride as he could without slowing down.

They raced through the night, a full moon lighting their way and Fist held on as well as he could while waking Justan through the bond. Once he knew that Justan and Gwyrtha would follow, Fist thought about what Jerrold had said. What had happened to Miss Nala's animals? How could they all be dead? Was it sickness? He asked Samson and the centaur shook his head.

"If all the animals are truly dead, it was not sickness. No illness would affect all of them or catch on so quickly. Besides, when the boy arrived, all he said before asking for you was 'blood'. There is something else going on."

"I see." Fist gripped the spear tighter and prepared his mind for battle.

As they approached the farmhouse, Fist could see that Jerrold's claims were true. In the light of the moon, he saw the still forms of Miss Nala's animals lying in the fields. The smell of their blood hung thick in the crisp night air. Even so, Fist was not prepared for the sight that awaited them on the family's porch.

Bindy wasn't just dead. She had been dissected and pulled apart piece by piece and her remains were strewn across the porch in a grotesque tableau. Fist climbed from the centaur's back and looked around the yard for any sign that the intruder was still around.

"It was done almost . . . artfully," Samson said, his face twisted in disgust as he stared at the grisly scene.

Indeed, the placing of Bindy's parts was deliberate. Each lump of flesh or shard of bone was placed in a precise pattern. Fist attempted to step onto the porch, trying to avoid stepping in the gore, but it would have been impossible. He caught a glimpse of Bindy's head sitting atop a coiled pile of intestines right in front of the door as if to greet the person opening it, and changed his mind.

He ran around to the back of the house.

"Miss Nala! I'm here!" He reached the back door, but before he could pound on it, the door opened.

"Fist?" Steffen peeked out with a sword in one hand, eyes wide, looking terrified but ready to do battle. When he saw Fist standing in the moonlight, the boy smiled in relief and opened the door wider.

"Don't come out!" Fist said and the door narrowed to a crack again. "Is everyone okay in there?"

The boy nodded.

"Tell Miss Nala that Jerrold is safe and me and Samson are looking outside. Do not open the other door!" Fist said, but by the look on Steffen's face, he could see that the boy already had.

Fist sensed that Justan was astride Gwyrtha and thundering down the road after them. He had Ma'am strung and ready. Samson headed to the other animal enclosures to check for signs of whoever had done this. Fist walked to the edge of the woods behind the goat pen with spear at the ready. He was so focused that he didn't even feel the frozen earth against the skin of his feet.

There was movement in the trees.

Fist ran forward, his hunter's senses taking over as he followed the sound and the slightest hint of movement the moonlight showed him. But whatever he was chasing was clever and he soon lost its trail. He searched around for a moment longer before Gwyrtha and Justan caught up to him. Justan slid off Gwyrtha's back and set her on the trail of the thing.

"Did you see it?" Justan asked, his bow at the ready.

“Some of it,” Fist said. “It was fast and I can’t . . . tell you right, but I will show you.”

He delved into the bond and showed Justan the moment of memory he had. He couldn’t make out exactly what it was, but a few things stood out clearly. Whatever he had seen had scales that reflected in the moonlight and it carried a sword on its back.

Chapter Twenty Six

Their search for the creature was fruitless. Despite Gwyrtha's superior tracking abilities, she lost its trail soon after Justan arrived. It occurred to them that whatever Fist had seen in the woods could have circled back to attack again and they rushed back to the farmhouse. To their relief, Master Coal and Qyxal had arrived and were tending to the family. Miss Nala and the children were shaken but unharmed.

The sky soon brightened with the morning light and Master Coal sent his workers out to assess the damage. Fist volunteered to stay with the family, while Justan left the house with Coal and Qyxal to figure out exactly what had happened.

From the state of Bindy's corpse, they knew that the attacker was both intelligent and twisted. They couldn't quite tell what message the placement of the goat's body parts was meant to send, but the attack was personal, designed to terrorize the family. Master Coal ordered some men to clear the remains from the porch. There was no need to make the family deal with it any further.

"Whoever did this knew the family well enough to pick their favorite goat to make an example of." Qyxal remarked. "Could it have been one of the other farmers? Is there someone that doesn't like her?"

"No," Master Coal replied. "There isn't that kind of animosity in this community. At least not in regards to Nala. Her husband was greatly admired by everyone and in the time since he passed, she has earned their respect."

"Maybe someone else they knew from their life outside the community?" Justan asked. "A relative?"

"I'll ask her, but I doubt it," the master said. "It wouldn't have had to be someone close to the family. Anyone that watched the children once with that goat would have seen the way they doted on it. Samson will be here soon with more information."

The centaur arrived a moment later to tell them the results of his search. Few animals had survived. Some of the sheep had broken out of the pen during the attack and were being rounded up. Two of the workhorses had been in Master Coal's stable waiting to be re-shoed and a few chickens had been overlooked, but the majority of Nala's animals were dead. It was a disaster.

"Nala will not be able to keep the farm going with two workhorses and a handful of sheep." Master Coal's face was calm as he considered the prospects. "Samson, have the men clean up the carcasses and haul them off for disposal. Tell them to salvage what wool they can from the dead sheep. Perhaps some of the meat from the animals is salvageable as well. We will see what she wants to keep and pay her for the rest. Oh, and something else . . ." From the look they exchanged, Justan could see that they were communicating further through the bond. The centaur nodded and galloped away. "Edge, would it be alright if Gwyrtha joined him? Samson is going to need a lot of help."

"Of course," Justan said and Gwyrtha trotted off after the centaur. "This is bad isn't it?"

"Miss Nala may have to give up the farm," Qyxal replied.

"We'll worry about that later," Master Coal said. "For now, let's focus on figuring out who did this."

"We know one thing," Justan said. "With the sheer number of animals killed in the short amount of time it was done, we are looking for multiple attackers."

"Or one very vicious creature," Qyxal said.

"How could one individual do all this in one night without being heard?" Justan asked.

"It could have been done," Master Coal said. "Samson says that all the animals were killed quickly. Their throats were cut or they were struck a single stab to the heart. It was done in a quick and efficient manner."

"I need to take a look at some of those animals," Qyxal said.

They went to the barn to examine some of the corpses and as they saw the attacker's handiwork in the light, it became evident that whatever had attacked was not bandits or men at all, but some kind of creature or creatures. The wounds on the animals were made by sharp teeth or claws, with occasional deep puncture wounds that could have been made by a horn or something. The attacker had been careful, but Qyxal eventually did find some strange tracks. Whatever had done this had claws on its feet at least.

"Fist saw a creature go into the woods last night," Justan said. "A scaly beast that carried a sword."

"But none of these animals were killed by a sword," Qyxal replied. "Are you sure that is what he saw?"

"Fist showed me the memory. He definitely saw what he described," Justan said. "Even if the beast was not what killed the animals, it must have been involved somehow."

"The mysteries continue to pile up," Master Coal said. "Qyxal, go around to the various attack sites and see if you can discover more. Edge, why don't you come with me? We should tell Nala what we found."

Justan followed Master Coal to the farmhouse. By the time they arrived, the workers had already cleared away Bindy's remains. Miss Nala and her oldest girl were scrubbing away the blood of their beloved goat from the wooden porch. She saw them arrive and walked towards Master Coal on trembling legs.

"So what did you find, Master Coal? How many of our animals survived?" Her tone was optimistic, but her face showed that she did not expect the results to be good.

The wizard told her what Samson and the workers had discovered. As she digested the information her lips trembled, but she did not cry. Nala nodded and her voice was clear and unwavering when she spoke. "Thank you for your help. I will go to farmer Tabot this afternoon and tell him the land is up for sale. He offered to purchase it when David died. Maybe he is still interested."

"Nala, that will not be necessary." Master Coal placed a

reassuring hand on her shoulder. "I had Samson send some men to tell all the other farmers what has happened. They are putting out a request for help. You know our community. They will be generous. Why, I wouldn't be surprised if your animals were replaced by the end of the day." Her eyes filled with tears as he spoke and she opened her mouth to respond, but no sound came out.

"If not, I will replace them myself," Master Coal added.

"I-I . . ." Miss Nala fell to her knees in front of the wizard and clutched his pant legs as if the weight of his kindness had pulled her down instead of lifting her spirits. "We owe so much to you, Master Coal. If it wasn't for your generosity, I don't know where we would be. I-I am sorry to be such a burden,"

Master Coal gently removed her hands and knelt beside her. "Nala, it is no burden. David was a great help to me when I first purchased my farm here. Without his support, my bonded and I never would have been accepted into this community. Helping you is just one small thing that I can do to repay him. Besides, you more than earn the assistance you get." Some firmness entered his voice. "I still expect our arrangement to be in force, by the way."

"Of course," she replied and Justan could tell that the weight of her guilt had been somewhat lifted. Master Coal stood and held out a hand to help her to her feet. Nala walked back towards the house and went back to scrubbing the porch with her daughter.

Justan reached through the bond to check with Fist. The ogre was inside carrying plates to the family's table. Giggling children were hanging from each of his mighty arms. They seemed to have recovered from the horrors of the night before. Justan told him what they had found.

Fist was upset about the loss of the animals, but relieved that the family's farm would survive. His main concern was about the creature's possible return. The ogre intended to stay there for the day just in case.

Justan turned to Master Coal. "Perhaps I should forgo my lessons today and stay here with Fist. The creature may come back."

"I'm sure they will be fine. Fist is more than capable of protecting them don't you think?" Coal asked.

"He wouldn't let anything happen to them," Justan agreed, thinking back to the horrible tragedy with Tamboor's family. "If any creature tried to attack Miss Nala or any of the children with him around . . . I would pity that creature."

"No you wouldn't," Master Coal replied with a knowing look. Justan smiled in response.

"No I wouldn't," he agreed. "It would deserve whatever Fist did to it."

"Very well then. Since Samson and Gwyrtha are hard at work elsewhere, why don't we start walking back to the keep? We can discuss today's lesson on the way."

"Yes, sir."

The day had become unseasonably warm and Justan shed his jacket as they walked. They started up the road, passing men who were cleaning up the carcasses of the animals. Justan waited for the men to be out of earshot before he spoke.

"Did you get my message to Willum last night?"

"Yes, I dictated your letter to him exactly as you wrote it. He said that your father is away on an important mission, but he will take the message to the rest of the council. Evidently Willum is quite close to Tad, the Cunning."

"Oh . . . good." Justan said, a bit disappointed that his father had not been able to receive the message directly. He had also considered passing along a message to Jhonate, but now he was glad that he hadn't. Justan didn't know how many people would have heard it.

"I also sent a letter off to Wizard Valtrek and told him to get Qyxal's message to the elves in the Tinny Woods. I would suggest you stop worrying for now. There is nothing more we can do. Hopefully Willum will tell me the council's reaction when I contact him later today. I will let you know what happens as soon as I hear back."

"Yes, sir. Thank you, Master Coal."

"Now, back to your lesson. I know that it was an eventful night, but did you get the chance to apply anything we spoke about yesterday?"

"Yes!" Justan said, suddenly remembering what he had been so eager to speak with the wizard about. He related what he had discovered about Fist's bond with Squirrel.

"Excellent! That was the surprise I wanted you to find!" Coal said with a wide grin. He looked more excited than Justan had seen him before. "Don't you find it fascinating?"

"Well, y-yes. But how is that possible? I mean, at first I thought he got the ability from me, but he says Squirrel felt the bond from the first time they met."

The wizard nodded. "That makes sense. The bond helps each of you by enhancing attributes you already have, but it would not give your bonded new abilities. How long has he known Squirrel?"

"About a year before we bonded. But . . . do ogres even have magic?"

"I'm not an expert on Fist's race," Coal said. "But I do recall hearing that there were ogre mages during the War of the Dark Prophet, so I see no reason an ogre bonding wizard couldn't be a possibility."

"So Fist is a bonding wizard . . ." It was the first time Justan had thought of it in that light.

"Yes. It would seem he is."

"But could that cause a problem? How will his bond with Squirrel react to mine? Are the bonds connected together in some way? Can I communicate with Squirrel directly or . . ?"

"Those are very interesting questions and I don't honestly know the answers. The concept of two bonding wizards linked together is one I have never thought about. If you want to try and reach out to Squirrel, you can I suppose. But I have no idea what kind of response you will get. I suggest asking Fist how he feels about it. At any rate, you will have to deal with it sooner or later. Fist could bond to something else, you know."

"Oh! I hadn't thought of that." Somehow, that possibility was a bit unnerving. Another thought came to him. "So since he has bonding magic . . . Shouldn't Fist be joining us in our lessons? I mean, he needs to learn too."

Master Coal laughed and when he saw the disconcerted look on

Justan's face, added, "Don't misunderstand me. I'm laughing at myself. You are absolutely right. He should be learning to use his magic. I am probably the only wizard in the world that would agree with you, but honestly, after all the creatures I have bonded to, I have no idea why it didn't cross my mind. It should have."

"So what should we do, then?" Justan asked.

The wizard scratched his head as he considered it. "He wouldn't understand the lessons you are currently undertaking. You were lucky enough to have come to me with a year of Mage School under your belt, but Fist would have little to no magical training at all. I am afraid that with you and Qyxal and all of my other responsibilities, there isn't time enough in the day for me to teach him all he needs to know."

"So it is up to me then," Justan said, unsettled by the idea. How was he going to undertake that kind of task? He would need to spend his every spare moment catching Fist up. "But Fist is learning so much already: how to speak, how to read and write . . . I wonder if it would be asking too much of him to take on this extra study on top of it."

Coal smiled. "Ask him how he feels about it. Just remember, you have an enormous advantage over any other teacher he could study under. When you are using the bond linked mind-to-mind, you don't have to overcome the barriers of understanding that most teachers have."

"I suppose not," Justan said. "But how would I go about showing him everything I know about magic? I'm not a good teacher."

"You don't have to be a good teacher to share knowledge through the bond. You have shared memories with him before, have you not?"

"Yes," Justan said. "Many times."

"In that same way, you could teach him about magic. It will take practice, but soon enough you will find that by using that same technique, you can explain whole ideas to him in an instant. Why I could teach you a week's worth of lessons in a few hours if we were bonded together."

"I should have thought of that." Justan frowned, having made the awkward realization that by overlooking such a simple application of the bond, he had been holding Fist back. How could he have gone this long without thinking of trying that? The ogre would be much farther along in all his studies if he had thought of teaching him that way earlier.

Master Coal smiled at the expression on Justan's face and placed a comforting hand on his shoulder. "Don't feel bad. The potential uses of the bond are staggering once you realize them, but it will take years. You can't expect to figure them all out right away. This is all part of learning what being a bonding wizard is about. One thing I have noticed about you, Edge. You have a tendency to put expectations upon yourself that just aren't reasonable."

The master's assurances didn't make Justan feel better. He was supposed to be smarter than this. He couldn't afford to learn at everyone else's idea of a reasonable pace when it came to his bonded. The world was too dangerous. For their sake and his, he needed to learn faster than what was reasonable.

Master Coal continued on with the lesson and as they walked, Justan's mind tackled each new bit of information from every angle, determined to put together every last application of his magic. He could not let Fist and Gwyrtha down again.

When the lesson was over, Justan went back to his room and took out the letter from Jhonate. He read over it again before pulling out a piece of paper and trying to write a response. He had tried the night before as well, but it was difficult to know what to say. He ached to tell her how he felt and he was pretty sure that he now understood what his feelings for her were, but there was no way he could come right out and say it. Could he?

What if he told her how he felt and it was too much too soon? What if he had misread the signals in her letter? If he rushed in, she could back off or knowing her, get angry. Maybe he should leave his feelings out of it and just tell her what was going on. But what if he said too little and she thought he didn't care about her? He started writing the letter, but spent so much time agonizing over every word that he eventually gave up and laid on his bed.

For a while he communicated with Fist and Gwyrtha through the bond. Gwyrtha was searching the outskirts of the farmlands with Qyxal trying to track the beast that had attacked Miss Nala's family. She had found an additional pair of tracks that were similar to the ones that Fist had found in the night, but unlike the other tracks, these new ones reeked of the blood of the animals that had been killed.

Justan's concern grew. So there were two creatures, perhaps even more and according to Gwyrtha these tracks were quite fresh, perhaps just a few hours old. The creatures were still around. He relayed her findings to Fist and promised him that he and Gwyrtha would stay at the farmhouse with him that night to help protect the family.

He left his room to seek out Lenny. In order to guard the farm with Fist that night, he needed some decent weapons. As Justan neared the smithy, the sound of the dwarf's curses along with hammers striking metal brought a smile to Justan's face. Lenny was truly in his element here. He left with two swords that Bettie had made as practice work. They were decently made and well balanced, good enough to be put to use in any king's army, but after seeing Lenny's work, he could tell that Bettie had a lot of work to do before she would be a master weaponsmith. Justan didn't dare tell her that though.

He headed to the practice area to get a feel for the swords. He started the sword forms Sir Hilt had taught him. He began working up a sweat and before he knew it, Gwyrtha had returned to the keep. She called out to him through the bond.

Ride.

When they arrived at the farmhouse, Samson had just finished making preparations for the night. All of the remaining animals had been moved to a different farm for the time being. Master Coal had foreseen that their biggest disadvantage in trying to guard the house would be the darkness. Magic orbs were affixed to each fence post around the house. When night came, the yard would be filled with a soft glow. It would be much more difficult for something to sneak up to the house now.

"It is good that you are here," Samson said, trotting up to them as they approached. "Coal wants us to patrol the other farms in case Nala's farm is not the only one being targeted. Can you help?"

"No," Justan said. "I'm sorry, but I promised Fist I would watch over the family with him tonight. I don't see why Gwyrtha couldn't come with you, though. She would be more help tracking anyway."

No. I stay, she said.

"Gwyrtha, it would be a great help to me if you could go with Samson."

She snorted in reply, not wanting to be away from him any longer. They had been apart for most of the day after all.

Please? he asked and promised to go on an extended ride with her the next day. Justan wasn't sure why he felt it was so important for her to go with Samson, but for some reason, it seemed right that he stay with Fist alone that night. It took a bit more prodding, but she went with the centaur.

Justan knocked at the front door and a disheveled and weary-looking Miss Nala welcomed him in.

"Fist will be just a moment. He is putting the children to bed," she said. Justan could hear their laughter in the other room along with the heavy clomp of Fist's feet. The youngest was too excited to sleep and the ogre was trying his best to tire him out. The two older boys were more than eager to shout out suggestions.

"Fist adores the children," Justan said.

"They love him so dearly, you know. They were so terrified this morning, but since he has been here, they haven't acted scared at all. He is like the best big brother they could have."

"He is," Justan agreed. "Evidently he has that effect on children. He has seen a lot of battle in his time, but in many ways, he is like a child himself. I think that's why."

"That's true. He's like a big sweet lonely child." A grin came to her face and Justan was surprised by the affection in her eyes as she spoke about the ogre. "Becca and I have spoken many times about it. From the moment we first saw him, both of us just wanted to reach out and mother him."

Justan chuckled. "I am grateful to you for it. The two of you have helped him a lot. Especially when it comes to his studies. I have had so much to do since we have been here, that I haven't been giving him the attention he needs."

The sounds from the boy's room had quieted down and Fist walked across the hallway to the girl's room. Shrieks of laughter erupted as they jumped on him from ambush points on either side of the door.

"It has been a pleasure. It really has," Miss Nala said. Then the smile faded a bit from her face and was replaced by a look of reluctance. "Sir Edge, has he told you what happened to the first human family he befriended?"

"Uh . . ." Justan wasn't quite sure how to answer her. "He has told you about them?"

"Tamboor's family," she said. "That's what he calls them. He talks about them all the time. Especially the children. Cedric this, Lina that. He talks about them with such fondness . . . But there is a sadness too. It may not be my business, but I must ask you, what happened?"

Justan hesitated for a moment but felt compelled to tell the truth. "They were killed. An army of beasts conquered the town and Fist fought hard for them, but he was captured."

"There is more though, isn't there?" she asked and reached out to grip his arm. Her eyes locked onto his. "Please tell me. I must know. It is important."

"After he and Tamboor were captured, the wife and children were tortured and . . . they were forced to watch." Fist's memories of that time were burned into his mind. They were so horrible that sometimes Justan woke up at night sobbing. Every time it happened, he reached out to Fist to find that the ogre was sobbing too. Justan felt a lump in his throat and he looked away as he continued. "When I first met Fist, he was broken by those memories. I . . . he still isn't over it. But we are working it out together. Being with your family has helped him a lot."

He looked back to see that tears were rolling down her cheeks. Nala pulled Justan into a crushing embrace. "He told me that you saved him and now I understand. Thank you, Sir Edge! Thank you for saving him."

Justan, stunned by her reaction, patted her awkwardly on the back. "I . . . now you know, but you mustn't tell him I told you."

She stepped back and lifted her apron to wipe the tears from her face. "I won't. I won't."

"Good, just take comfort in the fact that you are well protected tonight. There is no way he would let any of you be harmed."

"No. I would feel sorry for any beast that tried to attack this house with you two here tonight," she said.

"No you wouldn't," Justan said, a slight smile curving his lips.

"No I wouldn't," she agreed, but her eyes were deadly serious.

"The children will sleep now." Fist entered the room and from the sheepish look on his face, Justan knew that his cheeks had been soundly covered in little girl kisses. "It is dark. We should be outside."

"Of course," Justan said. "And Miss Nala, remember what I said."

"We will be perfectly safe tonight. I know. Thank you both. Oh!" She ran back to the kitchen and returned with a basket. It smelled of cookies and fresh bread. "Take this with you. You will need something to eat if you plan on staying out there all night."

She planted a kiss of her own on Fist's cheek and Justan walked with him outside into the looming night.

Chapter Twenty Seven

Did you hear that sound on the roof? Justan asked. He was watching the backside of the house while Fist watched the front.

I threw a cookie, Fist explained. *For Squirrel.*

Oh. In Justan's opinion, it was a waste of one of Miss Nala's delicious cookies. Surely Squirrel was perfectly happy with his little nuts and seeds. But he didn't say anything to Fist about it. Squirrel was keeping watch on the sides of the house from the rooftop. If Justan said anything derogatory, there was a chance that Squirrel would overhear it and find the worst opportunity to pelt him with rocks or something worse. The little beast had wonderful aim.

Justan thrust his hands into his armpits to ward off the chill and yawned as he watched the treeline for movement. The yard around the house was bathed in a soft glow from the lamps Samson had placed along the fence and with the temperature still too cold for insects, the night was awfully quiet. They had been watching for several hours and Justan was finding it difficult to stay awake.

I'm tired, he told Fist.

Ask Gwyrtha for strength, the ogre suggested.

Of course. Thanks. Justan could have slapped himself for once again forgetting one of the many uses of the bond. Gwyrtha and Samson were several miles away with Qyxal examining some older traces of the creatures. Evidently at least one of them had been sneaking around the farmlands for days.

Gwyrtha was happy to give him some energy. He reached through the bond to tap into her vast reserves and it didn't take much.

His eyes widened immediately and he felt like he could stay awake for another day without sleeping. What a handy thing it was, being bonded to a rogue horse.

Justan, Fist said. The ogre's thoughts were pensive. *Why did you tell her?*

Hmm? Who?

Miss Nala. You told her about Tamboor's family, I think.

Oh, you overheard that? Justan winced.

No, but I understand now. Miss Nala kissed my cheek. And she does not u-!

What?

The side! Fist shouted. The ogre was already running. *The corner of the house! Squirrel saw!*

Justan jumped to his feet.

Fist's thoughts were punctuated by a sharp spike of panic. *There it is!*

Justan ran around to the side of the house just in time to see Fist thrust his massive arm inside the open window to the girl's bedroom. How had it been opened? The windows had been secured and Justan knew that the children wouldn't have opened it after what had happened the night before.

Fist grunted and Justan knew that the ogre had grasped what he was looking for. He pulled and whatever he had grabbed onto resisted, but Fist's strong fingers weren't letting go. Justan could hear something overturn in the house and the children started screaming.

Fist strained and the sound of breaking glass accompanied his roar as he ripped a struggling form from within the house. He had whatever it was by the base of a long tail and Justan caught a glimpse of scales and claws before it turned on the ogre that held it.

The creature screeched and slashed at Fist with long claws on its hands and feet, tearing deep gashes in his flesh. He wrestled with it for a moment but it continued to thrash and the wounds were deep.

"Toss it to the side so I can shoot it!" Justan yelled. He had an arrow notched and ready. Ma'am was eager to fire.

Fist drew back the arm holding the beast and bellowed. It turned and dug its claws into his arm, but the force of the ogre's mighty throw ripped it free and the creature flew away with a speed that should have crumpled the beast to the ground. But somehow, it twisted its body in mid air and rolled as it hit to absorb the impact.

Gwyrtha! It is here! Justan shouted and drew back the bow as the creature rose to its feet and hissed. Seeing the creature fully in the light of the lamps for the first time, Justan froze in place. It was a lithe female figure with large reptilian eyes, two slits for a nose, and a mouth full of razor-like teeth. This was the creature that had roamed Ewzad Vriil's dungeons killing everyone in its path. This was the creature that had haunted the dark corridors of Justan's mind ever since.

Despite his terror at seeing its visage once again, one thought came clearly to his mind. This was all his fault. As he had feared the night before, Ewzad Vriil must have sent this creature after him.

"Fist!" Miss Nala's voice came from the window. "Fist, are you alright?"

Her worried voice shook Justan from his fear. He looked back at Miss Nala and yelled, "Get away from the window and stay in the house!"

"*Shoot it!*" Fist shouted, both aloud and through the bond.

He focused his arrow back on the creature, but before Justan could fire, she was on the move. She ran towards Fist, her eyes wide, her expression gleeful. She leapt up at him, claws extended.

Justan wasn't going to let her strike. There was a blur from the treeline and just as he released the arrow, the creature was hit mid-air with a flying tackle from another beast. This one wore a sword across its back.

The two raptoids hit the ground in a tangle of limbs and claws and the arrow ripped through the air where they had been, blasting into a stack of hay. Deathclaw and Talon screeched and hissed at each other as they rolled about slashing and biting. His heavier weight was an advantage in this sort of fight, but the sword strapped across his back hampered his movements.

Deathclaw wasn't sure why he had stopped Talon from striking the large wounded beast that protected the humans. Perhaps it was eagerness at finally having her in his sights, or perhaps he was just tired of coming across the corpses left behind in the wake of her insanity. In either case, the move had been foolish.

The best thing would have been to wait until she had killed the beast and the human archer before attacking. That way, she may have been wounded and easier to kill. As it was, he now had an enraged Talon attacking him at close quarters where he could not reach the sword and two more enemies at his back that would not know he wasn't after them. And by the sound the arrow had made as it passed mere inches from his body, the archer had magic.

Deathclaw knew that he had to end this quickly and escape or he could end up dying before accomplishing his task. Killing Talon was what really mattered. Once that was done, it didn't matter if he was alive or dead.

Talon bit into his shoulder and he gripped her throat with one hand. The claw on his thumb pierced her neck as he pushed her away far enough to get one leg up between them. He planted his foot on her chest. She clawed at him, scoring deep gouges in his skin, but he ignored the pain and with a heave, shoved her away before rolling and leaping to his feet.

He drew Star from its sheath. The blade sparkled with energy. This was the time of night when it was at its peak power. Talon launched herself at him and Deathclaw stepped aside, swinging the sword at her as she passed by. The tip sliced across her back. Flames spewed from the cut with a heat so intense that it left glowing embers behind.

Talon arched her back and screeched in pain at the burning wound, but still found a way to dodge his next strike. She then came at him, but their battle was interrupted by the bellow of the large wounded beast. It swung an enormous fist that Deathclaw had to fall to the ground to avoid.

Talon darted forward. The beast launched a mighty kick that caught her in the midsection. The blow sent her tumbling across the yard until she was stopped by a fencepost that cracked with the impact.

Deathclaw rolled to his feet. Talon was his only target, but if the beast would not back down, he would have to kill it as well. He tried to catch the beast's eyes and pointed to Talon with a chirp of explanation, showing that he was there to fight her, but the beast was not paying attention. Its face was full of rage.

It swung another punch and Deathclaw had no choice but to strike back. He dodged to the side and sent his tail barb out into the beast's thigh, tearing through enough muscle to slow it down. The beast roared in pain. Talon, despite what Deathclaw knew had to be multiple broken ribs, hissed in delight at his attack and leapt onto the beast. It staggered backwards.

She dug in with her rear claws, ripping deep wounds into its chest and side. The beast, already weakened from loss of blood, fell to its knees. She gave a cry of triumph and raised a claw for what Deathclaw knew would be a fatal slash at its jugular, but the beast grabbed her by the neck and lifted her in the air over its head.

She tore into its arm and Deathclaw saw an opening. He drew back his sword, but before he could strike, the arrow hit her.

Fist, I cannot get a good shot, move out of the way! The ogre, his rage broken by the enormity of his wounds, finally registered his frantic mental shouts. Fist gripped the creature by the neck and lifted her up in the air, giving Justan the look he needed. Ma'am thrummed with power as he let fly.

The arrow caught the creature in the side. The force of the shot ripped her from Fist's grasp. She hurtled through the air in a spray of blood to crash into the side of the barn.

The male creature hissed at the sound of the impact and Justan drew another arrow. It sheathed the sword and turned towards him, raising its hands palm out in a pleading manner. It started backing away, but Justan was not about to let it escape. He did not know why it had chosen to strike at the other creature, but it had attacked Fist and that was all he needed to know.

There was movement at the side of the barn and to Justan's surprise, the creature he had thought dead was stumbling towards the woods. He changed targets and fired again, but she took on a sudden burst of speed and the arrow blasted through the air just behind her, exploding into the dirt several yards away.

The male creature drew his sword and ran after her. Justan pulled another arrow but heard a thud behind him. Fist was face down in the dirt.

"Fist!" Justan reached the ogre and turned him onto his back. Squirrel leapt down from the roof and ran around the both of them chattering in concern.

"I am okay," Fist mumbled and tried to sit up, but Justan pushed him back down. The damage was severe. He had known it before, but hadn't been able to do anything about it during the thick of the battle. Through the blood and tattered cloth, Justan saw lacerations on the ogre's chest so deep that whiteness of rib bone was exposed.

"Stay there! Don't do anything. I told Gwyrtha. Qyxal and Master Coal are on their way here." Justan dove into the bond to inspect the damage.

"Are they gone?" Fist asked. His voice was faint.

Don't talk aloud. Save your strength. Just breathe, Justan sent. It was even worse from the inside. The ogre's blood supply was dangerously low and more was bleeding out of him every second. Fist was on the verge of death. *They are gone, but we will go after them as soon as Qyxal heals you up.*

Tell Miss Nala that I am sorry about the shirt. Fist tried to lift his head to look at the damage, but he had grown too weak. *Tell Becca to take money from my pay for her to make anoth . . .*

Fist's thoughts faded and Justan shouted, "*Fist! Stay awake!*"

The ogre stirred in response and Justan called out to Gwyrtha. She and Qyxal were close and Master Coal and Samson were not far behind, but Justan didn't think Fist had that long. He had no choice but to try to heal him alone.

Tired. Fist said even though Justan could tell his heart was racing. *Can I sleep?*

No-no! Stay awake just a little while longer. Justan pulled energy from Gwyrtha and channeled it to the ogre while he paused frantically. The damage was so extensive. Where should he start?

Fist's eyes opened wider with the increase of energy. *Can not see good. Hi Squirrel.*

Justan ignored Squirrel's panicked chattering and focused in on the major arteries that had been damaged. As he had watched Qyxal do in the past, he used water and air to hold the arteries shut while he manipulated the miniscule amount of earth magic he had to stitch the severed vessels together. It was intricate work, but when he released the blood flow, the wounds stayed closed. He then fed energy to Fist's bones, getting them to work harder at making the blood the ogre needed while he started working on the smaller vessels.

That feels funny, Fist remarked. His thoughts were muddled. *I-am . . . uh, I dying?*

No, Justan said, concentrating on his work. It was too difficult. The blood was leaving his body faster than he could repair him. *You will be fine. Tell Squirrel that I am fixing you.* The animal was chattering madly and pulling on his shirt.

Squirrel. Justan is fixinged me.

Justan finished the last major vessel, but his work on one of the arteries was leaking and he had to go back to it. If only he had been able to practice this work instead of just observing it. He wasn't fast enough.

Then he felt a hand on his shoulder and to his relief, Qyxal knelt beside him. The elf immediately took over the healing and Justan watched with intense focus as his friend set in with practiced ease, healing large areas of damaged flesh at once.

"Thank you so much." Justan said, his emotions bubbling over with gratitude. He had come so close to losing Fist and it was all his fault. "I-I wasn't good enough. I . . ."

"It is okay, Justan." Qyxal said, not bothering to use his proper title this time. He didn't look up, remaining focused on his work. "You showed good presence of mind. Fixing the arteries first was the right choice. If you hadn't, I would have been too late. As it is, the injuries are severe and with the blood loss, some of this will be painful. Fist, I am going to make you sleep now. When you wake up, you will feel much better, okay?"

"Yes, but Justan!" The ogre reached out and grabbed his arm. *Protect the children and Miss Nala.*

"I will," Justan said, but Fist was already unconscious. He reached down and gently pried the ogre's bloody fingers free from his leg. Justan grabbed his bow and stood.

"You should observe this," Qyxal said. "I didn't want to say this while Fist was awake, but these injuries are near the boundaries of my ability. This is going to be difficult."

"I know I should, but-."

The sound of hoof beats interrupted him as Master Coal arrived on Samson. There were a half dozen armed men right behind him on horses of their own. The wizard dismounted as he spoke to Justan.

"Are the creatures gone? Is everyone alright?"

"The two that we saw are gone, but Fist is badly hurt," Justan said.

"Qyxal, is he stable?" Master Coal strode to the elf and looked down at the blood-soaked ogre, his eyes filled with concern.

"Some of this is tricky if you would like to help," Qyxal said. The elf was deep into his work and the strain was evident in his voice.

Master Coal knelt beside him and raised his hands out over the ogre, but looked back to Justan who had already leapt onto Gwyrtha's back. "Where are you going, Edge?"

"She can't have gone far with that wound. Tell your men to search around and make sure that there are not more of the creatures," Justan said and willed Gwyrtha forward. *Find her.* The rogue horse eagerly complied, racing in the direction the creatures had gone. She wanted to take a bite out of the creature that hurt Fist herself. "I am going to kill that thing."

He had to. That thing needed to die. Something that would do the things that creature had done . . . He had to kill it. Then as soon as Fist was better, they would leave so that the farmers would no longer be in danger. He didn't know where they would go next, but now was not the time to worry about that. Now was the time to hunt.

The creatures couldn't hide their tracks this time. Gwyrtha had a clear trail of blood to follow. They didn't have far to go either.

A short way into the woods, they came to the top of a rise. Below them was a small clearing and Justan could see the two creatures doing battle. The fight wasn't going well for the injured one. She had several small glowing wounds from the magic sword.

It looked as though the creature with the sword intended to slay her. Even through the darkness Justan could see that she was horrifically damaged. There was a gaping wound where his arrow had hit her in the side. Yet she must have had a remarkable healing ability because she was no longer bleeding and somehow still managed to dodge the other creature's attacks. It was clear to Justan that the male creature was not trained with the sword.

Justan watched as she ducked a swipe of the blade. The moment the strike passed by, she twisted and sent out her tail with the wicked spike on the end. In an amazing show of dexterity, the male twirled around, knocking her tail aside with his own, and thrust out with the sword.

This time his strike was true. The shimmering blade pierced her belly just below the place where Justan's arrow had struck. Flames erupted from the wound, some even spouting from within the hole Justan's arrow had left.

She screeched and collapsed to the ground, chirping and hissing at the male in a pleading manner. The male creature took a step back and cocked his head before replying with a regretful sounding chirp of his own. He drew back his sword for a finishing strike.

Justan willed Gwyrtha forward. Once the female creature was dead, he couldn't let the male get away. He drew his swords.

The sky! Gwyrtha sent in warning.

Justan looked up just in time to see an enormous winged shadow descend from the night sky. It struck the ground in front of the female creature and as it touched the earth a wave of heat emanated from it with such force that it knocked Justan off of Gwyrtha's back. A nearby tree and the forest floor around the beast burst into flames. The male creature was thrown back several yards.

The female creature squealed as the beast scooped her up in one clawed hand and took off back into the sky. Once it cleared the trees, the beast banked and soared to the east. Justan watched its departure in stunned silence as the female creature's terrified screeches faded into the night.

He rose to his feet and checked to make sure Gwyrtha was okay. Despite some singed patches of hair, she was uninjured. He looked back into the clearing and in the light of the burning tree, saw the solitary remaining creature rise and look to the sky in the direction she had been taken. It let out a horrible keening sound.

A sudden lance of pain shot through Justan's skull. He fell to his knees, clutching his head in his hands. A scream nearly pierced his lips and an intense feeling of emptiness flooded his mind. It was over. She was dead. What was his purpose now? What was left? He was alone.

The thoughts were cut off as Gwyrtha struck the male creature, throwing it to the ground. She stood over it. Her claws dug in, cracking its ribs under her weight. The creature made no move to defend itself. Why bother? It, no, *he* was ready for death. Gwyrtha's maw full of teeth descended on his head, eager to oblige.

"*Gwyrtha stop!*" Justan cried out and forced his body to stand despite the pounding in his head. *Do not kill him.*

Why?

Just . . . don't. It was hard to think straight.

With reluctance, Gwyrtha backed off of the creature. It stayed on the ground for a moment, blinking its eyes in confusion. Then it sat up and regarded the two of them warily.

"You are not alone." Justan stumbled towards the creature and reached out. He absently noted that his hand was shaking. "I am Justan."

It cocked its head, sizing him up like a large puzzle. No human had ever approached it so. It did not take his hand but stood and took a few steps back. Why was there no fear in the human archer's eyes?

"Please," Justan said and extended his arm once again. With difficulty, he formed a picture of what he wanted it to do and sent it through the bond. He took another step forward. *Take my hand.*

Its clawed fingers reached tentatively towards his, but stopped a few inches short. A hiss escaped its mouth and it turned to run.

"Wait!" he shouted.

The creature only made it a few steps away, before stiffening and falling to the ground. It was then that Justan registered the sounds around him as multiple men on horses entered the clearing. The headache had been so intense, he hadn't heard them coming.

Master Coal leapt from Samson's back and strode over to Justan. As he approached, the creature on the ground screeched and struggled against the threads of air that bound it. The loneliness leeching through the bond turned to fear. Something about Master Coal terrified it.

"Master, please let it go." Justan's words were slurred. For some reason the pain wasn't going away this time. It had been over quickly in the past. Why wasn't it going away?

"But it is . . . Edge are you alright?" Coal looked. He stepped forward and opened Justan's eyes wider with thumbs and forefingers. "Did you take a blow to the head?"

"No, or I don't think so. My head hurts though."

"We need to find out the reason for the attack," the wizard said. "Why do you want me to let it go? What if it comes back with others?"

"He didn't have anything to do with the attack," Justan explained, his head still pounding. "He was only here to hunt the other creature down."

"But . . .?" Master Coal's eyes widened in understanding. He turned back to look at the struggling creature and Justan knew that the wizard had switched to spirit sight.

"How do you know?" Samson asked.

"His name is Deathclaw," Justan said, his head still pounding. "We've just bonded."

Chapter Twenty Eight

Justan awoke in his room at the lodge. At least he thought it was his room. The bed felt strange. The oddness of the sensation wiped the vestiges of sleep from his mind. Actually, it wasn't that the bed felt strange, it was more like there was too much of it. He sat up and tried to figure out how there could be too much bed.

He looked around and saw that he was indeed in his room at the lodge. He must have slept through the morning hours. His eyes ached as he noted the bright sunlight streaming through the one small window. The bed wasn't any different than it had always been. Instead, his perceptions of the bed had changed. He could feel every detail of the fabrics against his skin.

That wasn't all. The rest of his senses were intensified as well. He could smell the food cooking in the kitchens below: baked Honstule and eggs with some of Becca's famous bread. He could hear the excited chatter of women in the kitchen. All the intense sensations flooded his mind and that feeling of disorientation came back again.

Justan knew that these changes had something to do with the intense headache that had come on after bonding with Deathclaw. Something about that headache had worried Master Coal so much that he had put him to sleep. Justan shook his head. At least the headache was gone now.

He closed his eyes and checked on Fist. He felt a rush of relief. The ogre was alive and somewhere nearby. He was asleep, probably in his own room downstairs. Gwyrtha was also asleep, somewhere in the vicinity of the stables.

His new bond with Deathclaw had a different feel than the

others. He couldn't get an immediate grasp of Deathclaw's location. Had Master Coal been right the night before? Had his new bonded fled far away?

Justan switched to spirit sight and reached deep inside himself until he found the place where their bond began. It was somehow swollen and raw, almost like a newly healed wound. He felt around the edges of the bond and immediately felt a rush of agony pour through from the other side. Deathclaw was in pain; awful, searing pain.

Justan didn't hesitate. He pushed his thoughts through their connection until his mind was flooded with the creature's thoughts.

Deathclaw was in the woods somewhere not far south of the farms. He had burrowed deep into the leaves under a large bushy tree in an attempt to evade any humans that followed. He lay there without movement to betray his location, but his head was afire. It was like his brains were boiling in his skull.

The pain had started the moment Talon had been carried away and it had gotten worse the further he had fled from the humans. It had to be the wizard. That wizard had done something to him. He was sure of it. First it used a spell to bind him that he couldn't break and then it had planted this pain inside his mind. He should have killed the wizard the moment it released him from its spell. He had thought about it, but something had stopped him. Why?

Justan took Deathclaw's thoughts in. His immediate instinct was to dart in and ease the pain of his new bonded, but he did not quite know how to approach him. Such confusion churned within its-, no, *his* mind. The raptoid, or at least that was how he thought of himself, was quite intelligent, but he was still a creature. Would he take offense if Justan entered his mind without permission? Could he create a rift between them that could be impossible to heal?

He had to explain to Deathclaw what the bond was and what their connection meant. Only then could he ask permission and ease the raptoid's pain. But how should he go about introducing himself?

Um . . . Hello?

Deathclaw hissed. It took all his concentration not to move and risk giving away his position in the leaves. He had heard no approach.

He couldn't smell any humans. Surely one couldn't have snuck up on him without a trace of his presence. Was the burning in his head that great of a distraction?

My name is Justan.

Deathclaw still made no movements. He had heard this voice before, in the night, after Talon had been taken. Where was this human?

It is okay. I am a friend.

Friend? He did not know the meaning of this human word.

A friend is someone who cares for you. Justan sent. *We are bonded.*

How did it know his question? Deathclaw made the sudden realization that the voice was not coming from the forest above, but from inside his own head. The voice rang out from somewhere beyond the source of the boiling pain deep within his mind.

I am not causing the pain. Justan assured, hoping he wasn't wrong. *But I can help it stop.* Again, he hoped that he wasn't wrong. He began to pull up thoughts and images to explain to Deathclaw what the bond meant and how he could help.

Get out of me!

Justan was not prepared for the mental onslaught of the raptoid's fury. It tore at him with frightening intensity. He fled back through the bond and nearly fell out of the bed, gasping and sweating.

Justan heard a shuffling sound in the hallway outside his room and a slight squeak as the doorknob slowly turned. He pulled up the blankets and turned to see the door open. Master Coal peeked his head in. The intensity of the aroma that came through the doorway started Justan's mouth watering. When the wizard saw that he was up, a slight smile touched his face.

"Ah, it is good to see that you are awake. May I come in?"

"Of course, Master Coal." Justan wondered why the wizard seemed so hesitant.

Coal walked in and shut the door behind him. He carried a steaming plate filled with the foods Justan had smelled cooking below.

"I was sent to see if you would be able to eat something."

Justan snatched the plate from his hands. "Yes, thank you!"

"Uh, yes, well Becca was quite insistent. So . . . how do you feel this morning? Any lingering effects from last night?"

"Well . . ." Justan paused around a bite of food. "Actually, I do feel pretty odd this morning. This food is amazing!" The flavors of the food were alive in his mouth. They were intensified, not too strong, but complex. He tasted things in the food, he had never noticed before. He could pick out the individual spices Becca had used.

"Mind if I take a look at you?"

At Justan's nod, Master Coal put his hands to either side of Justan's head. His magic probed for a moment before he released Justan and stood back. He grabbed the chair by the small desk and swiveled it to face Justan before sitting down. He watched Justan eat for a moment before speaking again.

"Headache gone?"

"Yeah, but," Justan said, then took another bite. "Everything else feels strange."

"What do you mean?" Master Coal asked, his gaze intense.

Between swallows Justan explained the changes to his senses.

"I expected something like this. Headaches aren't all that uncommon among bonding wizards. Some days there can be a great deal of mental stress communicating with all of your bonded and keeping to your own tasks at the same time," Master Coal explained. "When the bond is first triggered, the pain can be excruciating. I figured that to be the source of the pain you were undergoing last night, but once I got a better look at you, I knew that this was different."

"In what way?"

"The bond was changing you," Master Coal said.

"But isn't that what it always does?" Justan asked. "When I bonded with Gwyrtha, I had more stamina and better control over my body. With Fist, I became stronger and started developing muscle in ways I was never able to before."

"You are right. As we have discussed before: when we bond, the magic changes us physically as well as mentally. However, last night I looked into your body and saw changes different than I have seen before. Your bonding with this beast-."

"Deathclaw," Justan corrected.

The master nodded apologetically. "Right, Deathclaw. Your bonding with him . . . What I saw was a concentration of spirit magic shifting the very tissues of your brain."

Justan blanched. "B-but the changes that come from bonding are always good, right? That's what you told me. The bond wouldn't change me in a negative way, would it?" The thought of his brain being altered was terrifying. He had always relied on his wits as his main weapon. What if he had lost intelligence from bonding with the wild creature? Would he even be able to tell?

"I don't think so, Edge. All my past experiences show only positive changes or improvements from the bond. Physically, at least. But bonding doesn't always go well."

"Master, Deathclaw is still in pain, he has a headache as bad as the one I went through but his hasn't stopped." Justan winced. "He is still suffering as we speak."

"Did you try to heal him?" Coal asked.

"Well, I wanted to heal him," Justan said, but seeing the look concern on Master Coal's face added, "but I asked for permission first."

"And how did he respond?"

"He . . . did not like that I was speaking to him from within his mind, he doesn't understand. So I let him be."

"He did not like it, hmm? Did he attack you?" Coal asked.

"Well . . . he-. Wait," Justan said. "You think my bond with him is dangerous."

The master slouched in the small chair and sighed. "Perhaps. I mean, it could end well and you could end up with an invaluable member of your bonded family, or . . . it could end very, very badly I'm afraid. That is what I want to talk to you about today."

"But how could it end up badly?" Justan said slowly. He sat back with his arms folded. "You just taught me that our mental connections with our bonded keep us from misunderstanding each other."

"Even if they understand you, Edge, they are still individuals. They have minds of their own and their own agendas. They may not want to be bonded to you. They may not like you. There have even been bonded that killed their bonding wizard."

"You are saying that Deathclaw could try to hurt me?" Though Justan didn't want to believe that was possible, the ferocity of Deathclaw's mental attack was still fresh in his mind. "He is wild and all, but he isn't malicious."

"I do not presume to know his intentions. I just want you to be aware of the dangers. You must be cautious with him. He is a wild creature. There are two quite uncomfortable ways this bonding could go." The master thought for a moment. "I think that for our lesson today I will give you two specific examples of situations very similar to yours with Deathclaw. Perhaps then you will understand what I mean."

"Okay."

"But first, why don't you get some clothes on?" The master smiled.

"Oh. Right, I'm not exactly dressed for company, am I?" His face turned red.

Master Coal stood. "I will tell Becca that you enjoyed the meal. Meet me in the study and we will continue this discussion."

Justan looked down at the plate with disappointment. He hadn't realized it was empty.

Chapter Twenty Nine

Master Coal settled into the high-backed chair in his study and peered at the student in the chair across from him over steepled fingers. The look the wizard gave Justan was both piercing and thoughtful. A few moments passed before he spoke.

"I will start by telling you about my first bonded, Honstule."

Justan leaned forward, his interest piqued. There had been so much talk of Honstule, but he still knew little about him.

Master Coal smiled slightly as he continued. "I know that you have heard many wonderful things about Old Honstule, but it was not always that way. We had quite a rough start. Like Deathclaw, Honstule was a wild beast when we bonded."

Justan was taken aback. He had always pictured Honstule as some wizened old man. "What was he?"

"Honstule was a goblin."

"A goblin?" Justan suppressed an internal shiver. The idea of being bonded to such a foul little beast was frightening.

Master Coal ignored the look on Justan's face and continued, "I was brought to the Mage School when I was twelve, but I didn't know about my bonding magic until a few years later. I had just become an apprentice at the time. My master was a healing specialist and had taken me with him to the Battle Academy for testing week. It was quite an exciting trip, actually. Then on the way back, we were beset by goblins."

"The same thing happened to me along that road," Justan said.

"Yes, well there were a dozen or so of them. The guards and the mages made short work of the nasty little things and my master took me with him to . . . dispatch any that were in agony. He called it a mercy.

"We came across one with a severed spine. It was squealing and feebly trying to pull its way through the grass. My master told me to take my dagger and end its suffering. I did so. It was the first time I had killed a creature. I felt quite horrible about it."

Master Coal's face twisted at the memory and Justan thought back to the first creature he had killed. It was at the beginning of the goblin attack on his own caravan to the Mage School. Justan hadn't felt bad at all, just exhilarated and worried about the rest of the attacking creatures. He hadn't even given it much thought. Now the first man he had killed, Rudfen Groaz, Justan would never forget how sick he had felt after that.

"Then we came upon another one," Master Coal continued. "It was Honstule. He hadn't been hurt during the battle, but while trying to run away he stepped in a gopher hole and had broken his leg. He was scampering backwards through the grass, his eyes glazed with fear. When I stood over him with my knife, he stared at me, keening loudly, pleading for his life in the goblin tongue. My eyes locked upon his eyes and . . . it happened. The bond came and Honstule's wild terror filled my mind.

"My master commanded me to kill the creature, but I couldn't do it. I don't know how I kept my composure with Honstule's scared and primitive thoughts attacking me, but I pled with my master to let me heal it and send it on its way. I argued that a single human kindness could change this creature. Perhaps it would change its attitude towards humans in the future. He laughed at my naiveté, but finally relented. He said I placed too much trust in such a nasty little thing.

"He seemed to be right too. I healed Honstule's leg and tried to show him kindness, telling him that it would be okay. The moment I finished, the mean little thing swiped at me and ran off through the grass. I could hear his thoughts as he ran. Honstule was laughing at my stupidity. If he ever came upon me again, he fully intended to kill me."

"So what did you do?" Justan asked.

"Nothing. I didn't know what to do. I didn't know what the bond was or how to use it. Honstule's thoughts were vicious and foreign and I was too unsettled by the experience to speak with my master about it. Besides, he was a hard man, not the sort one confided in. We traveled on to the Mage School and the further away we were from Honstule, the quieter his thoughts were until all that was left was the vague impression that he was still alive and to the northeast of the school.

"It was a year before I saw him again. He hid outside of the school and called to me from the bond. I stood atop the wall and stared down at him."

"Had he changed?"

"Oh, he was as mean spirited as ever, but the bond had changed him in other ways. He was larger, stronger, and much much smarter than before. He wanted to know more about the bond. He was tired of my constant presence in the corner of his mind and wanted me gone. I could tell from his thoughts that there were other goblins hiding in the trees around him. He intended to ambush me when I came out to meet him. So I declined.

"I told him that I didn't like him in my mind either. I didn't know anything about the bond at the time. I had searched through the library and could not find a single book about the phenomenon."

"Why?" Justan asked. He still didn't understand why the Mage School would willfully ignore such an important facet of magic. "Why are there no books about it? You keep suggesting that bonding magic has a long history in the world, yet so few know about it."

"I know it's frustrating, Edge, but once again we are going to have to leave that story for another lesson. Suffice it to say that I was just as stumped as Honstule about the whole situation. I had to threaten to call the guards before he finally left and went back to his hills. I began keeping track of him after that.

"Sometimes at night I would lay in bed and reach out to him through the bond. Sometimes I just monitored his thoughts. Sometimes I spoke with him. He was always mean and bitter about it, but after a while I knew that he began to look forward to those times.

"You see, he used the intelligence and strength he had gained through his bond with me to wrest control over the goblin tribes in his area. He had become chief over hundreds of the creatures and had all the power a goblin could have, but it wasn't enough. He grew weary of the company of his own kind. Their stupidity irritated and angered him. I was the only one he could speak to that understood his thoughts.

"For me it was different. I had this connection with him that I couldn't explain or get rid of and his existence was so very different from mine that I grew fascinated with him. I started to write a detailed paper on goblinoids, using his experiences as research.

"Well, a few years passed. Then I bonded again. His name was Neal." The master's face lightened up as he spoke. "He was an academy graduate sent to join the guards at the Mage School. He was a good man, strong, kind, though a bit dimwitted when we first bonded. He also had a facial deformity that others often found quite disconcerting. He was lonely, but we became fast friends.

"It was at this time that the one other bonding wizard at the school discovered my powers. He took me under his wing and became my new master."

"Who?" Justan asked.

"Unfortunately, Edge, I cannot tell you. His existence is kept quite secret. Very few know about it and the reasons why are, again, part of a lesson for another day."

"I see," Justan grumped. He had come to accept that this was the way Master Coal worked, but waiting for knowledge didn't make much sense as far as he was concerned.

"At any rate, that was a great time for me. Not so much for Honstule. As I spent more time through the bond with Neal I had less inclination to communicate with the goblin. Why talk to a creature that had evil thoughts and spent most of the conversation ridiculing you when you had a dear friend you could chat with?"

"How did Honstule take it?"

"He grew angry that he had been replaced. I ignored him more and more and that was a mistake. Honstule began planning retaliation. That fall it came time once again for the Training School exams. Neal and I were part of the caravan. As we crossed the same spot where Honstule and I had bonded, we were attacked by an army of goblinoids.

"There must have been forty in all. Over a score of screaming goblins, a dozen gorcs and orcs and one giant. All of them were armed with weapons stolen from caravans over the years. Honstule himself rode in a harness strapped to the giant's shoulders, protected from attacks by its bulk. It was a huge beast, maybe twelve feet tall and twice as wide as Fist. It wore a patch over one eye where Honstule had defeated it in battle.

"I was stunned. I never expected Honstule to actually attack us. I thought that we had gotten past that. I wasn't aware just how jealous he had become. As they surrounded us, he yelled at me through the bond, telling me that I would be sorry. In anger, I responded that I was finished with him. I told him to leave and never return and we would spare their lives.

"Honstule howled and shouted out orders to his goblinoids. It was very well organized attack. The leader of our academy escort was killed right away as part of Honstule's attack strategy. It was designed to put the rest of the caravan in disarray so that he could get to the mages, but after the initial surprise, Neal took charge and rallied the remaining guards, while I and the other mages supported with attack spells and healing. Honstule's goblinoids were decimated. He soon had only a dozen of his fiercest warriors left and they were a hairsbreadth away from fleeing. Neal went after the giant, knowing that if he could take the beast down, the attackers would dissipate and Honstule could be captured."

Justan could see the battle unfolding in his mind: the flames, the shouting, the screams of the dying goblins. It reminded him of his own first battle in the plains. He found himself holding his breath as Master Coal described the fight between Neal and Honstule's giant.

"Neal was nimble and good with his spear. He was able to avoid the swings of the giant's enormous club and counter attack. Soon the beast was wounded in several places and bleeding badly. Honstule could see that the battle was lost. He was screaming at his few remaining forces to rally and help the giant, but they scattered and ran into the hills.

"It should have been over then. I was wondering what to do with Honstule once we had captured him. The giant had grown weary from loss of blood and Neal was ready for the finishing strike, but one of the young mages grew too eager. He sent out a lightning strike . . ."

Justan shook his head. He had been on the receiving end of one of those spells himself. Lightning strikes were dangerous to use in close battle. They traveled along the ground as they hit and could cover a large area depending on the moisture in the soil, taking down friend and foe alike.

Master Coal halted the tale momentarily. He cleared his throat and took a sip of tea. His voice was thick as he continued, "The bolt struck at the giant's feet right as Neal's spear pierced its heart. Neal fell as the shock hit him. The giant fell on top of him."

"Was he okay?" Justan asked, though the grief in his master's eyes told him the answer.

"As the giant fell, the spear was still stuck in its body. The butt of the spear stuck in Neal's ribcage and the force of the giant's fall crushed his chest. He was dead instantly and felt no pain. But I . . ."

Justan understood. It was Master Coal that felt the pain. He shuddered at the idea of Fist or Gwyrtha being killed.

"Edge, the death of a bonded is something I hope you never have to go through. The pain you feel when bonding happens again when your connection is severed, but that is nothing compared to the mental anguish. It is like a part of your soul is ripped from you. The loss is greater than the lost of a friend or loved one. They are part of you in a more personal way than anyone but another bonded could understand. And I . . . I was with him through the bond as he died. I had seen the strike coming and was shouting at him to run, when he was torn away from me. I saw his spirit pulled away from his mortal form. I reached out to him trying to stop it, but he flew beyond my grasp and disappeared. The pain hit and the loss . . . I screamed, Edge. I screamed my voice out, both aloud and through the bond. When my voice would no longer go on, I continued screaming through the bond. I injured my throat. I was unable to speak for days, not that I felt like speaking.

"Honstule took the brunt of my impotent rage and pain. I think in a way it shattered him. He broke free from the body of the giant and ran off sobbing, holding his head with one hand, clutching at his heart with the other. Honstule had never felt loss like that. Goblins have emotions, but they don't have lasting connections. Their relationships are fleeting and based out of mutual need instead of attachment. As twisted as our relationship was, I was his first and only friend. Neal was his first loss."

Master Coal leaned back in his chair, exhausted from the telling. "I was catatonic for the most part for the next several days. I barely remember anything about the rest of the trip. The tests concluded. I stayed in the wagon for most of the return trip. Then, just as the caravan was about to enter the Tinny Woods, the wagon came to a stop. I heard a shout and went to the door. Honstule was kneeling in the middle of the road, his face in the dirt. He pleaded to speak with me. When I got there, he was surrounded by the guards, their weapons at his throat. They wanted to kill him. Part of me wanted to let them.

"Honstule pleaded with me through the bond to forgive him. He told me that his original intent in attacking the caravan was not to kill Neal. The plan had been to ransack the caravan and scatter us. He wanted to scare me is all. He wanted revenge for being ignored. He wanted me to fear him and therefore listen to him. It had all backfired and ended in tragedy. He offered his life up to me as compensation for his crimes. His guilt was palpable."

Master Coal leaned forward. "This is the important part of what he gained from me through the bond. The strength and intelligence and extended life span were but a side effect. I believe that the emotional connection and ability to know right from wrong, to feel guilt was what he really needed."

"What did you do?" Justan asked.

"I wasn't able to forgive him. Not right away. We bound him and brought him back to the school with us. He spent a short time in a cell, while the council tried to figure out what to do with him. The council knew of my bonding magic and put me in charge of finding out how much he could be trusted. I eventually overcame my anger enough to start spending time with him through the bond. Finally he was allowed to be released and lived as a worker in the gardens. It wasn't an easy life for him, surrounded by humans and referred to as 'Coal's pet'. I had been named at the Bowl of Souls by then and most didn't understand my attachment to the goblin. He learned to ignore the others and focused on the work. He became fascinated by horticulture. He would spend all his time either in the library doing research or in the garden practicing his skills."

"So that's how he came to create the Honstule plant," Justan said.

"It is his crown achievement," Master Coal said. "He didn't finish his work until he was old and wizened. Goblins have a fairly short lifespan. They are adults by the age of ten. They live a rough life and most only live to be in their teens. As far as I can tell, Honstule died at the age of sixty. It was about ten years ago now."

"There is one more thing I don't understand," Justan said. "The bonding comes when there is a great need from both of those being bonded, right? So I can understand why Honstule needed you. He had a broken leg and was about to be killed. But . . . why did you need him? Goblins are weak and as you said, short lived. They are mean and nasty creatures. What did you have to gain?"

"It is a bit hard to explain and it didn't make any sense to me at all for a long while, but Honstule explained it to me himself one day just before he died. The answer makes complete sense looking back on it now. You see, I was a smart young man back in those days, but I was also far too open and trusting. I think Honstule called me 'gullible' when he explained it.

"My whole life I was taken advantage of by everyone because I was too willing to believe whatever I was told. I needed to learn cunning. I needed to learn to distrust people sometimes. Both of those qualities were something that Honstule had plenty of. And it worked too. Looking back, I realized that it was around the time of our bonding that I had a great epiphany. Many of the people I thought were my friends really weren't. I began to be able to pick those people out and was much happier as a result."

"I see," Justan said. He gained some comfort from the fact that two vastly different people such as Honstule and Master Coal could come together. "I am glad that at least it ended up well."

Master Coal frowned, seeming a bit perturbed by his response. "Yes, but after years and years of painful trials. This isn't always the case. That is where the second story I wanted to tell you comes in. It has to do with the rock giant, Charz."

"What does Charz have to do with bonding magic?"

"The Master who taught me about bonding magic told me the story of Charz long before I met the giant myself," Master Coal said. "It happened over a hundred years ago. Charz was imprisoned in an arena in far off Khalpany. He was kept there for large gladiator battles and he had become legendary. He was undefeated. Then one day a powerful bonding wizard came upon the arena. As he watched Charz fight, they bonded.

"The bonding wizard spoke with him afterward and the giant was miserable. He was fierce and wild and loved the fighting, but he hated being captive. The giant longed to be free. He wanted to roam the wilds and fight bigger and better creatures. That night, the wizard freed him."

"Just like that?" Justan asked.

"Well I'm sure it was complicated. I don't know how he was able to accomplish the feat. At any rate, they escaped the arena. The ruler of Khalpany was displeased and sent armies to retrieve his prized fighter. Charz defeated every force that was sent after them."

"So how did Charz get along with the wizard?" Justan asked.

"He liked having someone along that could heal him after injuries. He enjoyed the wizard's wit and the companionship of the wizard's other bonded. But he disliked being told what to do. He was always searching out fights. He put them in danger countless times. When the wizard tried to get him to stop, he ignored him. The wizard tried countless things to get him to stop. Finally Charz left the group in anger and went on a spree. He challenged every fighter or creature he could find, leaving dead and wounded in his wake. The wizard followed behind, healing those he could and making reparations when possible.

"But Charz went too far. He sought out a retired academy graduate, a named warrior known as Sir Slash. Slash had settled down near the Razbeck border and had become a fisherman. He had a pregnant wife and refused to fight. Charz goaded him by killing his horse. When that didn't work, he crushed Slash's house. Finally he attacked Slash's wife. Charz broke her arm before Slash finally agreed to go to battle.

"When the bonding wizard arrived, Slash was dead. His pregnant wife with the broken arm nearly lost the baby. Charz, who was gravely wounded was ecstatic over his triumph and demanded to be healed. The wizard realized that Charz was uncontrollable and too dangerous to be left free. But a bond is forever and he could not make himself kill him. Instead, he gave him an ultimatum. Either Charz gave up challenging people to fight, or he would imprison him again. Charz refused to change his ways.

"So his master used powerful earth magic to bind Charz's body to a nearby cave. The spell had provisions. As long as the rock giant stayed by the cave, he would heal from anything, but the further away he strayed from the cave, the weaker the healing magic would become. Also, there was a limit. If the giant wandered too far from the cave, he would collapse and be unable to move. The wizard told him that the spell would stay in place until he had a change of heart. Then he left Charz there and never returned."

"What a sad story," Justan said.

"Yes, it's sad. Do you see? Charz has been captive in his little territory for a hundred years and still he has not changed his ways. I myself tried for years to get him to reconcile with his bonding wizard. Some people will never change."

Justan knew what he was trying to say. Doubtless Master Coal expected the story to fill Justan with dread and temper his interactions with Deathclaw. But what Justan thought of wasn't the Charz he met in the forest; arrogant, angry, and evil. What came to mind as Master Coal finished his story was Charz as he last saw him on the bank of the river; lonely, weeping, and utterly defeated. Justan was determined not to let Deathclaw meet such an end.

Chapter Thirty

"Oh how I loathe him," the sultry voice said.

Arcon watched the wizard Ewzad Vriil pace back and forth at the balcony's edge while his Mistress' frustration echoed in his head. The mistress wanted Ewzad to set their plans in motion, but he was too busy waiting for his plaything to return. Hamford stood silently next to Arcon. They had been standing there since lunch, waiting for hours until the sun had set. The mistress hated being made to wait.

"Why am I stuck with this fool?" she snarled. Arcon tried not to have an opinion. The wizard and his mistress were always at odds it seemed and yet they still continued to work together. He did not understand why, but he didn't ask. Unwanted questions could lead to punishments.

"He should be back by now," Ewzad grumbled. "Yes-yes, he should. Still, closer, closer. He is coming I feel it. Why does he take so long?"

"I wish I could command you to push him over the edge," she added. *"It would be so easy."*

Arcon did not let his expression change, knowing that the wizard would notice. His mistress was wrong. It would not be easy. Ewzad did not trust him. Ewzad knew where his loyalties lied and watched him like a hawk. Even if he was lucky and somehow successfully pushed the wizard over the edge, Ewzad Vriil would reach out one of his writhing arms and cause Arcon's neck to grow and grow until it dangled long enough to grab onto and haul himself up. Then . . . Arcon repressed a shudder. Whatever the wizard decided, it would mean a grisly death for him.

"How little faith you have in me," his mistress sneered and yanked the pain centers of his mind. Arcon's knees nearly buckled and sweat popped out on his forehead but still he did not allow his expression to change.

No mistress, please, he replied trying to keep his tone even despite the searing pain, *I would do whatever you asked of me even if it meant my death.*

"Of course you would, my dear." She stroked the pleasure centers now and his knees nearly buckled again. "*But then why do you doubt me? Why doubt my wisdom? I would not send you to your death.*"

I know, mistress. He almost thought the words, "unless it served your purposes", but shoved the rebellious phrase down deep into his subconscious and locked it away before she could hear it. Instead, he thought, *You love me. You would not let me die.*

"Oh really?" Ewzad spat. He was talking to the mistress again. Arcon could tell. "You think I don't know this? The army will wait a moment longer. She is returning to me!"

I am your servant Mistress. Always, Arcon said. He spoke with his mind and not with his lips as Ewzad Vriil did. Arcon was puzzled by the wizard's eccentricities. Like Arcon, Ewzad had a moonrat eye embedded in his flesh. She would hear his thoughts, surely the wizard knew this. How could one so intelligent act so foolishly? It didn't matter who was around, the queen, nobles, soldiers, he always jabbered away, embarrassing himself in front of others.

"It is his pride, sweet Arcon," she said, her irritation like a knot in the back of his head. "*He cares not what others think. They are insignificant to him. His own vanity and desires are all he cares about. Nothing else.*"

He felt the urge to think, "So unlike you, mistress," but pushed the sarcastic thoughts back in his mind to lock away with the others. Arcon was getting better at controlling his thoughts. It wasn't easy. When he had first set out of the Tinny Woods with his mistress' gift inside him, he had been open with his frustrations. Weeks of constant punishments had trained his mind since then.

Arcon had finally found one small corner of his mind where she could not hear. He had learned to put all his rebellious thoughts there and sometimes, when she seemed preoccupied he would escape to that safe place. There he could brood, laugh, or scream in horror without her knowledge. But times like that were brief. The mistress was always monitoring him. He could not understand how she could listen to his thoughts, argue with Ewzad Vriil, and command an army of monsters all at once.

A sultry laugh echoed in his head. *"I am just that good, dear one."* This time he could not repress his shudder.

"Ah! Ah!" Ewzad shouted, leaning far over the balcony's edge, pointing one finger at the night sky. "He comes! I told you, they return! Yes!"

Ewzad backed out of the way and Arcon saw the enormous shadow coming. It blocked out the stars and then the red and black beast soared in through the open balcony to skid across the polished marble of Ewzad's greatroom. Its claws scrambled, knocking over chairs and a heavy wooden table, but it could not find purchase. As it slammed into the rear wall, its massive body gave off a blast of heat that set half the room to flame.

Arcon backed away, his arms raised to ward off the heat. The enormous beast must have been badly wounded. He could see a boiling trail of blood that followed it to the wall. There was a great hiss and a creature darted out from under of the beast's wings. It was a nightmare. Badly burnt, half covered with blistered and blackened scales, it screeched gleefully. Arcon saw its disturbingly female body arch in triumph and noted that its claws and teeth glistened with the same boiling blood the great beast had left behind.

"Kenn!" Hamford shouted, but the big man dared get no closer than Arcon had.

"Oohoo!" Ewzad shouted, clapping his hands and jumping up and down with joy.

The female creature's head whipped around at the sound of the wizard's voice. Its eyes narrowed. Then, so fast that Arcon could barely register its movement, the creature leapt at Ewzad Vriil.

A buzz filled the room and the creature froze in mid air, mere inches from the wizard. Its mouth was open, exposing razor sharp teeth, and both arms and legs were extended, claws ready to tear flesh. Ewzad did not seem fearful. He grinned eerily and extended a curving arm towards its face. One finger touched it right on its slitted nose.

"Boop!" Ewzad giggled. He leaned in and wrapped both arms around the creature in a snakelike hug. "There-there. Shhh, its okay, my dear Talon. You are home with me. Yes you are!"

Hamford rushed forward and tore a tapestry from the wall. He began beating at the flames. Arcon turned and reached out over the balcony with his magic, condensing the moisture in the air. He pulled the water into a great ball, brought it into the room, and dropped it onto the burning furniture. With a great hiss, most of the flames were extinguished. Hamford rushed to the great beast's side.

Ewzad Vriil stepped back from his embrace with the creature. The side of his face and his robes had become caked in clotting blood. The wizard frowned as he assessed the damage to his beloved Talon.

Arcon saw now that the creature's wounds were more garish than he had previously seen. There were deep slashes in several places along her body and a gaping hole in her abdomen. He could see through the hole to the other side. How was this hideous creature still alive?

"Oh my dear-dear Talon. This won't do. No-no-no," Ewzad clucked, peering into her wounds. "Very near death, aren't you? That won't do. That won't do at all. Hmmm." The wizard closed his eyes, pointed his hands at her and concentrated. His arms waved slightly back and forth while his fingers undulated. "I see. The wounds were cauterized."

Blackened dead flesh popped out of the wounds as they began to close. Dead skin fell to the floor in sheets as new skin grew to take its place. Ewzad snickered. Her claws, teeth, and tail spike grew ever so slightly longer. "You somehow got rid of the seed I planted inside you, didn't you sweetheart. Yes-yes, well that is over. You are mine once again."

The wizard left her there frozen in mid air. The door burst open and several guards entered with swords drawn. From the livery they wore, Arcon knew that these were some of Queen Elise's house guards, evidently raised by the ruckus. They saw the ashes and carnage and beasts and halted in their tracks. One brave man stepped forward.

"My Lord Protector . . . is everything alright?" the man said stupidly.

"And what took you so long, you foolish little men?" Ewzad griped, one finger pointed accusingly. This time his arm did not waver. "Were you hoping to arrive after I was dead? Hmm?"

The guard blanched. "No, my Lord Protector. We-we rushed here as soon as we were told of the commotion."

"Look at these foul beasts!" Ewzad said, gesturing to the frozen Talon and the red and black beast collapsed against the wall. "Were you going to come to my aid with but five men? No-no that would not do at all. Be gone and be glad I don't flay the skin off your bones!"

"Yes my Lord!" The guards turned to run.

"Wait, you fools!" Ewzad commanded. "Visit the kitchens on your way and have them send up a fattened pig from the stocks. And have it raw, yes, raw mind you!"

The guards bolted and Ewzad walked to the enormous red and black beast, who still lay unmoving. Heat no longer emanated from its skin. Hamford was tugging on its arm, calling out to it in concern. Ewzad nudged the large guard with his foot and Hamford slowly backed away.

"Kenn!" the wizard barked. He raised one hand and slowly made a fist. A wave of heat shot forth from the creature and it slowly stirred. It raised its head and Arcon saw that it was a demon. Two enormous horns grew from its head and its eyes glowed a smoldering yellow.

"M-MASTER," came a deep booming voice. The temperature rose a few degrees from its breath alone.

Ewzad winced at the heat. "My-my dear Kenn. You dare talk to me like that? In that form? While oh so much bigger than me? No-no that won't do. Come on now . . . Come along . . ."

To Arcon's astonishment, the great beast began to shrink. Its great form decreased to the size of a large man. The tail shriveled and disappeared into its body. The great horns shrunk down until they were but little nubs on its head.

"Master I hurt," it said and this time its voice was not so loud and horrible, but still gave Arcon a shiver. The wounds were obvious. Its abdomen had been clawed repeatedly until some of its innards had spilled, and its right arm had been torn and bitten to shreds.

"Oh, poor thing!" Ewzad cried and raised a serpentine arm. Its wounds closed and soon the beast stood healthy and invigorated.

"Thank you, Master."

"Ah dear Kenn, you served me well this time. You brought her! You brought my precious Talon home and I thank you." The wizard said sweetly. Then his visage darkened. "However, you brought her damaged. Some wounds were unavoidable, but she was nearly dead, yes, VERY nearly. So I ask you oh sweet Kenn. What happened to her?"

"It wasn't me, master. Well only a small part of it was, but that was after she awoke and started attacking me." The beast called Kenn looked at Hamford. "It was Hamford's demon, Master. It was fighting her as I arrived. And it carried a blazing sword."

Hamford's eyes widened. "Good lord."

"Oh!" Ewzad's hands sprang to his lips. "Oh! Oh! Oh! Kenn, dear Kenn you saw him? You saw him again?"

"Yes, Master."

"And you did not take him too?" There was an angry twist to his words.

"I could not. There were men nearby and your command had been to bring Talon back."

"Oh! I must have him. I must! You must go get him for me!"

"Not now!" the mistress said in Arcon's mind. "*The fool. We need this pet beast for the battle*." She must have spoken to the wizard too, because Ewzad wrinkled his nose in irritation.

"No-no, you foul creature. I am sending Kenn and that is final. We have enough beasts for the assault. Yes-yes, we will be fine!"

There was a hesitant knock at the door. The servants had arrived with the pig Ewzad had ordered. They laid it at his feet and backed out the door as quickly as they could. The pig must have weighed at least three hundred pounds, but with one swipe of Ewzad's hand, it fell in two.

He grasped one leg and effortlessly tossed the smaller rear half over to Kenn.

"Eat, dear Kenn. Yes, the healing will have taken much out of you. You need nourishment. Eat-eat, I wish you to leave tonight."

Kenn caught the heavy half of pork with one hand, hunger in his eyes. He tore one haunch loose and raised it to his mouth.

"Are you going to eat that raw?" Hamford asked.

"Raw?" Kenn laughed. It was a haunting, evil sound. He bit into the haunch and steam poured from his lips. Grease rolled down his chin and caught fire on his red-skinned chest. The smell of cooking pork filled the air. He chewed a couple times and swallowed. "Nothing I eat is raw anymore."

Ewzad giggled. He pulled the rest of the carcass over and dropped it in front of Talon. "Here you are, sweet-sweet thing. Your wounds were even greater. I can't have you starve, no-no I can't. Be good, now."

The wizard snapped his fingers and she dropped to the ground atop the half-pig. Talon whipped her head around, her eyes taking in the room. A hiss escaped her lips. Arcon and Hamford took a few steps back in alarm, but she simply tore into the pig rending it into pieces and occasionally tossing flesh into her mouth.

Ewzad gave her a loving smile. Arcon did not want to take his eyes off of Talon, afraid that the creature would not find the pig to be enough. He backed further away, making sure that Hamford was between the creature and himself.

Kenn had already demolished the one haunch and was tearing into the other. Flaming grease pooled on the floor around him. Arcon had missed dinner waiting for Kenn to return with the wizard's prize. The smell of fried pork would normally have made Arcon's stomach growl, but the sight of the two creatures' gorging just made him nauseous.

"Steel your stomach, my Arcon. You are no child. Ewzad Vriil stages this feast in part to frighten you," his mistress purred.

Ewzad tapped his foot. "Finish up, Kenn. I don't want you to lose that beautiful beast, no-no I don't."

Kenn swallowed. “Then I will leave, Master.”

“Before you go, head down to my dungeon and pick out a few of my sweet new babies to take with you. Whichever ones you like. This must be done quickly, yes? I do not want you to have as much trouble with this prize as you did with Talon. Hamford will show you the way.”

“Of course, Master.” Kenn continued to eat as he followed his brother to one of Ewzad’s secret passageways, leaving a trail of flaming oil in his wake.

“He has the beast take two more with him? The fool! The Fool! The ignorant fool. He weakens our force even more with his little distractions!” His mistress’ anger was so intense that Arcon’s vision blurred. He felt his nose begin to bleed as it sometimes did when she was in a rage. This often happened around the wizard. He hoped that there would not be permanent damage.

Ewzad scowled. “Enough of your prattle, woman! Silence yourself or I will punish you again! Yes I will!”

Arcon could feel his mistress glower, but she must have remained silent because Ewzad smirked with satisfaction. Arcon’s nose bled again, but it was worth it. Ewzad was the only person alive except perhaps the Dark Prophet himself that could do his mistress harm. Arcon heard her squeals of pain and outrage whenever this happened. But any pleasure he took from her punishments was shoved back to that safe little corner of his mind to be enjoyed later.

“Still, you are right. Yes indeed,” Ewzad said. “It is indeed time. Unleash our hordes. Yes-yes, tell my army to begin. Tell them Envakfeer says close the noose. Close it! It is time we started our conquest. Yes. The Dark Voice shall be pleased.”

“Finally.” Arcon felt her satisfaction in his mind and her presence lessened as she spread her focus out amongst her contacts in their army.

“Yes-yes, of course you are pleased. The army goes and plays while I have to sit here and pretend to be the loyal protector. Pff! Necessity-necessity. Always necessity. Elise had better give me that heir soon,” Ewzad mumbled and padded over to Talon. The creature had finished her play and was now simply devouring the bits of flesh she had torn from the carcass.

"Now you, my little beauty . . ." he crooned, petting her scaled head. Talon chirped and nuzzled his hand. All traces of her former rage towards the wizard were gone. "It doesn't do to have you defeated. No-no. We have some improvements to make, don't you think?"

Chapter Thirty One

Jhonate sat on the lowest pine bough perfectly balanced, her legs folded beneath her and her arms folded in front of her. Her eyes were closed as she breathed in the crisp air of the mountain winter. The cold pressed against her, bit at her face, and tried to invade her padded armor, but Jhonate was not chilled. She felt all, observed all, but her thoughts were turned inward. Inside her mind, a small figure prepared for battle.

There was a stirring at the edge of her thoughts. She heard the light crunch of the snow as someone walked closer. One of her comrades was approaching. It was that blond mage. Jhonate could smell the sweet flower water the girl brushed into her hair every morning. Jhonate was beginning to hate the smell of flowers.

Ever since the journey started, Faldon had insisted that she stay near Vannya and Wizard Locksher while the rest of the group did the real work. She had protested, but Faldon told her it was because she was their best fighter and he needed her to protect the magic users in case of attack. That was his excuse, but she knew the real reason. Though Faldon left it unsaid, it was Jhonate's job to make sure that the other students left the girl alone. She supposed that it was necessary. The girl was a distraction. When she was around, the intelligence of the other students dropped below trainee level. Jhonate had been forced to send each of the male students away at least once, Jobar several times. Vannya was no help. She flirted away any time the men came near.

It shouldn't have been so bad protecting the two. The wizard Locksher himself was pleasant to be around. He was highly intelligent and even somewhat knowledgeable about her people. But the girl was insufferable. She was so frail and dainty, constantly complaining about the hardy mountain bugs, the cold, the lack of showers, and her feet. Oh how Jhonate was tired of hearing about her poor little mage feet. Vannya would not have lasted a day in the wilds around Jhonate's home. She itched to be away from the girl, but above all else, Jhonate itched to be part of the action.

"What are you doing?" came Vannya's puzzled voice.

"I am training," she replied.

"Look's more like sleeping," Vannya remarked.

Jhonate kept her mind quiet and calm as a hawk waiting to strike, letting the irritating woman's words flow past her without effect. She said mildly, "That would explain my dreams of you slipping and falling on that face of yours."

"Why, I-!" She heard the mage stomp her little foot. "And what did I say to deserve that?"

Though she could not see it, Jhonate could sense the dropped jaw on the girl's little face. Only her vigilant training kept her mouth from curling into a smile. What did the girl expect? She had fired the first volley.

"Did I offend you?" Jhonate asked.

"Yes indeed!"

"Then move along, child, and leave me to my training."

"Child?" Vannya said. The sheer outrage in her voice nearly caused Jhonate to lose her composure again. Instead, she kept her eyes closed and breathed steady. Vannya on the other hand could not hold her feelings in check. "How much older than me are you? A year? Maybe?"

"Vannya, come, leave the daughter of Xedrion alone," Wizard Locksher said from several yards away. "Can't you see that she is training?"

Vannya huffed and sputtered a bit before saying, "No wonder Sir Edge had such a hard time with you as a trainer. Two weeks merely sharing a tent and I am ready to pull my hair out. I can't imagine a year." The girl then stomped away to join her master.

Jhonate's brow furrowed a bit at the mention of Justan, but just slightly. She was quite proud of herself. She had not let the girl distract her. She was still as calm as the cold mountain air around her. She hadn't even reached for her staff. There had been times during the last two weeks she had let the girl rile her up. Luckily for Vannya, Faldon had commanded her not to strike the girl.

Vannya seemed to resent the time that Jhonate had spent training Justan. She always brought him up in conversation, bragging about the time they defeated the orc captain, going on and on about the way Justan single handedly destroyed a giant golem that attacked the Mage School. Then she would bring out this letter that Justan had written her. Vannya never read it aloud, but often commented on how dear their friendship had been, and how Justan had said that he was looking forward to seeing her again.

It hadn't bothered Jhonate, of course. Justan may not have written her such a letter, but why should he? It was not as if a trainee should keep in constant contact with his trainer. Besides, she did not need a letter to know his esteem for her. After all, he had given her a parting gift, a plain silver ring with a thin line of gold around the edge. The ring didn't look to be all that valuable, but Faldon had told her that it was a precious family heirloom. Wearing it made her feel close to Justan and in an odd way protected, which was ridiculous because she . . . With a start, she realized that she was twisting the ring on her finger again. Jhonate fumed at her lack of concentration. She needed more training.

"Is something bothering you, daughter of Xedrion?" Poz, son of Weld asked. He and Jobar Da Org had just returned from scouting the road to Jack's Rest and the two men were on their way to talk to Faldon the Fierce.

"No," she said. Her thoughts were calm and collected. "I am merely preparing for the battles ahead."

"Then why do you look like you just bit into a lemon?" asked Jobar.

Her eyes flashed open and she reached for her staff. Faldon had given no commands about striking her fellow students. She hit the ground, soft as a cat and Jobar was already running. Fleeing was a futile gesture.

A short time later she received a short message on her message stone. Faldon wanted everyone assembled. Locksher, Vannya, and Poz were already there when Jhonate and her fellow students, Qenzic and Jobar arrived, the latter grumbling about the new knot on his head.

"So," Faldon said. "Poz has reported signs of battle all along the road to Jack's Rest. The interesting thing is it's all been cleaned up. No bodies or broken weapons. He found a large burn pile just off the road not too far ahead where all the corpses have been tossed."

"If the battle's been cleaned up, doesn't it mean that there are at least some villagers left alive?" Qenzic asked. "The goblinoid army hasn't exactly been cleaning up after itself in the other locations we've seen."

Jhonate hoped he was right. The first week of their journey into the mountains they had traveled from village to village to warn the people. Most of them already knew of the goblinoid army from the refugees who had been trickling in for weeks. The villages had been reinforcing their defenses, but once they learned that the Dremald soldiers were being recalled, leaving academy patrols sparse, villagers streamed out of the mountains in droves. Reneul was going to have a lot of new mouths to feed.

Once they had reached the higher elevations, signs of the goblinoid army were everywhere. They hadn't run into any enemy forces, but Faldon's group had encountered multiple empty villages and homesteads that had been razed to the ground. The invaders had left corpses and destruction in their wake. Unfortunately, their orders did not allow for them to take time to bury the dead.

"Qenzic has a point," Locksher said, but the wizard had an eyebrow raised, an expression that Jhonate had come to know meant that the wizard found something interesting. "These goblinoids are uncivilized to be sure, but large sprawling armies like the one we have been following have to clean up after themselves to a certain extent if only to avoid diseases. This is especially true if it is a major route for their supply lines. Poz, did you get close enough to see what was in the burn pile?"

"No, sir. It was right next to the main road and too exposed. I did not want to risk being seen." Poz didn't mention that he hadn't thought to do so, but the reddening of the cheeks on his freckled face told the story. Jhonate would have checked it out if she had been the one scouting ahead. Such attention to detail was important to their mission.

Locksher didn't chastise the student. The wizard never did. He left that to Faldon, which was one of the reasons that the academy students respected him. Locksher simply turned to Faldon and said, "If possible, I would like to check out this burn pile before we continue to Jack's Rest. It may help us know what we'll be facing."

Faldon nodded. The veteran leader had been relying more and more on the wizard's advice as the journey went. It would have irritated Jhonate, but the man had not steered them wrong. "Jobar, Qenzic, and I will scout ahead and make sure the road is clear of enemies. Once we signal, Poz and Jhonate will take Wizard Locksher and Mage Vannya to the burn pile."

"Yes sir," she said, pushing down the frustration that tried to bubble to the surface. Once again she was forced to take up the rear with the mage.

The group quickly dismantled their tents and the three scouts went on ahead. Poz and Jhonate hid their supplies for quick retrieval later. While they worked, Locksher busied himself quizzing Vannya on various deduction techniques. She did well enough, but as far as Jhonate was concerned, the mage's mind was little more than average.

A short time later, Jhonate received a badly handwritten message on her stone.

Road safe. Holding position.

Poz led them down to the road and they traveled to the spot where the corpses had been burned. Sure enough, Jhonate saw the heavy tracks of man and beast and the discoloration of blood under the snow that showed a battle had taken place there not too long ago. There was more evidence once they reached the burn pile.

"From the smell of it, that is giant spoor," Jhonate observed.

"You can't tell from the size of it?" Vannya smirked. Jhonate once again considered beating the girl.

"Vannya, look at this," Locksher said. The wizard was standing near the burn pile. "What can you see?"

The mage padded over to the wizard, the enchantment he had placed on her boots muffling the sound of her feet in the snow. Both of them used the spell. It was necessary to keep them from being a hindrance to the stealthy group. But for the hundredth time since starting, Jhonate shook her head in disgust at the spell. Such magic was cheating.

"Hmm, let's see." The mage tucked a lock of blond hair behind one perfect ear and crouched next to her master. "The pile is quite high there must be . . . thirty or so corpses in there." She stuck out a hand just over the pile. "It isn't smoking and there is no residual heat so it is fairly old, at least a couple days."

Jhonate had to admit that the girl wasn't completely vapid. She was right on with her assessment. Once a pile of corpses this size got burning, the fats and moisture in the tissues kept it smoldering for a long time.

"What else can you see?" Locksher prompted.

She crinkled her pert little nose. "Well, I see no pieces of metal, maybe some bone weapons. It looks like this is all from the goblinoid army but it is kind of hard to tell exactly because there are-."

"No skulls," Jhonate finished.

"Right." Locksher said. "Very good. Where are their heads? But I agree. From the bones and bits of burnt tissue that are left, there are no human bodies here. So what does that tell us?"

"Humans won," Poz said with a smile.

"It certainly looks that way," Locksher agreed.

Jhonate sent their findings to Faldon. The scouts moved ahead and Jhonate led the rest of the group through the trees parallel to the road. Faldon, Qenzic, and Jobar met up with them just before they reached the village. There were no signs of goblinoid forces around. But there was quite a bit of noise coming from the village ahead.

Fortress was the word that came to Jhonate's mind as Jack's Rest came into view. The forest had been cleared for a hundred yards around the village and it was surrounded by high walls made of thick logs. The work had been done with the practiced hands of war veterans, she could tell. There were no gaps between the logs and they had been cut smooth to prevent easy hand holds for invading forces. A trench had been dug around the perimeter of the wall and Jhonate was sure that it was filled with sharpened stakes. She could see a couple men in a guard tower above the gate.

"This looks far different from the Jack's Rest I remember," said Poz.

"Those are no slip-shod defenses," said Qenzic. "To put up fortifications like that must have taken . . ."

"Months," Faldon said in disgust. "They have been alone for months fighting off an army and we have sat behind the walls of the academy, leaving them to fend for themselves." With that, he stepped out of the trees and walked down the center of the road towards the gate. Locksher was right behind him and after a few nervous glances, the others followed.

The smell of decaying flesh hit them as they exited the trees. On both sides of the road leading up to the gate were hundreds of goblinoid heads mounted on stakes. All manner of beasts from goblins, gorcs, and orcs, the occasional ogre, and even a few giants were represented. The freezing winter air had kept them from decomposing, but the heads had been half pecked bare of flesh by scavenging birds.

Jhonate saw a troll's head impaled, the end of a stake protruding from one eye. It was still moving, its remaining good eye darting back and forth, its maw of pointed teeth opening and closing. Its neck had been cauterized to prevent it from regenerating, but Jhonate knew that the creature would stay moving like that for weeks until the tissue died from starvation. Evidently these men did not know how effective a little pepper would have been when killing the beast.

Jhonate had not seen a display like this in years. Not since leaving her people to enter the academy. It gave her a chill as she remembered that day. Smoke had filled the jungle and the air had been full of screams as her father's men destroyed the bandits responsible. The men of Jack's Rest had indeed been left to battle alone for too long.

"Look," said Qenzic. "Moonrats." Sure enough, next to the gate was a cluster of dozens of moonrat heads. All of them were missing their eyes.

Jhonate frowned. Why did they have to be missing the eyes?

This was the first glimpse of a moonrat she had seen since leaving on their mission. She itched to get her hands on one.

"By the bloody gods! Is that Faldon the Fierce I see?" said an excited voice from the watchtower above the gate.

"It is!" Faldon shouted. "But I can't see who's talking!"

"Just a minute!"

They heard the thump of heavy boots climbing down. There was a grunt behind the gate as a bar was lifted and the gate slowly opened outward on heavy hinges. The loud sound of men working poured out as a weathered, squat, but heavily muscled old man walked out from behind the gate. Two full quivers bristled on his back.

"Rickon the Bug!" Faldon said and clasped the man's hand.

"Yer a welcome sight, Faldon!" the man replied. "Is the academy sending up reinforcements?"

Faldon's smile faltered. "I'm sorry, Rickon. The academy is overwhelmed. We are all that could be spared."

The man nodded resignedly. "Well come in then. We haven't been attacked fer a while but you never know."

Chapter Thirty Two

Jhonate was impressed as they walked through the village. They had come expecting to find either no survivors or a small few hanging on for dear life, but Jack's Rest was bustling. Refugees, both men and women packed the street hard at work. Most were dirty and their clothes were tattered, but everyone seemed healthy.

The village center showed signs that it had been attacked just months ago. The old original log buildings that still stood were fire damaged and hastily repaired. Smaller shacks and shelters had been packed between them and several wood frame houses were being built.

"People are sheltering here from villages and homesteads all around," Rickon explained. "We bring back any survivors we find."

"Why do they still build when the army could attack at any time?" asked Qenzic.

"We're mountain folk. It's what we do," Rickon said.

"Who's in charge?" Faldon asked as they walked.

"Why yer old friend, Tamboor the Fearless."

"Tamboor?" Faldon laughed. "Of course Tamboor's alive. It would take more than an army to take him down."

"Yeah, I guess." Rickon shrugged. "If you can call that living."

"What do you mean?" Locksher asked, struggling to keep up with the conversation as they weaved through the crowded road. Jhonate didn't have as much difficulty. A few sharp glares and people gave her a wide berth.

"I might as well warn ya about Tamboor," Rickon said. "He ain't right in the head. Had his wife and two youngest killed right in front of him the first day of the attack. He was hauled off to some dungeon somewhere and when he came back . . . well, Tamboor don't talk much anymore."

"Then how is he in charge?" Vannya asked.

The old man laughed. "We can't help but follow him. His craziness is the only reason we're alive."

"Can you take us to see him?" Faldon asked.

"Sure. Headquarters is right around the corner, but he's probably down training. I'll take you there."

They walked down the center street. The sounds of wood being chopped and the grunts of men laboring mingled with the chatter of women and the occasional laughter of children. The smell of various simple dishes being cooked for noon meals filled the air and set Jhonate's mouth to watering. She realized that she hadn't eaten that morning.

"Those moonrat heads back there at the gate," Jobar said. "Why are they missing the eyes?"

Rickon snorted. "Any rat we find, we burn 'em out. That's the rules. They are *her* eyes, you know. The witch that commands this army. It is how she keeps track of her soldiers. How she gives orders."

"The mother of the moonrats," Jhonate said with a scowl. "I know her."

"Yep. Uh . . . that's the one," Rickon the Bug said. He gave her a wary sidelong glance, but she ignored it.

They left the busiest section of town. The buildings and shacks were spread farther apart now and they passed several blacksmiths hard at work making weapons. Then the clang of hammers against anvils was replaced by the ring of swords clashing and the whistle of arrows firing.

As they rounded the corner, a busy archery range came into view. A dozen grizzled men were taking shots at straw targets while a younger few sat at benches making arrows. On the far side of the street, men practiced sword forms and axe play. Jhonate quickly noted the skill of each participant. Most of these men were past their prime, but all were well trained. These men were veterans. Surely these were the academy retirees Faldon had told them about.

"There he is," said Faldon. Jhonate followed his eyes to a man on the edge of the training area. They weren't the only ones watching. Half the men in the area had stopped to watch him.

Tamboor was practicing sword forms at a furious pace. Sweat streamed from dark hair streaked with gray and poured down his scarred and thickly muscled frame as he worked bare-chested. Steam rose from his skin in the crisp winter air, but he seemed unaffected by the cold. His face contorted in anger as he spun and jumped and parried and stabbed invisible foes in a series of forms Jhonate had not seen before. Each slice of the sword was quick and strong and full of rage. Even in their ferocity, the moves were tight and precise. Jhonate did not see an opening in his movements. She was struck by the realization that she would stand no chance against this man in battle.

"I would suggest you let him be for now," said a man standing nearby. He was tall, dark haired, and with a warrior's build. He wore a chain hauberk under scalemail and a long sword was sheathed across his back. The man was young, probably in his twenties as far as Jhonate could guess, but his eyes were lined and full of sorrow as he watched Tamboor work. Something about him seemed familiar, but Jhonate could not place it.

Faldon shook his head. "Interrupt Tamboor's sword forms? I wouldn't dream of it. Even back at the academy we knew not to bother him while he was training. He looks mad, too. Angrier than I've ever seen him." Faldon looked at the man and gestured to the weapon on his back, "Excuse me, son, but why is it that you wear Tamboor's sword? I would recognize Meredith's pommel anywhere."

The man reached up and touched the hilt of the weapon lightly, but did not take his eyes off of Tamboor's dance. "It is part of our agreement. Father is only allowed to wield Meredith in battle. At all other times, he is to wear my sword, Elise. She's a healing sword, you see. He's calmer when he has her in his hands-." The man turned to Faldon with a puzzled look. Then his eyes widened in recognition. "I'll be thrice hung . . . Faldon the Fierce!"

He walked toward Faldon hand extended, but was intercepted by a flash of blond hair as Vannya rushed in. She threw her arms around him.

"Zambon!"

The man looked a bit embarrassed and patted her awkwardly on the back. "Uh, yes and you are . . . Vannya, right?"

She stepped back. "What are you doing here? You left the school with Sir Edge. Is he around here somewhere?" She looked around excitedly as if expecting to see Justan walk around the corner. She seemed so certain that Jhonate had to struggle not to do the same. What would Justan possibly be doing up in the mountains?

"Well . . . no." Zambon said. "I-."

"I recognize you now," Faldon said with a grin. "Zambon, I haven't seen you since you graduated. You know my son?"

"Where is he?" Vannya asked.

Zambon looked at the two of them flustered as if not sure whom to speak to. "Well, uh yes, I know him. No, he is not here. I last saw him a few months ago at Ewzad Vriil's castle."

This response sparked another series of questions and Zambon was forced to start from the time they left the Mage School. He told them of their journey and of Justan's capture and imprisonment and subsequent bonding with the ogre, Fist.

Jhonate was stunned by Zambon's tale. Her memories of Justan blurred a bit with each new detail. The young man that left her at the edge of Reneul seemed so different from the Sir Edge Zambon spoke of. She twisted the ring on her finger. Had he really changed so much in such a short time? If she saw him again, would she even recognize him?

"With Ewzad Vriil dead, the rest of the soldiers gave up easily." Zambon said. "Captain Demetrius took charge and Sir Edge went on to meet that master wizard he had been sent to find. My father and I brought Sneaky Pete's body back here to Jack's Rest. We fought goblinoids and gathered any men we met along the way. When we got here, the place was destroyed for the most part. A few goblinoid patrols were camped here but we took the place back and fortified it. Now we harass the army as best as we can, and new men stream in from all around every day." He noticed the uncomfortable looks on a few faces and his brow furrowed in concern. "What? What's wrong?"

"Son, I hate to tell you this, but . . . Ewzad Vriil is not dead." Faldon said.

Zambon's face went pale. "That's not possible. I saw him disappear. I saw Elise stab him and I saw him melt away."

"Nevertheless, he is back and staying at the palace in Dremald. King Andre is dead and now Ewzad has Queen Elise's ear. He is probably the most powerful man in the kingdom."

Zambon swayed on his feet for a moment. Then he glanced at his father and the look of despair quickly evaporated. His lip curled into a snarl and for a moment, his face looked much like Tamboor's. "We'll have to find a way to remedy that."

"I am afraid you are correct," Locksher said. He had been silent during the telling of the story, just taking it in. Now his eyes were wide with horrible realization. "Dear gods, do you see, Faldon? This has all been about Ewzad Vriil! He always had a thirst for power. Remember the mission we undertook years ago to defeat that vampire? Remember what Ewzad Vriil had been up to then?"

"He was coercing others into drinking elven blood just to see what would happen," Faldon said.

"I think he was trying to decide whether the powers gained would be worth it. Those others were just his test subjects. He was about to drink it himself when I caught him." Locksher looked as if he had swallowed a bug. "We thought him harmless once the king had banished him. Now it seems he had been hiding powers from us. I should have seen it. I should have tested him back then while he was still in my hands."

"I had him at sword point!" Faldon said, his teeth gritted together.

"Both of us had him," Locksher agreed, pacing back and forth. "I let him go even though something didn't feel right about the boy. I told myself to keep an eye on him but time passed and I forgot. Even when he popped back up in the kingdom at young King Andre's side, I did nothing, too distracted with my studies to look into his movements."

"What are you saying?" Vannya asked.

It was just dawning on Jhonate. The pieces fit together too well.

"Zambon," Locksher said. "When you were speaking of Ewzad's disappearance in the throne room earlier, you said that Princess Elise accused him of killing her father just before she stabbed him. Well, think about it. It makes sense. King Muldroomon revoked Ewzad's rights and titles, banished him. Then mere days after the king dies, Andre pardons Ewzad and makes him a duke. An army of beasts appears in the mountains and who leads them into Jack's Rest? Our friend Ewzad. Zambon, would you be so kind as to tell us again? When Sir Edge led the prisoner revolt into Ewzad's throne room, what did the duke call himself?"

Zambon blinked. "The messenger of the Dark Prophet."

Vannya gasped. "The villagers have been reporting that the goblinoid army attacks to the cry of, 'for the Barldag!'"

"Yes! The Barldag." Locksher said. "Exactly! That is what the goblinoids called the Dark Prophet two hundred years ago."

"Could it be?" Faldon's voice was calm, but Jhonate saw the worry in his eyes. "No, the Dark Prophet is dead. My instructor took us to the palace of the Dark Prophet when I first entered the academy. I saw his twisted bones in the ruins of his throne room."

"It is impossible of course." Locksher paced back and forth excitedly. "Yet somehow Ewzad Vriil has united all the mountain tribes of the goblinoids by convincing them that he speaks for the one they call Barldag. Now he sits in power at the palace in Dremald. Tell me, what would stop him from giving Queen Elise an heir and becoming king by default?"

"The Mage School would hunt him down as soon as it was proven that he was practicing dark magic," Vannya said. "The queen couldn't stop them. Those laws are older than the kingdom. They take precedence over any laws a Dremaldrian ruler enacts."

"And the Battle Academy would back them," Jhonate said.

"Yes, the academy is a threat. But now, with Ewzad at her side, our new Queen has recalled all troops from the border. Meanwhile his army gathers its strength. I have been worried that we have not run into any goblinoid forces on our journey."

"And we haven't been attacked for over two weeks," Zambon said. "Ben the Blade took fifty men out two days ago to find out what the beasts are up to."

"I fear that the army is on the move," Locksher said.

"The academy's defenses are stretched thinner than they have been since the War of the Dark Prophet, especially in the east, where there are few attacks," Faldon said. "Now would be a perfect opportunity for Ewzad to assault the academy. If he took the army around the eastern edge of the mountains, he would have a distinct advantage."

Qenzic swore. "If the academy was defeated, he could roll right on to the Mage School and if he succeeded there, nothing could stop him. All the known lands would be next."

Locksher nodded, massaging his temples. "We need to warn them both. But when will he strike?"

"I know how to find out," Jhonate said. All eyes turned on her. "We need a moonrat eye."

Locksher's eyes met hers and she could see that the wizard understood. "She's right. It would be the fastest way."

"We burn all the eyes, remember?" said Rickon the Bug.

"Not all," Zambon said. He walked over and rummaged through a well stuffed pack near the site where his father trained.

Jhonate glanced at Tamboor. The man was still hard at work on his forms, oblivious to his visitors or their revelations. How did he continue with so much focus when such commotion was around? "*He ain't right in the head,*" Rickon the bug had said. She fought back a shiver.

Zambon returned with a leather pouch in hand. "Father slew one of the army's leaders the day we retook Jack's Rest. It was a huge fat giant. This eye spilled out of its belly. We think the giant had swallowed it. We went to dispose of it, but the witch soon had five of our own men trying to keep us from tossing it into the fire. She went after me too. The witch almost had me ready to attack my own father until he tucked the eye into this pouch." His face twisted with distaste. "I don't like being even this close to it. I've wanted to destroy this for a long time, but father won't let me. He likes to take it out from time to time and wrestle with the witch. From the look of satisfaction on his face, I think he wins."

Zambon loosened the strings and started to open the pouch. Everyone leaned in to take a look. He jerked it away. "Careful! Remember what I said? There is something different about this eye. Its power isn't as great as it was when we found it, but the witch is still protective of it. Sometimes she attacks even if you just look at it."

Zambon opened the pouch fully and this time only Locksher and Jhonate leaned in. The eye was a dull orange color. It was shriveled and veiny and did not glow, yet it had a presence almost as if there were still life inside.

"Orange," Locksher said with a pensive look. "I've never seen that in a Moonrat. I have seen a few with green eyes, but the majority of them are yellow."

"All of the moonrats we've found up here have green eyes," Zambon said. "Except this one."

"It must be special in some way," Locksher said.

"The moonrat we killed in the mountains last year had orange eyes just like this one," Jhonate said. She reached for the orb.

"Wait!" said Locksher. "What are you doing, daughter of Xedrion? It is best that I handle this."

"What are you planning to do?" Faldon asked

"*I* am scouting ahead," Jhonate replied. She gave Locksher her most stern stare. "Have you trained for mental attacks?"

"Professor Locksher has a perfectly well trained mind, thank you," said Vannya.

Jhonate ignored her and raised one eyebrow at the wizard, her arms folded.

The Wizard of Mysteries shuffled his feet a little before admitting, "Well, I haven't specifically trained for it, no. But I am no stranger to mental battle. I have been through a scrape or two."

Jhonate snorted. "Wizard Locksher, my people have long been plagued by witches that control the mind. They lure children away in the night. They seduce warriors into murdering friends and loved ones. Since I was but a small child, my father assigned tutors to teach me how to guard against mental intrusion. I have also been trained to strike back. Since my first encounter with the mother of the moonrats last year, I have intensified that training. I am the only one here qualified for this mission."

"Well then," Locksher said with a slight bow. He gestured to the bag. "The eye is yours."

"Hold on. I am the one that gives out missions," Faldon said. He placed a hand on Jhonate's shoulder. "Are you sure about this?"

"I am prepared, sir," she said firmly.

Faldon stared into her eyes for a moment, then nodded.

Jhonate sat right there in the dirt, crossed her legs and held out her hand expectantly. Zambon stared at her hand but after she gave a few impatient gestures, he understood and handed the pouch down to her. The weight of it was a bit ominous. It seemed heavier than it should be. She closed her eyes and slowed her breathing, then shut out the sounds and sensations around her and cleared her mind of all distractions. Soon all was gone but a white emptiness. Slowly, Jhonate built up in her mind a representation of herself, staff in hand, armored, and ready for battle. Once ready, she reached her hand into the pouch and grasped the eye.

Nothing happened immediately. She had expected to be attacked by the voice at once. After a few short moments without result, she focused on the eye in her palm. The world outside her body faded and a low hum began to fill the whiteness. The small version of Jhonate in her mind sprouted large feathered wings and began to soar towards the hum. Then she saw it, a black square in the distance. She picked up speed. The square grew larger and larger as she approached.

Jhonate burst into empty space, a black nothingness. She glanced behind and saw a small window of light behind her in the darkness. It was the way she had come, the way back to her own world, and it would be her escape route when it came time to leave. A silvery wire trailed from the window, connected to her somewhere along her spine. With a mental nudge, Jhonate lengthened her staff and hardened her armor before gliding further into the darkness.

She soon saw other tiny points of light in the blackness around her and knew them to be portals to other eyes, other minds open to the call of the mother of the moonrats. Jhonate became aware of movements in the darkness, hundreds of tendrils somehow darker than the nothingness around her. They moved quickly, darting through the ether, piercing through the tiny points of light in rapid succession. The mother of the moonrats was busy communicating with her army. This distraction was why she had gotten this far.

Jhonate soared towards the source of these tendrils, an amorphous black mass in the center of the darkness. The tendrils shot by faster and closer together the nearer she came to her goal. She darted and dodged nimbly around them knowing that if one of the tendrils even touched her, she would be found out.

Soon the tendrils were so thick in the air that it became difficult to proceed. She searched until she found a calmer area in the center mass. Once close, she extended her grey staff. The tip narrowed itself to a fine point and she thrust it inside the black.

A barrage of thoughts and images filled her mind. The mother of the moonrats was old, very old, ancient. Her mind was full of memories and it took Jhonate a moment to focus her search. A blur of thought processes flew past her, individual conversations, no, orders. The shape of the army emerged in her mind, she saw their numbers and formations. It was bad. Very bad.

Quickly she sifted through thoughts digging deep into the mother of the moonrat's mind looking for something, anything that might be of help. Finally she saw it, a secret so well protected so well guarded, that the moment she touched upon it, all other movement stopped.

"YOU!"

Jhonate withdrew her staff and darted back the way she had come, following the thin silver wire. A swarm of tentacles pursued her, reaching, grasping. She soared and banked and slashed about with her staff, now sharp as any sword. Each tentacle she cut hissed in the ether.

"HOW DARE YOU COME HERE?"

The roar was thunderous and Jhonate realized how precarious her situation was. She was within the mind of a creature so old, so experienced that if she was captured, her soul would be overwhelmed and torn asunder. Jhonate would be gone, her mind an empty shell, her thoughts replaced by the commands of the mother of the moonrats.

"YOU WILL NOT ESCAPE!"

If she had true ears in this place they would have been bleeding from the intensity of the roar. She whirled her staff around, severing hundreds of tendrils, but some of them made it through her defenses and touched her. Each time there was a searing pain as if a bit of flesh had been ripped from her body. Bit by bit, her armor melted away, pulled into the darkness. She battled for what felt like hours, flitting around, always following that silvery trail. Her wings were in tatters. Her skin throbbed. Finally she saw the window she was searching for. Jhonate flew towards it with every bit of her strength. Tendrils grabbed her staff, pulling it away from her. More tendrils wrapped around her legs, tugging, yanking, melting her flesh. They pulled at her and she surged ahead, throwing all her strength into one last lunge. There was a tearing sensation and she shot forward.

Jhonate burst through the window and into the comforting light of her own mind. She shouted for joy, but her triumph was short lived. The window to the moonrat mother's mind was still open. Tendrils poured in, gripping the light around them. More and more tendrils came through the portal. They swarmed and rippled and twisted together.

A shape emerged from the tangled mass, black and shining and feminine and beautiful and horrible all at once. A face formed, full lips, a dainty nose. The eyes that opened in the center of that perfect face glowed red, the red of living blood.

Jhonate tried to stand, but she could not. Her small form was naked and bloodied, her legs ended in ragged stumps where the tendrils had torn her feet from her. She told herself that this was not real. It was a mental representation of her body. She was in her own mind. She was in charge.

"I think not," the black figure said. Jhonate gasped in surprise.

"Oh, so you think you accomplished something with your little trip inside me, do you, dear? Now that I am here, your mind is no longer yours."

"You are wrong," Jhonate said. Her feet had grown back as instructed. She stood and faced the creature. Clothes reappeared on her body. "I am not so weak as you think."

"So you grew a couple feet? You think that a few years of training make you equal to me?" She snarled and thrust out an arm. Long black fingers shot from her hand and wrapped tightly around Jhonate, holding her in place. *"Shall we see what you found out on your little trip?"*

The moonrat mother reached her other arm into the whiteness. Jhonate could feel the creature rooting through her memories. As she had been trained, Jhonate moved the important thoughts out of the reach of the grasping arm. The small success increased her confidence. She spat onto the fingers binding her. Her spittle sizzled, melting through one of them. The moonrat mother's eyes narrowed and another black finger grew out to replace the damaged one.

"You did not like it, did you? Having me inside your mind," Jhonate said. "How many centuries has it been since you felt invaded?"

She chuckled. *"You know nothing of me, girl. My idle thoughts could fill your mind a thousand times over. What little you saw was insignificant."*

"Then why are you so worried?" The black fingers kept searching in her head, leaving a slimy residue behind, but she continued to shift those important memories aside. She had fought too hard to have them taken away now. She flexed her mind, and armor appeared back over the clothes on her body.

"So you insist on keeping those thoughts from me?" The black figure withdrew her arm from Jhonate's mind and moved forward until her face was inches from Jhonate's own. *"It is futile. I will have them."*

"Why are you so proud?" Jhonate glared into the creatures red eyes. "For all your power, you are trapped. Enslaved. I saw that much."

"Trapped?" A peal of horrible laughter ripped forth from her throat. *"Trapped? You caught but a tiny glimpse of my vastness. My eyes are everywhere. I have long ago escaped the bonds of a human mind."*

"So what I discovered was real. You were human once. What warped you into this thing before me?"

The face contorted into a snarl. The bands around Jhonate squeezed. It became harder to think. The armor began to melt away again.

"I marked you for death a mere year ago." the creature said. *"And now I have you. When you are dead, it will not matter what you learned."*

"And yet I live," Jhonate responded, struggling to remain conscious. There was something she had learned, something important. What was it? What?

"Not for long."

There was a crunch somewhere inside her. Jhonate's thoughts faded. The whiteness surrounding them dimmed. What was it? What had she learned? Something important had resided in the center of the creature's mind . . .

"I know your name," Jhonate said. The perfect face was filled with terror. "You are Mellinda."

A howl of rage filled the air. The bonds tightened again.

"Release me," Jhonate commanded.

The creature stepped back and Jhonate was free.

"You will have no power over me!"

The creature named Mellinda swelled. More and more blackness flooded through the window. Before Jhonate could issue another command, hundreds of black arms shot forth into the whiteness. The hands grasped, searching for the name. Jhonate tried to hide it, but there were too many. She was not fast enough. The hands seized the memory and tore it away.

"Now your commands are nothing!" The mother surged towards Jhonate's small form.

Suddenly, an enormous gray arm came from nowhere, or possibly from everywhere at once, and seized the creature in its fist. The black tendrils withered. The beautiful face began to dissolve.

"Let me go, soulless one! Let me-!"

The voice cut off. Jhonate's white world dissipated. She heard concerned voices and felt the chill mountain air on her face. She opened her eyes, but her vision was dimmed. A rough hand ripped the orange moonrat eye from her grasp.

Jhonate's eyes cleared. Tamboor the Fearless, his glistening body still steaming in the winter air, brought the eye up to his face.

"Thank you, Tamboor the Fearless. She did not get it all," Jhonate said. "She did not get everything."

Jhonate felt hands trying to help her up and shook them off. She took a deep breath and let it out slowly, forcing her nerves to relax. Her head ached and her mind reeled from the mother of the moonrat's last attack. She had torn such an important discovery from her grasp. What had it been? Jhonate remembered feeling such a sense of triumph before . . . but whatever she had lost, the creature had failed. She hadn't gotten everything.

Jhonate stood. One important fact loomed large in her mind. She turned and looked at Faldon and Locksher's concerned faces.

"We are too late. Ewzad Vriil's army has begun the attack on the academy."

Tamboor growled and squeezed his taught fist. Muscles bulged in his forearm and with a pop, orange ichor squirted from his hand. Tamboor threw the remnants of the eye to the ground.

Chapter Thirty Three

Justan exited the lodge, his belly filled with a hearty breakfast. He stepped into the street and took a deep breath of the crisp morning air, inhaling the scent of the pines in the forest mixed with the smell of hay and manure from the stables and the faint whiff of smoke already coming from the smithy. He stretched, feeling each individual muscle in his back tighten in a satisfying manner. His senses were sharper now, his body more aware. It was an exhilarating way to begin the day.

He walked towards the stables, but stopped before entering. He turned to look up past the log walls of Coal's Keep and into the trees beyond. In the highest boughs of one tree he caught the briefest glint of eyes watching.

As he did every day, Justan greeted his new bonded. *Good morning, Deathclaw, will you please let me fix that headache?* The raptoids head still throbbed. The pain hadn't faded like Master Coal had said it would. Justan had no idea how Deathclaw functioned as well as he did. Justan had to mute the sensation to avoid getting sympathy headaches of his own. As usual, all he received was an irritated hiss in response. Deathclaw did not like that Justan always knew where he was. *Very well then. Will you be joining us again today*?

Deathclaw hissed again. Still, Justan knew that he would follow.

Fist and Gwyrtha were waiting in the stables. Justan smiled. "Ready to work?"

"Yes!" Fist said. "Miss Nala said that she would be making meat pies this morning. I hope she also makes fruit pies."

"So do I," Justan said.

Gwyrtha nudged him. *Ride*.

Justan grinned and scratched her behind the ears. “Let’s go then.”

He mounted up and they left the keep, Fist walking beside them. Justan sensed Deathclaw nearby, shadowing them in the trees. The raptoid tried his best to remain undetected, staying downwind and keeping to the shadows, but he couldn’t hide from the bond.

He follows, Gwyrtha said. Evidently he couldn’t hide from her either.

“Yes he does, Gwyrtha,” Justan said, patting the side of her neck. “It’s okay.”

On a hunch, he decided to widen his connection to Deathclaw’s side of the bond. The pain of the raptoid’s headache leaked through, but it wasn’t intolerable. Now Deathclaw would hear their conversation despite the distance. A brief sound in the forest beyond told Justan that Deathclaw had been startled by the sensation.

Fist glanced in the trees. “Why does he watch us?”

“He is curious,” Justan answered. “He can sense the bond, but he does not understand it.”

“Tell him then,” the ogre said.

“It’s not that easy. I’ve tried. But he doesn’t like it when I contact him directly.”

“Why not?”

Fist was asking “why” questions a lot lately. Why do all humans sleep in separate rooms? Why are rocks heavier than wood? Why is the sky blue? Justan supposed that it was a good thing the ogre wanted to understand the world, but that didn’t keep it from being annoying.

“Deathclaw is different from you and me, Fist,” Justan said. What little he knew about Deathclaw came mostly from what he had learned the night they bonded. At the time, thoughts and memories had flooded Justan’s mind and he hadn’t been able to process them all. Deathclaw had fended off every attempt to learn more since. “He wasn’t always like us. He used to be a wild beast before the wizard changed him.”

"He is no longer a beast?" Fist didn't quite believe it.

"Not truly," Justan said. "He is just afraid."

"What is he scared of?"

"I'm not quite sure. Himself maybe. He doesn't quite know what he is."

"Either do I," Fist said candidly. "Am I still ogre? Am I now part human?"

Fist is Fist, Gwyrtha said.

"Yes." The ogre grunted in agreement. "I am me. Squirrel is Squirrel. Gwyrtha is Gwyrtha. And Justan is Justan. That is all I know."

Justan is Justan, Gwyrtha agreed.

"Good point, Fist," Justan said with affection. "We have all been through a lot of changes. But we are still us. That's all that is important. Deathclaw on the other hand hasn't come to grips with that."

Justan felt a tightening on Deathclaw's side of the bond, as the raptoid somehow squeezed it shut. The pain of the headache left as well. Evidently he no longer wanted to hear exactly what they were saying. Still, that didn't stop Deathclaw from watching them through the trees as they worked.

That afternoon, Justan arrived at the study before Master Coal had arrived. He was trying to decide whether to wait inside for the wizard when he noticed Qyxal kneeling next to the honstule garden that stood in front of the study. The elf had a large leather-bound book open on the ground in front of him and was transcribing notes into a smaller notebook with a quill pen. It wasn't the first time Justan had seen him like this. While Justan spent his spare time working and training, Qyxal seemed to always be tending the gardens.

"Kind of an odd place for a read, isn't it?" Justan asked. "Aren't you uncomfortable reading all hunched over like that?"

"Just a second." Qyxal made one more quick note and looked up at Justan with a half grin. "It's fine. My feet may get numb after a while and I'll have to sit. What are you up to? Is Master Coal not in yet?"

"He's not. I wonder what's keeping him. He's usually leaning back in his chair, sipping a cup of tea by the time I get here." Justan walked around the edge of the garden to where Qyxal knelt. The sweet smell of honstule blossoms hung in the air and Justan felt the warmth radiating from the soil. Coal kept the garden heated year round. "What are you studying?"

"This is one of Old Honstule's field journals," the elf said. "At the end of his life, he devoted all of his time to the development of this vegetable. He calls it 'specimen p405'. They didn't start calling the plant honstule until after his death."

"It's pretty impressive, isn't it, a goblin creating something new like that?" Justan said.

"Pretty impressive?" Qyxal shook his head and laughed. "Justan, don't you know how amazing this plant is?"

"Well it certainly tastes good." Justan replied. "And everyone says that it's great for energy."

"Justan, this plant is much more than that. It is a miracle. That little old goblin created a plant that is practically perfect for cultivation. It grows all year round. You never have to replant it. It lives on a minimal amount of water and you only rarely have to fertilize it. You can harvest the entire plant by cutting it down a few inches above the ground and it will regrow within a month. Every part of the plant can be eaten."

The elf was so animated that Justan couldn't help but smile. "Master Coal says that it should be a staple in every farmer's garden."

"Farmers that grew this plant wouldn't need anything else. Justan, lean in close and look at this plant. Come on, kneel down," Qyxal said and Justan did so. "Now switch to mage sight."

There was a faint but unmistakable glow of magic radiating from the plant; an intricate mix of earth and water and air magic interwoven throughout the fibers. "I see it."

"This is the same type of magic that you would see in an apple grown from a tree in an elven homeland," Qyxal explained. "This plant has elven magic."

"How did Honstule accomplish that?" Justan asked.

The elf pointed to the large leather-bound book. "According to his notes, the majority of Honstule's work on this plant was done while he lived at the Mage School. He says that the soil in the gardens at the school was mixed with soil gifted to the wizards by various elven tribes over the years. This means that several small sections of the Mage School gardens are actually elven homeland."

Justan was impressed. An elven homeland took hundreds of years to create. When Elves moved into an area they seeded the ground with their hair, their waste, and the bodies of their dead. Over time this imbued the soil with their life essence. Trees and other plants that grew in that soil stayed green all year round and never rotted. Justan had eaten elf-grown food before and he had actually been able to feel the life of it enter his body.

Qyxal reached into a pouch tied at his belt and pulled out a small handful of seeds. To Justan's mage sight, they glowed black with earth magic. "See Justan, Honstule developed a plant that produced seeds that were themselves full of elven magic. If you take a seed from an apple grown in an elven homeland and plant it somewhere else, it doesn't grow to produce magic-enhanced apples. The magic in those seeds would be borrowed magic. If not planted in the soil of an elven homeland, the plant would grow heartily, but the magic is long gone by the time the tree is big enough to bear fruit. But this plant is different. Its magic isn't borrowed. Its magic is inherent like the magic of the elves themselves!"

"So . . ." Justan tried to wrap his mind around the concept. "What you are saying is that this plant will produce magicly-enhanced fruit no matter where it is planted?"

"Yes! And look at this." He picked up a handful of soil. "Master Coal says that this garden was planted just ten years ago. Look at the magic within. Each honstule leaf or flower that is allowed to re-enter the soil as fertilizer has left its own magic traces behind. Its very growth cycle creates homeland!" Qyxals eyes were brimming with excitement. "My people are living in constant battle with the decay of the moonrats. There has been a stalemate for years. For every foot of new homeland we create, another foot of forest begins to rot. With honstule plants my people could create new homeland five times as fast."

"That's great, Qyxal," Justan said, clasping the elf's shoulder.

"This is why I joined the Mage School. To find a way to help my people with my talent! When we leave here, I will be able to return to the forest. With these seeds and all the growing techniques I have learned while we have been here, we will win the fight. That's what I have been up to while you were learning bonding magic." Qyxal picked up the book he had been writing in. "It is all right here. And when the battle in the Tinny Woods is over and the moonrats are driven out, I can take Old Honstule's plant from farmstead to farmstead and village to village."

"With a plant like this, a farmer could live anywhere," Justan said. He was catching on to Qyxal's dream. "It is a great ambition you have, Qyxal. All I'm trying to do is master my magic and enter the Battle Academy. I haven't thought much further than that."

Qyxal chuckled and shook his head. "Justan, I have known you for nearly two years now. In that time you have saved the Mage School from a marauding golem, become named twice, liberated a dungeon full of prisoners from an evil wizard's castle, defeated a rock giant, and you have even found time to teach an ogre to read. I think that you will find a way to make your future important."

"Well, that's an exaggeration," Justan said. "But I'll tell you what, Qyxal. If I can help you with your dream I will. That is a promise. Maybe when I am done with my time at the Mage School, I will stop in to help your people fight off those moonrats for a while."

"I will hold you to it," Qyxal said.

Justan took his leave and walked back to the door of the study. The wizard still hadn't arrived, which was strange. He sat on the top step and decided he might as well get some practice in while he waited.

Justan leaned back against the door and closed his eyes. He immersed himself in the bond. Deathclaw was up in a tree beyond the wall, still watching and eating a fox or something as close as Justan could tell. Fist was at Miss Nala's and he didn't know where the wizard was. Gwyrtha was out on patrol with Samson. Coal wasn't with them and she didn't have a way to ask the centaur about his whereabouts.

With nothing else to do, Justan tested his other bonds. They were fainter, and without a person on the other end to communicate to, he still wasn't quite sure how to use them. Ma'am was in his room back at the lodge and as usual, he felt only an eagerness from her. She wanted to shoot. His link to his naming dagger, or to be more precise, his links to the two individual blades of the dagger, were odd. Lenny had been working on a way to incorporate them into his sword designs and a few days ago the signals had been jumbled and strange. Today they were as clear as ever. They were at the forge and close together. Perhaps the dwarf had given up. Justan hoped that wasn't the case.

Finally, and most reluctantly, he delved into his connection with the rune on his chest. He was leery about trying to communicate with whatever living thing the Scralag had placed inside of him, but it was something he made himself do every day at Master Coal's urging. As usual, the bond ended abruptly as if blocked by a wall. Justan had tried coercing it, yelling at it, assaulting it; nothing had changed. This time, he eased his presence up to the blockage and ran his senses across it. The blockage was smooth as glass and unyielding. He switched to his mage sight and was greeted with a spiderweb of glowing blue and yellow. It was frost magic, just like his own.

Out of curiosity, he stretched a strand of the bond across his eyes and switched to spirit sight. Each blue and gold strand of magic was coated with a fine smoky twist of spirit magic. He reached out with his own magic and used his miniscule talent in fire magic to produce two small red strands. He shaped them like a tiny pair of clippers and tried to cut one of the threads. To his surprise, it snapped in two. As he had done with the barriers in Ewzad Vrill's castle, Justan began plucking at the strands in an attempt to pull the magic apart.

A stab of pain shot through his chest and an icy cold radiated from the rune. Justan reached up and felt frost caking the front of his shirt. He let go of the web of magic blocking the bond and eased back. To his relief, the tiny bit that he had unraveled stayed in place, the frayed ends of the magic unmoving. Justan was paralyzed with uncertainty. Should he continue to destroy the spell and find out what was behind the blockage? Should he try to weave it back together?

"Sir Edge!" Justan felt rough hands grab his shoulders.

Justan switched off the mage sight and opened his real eyes. Master Coal stood in front of him. His eyes were ringed with worry. Qyxal had put his book down and was running over to them.

"I am okay, sir. I was just-."

"Gather your friends together," the Master said. "I have been speaking with Willum. The Battle Academy was attacked early this morning. They are under siege."

Chapter Thirty Four

"What about Wobble, Coal?" Lenny asked. "Were the dwarves attacked?"

"I am sorry. I don't know, Lenny. I will ask Willum the next time we speak. He's on duty at the academy's outer wall until late tonight and I cannot communicate with him from this distance unless both of us are completely focused."

The air was tense in the main room of the lodge. Everyone had questions for the master, but Coal had refused to give any details on the siege until his wife, Benjo, Lenny, and Bettie had arrived. Fist was on his way from Miss Nala's farm, and there wasn't room for Gwyrtha in the lodge, so Justan kept the ogre and rogue horse abreast of the situation through the bond.

"We should leave tonight," Justan said. "The sooner we arrive, the less entrenched they will be."

"Just a minute, now," Becca said, her lip quivering with fear. The news had come while she was preparing the baked goods for the evening meal and her arms and apron were still covered in flour. "I am afraid for Willum too, but there are not enough of you to take on an army."

"Becca, dear," the wizard laid a hand on her arm. "We aren't going to do anything foolish."

Justan didn't like the sound of that. "I don't care how big that army is. I can't just sit here safe, while-!"

Coal slammed his fist on the table. "Sir Edge! Don't get ahead of yourself. We must let all the facts be known before we make any decisions."

"Coal's right," Lenny said. "Yer the one with the strategic mind, Edge. You dag-gum know to think before you strike."

"What more do I need to know?" Justan said. "I can tell you already that the academy has withstood sieges before. They have defenses in place and stores in supply for just this kind of situation. But this army is different from the ones they have faced in the past. It is led by Ewzad Vriil."

"I know what yer sayin' son, but-."

"My mother lives in Reneul, Lenny," Justan said with a glare.

"If you would have let me speak, I could have told you already," Coal said. "I asked Willum about your mother specifically. She is safe inside the academy walls along with any of the citizens of Reneul that had nowhere else to go. The rest fled elsewhere."

Justan sighed in relief. Darlan was okay.

Coal continued, "Thanks in part to the report we sent to the academy, they had already begun preparations before the attack began. For the last several weeks they had been building up their stores and are prepared to stand firm for months. The army will starve before they do."

"That's well and good, but Ewzad Vriil doesn't seem to be a patient man," Qyxal reminded. "What if he uses his magic to tear the walls down?"

"He can't," Justan admitted. "At least not directly. The Mage School reinforced those walls after the War of the Dark Prophet. They are just as impervious to magic attack as the walls surrounding the Mage School."

"We may not have to worry about Ewzad Vriil getting involved directly," Master Coal added. "Right now his position is Lord Protector to the Queen. He has to stay at her side."

"Coal's got a point," Lenny said. "The gall-durn made-up threat against the queen is the only thing they got keepin' the Dremald armies out of the fight and Vriil worryin' about Elise's safety's the only thing keepin' the people on the wizard's side. I tell you right now, I done been in Dremald a long time. The nobles hate that varmint. I bet you they're just itchin' to get rid of his blasted hide. If Ewzad Vriil was seen among the army assaultin' the academy, the nobles'd cause such a scene that the next thing you know, there'd be a revolt."

"Still, even if he isn't on the actual battlefield, he could be a problem. Who knows what kinds of beasts he could send with the army?" Justan imagined enormous armored beasts designed for the purpose of climbing the walls and shuddered.

"But surely the Mage School will help," Becca said, a gleam of hope in her eye. "With all those wizards, there's no need for you all to get involved."

"The Mage School will help in whatever way they can to be sure, Becca," Coal said. "But they're not soldiers. They cannot fight on an open field without an army to stand behind."

The door opened and Fist ducked inside. The ogre was sweating from his run to the keep. He lumbered over to sit next to Justan and laid a heavy arm across his shoulder. *I will fight*, he promised.

"How badly is the academy outnumbered?" asked Benjo. The man had been sitting there so silently that Justan had forgotten he was there.

"The last count Willum had heard was thirty-five thousand goblinoids to their four thousand inside the academy walls," Coal said. "And more beasts stream in from the hills every hour."

"Them odds don't sound good," Lenny said. "Goblinoids ain't usually that hard to fight, but . . . dag-gum."

"The numbers are pretty overwhelming," Justan said, his head down. "Four thousand sounds optimistic. The last count I heard before I left was about five hundred graduates and teachers and two thousand students. The rest of their numbers most likely come from this year's trainees and any of the citizens of Reneul they could find that knows how to lift a sword."

Even Master Coal had nothing to say to that. The room fell silent as everyone brooded. Then Fist's enormous hand clenched Justan's shoulder.

We will win, the ogre sent. *Tell them.*

Justan looked over at Fist in surprise. The ogre's gaze was firm and he gave an encouraging nod. Justan could have slapped himself. Fist was right. What was he doing bringing everyone down?

"But then again, numbers are deceptive," Justan said, his voice raised. He did his best to exude confidence. "The academy is actually pretty well situated. They only need a couple hundred men to hold the walls. With four thousand, they will be able to take shifts even during a concentrated attack. They have their own protected well in the center of the fortress. Until they run out of pitch, arrows and food, they should be fine."

"Yes!" Fist pounded the table with one great fist in agreement. "The Barldag Army will fight each other. Goblins hate ogres. Ogres hate giants. Everyone hates trolls. Trolls eat everything."

"Hah!" Bettie said. "That's right, ogre. All the academy has to do is sit tight and that goblinoid army will defeat itself!"

Coal nodded. "I don't know how Ewzad Vriil has been keeping the army together this long but I hope Fist and Bettie are right."

"So what do we do?" Qyxal asked.

All eyes were focused on Master Coal. No matter what the wizard said, Justan knew what he was going to do. He just hoped that he wouldn't have to do it against his master's wishes. Coal placed a gentle hand over his wife's and she smiled at him hopefully. He gave her an apologetic shake of his head.

"We leave tomorrow." He stood. "We can't just sit back here and do nothing. If this army overtakes the Battle Academy, the Mage School could very well be next."

Justan smiled with relief. *We fight,* he thought.

We fight, Fist and Gwyrtha replied.

"Don't I have any say in this?" Becca said, her eyes filling with tears.

"Dear, would you have me leave Willum there without my support?"

"Of course not!" she said. "But wouldn't you be of more help if you stayed here and tried to raise support from Razbeck?"

"I will send new messages to the Mage School and to the king of Razbeck asking for assistance this very evening. But I know already that their support will be limited. I am going with Sir Edge. Together we will make sure that Willum is safe."

"I'm going too," Bettie said. "And so is Samson, of course."

"You can't just pile out and leave us all alone!" Becca turned to Fist, her voice shaking, her eyes pleading. "What about you, Fist? Will you stay here with us? Nala and the kids would miss you so."

"No. Justan leads the Big and Little Peoples. If we go to war against the Barldag army, he needs me." The ogre pounded his chest with one hand. "I am his fist!"

"Becca, dear, you are right. We can't all go," Master Coal said. "Benjo, I am sorry, but I need you to stay behind."

The large man's jaw dropped in surprise. "But father! I can fight!"

"I know, and that is why you must stay. With Samson, Bettie, and I gone, we can't leave the community unprotected. Becca will be in charge of running the farms, but I need you here to defend them."

"You can do it, Benjo," Justan said. "You are one of the best I have ever seen with the spear. You would have made the academy for sure."

"Yes you are," said Fist.

"They're right," Bettie affirmed, slapping one greenish hand on the man's shoulder. "You've been training with that group of guys from the farms. They're getting pretty good. You keep it up every night and you'll have your own military. The farms won't even miss us."

"And Becca," Coal said. "I am sorry, but-."

She ripped her arm from his grasp. "You will need provisions for the journey," she said. She straightened her apron and fled into the kitchens.

"What about you, Lenny?" Justan asked. The dwarf was heading for the door.

"Well of course I'm goin', dag-blast it! I was gonna go back to Wobble sooner or later anyway. Now 'scuse me so's I can go stay up all night finishin' my gall-durn work!" The dwarf scowled and threw the door open before storming outside mumbling to himself, "What're they thinkin'? Leavin' first thing in the mornin', my hairy dwarf . . ."

"I'm going with you too," Qyxal said. "At least part of the way. I need to get to my people. Maybe I can convince them to come and help."

"Thanks, Qyxal," Justan said.

Everyone filed out of the lodge to prepare and Justan stood wondering what to do. He itched to act now. It was only midafternoon and they weren't leaving until the following day. His regular schedule was thrown out at this point. Perhaps he should pack, but in all truth, he had nothing much to pack. The only thing that he had accumulated in Coal's Keep was knowledge, a few extra shirts, and of course, Deathclaw.

"Oh," he said aloud. What was Deathclaw going to do about this new development? Would he follow them as they traveled to the Battle Academy? The raptoid didn't particularly trust them. This made things even more complicated. Justan had no idea how to handle his new bonded while standing still, much less on the move.

Justan headed up to his room and gathered his belongings together. He opened his pack to put them away and frowned. In the bottom of the pack was a torn bundle of richly embroidered silk. Why was that there? He couldn't remember where it had come from.

He reached in, and as soon as his fingers touched the fiber, a sense of unease crept up his arm. Then he remembered. It was the dark jeweled dagger he had taken from Ewzad's castle. He had brought it with him all this way intending to show it to Master Coal. Why hadn't he? Perhaps there was still time before the wizard became too busy. But . . .

Justan withdrew his hand. There was no need to show it to Master Coal now. The wizard didn't need another distraction with all the preparations going on. He closed the pack and reached for his extra clothing, but paused. The very fact that he felt reluctance to show Coal the dagger made Justan think that it might be best if he did.

He reopened the pack and stared at the bundle with indecision for a moment longer before finally placing the rest of his belongings inside. He couldn't see how the dagger would help them with their current situation. He would find time to show it to Master Coal while on the trail. They had a long journey ahead after all and there would be plenty of opportunities. He definitely wouldn't forget again.

Justan finished packing and sat on his bed. He mentally prepared for a moment, then closed his eyes and reached out to Deathclaw. The raptoid was once again high in a tree outside the keep, nursing his searing headache while watching the movements of the humans walking about. Justan didn't quite know how to phrase what he needed to say, so he delayed and just listened.

Deathclaw was waiting for Justan to appear. He wasn't sure why the human was so fascinating to him, but he knew that their connection, no matter how disturbing, was somehow important. He was also pretty sure that Justan was somehow responsible for the pain in his head. He had considered leaving several times, thinking that the pain might fade with distance, but whenever the thought had come up, he hadn't been able to force himself to leave. The truth was that he really had nowhere to go.

That was the thought that Justan needed to hear.

We are leaving, Deathclaw, he sent. *Will you come with us?*

Deathclaw hissed at him and pushed his presence away. Whenever the human spoke, his headache roiled. Why did Justan's thoughts continue to assail him? *Get out!*

Justan held firm, refusing to budge. He wanted to try again to explain the bond, but knew that Deathclaw would not understand. Then he thought of the memories he had seen in Deathclaw's mind the night they were bonded and knew what he needed to say.

In the morning we leave to make war. Justan sent an image of Ewzad Vriil through the bond. Deathclaw stopped fighting. For a moment, his headache faded as fear and anger flooded the bond and Justan added, *We fight the wizard you hate.* Justan inundated Deathclaw's mind with Fist's memories of the wizard marching into Jack's Rest and commanding Tamboor's family put to death. He let him feel some of the ogre's horror and pain. *We hate him too.*

He showed Deathclaw his own memories of being paralyzed by Ewzad, the fear he had felt as the man with the writhing fingers had commanded him dragged through a portal just like Deathclaw's sister had been. *We have fought him before.* He showed the raptoid the battle in the throne room in Ewzad's castle.

He marches on my people now. Justan sent him images and memories of the Battle Academy and its proud history, of the city of Reneul and of the love Justan felt for his mother. He showed him a vision of Ewzad leading an army against the academy and Reneul. Showed him the people trapped by his army. Justan stopped the flood of images. *We go to fight him again. Will you join us?*

Deathclaw was shaken by the assault to his senses. He did not understand how the human had shown him these things. Many of the feelings that had been poured into him were so foreign and yet at the same time, he understood. The wizard that had changed him, this Ewzad Vriil, was still out there. He clenched his jaw and hissed. This was what he had been searching for. This was a purpose he could latch onto. Yes, he could fight the wizard. He could destroy the wizard.

I will go, Deathclaw sent.

Good, Justan said. *We will need you.*

Deathclaw's headache chose that moment to rush back in. The raptoid pulled away from Justan's presence slightly. It was true that he intended to kill the wizard but he still did not know if he could trust this human.

Justan's own head was reeling from the intensity of Deathclaw's pain. *Will you allow me to heal you?*

No. Deathclaw pushed him away. *Leave me.*

Very well. Justan backed out through the bond satisfied that he had at least made some progress. A foothold was there. Perhaps along the road Deathclaw would be able to acclimate with the rest of them.

As Justan left the bond, he became aware that the room was very cold, bitterly so. His breath fogged in the air. A sudden searing pain tore from within his scar. He raised a hand to his chest to find that his shirt was caked in frost. With everything that had happened, he had forgotten about his encounter with the rune. He tore off his shirt and looked down at the scar on his chest, half expecting to see some creature trying to claw its way out.

To his relief, there was no creature, but the frost encrusting the puckered scar on his chest was thicker than usual. A faint mist flowed from the edges as the very air around the rune froze. He dove back into the bond and found the blockage he had begun to dismantle earlier in the day. The edges of the magic web he had begun to unravel were frayed and the blockage in the bond was bulging out.

He became paralyzed with indecision. Surely the best thing to do would be to run to Master Coal. He started for the door, but stopped. What if the wizard became concerned and delayed their departure? He couldn't afford a delay. Justan reached for the loose strands of magic and tried to weave them back in place. Exactly how had the magic been placed? He couldn't remember. Justan grew angry with himself. Why hadn't he at least attempted to memorize their position in case this sort of thing would happen? Why had he been so stupid as to mess with it in the first place? He knew nothing about the spell. Why hadn't he researched it first? He used to be so thoughtful and methodical. When had he become so reckless?

In desperation, he tied the magic back together as well as he could, envisioning strong knots. He pulled back and surveyed the results. The resulting work looked crude and haphazard at best. The blockage still bulged, but the knots were holding. Cautiously, he retreated through the bond and looked back down at the scar. The frost clinging to the rune was still heavier than normal, but cold no longer leached from it.

Justan sighed. His hasty repair seemed to have worked. He knew that he needed to talk to Master Coal about what had happened, but now wasn't the time. As long as it didn't get worse, he would wait and bring it to Master Coal's attention once they were far down the road on their journey. He would discuss it when the right moment came.

The decision brought some relief to his mind, but at the same time, he felt uneasy. He now had two secrets he was keeping from Master Coal. How could that be a wise thing to do?

Justan? Are you okay? Fist asked through the bond. The ogre had noticed his panic.

Yes, Fist. I was just getting ready to leave. The lie sounded lame to Justan's ears, but Fist did not seem to notice. From the sense of frustration leaching through from Fist's end, the ogre was dealing with his own problems. *What's going on?*

I . . . Squirrel does not want to leave. He likes it here. And-. Justan could see it through the ogre's eyes. Squirrel was holed up in his little house and Fist was surrounded by a jumbled mess. *They say to pack it, but how? I don't know how to take it all. Help? Please?*

Chapter Thirty Five

"Another!" Ma'am commanded, whacking Justan in the back with her stick. She was running him ragged once again. Fifteen laps around the Training Grounds and still she wouldn't let him stop. His bond with Gwyrtha had given him a lot of stamina, but even that wasn't enough with Ma'am around.

"Come on, Justan!" Fist yelled as he ran by, lapping him for the third time. "Running is fun!" Squirrel sat on his shoulder and jeered, chattering a squirrely laugh.

"Faster, boy! Straighten that gait." Ma'am was running beside him now as she did from time to time, easily keeping pace. Justan watched her face as she ran. She was beautiful, with her stern green eyes and fine lips. Her dark hair streamed behind her, the green ribbons fluttering in the breeze. He could smell her then, that familiar smell, and it was intoxicating. His heart swelled and he had to tell her how he felt. He could wait no longer. He reached for her and she looked back at him expectantly.

"Jhonate-."

"What are you doing Justan?" Vannya asked. The mage ran up on his other side. The wind blew her robes tightly against her body, revealing every voluptuous contour and the sweeter, more flowery smell of her blond hair overtook Jhonate's. She linked her arm in his and leaned her head on his shoulder. It felt nice. He felt a painful jab in his ribs.

"Hey!"

He looked back at Jhonate apologetically. Her scowl was

intense; her fierce eyes uncompromising. She drew back her staff to strike him again. The tip sharpened to a fine point.

"Hey!"

Justan awoke to a hard nudge in his side. The pleasant smell of the two women vanished, replaced by the sharper scents of smoke and blackened metal.

"Hey! Son, get yer butt up. I got somethin' to show you!" Lenny said.

Justan sat up, wincing at the light of the lantern the dwarf held. His newly heightened senses were a burden at times like this. He glanced at the window. It was still dark out. Justan scowled. It had taken him such a long time to fall asleep and the dream had been so . . . interesting. Frightening, but interesting.

"What? It's mornin'! Don't dag-gum look at me like that. I ain't slept at all." The dwarf looked it. He was still wearing his black-stained apron and reeked of the forge and his eyes were bloodshot and weary. Still, he wore an energetic grin under his slightly disheveled moustache.

Justan yawned. "But why now? Surely it will be a few hours yet before we leave."

"It's gonna take some time to show you yer new swords, don't you think?" Lenny said, raising a bushy eyebrow.

Now Justan was awake. "You're done, Lenny? They're finished?"

"Yer darn tootin'," he said. "Now wake up yer friends. I got presents fer ever'body."

The dwarf went to roust Qyxal while Justan woke Fist through the bond. It had taken a long time to sort Fist's belongings the evening before. The ogre wanted to keep everything. Finally Becca came through with an oversized pack that she had modified from two of Samson's old saddlebags. After tossing aside the shirts and pants that were torn or too badly stained for cleaning, they had been able to whittle it down to a pile that just barely fit.

Justan dressed and made one last quick check of his belongings to make sure that he was ready to leave. Fist was waiting in the main room of the lodge, still rubbing his sleep-encrusted eyes, when Justan came down the stairs. The elf and dwarf soon joined them.

"So why do I need to be here?" Qyxal was saying grumpily. Somehow his hair looked perfectly brushed and braided despite the rude awakening.

"Cuz I made you somethin' too, durn elf!" Lenny grumped back.

"Really?" Qyxal smiled and clapped the dwarf's back. "Why . . . I am surprised. How nice of you."

"Edge made me, all right?" The dwarf stomped out the door. "C'mon."

They arrived at the smithy just as dawn was beginning to break. Bettie was up cussing Benjo around the place, barking out instructions. Benjo was going to be the sole trained smith in the community while she was gone, and the half-orc seemed determined to shove every last bit of information she could into his head before they left.

"Just a minute, boys," Lenny said. "I'll be right back." The dwarf walked through the doorway and gave Bettie's rear end a sharp slap on his way past. She clouted his head with one clenched fist in response.

"So you're back already?" Bettie said to the dwarf with a surprising lack of anger. She peered out of the forge at Justan and walked outside. It was the first time Justan had seen her without soot-stained clothes. She was dressed for the road. Travel leathers and a light woolen shirt strained against her heavily muscled form and her heavy forge-blackened boots had been replaced by trail-worn leather ones.

"Edge, Fist, Elf," she said with a polite nod. "I dunno why Lenui's been keeping all this a secret up till now, but wait till you see what he's been up to. You'll crap your pants, I tell you." Bettie smiled and rubbed her hands together. Justan had never seen her in such a good mood. It suited her. With a smile on her face, she was quite attractive.

Lenny shuffled around in the back of the forge and barked out a few curses and commands to Benjo. Finally he emerged carrying several cloth bundles. Benjo was right behind him, carrying even more. The dwarf's gap-toothed grin was even wider than usual.

Justan could feel his new swords calling out to him. They were in one of the bundles Benjo held. He could feel it. They seemed . . . content. Lenny's attempt at setting the dagger's blades into the swords must have gone well.

"First you, Elf," Lenny said. He unwrapped one of the bundles to expose a steel bow and a dark leather quiver full of arrows with scarlet fletching. "Lemme tell you somethin'. Makin' properly tensioned steel ain't easy."

Qyxal laughed in surprise. He lifted the bow. "Amazing. And it's light! Thank you, Lenny. Imagine me, an elf mage with a dwarf-made bow. I will cause quite a stir in the Tinny Woods when I appear with this. I-." He leaned in closer and gazed at the surface of the bow. "Are those magic runes?"

"Course it is. I made you a singin' bow. What'd you think, that I'd skimp on you just 'cause yer an elf?" Lenny shook his head in mock offense, but Justan was pretty sure that the dwarf had at least considered doing just that. "It's got protective runes. It'll never rust or lose tension. You can even keep it strung if you want. That's a reinforced steel cable string. Now I know how you elfs'd prefer wood bows, so I gave you a wood grip. Coal magicked it and Bettie carved it so it'll always stay dry, even if yer palms'r sweaty or slick with moonrat blood."

Qyxal ran his hand across the steel, his eyes full of appreciation. "My friend, this is truly a gift better than I deserve."

"Don't forget this." Lenny lifted the quiver. "Firedrake leather. You'll need it fer these." He pulled out one arrow. The steel head had a polished sheen and Justan could see tiny runes inscribed into the metal. "Fire arrows. They work the same way my hammer Bertha does. If they rub on anythin', instant flame. So we had to use specially treated wood and firedrake feathers so's they wouldn't all go up in smoke when you drew one. We made you twenty but be careful with 'em, the heads can be reused but the shafts and fletchin's'll burn up sooner or later. You should probly get another set of reg'lar arrows." He frowned. "Dag-gum it, Bettie, why didn't you think of that?"

"I was busy making the arrowheads, you idiot," she replied.

"They're her first magic work in steel and she done a perty good job," Lenny said.

Qyxal accepted the quiver with a bow and made as if to hug the dwarf. "Thank you. Both of you."

"Enough thankin'," Lenny said, avoiding the elf's embrace. He reached for another bundle. This one was long and bulky. It seemed quite heavy from the way he hefted it. "Fist. Yer next."

"Me?" The ogre stepped forward with a wide grin.

"Yeah, I dun told you I was replacin' yer mace you busted on that dag-blamed rock giant."

"Oh! It took so long I thought you forgot," Fist said.

"You want it or not?" Lenny grumped.

"Yes!" Fist said, a bit of panic entering his eyes.

"Fine, then." Lenny unwrapped the bundle and lifted an enormous mace. It was a thing to behold, long enough that a normal man would have to wield it two-handed. The leather grip and shaft were covered in runes and the spherical head was unlike any mace Justan had ever seen. He could feel Fist's excitement bursting through the bond. Squirrel must have felt it too, because he left his furry pouch and bounded away from the ogre. He scampered up the side of the forge to take a perch on the roof and watch from a safe distance.

"I know what yer thinkin'," Lenny said. "It looks kinda weird. But I had fun with this one. Half the head's set with spikes for puncturin' and the other half is ridged for bashin' and tearin'. The runes make it tough enough to handle the punishment yer gonna unleash on yer enemies. You ain't gonna break this-un, that's fer sure." Lenny chuckled and grinned his gap-toothed grin. "And this is the part that makes me a genius. You wanna guess what it does?"

"Does it bash like Buster?" Fist asked, his eyes aglow.

"Naw. I figgered that help bashin' was the last thing you needed. Yer plenty strong. No, what you need is speed. This thing'll make you faster."

Justan laughed in amazement. His mind buzzed with the possibilities. "Really?"

"Yeah! I said so, didn't I? Fist, when yer holdin' this, you'll run faster, swing faster, and defend faster and-!"

Fist caught the dwarf up in a crushing hug. “Thank you!” He put the stunned and sputtering dwarf down and picked up the mace. He gripped thc pommel and his arm lifted the mace so fast he nearly gave himself a face full of spikes.

“Whoa, son. Dog-gone it, stop swingin the blasted thing around! It’s gonna take some gettin’ used to. Take it easy at first ‘till you get the hang of it. One other thing. It’ll make you faster, but you’ll also get tired faster ‘cause yer movin’ so quick.”

“Okay!” Fist swung the wicked weapon in quick strokes. Justan and Qyxal took a few careful steps back just in case.

“Lenui, don’t forget-!” Betty said.

“I ain’t forgettin’ nothin’!” Lenny snapped. “Benjo, bring it out.”

Benjo went inside and came out burdened with an enormous oval shield. The main body was stout wood that had been edged and backed with iron. The entire surface was covered in runes.

“That thing is massive,” Qyxal said, and Justan had to agree. The biggest shield he had ever seen was the iron shield of Stout Harley, the defense specialist on the Battle Academy Council. This one was half again that size.

“I did the runing on this one,” Bettie said. “The wood won’t rot or splinter and the iron won’t rust, though it’s damned heavy.”

“Thank you!” Fist said. Bettie saw him coming, but with mace in hand, he was too fast for her to avoid. He caught her up in an embrace as eager as the one he had given Lenny, lifting the muscular half-orc and swinging her around. He stumbled, still unused to the extra speed and they nearly fell to the ground.

“Whoa! Settle down, you big ogre!” Bettie laughed as she extracted herself from the ogre’s grip. She walked over and took the heavy shield from Benjo. She handed it to Fist. “Try that on your other arm and see how it feels. That’s right, slide your arm through the straps.”

Fist slid his arm through the reinforced straps on the back. He lifted the shield and mace in the air and laughed aloud. Justan thought that the sight of the enormous ogre so heavily armed was one of the most terrifying things any enemy was bound to see. He was getting more and more excited for the battles ahead.

Justan wanted to see his new swords more than ever.

"Dag-gum, he's a big target," the dwarf mused, stroking his moustache. "We really need to get him some armor."

"A half-helmet and breastplate maybe?" Bettie asked.

"Hmm . . ." The Dwarf nodded.

"Fist, have you ever used a shield before?" Qyxal asked.

"No!" Fist said. "But I will now." He mimed being attacked, swinging his mace and lifting his shield to ward off an invisible blow.

"We'll have to spend some time practicing with that along the way," Bettie said, with a shake of her head. She looked at Justan. "Samson and I have experience with shields. We'll help him. Fist! C'mere, let me get you your shoulder harnesses so you can put your mace away!"

"Harnesses?"

"Yeah, you can't put that nasty thing in a sheath. It'd even be hard to hang it from a belt. The spikes would smack into your legs and cut you up while you were running. Benjo and I put together a rig so you can sling the mace over your back. Then it won't be in the way. I even made some hooks to hang your shield on so you can walk with your mace and shield on your back and leave your arms free." Bettie lifted a rather complicated looking bundle of runed leather straps and marched towards the ogre.

"Where's the rogue horse?" Lenny asked.

"Still asleep." Justan hadn't woken her, knowing that she had a long journey ahead.

"Get her over here. Benjo's finished her saddle."

"Really?" Justan said. He turned to Benjo. "Can I see it?"

"Sure, Sir Edge. I'll get it for you," the large man said and ducked back into the forge.

He came out carrying what Justan could only describe as a work of art. Justan walked up and ran his hand over the leather, marveling at the exquisite craftsmanship.

"It's beautiful," Qyxal said, his eyes wide.

Benjo blushed. "I-it had to be beautiful for Gwyrtha." He had spent some time with her over the last few weeks while he had fitted her for the saddle. She had even let him ride her a couple times.

He began pointing out the features, "It has a low cantle and front and rear self-adjusting cinches because of the way she runs; you know, more catlike than horselike. I-I also made it with low forward jockeys for slow riding and a set of rear grips for your feet for when you're laying forward against her while she's running at speed. There's no horn because it would just get in your way."

Gwyrtha! Come see this! Your saddle is finished, Justan sent.

Yes! she replied, switching from sleep to wakefulness almost instantly.

"She's coming," Justan said.

"Gwyrtha is going to love it," Qyxal said.

"And we didn't let the dwarf add any of his extra metal bits," Bettie added.

"Nothin' would blow up!" Lenny exclaimed.

"It would!" Bettie retorted. "Rogue horse chunks everywhere. How would you replace that? I tell you, you don't know what you're doin' when it comes to mixing leather and metal magics on horses."

"Yer wrong! I been on horses since I was a dag-burned stub of a young dwarf. There's lots you don't know about me, woman!"

"And what happened to the fat sow you tried your little 'test harness' on?" she said, hands on hips.

"That pig was good eatin'!"

Gwyrtha arrived and ignored the rest of them, trotting right up to Benjo. She sniffed the saddle, gave it a snort, and rubbed her head against him. *Put it on.*

Benjo cleared his throat. "As you requested, it's been runed to keep you warm in the winter and cool in the summer. The leather will stay supple far longer than normal leather will."

Gwyrtha turned her side to Benjo, and gave him an eager nudge, causing the big man to stumble back a few steps. *Put it on!*

"Um, she wants us to put it on," Justan said.

"I can see that," Benjo replied. "Give me a hand, Sir Edge. I'll show you how to properly secure it."

Justan nodded and helped Benjo place it over her back. The large man described the saddle's features in more detail as they cinched the straps, more talkative than Justan had ever remembered seeing him.

When they finished, Gwyrtha moved over to bump Fist. The ogre was examining the details on his new mace, showing them to Squirrel, who had retaken his customary perch on the ogre's shoulder.

Look, she sent.

"It looks good, Gwyrtha." the ogre said, patting her head. Squirrel leapt from his shoulder and ran from the top of her head, down her mane to sit on the saddle expectantly. Gwyrtha strutted about a bit before taking a quick run down the road to test it out. Squirrel began to slide on the leather and darted forward to clutch her mane in desperation.

Fist laughed.

"Benjo," Justan said. "You outdid yourself."

The large man shuffled his feet, "Well I-."

"Yeah, boy. You done good." Lenny clapped him on the back. Then he bent over to pick up the final cloth bundle. He turned to Justan. Justan's heart skipped in his chest.

"Okay son, now here's the best part. I gotta tell you, these were the hardest dag-blasted swords I ever made. Everthin' was a mess to begin with. The magicked metals were stubborn to work with even with the meltin' powder, and I had no idear how I was 'posed to set yer rune-dagger blades into the swords. It took every garl-friggin trick and bit of Firegobbler know-how I had to get the metal shaped just right. Bettie could tell you, I was sweatin' buckets-full tryin' not to make a mistake."

"He didn't curse for almost a full day, he was so blasted focused," she confirmed.

Lenny nodded solemnly. "Finally I got 'em ready. I heated up yer rune blades as much as the magic'd let me and slid them into the slots I made in the swords." The dwarf whistled through his missing tooth. "Lemme tell you, son, it was amazin'. Everthin' clicked into place and the magic sealed in by itself and-. Just . . . well, look."

The dwarf opened the bundle and Justan's breath caught in his throat. The blades were exquisite. As Justan had envisioned, each blade began below the hilt and curved out to the tip like slender quarter moons. The hilts were inset into the back of the blades with a gap carved out just wide enough for his fingers. The sides of the blades were finely runed in a starburst pattern and at the center of the patterns were the naming runes. The rune on one sword matched the rune on the back of his right hand while the other matched the rune on the palm of his left.

"I can't even see where you inserted the dagger blades," Justan said.

"Yeah, well, when I put them blades in, they just sorta melted in with the rest of the metal and yer namin' runes appeared. It was like it was meant to be."

Justan reached for the swords. "What do they do?"

Just before Justan's hands touched them, Lenny pulled them out of his reach. "So you see, the thing is, I couldn't rune the swords too much before-hand. If I tried to force a particular magic on it, yer namin' runes might've rejected them. All I could do was prepare 'em fer whatever magic yer rune-blades were gonna bring with 'em."

"What are you saying?" Justan asked.

"Well, the thing is, I don't rightly know what they're gonna do."

"How is that?"

The dwarf winced uncomfortably. "Yer blades basically runed themselves. Once it were sealed, I couldn't add nothing to em. I can tell you this much. Like all namin' weapons, they're indestructible as long as yer alive. Also this one-." He gestured to the sword emblazoned with Justan's wizard rune. "When you touch it, somethin' funny happens. All yer emotions and feelin's just vanish. Poof! Yer anger, yer pain, whatever, they seem to go away. Dunno why. The other one, I ain't got no idear what it does. But it does somethin'."

"Damn near raises my hackles, that one does," Bettie agreed.

"I'll tell you one thing, though," Lenny added. "Them's the best dag-gum swords I ever made and that's the truth." He held the swords back out to Justan.

The moment Justan's hands grasped the hilts, there was a small click within his mind, somewhere deep within the bond. A voice, quiet but firm echoed out, EDGE.

His excitement at finally touching the swords disappeared, replaced by a calm assurance that all was right. These swords were the last swords he would ever need to own. They were a part of him.

Justan lifted the blades and though they were long and were heavier than the swords he was used to, they seemed like extensions of his own arms. Any worry he had about being able to learn to use them disappeared. He extended the right sword out and with a flick of his wrist, flipped the left sword around so that the dull back of the blade rested against his forearm. They were perfect.

He could feel the left blade siphoning off his emotion, leaving only cool calculated thought behind. The right blade, however, burned with a hunger. Justan switched to spirit sight. It came much easier to him now. He saw a thin cable of silvery spirit magic that linked the hilts of the two swords together. All the emotions that were siphoned off by the left sword were flowing into the right, though he did not know for what purpose.

"Edge?" Bettie said. "Are you alright?"

"You feel strange," Fist agreed. The ogre had felt the absence of Justan's emotions through the bond.

"No everything is fine," Justan said. He looked at Lenny. Though he didn't feel the emotion, Justan knew that there were tears in his eyes. "They are wonderful, Lenny. They are perfect."

The dwarf smiled and patted Justan's arm. "I told you I'd make you swords that sing."

"Um, is there a way to turn these things off while I'm fighting? The way it takes my emotions away is a bit unsettling."

The dwarf shrugged apologetically. "They're yer rune-swords, son. Like I said before, I didn't form the magic in 'em. Yer gonna have to figger that out on yer own."

"Here," Bettie said. She held out two leather half-scabbards attached to harnesses. "These will strap to your back so you can sheath your swords over your shoulders."

She helped Justan strap them on. The moment he sheathed the left sword and let go of the hilt, his feelings rushed back in. “Whoa,” he said, and wiped the tears from his eyes. He sheathed the right sword, put his arms to his sides, shook his hands, then in one fluid motion, reached back up and drew both swords again. He felt that strange peace settle over him again. This was going to take some getting used to. He re-sheathed the swords.

“Thank you, Bettie,” he said. “You did marvelous work on the sheathes. How much do I owe you?”

“Ah! Don’t worry. Lenui subcontracted ‘em out to me. I got paid for my work already.” She winked at Lenny and whacked Justan on the back hard enough that he nearly stumbled. She looked over at Fist, who was trying to strap the shield to his back while still holding his mace. His every movement was fast and awkward. The shield slipped from his fingers and hit the ground with a thud. Bettie yelled, “Not like that, Fist! Here, let me help!”

“Lenny,” Justan said, watching Bettie storm over to the ogre. She made Fist put the mace down so that he could stand still long enough for her to help him with his shoulder harnesses.

“Yeah, son?”

“You and Bettie . . .”

Lenny’s eyes narrowed and there was a warning tone in the dwarf’s voice. “Whadda you want?”

“It’s just that the way you two work so closely toge-.”

“Shh!” The dwarf reached up, grabbed him by the collar, and pulled him down until Justan’s ear was level with his moustache. He whispered, “Don’t you dare say nothin’ to no-one. All’s I know is it’s goin’ good, so shut yer dag-gum face about it, afore you screw it up.”

Justan looked at Lenny with raised eyebrows. “I didn’t know you could whisper.” At the dwarf’s scowl, he added, “All I was going to say was that you two produce good work together.”

“Yeah I know, son,” the dwarf said, releasing him. “We work too dag-gum blasted well together.”

“What’s wrong with that?”

"One day it's gotta end."

Bettie finally had the shield and mace hung on Fist's back. The ogre stretched, rotated his neck, and nodded. "Feels good. I could carry this."

"Good. Now you just gotta learn how to-." Her mouth hung open mid-sentence and her eyes looked distant as if she was listening to something. Bettie nodded and yelled, "Alright, boys! You can play with your pretty new weapons later. Coal says Becca wants us to come eat! Then we gotta go!"

Justan smiled and his heart jumped. It was time. They would be on the road soon. Somehow they would find a way to help the school, he knew it. He would be able to see his father and mother and Jhonate would be there . . . He pulled his swords once again and felt his excitement sucked away by the magic of the left sword. His pulse evened and he felt calm once more. This could be useful.

He looked over at Fist. The ogre wasn't as happy about leaving. "I'm sorry, Fist. I know you are going to miss this place."

The ogre grunted. "I will be sad to leave Miss Nala and the children."

Justan sheathed the left sword and felt the ogre's sorrow wash over him. He suddenly felt guilty. "I can't make you leave, Fist. You could stay and help Benjo watch over the community and keep farming."

Fist gave a sad half smile and shook his head. "I am with you. You are the leader of The Big and Little Peoples."

"It doesn't have to be that way. We will stay bonded forever whether you come with me or not. I can return for you when the siege is broken."

"No. I will go with you," the ogre said firmly. "If I stay here too long . . ." *I won't be able to leave.*

"But you will be happier here," Justan said. Fist didn't understand. "Everyone accepts you here! Where I am taking you . . . it's going to be hard. People are going to look at you and-and-."

"I know! They will see an ogre." He grabbed Justan's shoulders with both hands. *But I have decided. I am not an ogre. Not anymore. I am just Fist. You will tell them. You are Edge. They will have to listen.*

Justan looked him in the eyes. *What if they don't?*

Fist let go of his shoulders and shrugged. *Then we shall show them.*

"And what about your friends here?"

"They are my friends." Fist placed one large finger on Justan's forehead and said both aloud and through the bond, *"You are my family."*

Justan swallowed a lump in his throat. "Thank you Fist. I-I am happy that you are coming."

Fist nodded and headed towards the lodge.

Justan felt a confused bundle of emotions at the edge of the bond. He looked up past the wall at the tree he knew Deathclaw was sitting in. The raptoid had been listening. *We leave soon, Deathclaw.*

From the upper boughs of the fir tree, Deathclaw nodded, ignoring the waves of pain the movement caused him. *We leave.*

Chapter Thirty Six

Fist walked into the lodge with his new mace and shield strapped to his back. The smell of the morning meal usually made his belly rumble, but this time he hardly noticed. His belly was too busy churning with turmoil. He was excited to leave, excited to experience the long journey with his tribe, excited to see Justan's homeland, and perhaps most of all, excited to use his new weapons in battle. But sadness weighed him down. This place felt like home.

He headed past the food-laden table, waving and smiling weakly at the men who called out to him in greeting. Justan was right. He had found a unique place here in Coal's keep; a place where he was befriended by the humans. Fist had tried to show confidence that he would be accepted elsewhere, but in truth he shared Justan's fears. What if he was leaving the only place in the human lands where he would be seen as an equal?

Fist passed the busy kitchens and opened the door to his room. He let out a sad sigh as he bent over to step through the low doorway. Squirrel emerged from his pouch, scampered across the floor, jumped nimbly over Fist's oversized pack, and darted inside his own little home. Fist sensed his friend's sorrow and received a mental scolding through the bond. Squirrel did *not* want to leave.

"Sorry, Squirrel," he said. "Maybe we will come back. Oh, I am going to miss that bed."

"I'll keep your bed here for you," said Becca from behind him.

Fist turned and smiled at Coal's wife. "I will miss it a whole much. I wish I could take all of it with me. Especially my pillow."

"I don't think we could fit as much as a single straw inside that pack without it bursting." She edged past him into the room and put her hands on her hips. "I do think, however, that I might let you take that pillow with you on two conditions."

"Really?" Fist's grin grew wider.

"First of all, you must promise not to get it dirty. You keep taking off the leather cover I made for it."

"But it's sooo soft without the cover," the ogre protested.

She scowled and shook a finger at him. "That cover keeps the pillow clean. You sweat and drool in your sleep, you know it. Besides, on this journey you could be sleeping in the dirt and rain and who knows what else. That cover has been treated to handle dirt. You will keep it on, or I will not let you take it. Are we understood?"

"Yes," he grumped.

"Alright then. My second condition is that you keep the promise you made to your little friend there." Her look grew stern. "You must come back and see me. Do you understand?"

Fist hugged her. "Yes Mrs. Becca. I will come back. We all will."

"You had better." She hugged him back, then pushed him away. "I'll strap your pillow on top of that pack. Have you eaten yet?"

Fist shook his head.

"Good, Nala heard that you were leaving and wanted you to eat breakfast with them before you go. Now, you go down and say goodbye. I'll make sure that Sir Edge brings your pack down with him when they leave."

Fist nodded. "Thank you, Mrs. Becca. Thank you for everything."

She opened her mouth as if to say more, but her eyes welled with tears and she shooed him away. Fist patted her shoulder, then bent over and walked through the doorway. "Squirrel. It is time to go."

Squirrel reluctantly left his little house and stopped in front of Miss Becca. He unloaded a cheek-full of seeds at Becca's feet and chattered at her, then darted into his pouch at Fist's side and sulked.

Fist exited the lodge and walked out of the keep towards Miss Nala's house. He started down the long hill towards the farmlands just as the sun broke over the trees. Light poured over the long expanse of fields and the smell of tilled earth filled his nostrils. Fist's breath caught in his throat. What if this was the last time he walked this road? He hoped he hadn't lied to Becca. He fully intended to return, but what if he couldn't? What if-.

Fist stopped and reached for his mace. Something was in the woods on the left side of the road. He listened, but there was only silence. *What do you think it is, Squirrel?* Squirrel poked his head out of the pouch and sniffed a few times before ducking back in. Fist grunted. *I see.*

"Why are you following us, Deathclaw? Justan is not here," he called out. What did the raptoid want? "Do you want to talk? Come out and talk!"

There was no response, but Fist hadn't really expected one. As far as he knew, Deathclaw couldn't talk. Though they were both connected to each other through the same bonding wizard, they couldn't communicate directly unless Justan willed it, and Deathclaw had never cared to communicate before.

"If you do not want to talk, do you want to race?" There was questioning chirp from the trees beyond. Fist chuckled. "Good. Can you beat me to Miss Nala's farm?"

He reached up, grasped the handle of his mace, and ran. Fist was a good runner. He had long powerful legs and plenty of stamina. Normally he wasn't too fast, but the magic of the mace gave him twice the speed. He felt like he was soaring. It was exhilarating. Squirrel even left his pouch to perch on Fist's shoulder as he ran. Fist heard skittering in the trees and knew Deathclaw was right behind him, but the sounds grew fainter and soon he was sure that he had left him far behind. Fist laughed as his long legs ate up the distance.

Miss Nala's house came into view before he knew it. Reluctantly, Fist slowed and stopped. The moment he let go of the mace, he became overwhelmed with weariness. He leaned against a stout fencepost. Lenny had been right. The mace's magic did make him tired.

A rock hit the ground near his foot. Fist looked up towards Miss Nala's house and didn't see anything at first, but then his gaze moved to the trees. Deathclaw's lithe form was outlined in the sunlight for a brief moment before he scampered up a tree. The raptoid had arrived first. He must have taken a short cut.

"You win, Deathclaw!" Fist yelled. "But not next time!"

At the sound of his voice, the door to the house burst open. Miss Nala's children ran out the front door. "Fist!" they cried. The youngest girls grabbed his hands to pull him towards the house and peppered him with questions.

"Is it true?" "Mom says you are leaving!" "Please tell us it's not true!" "Whoa, is that your new mace?" "Can I see it?" "Can I hold it?"

They reached for it and Fist had to hold the weapon up out of their reach. The spikes were sharp and one of them might get hurt. Besides, the children were fast enough as it was. This only encouraged them and they tried to climb his body to get to it. Fist protested and turned and gently pried them off until Nala finally arrived to save him.

She pursed her lips and let out a sharp whistle. Fist winced. That whistle always hurt his ears. "Stop it this instant! You get inside and finish setting the table! Fist is going to have breakfast with us this morning before he leaves." She paused to look at him. "Aren't you, Fist?"

"Yes, Miss Nala," he said.

Fist hunched over as he entered the house and leaned his new shield and mace against the wall just inside the door where he could keep an eye on them. The smaller children were busy at the table now but the two older boys, Steffen and Jerrold, were eying the mace with fascination and he didn't want any mishaps.

Miss Nala saw their looks and called the boys to the table right away. Fist walked over and sat at his regular spot while the children started their usual squabbling over who would get to sit next to him. Nala had long ago developed a system for this situation and quickly sorted it out.

Meals at Nala's table were much simpler than the meals at the lodge. She didn't have all the resources that Becca's kitchen had, but in

Fist's mind, she made up for it with the quality of her cooking. The morning meal consisted of freshly baked bread, eggs from her new chickens, and the ever present honstule plant. The bread was crusty and warm and she made the eggs just the way Fist liked them, fried on both sides, but with the yolk still runny. He liked to pile the eggs in between two thick pieces of bread along with a few pieces of honstule and eat it in one big sandwich.

As they ate, the children continued to ask him questions about why he was going and where, where did he get his new mace and shield, and when he was coming back. Fist tried his best to answer around mouthfuls of food. Miss Nala said nothing. She just directed the children when necessary and pushed the food around her plate.

When they had finished eating, Fist went to help her with the dishes as usual, but she suggested that he go play with the children instead.

"I do not have much time to play," he said. Justan had finished eating and they were loading up the horses for the journey. "They are coming soon."

She stood in the kitchen with her eyes fixed on the floor, her hands clenched at her sides. "Must you go, Fist?"

"Yes, Miss Nala," he said.

She stepped forward, reached both hands up to his ears and pulled him down to kiss him gently on the forehead. Her lips brushed the scar left behind by the arrow that had struck him the day Tamboor's family had been killed, and Fist felt a lump in his throat.

"We will miss you," she said, looking into his eyes.

"I will miss you too," he promised.

She took a step back and lifted a heavy linen bundle from the edge of her stovetop. "I have prepared a few goodies for you to take along with you. The girls helped me make cookies last night. There should be enough to share with your friends."

"Thank you," he said with gratitude and took the bag from her. "Um . . . Benjo will be watching over you while we are gone. He will make sure that you are safe."

She gave him a sad smile. "I am sure he will do just fine. Now go on outside and say goodbye to the children. And play with them as long as you can. They need that."

"Yes, Miss Nala." Fist gathered his mace and shield and stepped outside.

He immersed himself in the children's play forgetting about his departure for a time. It was over too soon. Justan and Gwyrtha appeared first, with Qyxal and Lenny mounted on Albert and Stanza close behind. They waved to him and he nodded before turning to the children.

He said his goodbyes. The older boys took it stoically and hugged him farewell. The younger children cried and pleaded with him not to go. It nearly broke his heart to do so, but he gently extracted them from his legs with their brothers' help and joined his companions at the road. He watched the door, but Miss Nala didn't leave the house.

Master Coal soon arrived astride Samson and Bettie astride her favorite horse Pansy and it was time to go. Fist put the extra food she had given him in one of Gwyrtha's new saddlebags, settled his shield and mace to the harness on his back and walked down the road away from Miss Nala's farm, having no idea when he would ever return.

Gwyrtha nudged him, excited about the journey and he patted her head, but couldn't summon up any excitement of his own. Justan tried to cheer him up, talking about the wonders of Gwyrtha's new saddle. Normally he would have been enthusiastic, but now it just reminded him that there was going to be a lot of walking ahead. Justan finally understood his mood and patted him on the shoulder, letting him walk in silence.

The road soon left the farmlands behind and moved through a series of sparsely forested hills. Justan moved back to talk with Master Coal and Bettie cantered up alongside Fist as he walked. She pulled out her new weapon, a great hammer much like Lenny's but with a longer handle. She showed him the two sets of runes on its head.

"One set makes him work like Lenui's Buster, hitting with twice the power of my swing, but if I twist the handle like this," She twisted until there was a click. The handle rotated and clicked into place again, causing the second set of runes to line up. Bettie giggled. "Now he's a fire hammer like Lenui's Bessie, except mine's better because all I have to do is click it back and it don't burn anymore." She looked back over her shoulder at Lenny. "Look at him. The dwarf's still mad he didn't think of it first."

Fist smiled and nodded politely, but couldn't think of anything to say.

"I call him Maker," she added. "Because sometimes I'll be using him to make things and other times I'll be using him to send things to their maker. Get it?"

"No," he said. "But it is a good name."

She scowled and trotted along side him in silence for a bit longer before leaning over and swatting him upside the head with her open palm. "What's wrong with you, ogre?"

Fist raised his hand to the side of his face in surprise. The blow had stung. The half-orc was strong. "Why did you hit me?"

"So you're going to miss people? Big deal, ya baby!" she said sternly. "You think you're the only one leaving friends behind? We're on a journey. Moping and missing folks is for late at night when you're sleeping on the cold ground. Right now you're traveling with a group of friends that accept you far more than anyone else. Enjoy it! Believe me. I'm half orc. Everyone hates half-orcs. These trips may be the best times of your life."

Fist stared at her dumbfounded. Squirrel emerged from his pouch, climbed to his shoulder and shook a finger at him, scolding in agreement. *Okay, Squirrel.* "You are right, Bettie. I will try to be happy."

She nodded and trotted over to throw curses back and forth with Lenny. Fist reached up and scratched Squirrel's back, feeling the tiny creature's pleasure through the bond. A smile slowly spread across Fist's face. She was right. There was no room for sadness. This was an adventure.

They soon reached the bank of the Wide River and traveled a few miles downstream until they came to the shallows. Master Coal had traveled this route many times and knew the way, so he and Samson took the lead, followed by Bettie, Lenny, and Qyxal, while Justan and his bonded took the rear.

The water was icy cold, but unlike last the time they had crossed, Fist wasn't delirious with a fever or running for his life. Crossing the river at Justan's side wouldn't be so bad. They made good time, following Master Coal's direction, but a third of the way across, Justan reigned in and looked back.

This could be an issue.

Fist followed Justan's gaze back to the shoreline. "What is it?"

Concern creased Justan's brow. "Deathclaw's afraid of the river."

Deathclaw stood at the river's edge, staring at the water, cold and swift, that spilled across the rocks of the shallows. There were places where he could see the river bottom, but there were also places where the water was dark, deep, and swirling. Deathclaw forced his fingers to unclench. He hadn't known how hard it was going to be to cross the river again.

A note of concern drifted from the back of his mind and he glanced up, to see Justan sitting safely astride his strange beast looking back at him. Deathclaw hissed inwardly, his head throbbing in time with his swiftly beating heart. The human felt his fear. He hated that it knew his weakness.

Do you want me to come back for you? Justan's thoughts intruded. *Gwyrtha would let you ride across on her back.*

A vision was pushed into Deathclaw's mind. He saw himself astride the beast, riding comfortably as it took him across unscathed. Ride another creature? The concept was so foreign that he immediately thrust the vision away. Ridiculous. He would cross on his own . . . somehow. *Go! I will cross.*

He waited until Justan had turned and continued on before wading into the shallows. The water's chill caused him to gasp, yet he moved forward, careful to keep his tail up and dry. The trail Justan and the others had taken was easy at first. The water never rose above his shins, and the pull of the current was not enough to make him lose his footing. His confidence grew, but the water's cold began to stab his feet like daggers and his headache increased in rhythm. Deathclaw slowed and focused on his feet, willing his body's magic to kick in. His legs throbbed and warmth spread downward, lessening the pain. He picked up his pace, completely focused on the path in front of him. Then the path disappeared.

The water before him was muddied and swirled slowly so that he could no longer see the bottom. His heart thumped in his chest. Deathclaw looked up. Justan and the others were now far in the distance.

Justan sensed his indecision and sent reassurance that the path was still there. A flood of Justan's recent memories echoed through Deathclaw's mind, showing him the route that the others had taken. The ogre Fist was afoot just as he was. Justan linked the ogre's thoughts to his and Deathclaw saw that the water ahead had never been more than waist deep. These deeper parts were mainly swirling pools where the river's current had dissipated and would not sweep him downstream.

Deathclaw nodded, reassured, and stepped into the muddy water. The bottom gave out from under him and he sunk chest deep. He thrashed frantically forward, hissing angrily at Justan and the ogre. Finally he climbed out of the pool, back to the shin-deep water, and stood shivering as his body slowly adjusted once more.

Sorry, the ogre's thoughts rumbled. *You are shorter than me.*

Deathclaw hissed at him and looked back. The shoreline was distant but visible. He was only a third of the way across. His head pounded and he doubted himself once more. Was it really worth following this human just to satisfy his own curiosity and have the vague chance to kill the wizard Ewzad Vriil?

He pushed on. The route Justan showed Deathclaw took him around great rocks that jutted out of the water like great curving fingers. Some were just taller than him, while others were nearly small islands in and of themselves. There were times that he lost sight of the distant party all together. Only Justan and the ogre's assurances kept him moving forward. The water churned and swirled but was never more than waist deep.

Deathclaw sloshed past the last of the craggy spires just as Justan and the others reached the far bank. He could see them gathered in front of the tree line and felt frustration come from Justan's mind. They were arguing about something. Finally, the human's voice came again.

Deathclaw, we cannot wait for you here. Memories of a fearsome rocky giant were sent into his mind. The riverbank was the edge of this monster's territory and they were afraid that their presence would draw its attention. *We will head up the hill to the outskirts of Charz's territory and wait for you to finish crossing. Hurry as quick as you can.*

Deathclaw understood their urgency. His years in the Whitebridge desert had made him familiar with the necessity of avoiding the territories of stronger creatures. He watched as Justan and the others traveled down the shore and up a grassy hill. They faded from sight and he redoubled his pace, more confident in the directions he was given and in his own ability to traverse the shallow waters. Soon the bank sprawled before him. Deathclaw's body was weary and numb with the cold, but he exulted in his achievement. He had not let the river beat him.

A short distance from the shoreline, a large shadow flowed across the bank. Deathclaw looked and saw an enormous beast circling in the sky above and forgot about his triumph. He knew it immediately. That night, so much had been hidden in shadow, but he remembered the great horns on its head and the heat of its passing. This was the beast that had taken Talon. Its skin was scaled a deep red; its wings, claws, and horns a deep black.

It swooped down close to the shore and a figure leapt from its back, rolling as it hit the ground. This green-skinned creature, about Deathclaw's size, stood from the pebbled ground of the riverbank and brushed itself off. It wore some kind of thick green overlapping plate armor.

Deathclaw crouched and watched it warily. It saw his stance and copied his motion, settling into a crouch of its own. Neither of them made a move for several seconds. Then in a smooth motion, it drew two daggers from a belt at its waist and charged.

It was fast.

Chapter Thirty Seven

The party had been waiting at the outer edge of Charz's territory only a short time when they saw the red beast glide overhead and bank towards the shoreline.

"What the blasted hell was that?" Bettie said, from atop her chestnut mount.

"It was huge. Was it a dragon?" Qyxal asked.

"No," said Master Coal. He placed a hand on Samson's shoulder. "Do you recognize it?" The centaur shook his head.

Justan had no idea just what it was, but it was headed towards Deathclaw's position. Lenny opened his mouth to speak just as Justan felt Deathclaw's recognition of the beast.

"We need to head back," he said.

"But I was gonna tell you-," Lenny began.

"Don't worry. Charz has no way to know we're here." Justan said. "Deathclaw recognized that thing. It was the beast that took his demon sister the night we bonded. What if it attacks him?"

Fist pulled his new mace from its place at his back. *I'm ready.*

Me too, Gwyrtha added.

"Surely he knows to stay out of sight," Master Coal said, obviously hesitant to re-enter the giant's territory.

Justan's eyes widened. "He's under attack!"

Coal frowned, then nodded. "Let's go."

"Wait a dag-gum minute, son!" Lenny said. "I think I might-!"

Gwyrtha was already running down the steep bank along the tree line. Justan leaned forward in the saddle, clutching her mane. Fist was right behind, his long powerful legs churning the earth with the increased speed brought by his mace. With a curse, Lenny and Qyxal charged after them and Coal and his bonded brought up the rear.

Deathclaw's predicament came into view as they turned the corner at the forest's edge. The raptoid stood knee deep in the flowing water, fighting toe to toe against a small quick figure. Justan and Fist picked up speed just as the enormous winged beast reappeared in the sky above. It dove right for them.

The great red beast soared just over Justan's head and Coal saw one of its hands release a huge ball of writhing tentacles. The ball struck the ground right behind Fist, throwing up a cloud of earth.

It instantly opened up into a wide tangled mass of waving tentacles. Lenny and Qyxal were barely able to swerve around it and reigned in just on the other side, looking back in surprise. Feelers shot out in all directions as the thing grew and expanded, taking up the road. Some of the feelers plunged into the ground like roots digging into the soil and a long stalk-like head rose from the center of the mass. A large unblinking eye opened up and gazed right at the wizard.

Coal and his bonded found themselves divided from the others. The wizard recognized the danger and shouted, "Qyxal, Lenny, go on and help them! We'll be right behind you."

"Dag-blast it! Right," Lenny replied, giving one worried glance to Bettie before he wheeled Stanza around and galloped after Justan, Qyxal riding in his wake.

Coal reached for the spear strapped to the pack behind him, and handed it to Samson. He slid from the centaur's back and switched to mage sight, studying the beast before them. What he saw surprised him. The creature was ablaze with magic. Each part of its body was held together with tiny strands of all four magical elements. The mix was wildly unstable. By all rights, such a creation should have fallen apart, but as he looked closer, he saw that each elemental strand was anchored together with wisps of spirit magic. A wizard with spirit magic had created this thing.

As he formulated a plan, Bettie lost patience. She rode forward and charged the beast, her new hammer held high. *Wait!* Coal cried through the bond, but she had come too close. One thin, whip-like tentacle lashed out from the center of the thing. It struck her horse at the shoulder, shearing off its left front leg.

The horse squealed and fell towards the beast. Bettie instinctively pulled her foot out of the stirrup and dove off the right side of her horse as it fell. She landed on her side, and scrambled backwards in the dirt, trying to put more distance between herself and the creature.

Her mount crashed at the base of the root-like structures that anchored the beast to the ground. The horse screamed in pain and thrashed, trying to get up.

"Pansy!" Bettie cried, getting to her feet. She had somehow managed to hold onto her hammer as she fell. The half-orc swung her weapon back, intending to run to her horse's rescue.

"*No, Bettie!*" Coal shouted.

The whip creature lashed out with quick cracks of its razor sharp tentacles. Pansy's horrible screams were silenced as the creature divided the poor horse into quarters. It kept lashing repeatedly, cutting the horse into smaller chunks. All the while, the eye on its stalk of a head never looked away from Coal and Samson.

"Bettie, come back over here!" Samson called. "We need to do this right!"

Pansy! Bettie, tears streaming from her eyes, ran over to them. Coal laid a comforting hand on her shoulder. The roots at the whip-creature's base churned through the ground, pulling it forward until it was on top of the horse's still-quivering remains, then it settled down and hideous slurping noises told them that it had begun to feed.

I'm sorry, Bettie. Coal shared in her sorrow through the bond. Bettie had raised Pansy. He had given the horse to her right after it was foaled in an attempt to help with her loneliness.

"How do we kill the damned thing?" she asked with gritted teeth.

"Like Samson said, we do it right," Coal said. Bettie nodded.

As soon as Justan saw Deathclaw's assailant, he knew that this was no random attack. This new figure and the great red beast in the same area? The whole thing stank of Ewzad Vriil. He spurred Gwyrtha forward, intent on getting to Deathclaw before the raptoid was overpowered.

Justan barely saw the great red beast dive from overhead. He was aware of the commotion behind him, but he didn't stop. He trusted his friends to handle the attack and focused on helping his new bonded.

Deathclaw was holding his own at the moment, but he was sorely pressed. The attacker was unnaturally fast and Deathclaw hadn't even been able to draw his sword yet. His complete attention was focused on avoiding the beast's slashing daggers.

Justan saw the green overlapping platemail and made a sudden realization. This creature was similar to Huck, Ewzad's creation that he had faced on the way to Dremald. Justan gripped Gwyrtha with his legs and sat up in the saddle, reaching back to grab his bow. He sent a mental command to Gwyrtha. She slowed to a stop and Fist arrived at their side breathing heavily but ready to fight. Squirrel left its pouch at Fist's side and darted across the ground, headed for the trees.

Justan drew an arrow. They were close enough. He had a clear shot on the beast. He aimed for the base of its neck. Surely whatever armored plates Ewzad Vriil had given it wouldn't be able to withstand a shot from Ma'am at such a critical spot.

Before he could release the shot, a great shadow appeared over them. Justan looked up just as the enormous winged beast darted in. It struck the ground several yards in front of them. A wave of heat blasted forth, causing Gwyrtha to stumble back several steps. Fist raised his shield, but had to strain to keep his footing.

The creature rose on two scaled feet and stretched, spreading its wings like a great demon out of legend. The air blazed hotter still. It was no dragon. It had arms and legs shaped and muscled like a man's, but stood at twice Fist's height. Two huge horns grew from its temples and its eyes were a fiery yellow, but its facial structure was clearly humanoid.

"Why are you here?" Justan called out, hoping that a creature this human-looking would somehow be able to be reasoned with.

The beast's eyes widened in recognition and smiled, showing a mouth full of sharpened teeth. The voice that came out was both loud and terrible, "JUSTAN, SON OF FALDON THE FIERCE? AGAIN?"

Again? Surely he would remember such a beast. Justan recovered from the shock of its speaking to ask, "Why do you know me? Who are you?"

"YOU DON'T RECOGNIZE YOUR DEAR FRIEND, KENN?" The beast laughed, a deep unpleasant sound. "BUT WHY SHOULD YOU? KENN WAS WEAK! I AM MAGNIFICENT!"

Justan's jaw dropped. Kenn? The facial similarities between the enormous beast before him and the sniveling man he knew were faint, but Justan could think of no reason to doubt the thing. A surge of pity rose inside him. "I'm sorry Kenn. Ewzad Vriil did this to you, didn't he?"

"DID THIS TO ME?" The beast that was Kenn spat and its saliva sizzled in the mud. "THIS WAS A GIFT FOR A FAITHFUL SERVANT."

Justan saw no reason to argue with his delusions. "Why are you here, Kenn? Why are you after Deathclaw?"

"THE DEMON?" Kenn shrugged his scaled shoulders. "MY MASTER LIKES HIS PLAYTHINGS. THIS ONE GOT AWAY." His eyes narrowed. "WHY DO YOU CARE?"

"What matters is that I do care." Justan knew Kenn well enough to understand that he wasn't going to be able to talk his way out of this fight. Even so, he had to give Kenn a chance to back out. He laid the bow across Gwyrtha's back and showed Kenn the runes of the back of his right hand and the palm of his left. "You are different now, Kenn, but so am I. I am Edge. I was named as warrior and wizard at the Bowl of Souls! Let Deathclaw go and there is no reason for us to fight."

The great beast scowled. "YES, I HEARD OF YOUR SO-CALLED NAMING. THE MASTER *MENTIONED* IT TO ME MULTIPLE TIMES. EVEN IF I WASN'T HERE FOR THE DEMON, I WOULD HAPILLY KILL YOU JUST FOR THAT HUMILIATION

ALONE."

Justan picked up Ma'am again. *Fist, when I distract him, go help Deathclaw.* The journey across the river had taken a lot out of the raptoid and Justan could tell he was about to be overcome. Fist hesitated, not wanting to leave Justan's side, but he tightened his grip on his new mace and nodded. Justan sent him every memory he had about his fight with Huck.

Kenn stepped forward and Justan raised his bow. But before he could draw back the string, a small fiery streak arced through the air and struck Kenn in the chest. Qyxal arrived on Albert with his new bow in hand, followed by Lenny on Stanza. A small gout of flame spurted from the place Qyxal's arrow had struck. Kenn looked down and snorted in derision.

Now, Fist. Ma'am thrummed with glee as Justan drew and fired. The arrow was nearly too fast to follow. It struck Kenn right between the eyes, the impact rocking his enormous head back. Kenn let out a gasp of surprise, but the strike lacked its usual explosive effect. The arrow had barely sunk in past the tip. Kenn looked back down at Justan and his demonic face twisted in anger. The tiny arrow went up in flames.

Deathclaw could feel the heat at his back, but dared not take his attention off the green-armored creature before him. It stood at about his height, but each limb and segment of its body was covered in solid armor. Each plate overlapped another and Deathclaw had not been able to reach a seam to strike into. Its head was covered in a helmet with a rectangle cut out for its eyes and was otherwise featureless except for a thin vertical slit that extended from just under its eyes down to its chin.

Such thick armor should have weighed it down, but the creature didn't seem to be encumbered at all. It was faster and stronger and harder than him. Every strike he got in with claw or tail barely scratched its bony plates. Only the precise control he had over his body had kept him alive so far. If only he had a brief moment to draw his sword, the fight might be even, but every time he reached for the hilt, the creature went on the attack.

He moved his head to the side, narrowly avoiding a slash from one of its daggers and at the same time, rose his foot to block the follow through of the blade in its second hand. The claws on his foot scraped along the hard plates on its forearm, but did no damage. He twisted and sent his tail out just under its guard. His tail barb struck at the joint of the beast's armor in its armpit. Deathclaw felt flesh give and knew that he had finally done some damage.

The creature didn't so much as grunt. The narrowing of its eyes were the only sign it had been hit. It twirled and whipped its leg around so fast Deathclaw almost didn't see the kick coming. He raised his arm at the last possible moment and felt a crack as its heel struck.

Even before the pain hit, he knew that one of the bones in his forearm was broken. He dodged around the creature, trying to buy time while he forced his fist to close. He clenched his muscle around the bone, forcing it to set in place. He willed the magic within him to heal it and felt the bone tingle as his body started to work. Normally with a break this minor, his magic would have it partially healed in minutes, but this creature was not going to give him time.

It leaned forward and stabbed both daggers out in a double thrust. Deathclaw had to leap back to avoid being impaled. He wrapped his wounded arm around his back to protect it, knowing that he was going to have to defeat the beast without the use of one limb. He really needed to get to his sword, but now the hilt was even harder to get to because it was on the same side as his wounded arm.

Fist is coming, said Justan's voice from within the bond. Deathclaw felt a tiny click in the back of his mind and he could hear the ogre's thoughts. His headache thumped with the increased stress. The human had somehow connected them together again. The ogre was running towards him, confident that he would be able to help kill the beast, but reluctant to leave Justan. Fist intended to end the fight quickly and get back to help the human.

Deathclaw hissed in irritation. The ogre would likely get killed. He chirped a command through the bond. If the ogre had been one of Deathclaw's pack, he would have understood the tone of the chirp to mean, 'hang back and wait for an opportune time to strike,' but Fist charged on oblivious to the tone.

The creature saw him coming. It sent a quick kick into Deathclaw's midsection and edged its way to the side. Now Deathclaw was between the beast and the oncoming ogre.

It is fast, Deathclaw warned. *It is hard.*

So am I, Fist said and charged on. *Justan said it is not wearing armor. That is its skin. The wizard made it hard.* Fist gathered the memories Justan had showed him and threw the information into Deathclaw's mind.

When Justan had sent memories into Deathclaw's mind, it had been done gradually, and felt almost as if he had experienced them himself. This was different. Fist just shoved them over. The overwhelming pile of thoughts inflamed his raging headache and threw off Deathclaw's concentration. The beast took advantage.

The orc, for that is what Deathclaw now understood it to be, jumped and kicked out with both feet. The blow landed on Deathclaw's chest, blasting the air from his lungs, and sending him sprawling right into the path of the oncoming ogre.

Fist reacted quickly, jumping over the raptoid with mace raised, intending to strike the beast down with one mighty blow. The orc stepped aside, and as the mace carved the air where it had been standing, slashed out with his dagger, scoring the ogre's hip.

Fist grunted and swung the mace in a vicious backswing that the orc ducked under. It darted in with dagger extended, but Fist brought his large oval shield around with his other arm and connected with its wrist, knocking the dagger from its hand. He raised the shield and kicked out with one heavy foot. The orc rolled to the side to avoid the attack and as it came back to its feet, Deathclaw's tail barb was there to meet it.

He aimed for the orc's eyes, but it turned its head at the last moment and the barb merely scraped along its hardened skin. It crouched and backed away quickly, its one remaining dagger clenched in its left hand, and watched as the raptoid and ogre advanced.

Finally Deathclaw had the reprieve he was waiting for. He reached back with his good arm and worked Star free from its sheath. Hopefully the enchanted blade would do more damage than his claws.

We rush it together, Fist announced. Though Deathclaw did not like taking orders, he didn't disagree. It seemed the smartest course of action. He gave a mental nod and they charged forward.

The orc reared back and the vertical slit in the front of its face split open. To Deathclaw's surprise, there was no nose or mouth within, just a toothless glistening maw. It lurched forward at Deathclaw and spewed a long stream of yellow liquid.

Deathclaw tried to dodge, but wasn't fast enough. The stream spattered along the left side of his body. His scaled skin steamed and bubbled on contact with the substance. Deathclaw screeched. He dropped his sword and rolled in the mud of the riverbank, trying to quench the searing pain.

It turned and spewed another arc of acidic liquid at Fist. The ogre got his shield up just in time. The shield smoked on impact and he hoped that Bettie's runes would hold up. The creature took advantage of the shield obscuring Fist's view. It ran forward and when Fist lowered the shield to continue his charge, the orc was already in front of him.

It slashed the dagger over the top of his shield, slicing the tip of Fist's nose. As the ogre flinched back, the orc grabbed the top edge of the shield, jumped up, braced its feet against the bottom of the shield and pulled back.

Fist was caught off guard by the move. He tried to hold firm to the straps on the back of the shield but the orc had greater leverage. It wrenched his arm and ripped the shield from his grasp. It landed on its back and kicked the shield away before rolling to its feet.

The orc ducked a swing of Fist's mace and stabbed out with the dagger, piercing the ogre's forearm. Fist swung again. It countered. Fist realized that he was slowing down. Even with the increased speed the mace gave him, he wasn't fast enough.

On his next swing, the orc ducked, then spun and kicked low, catching the back of Fist's ankles. The orc's weight wasn't enough to knock the ogre from his feet, but it did knock him off balance. It then leapt up, launching its shoulder into his chest.

As Fist fell backwards, it reared back and opened its mouth slit ready to spit again.

Coal stepped behind Samson and Bettie. Once out of the view of the whip-creature's stare, he laid down on the dirt. He cast a spell into the ground beneath him and swiftly burrowed down several feet into the earth. Once submerged and safe from the battle he was able to focus his entire mind on his bonded. He linked Samson and Bettie together and sent his consciousness into their bodies.

This creature is a plant, he told them. *Those tentacles are vines and roots.*

So where do I hit it? Bettie asked.

It doesn't have a central organ structure that we can reach out and strike. It doesn't have a heart or lungs, Coal said. *Think of it as a giant weed.*

We can't just pull the thing out of the ground, Bettie grumbled.

What about that stalk? Samson asked, watching the large eye that gazed back at them silently while its roots continued to feed on Pansy's remains.

It is a possible weak point, but it's well protected at the center of that mass of tentacles.

I could throw my spear, destroy the eye. Samson suggested. He was an excellent marksman. Coal had no doubt he would strike true.

And if it doesn't kill the thing, we just lost your damned spear. Bettie said. *Then what're you going to do, punch it?*

True, Coal said.

Do we have to fight it at all? Samson asked. *It is pretty slow. Why don't we just cut through the forest and leave it here.*

Good point, Coal said, glad that Samson had been the one to suggest it. He was pretty sure he already knew what Bettie's response was going to be. *With how slow it moves and the way it took up the road, I'm guessing that this creature was created as a barrier. It's not attacking. I think it was set here to separate us from the others.*

Then we kill it quick and catch up to them, Bettie replied.

Samson wasn't ready to concede. *If we cut through the forest, we can be there so much fast-.*

No! It killed Pansy. I ain't leaving it alive. Bettie twisted the handle on her hammer until it clicked into place. *Maker can set it on fire.*

Coal felt her determination and knew there was no use arguing with her at this point. *How do you plan on getting close enough to use your hammer?*

"I'm taking your shield, Samson," she said aloud. Bettie often tired of speaking through the bond when she had perfectly good lungs to use. The half-orc grabbed the shield from its place strapped to one of their saddlebags. "What we do is we come at it together. You take the left, slashing with your spear. I'll set the right side on fire."

Will the shield stand up to an attack from that creature? Coal asked.

She snorted. "I runed the wood myself. It'll handle anything that plant can do."

"And what do I do without my shield?" Samson asked.

"Do your rogue horse thing," she responded.

Very well, Bettie. Master Coal said and asked Samson, *Are you okay with this?*

As always, Samson responded and Coal began making the necessary changes to the centaur's body.

At his current size, Samson was a large target. Coal shrunk him down until he was just over Bettie's height. Then he worked on the centaur's defenses. He hardened the skin on Samson's human torso until it was as tough as stone, careful to leave more supple joints so that he could have full movement. Along his horse-like half, Coal thickened his pelt and stiffened each hair until it was as tough as wire.

"Good enough," Samson said. *When are you going to teach Sir Edge how to do this? Gwyrtha would be even better suited to this kind of thing than I am.*

He's got to learn one thing at a time. Coal explained. *We have a long journey ahead of us before we reach the Battle Academy. There will be plenty of time.*

Samson and Bettie spread out and approached the whip-creature from opposite sides, eying it warily. Coal monitored their bodies, ready to heal them if either one was injured. The stalk at the center of the tentacles turned back and forth, unsure who to follow. Then the base of the creature shivered and another stalk rose to join the other. This new stalk focused its single eye on Bettie.

That answers that question, Samson sent, glad he hadn't wasted his spear.

Bettie edged forward, shield raised in front of her. She kept her hammer at the ready, watching for the first sign of movement. Coal watched it through her eyes and from the length of the tentacles, estimated that it had just over a twelve foot reach. Both bonded noted the information and edged closer.

A tentacle lashed out at Bettie. She took the strike on her shield and true to her word the shield held. She swung her hammer forward as the tentacle withdrew and nicked the edge. With a puff of smoke, a small flame erupted from the tentacle's surface and the creature shuddered. Another tentacle lashed out and then another. Bettie took both strikes on her shield, but the tip of one tentacle whipped over the top and slashed her forearm.

Bettie winced. The cut was deep but Coal was already working on it from within. He coaxed the wound closed within seconds. Bettie's return attack was head on, setting the tentacle fully ablaze.

Samson swung his spear at an incoming strike and batted the tentacle away. More came in quick succession and each time the centaur's rune-reinforced spear knocked the attack aside, finally slicing one tentacle in half with its sharpened tip.

Coal saw another tentacle rise from the center of the mass to replace the one Samson had severed. He instantly knew that they were approaching this wrong. The creature was built with such intense and chaotic magic, there was no telling how many tentacles it could regenerate. Sooner or later, it was going to land some direct hits and Coal wouldn't be able to heal either one of them if they were cut in half.

Come back, he said. *This won't work*

Bettie started to back up, still using shield and hammer in concert to set the tentacles ablaze, but Samson was too close. It wasn't easy for the centaur to back up while working his spear. A tentacle slipped past his defense and scored the side of his equine lower body. His thickened wiry pelt saved him from a possibly fatal wound, but a long and deep gash opened up.

Samson gasped and tried to back up. Coal went to work healing the wound as two more tentacles slashed out at once. The centaur batted one aside, but the second struck his arm. The rocky hide was gouged deeply, but did not bleed.

Bettie backed out of the creature's reach just as the next lash cut deeply into Samson's flank. She saw the centaur's distress and rushed to help.

Wait! Coal was already healing the wound and knew that Samson could take more punishment but the half-orc could not. Bettie stopped just out of the reach of the tentacles, but Coal knew that if Samson was wounded again she might go in anyway.

A plan formed in his mind. *Bettie, come here, quick! I need you!* She glanced worriedly at Samson, who was still swiping tentacles aside as fast as he could, then screamed in frustration and turned and ran to Coal.

The wizard cast a spell and rose out of the earth as easily as he had submerged himself. Coal shook the dirt from his robes as he pulled his naming dagger from its sheath at his waist. He held it out to Bettie and sent her instructions on what to do. *Strike true.*

Samson was almost free from the whip-creature's reach. It did not want to let him go. Its root-like feelers churned through the earth, slowly dragging it closer. The centaur swore as another tentacle deeply gouged his torso.

Bettie snatched the blade from Coal's hand. She had never been very good at knife throwing, but she was at least better than the wizard. *You had better start practicing*, she told him. She took a deep breath, focused, and hurled it forward.

Master Coal's weapon hurtled end over end and plunged into the center of the whip-creature's tentacled mass. The strike itself did no damage, landing hilt first and tangling itself, but the dagger was right where he wanted it. The spell he planned to use had a very short range.

He wove his spell, reached through the bond and cast it through the dagger. The effect was immediate. The creature shuddered and its feelers plunged deeper into the ground. Its attacks slowed and Samson was able to back out of its reach.

Coal nodded in satisfaction. A fireball would have done the work much quicker, but he was weak in fire and air. His strengths were water and earth. Wizards with that combination of abilities were often jokingly called "mud wizards". The spell he had released was usually reserved for drying out marshy areas in the farmland.

The dagger sucked in moisture far faster than the whip-creature could replace it from the ground. Its tentacles began to wither, the stalks shriveled and collapsed. It shuddered and shrank in size.

Now, he sent.

Bettie threw her hammer and the creature went up in flames.

"That ain't gonna work, son!" Lenny spat. "I tried to tell you before, but you weren't friggin' listenin'. It looks like a dag-blasted bandham! I done seen one back in my younger days. Mean bastards. They're the only beasts alive that hunt dragons."

"A bandham? How does that information help me here, Lenny?" Justan said, firing another arrow. The shot caught Kenn in the shoulder, staggering him, but doing as little damage as the strike before.

"They're immune to dragon magic, that's how! Yer dragon hair string ain't gonna work on him."

"So that explains it," Justan said and Ma'am thrummed in glee as he fired again. Kenn growled in irritation as the arrow knocked him back once more. Justan's mind whirred. How were they going to defeat Kenn without the bow? The heat he gave off was too intense for close fighting.

"So how do we fight it, Lenny?" Qyxal asked.

"I dunno." The dwarf shrugged. "Keep hittin' it and hope you kill the blasted thing 'afore it burns you to death?"

"Thanks," Qyxal said with a scowl.

"Spread out," Justan said. "He can't attack all of us at once. Look for an opening."

"AN OPENING?" Kenn laughed. He flexed and another wave of heat emanated from his body. "I'LL KILL YOU ALL."

Qyxal galloped towards the forest, Lenny towards the river's edge, and Justan cocked another arrow. He switched to Mage Sight. The heat Kenn gave off wasn't physical. It was magical. Kenn's body was a mass of magical energy; a chaotic tangle of fire and air that swarmed about him with an orange glow. It was like a spell was being cast by his body. Justan had no idea how he was able to control it.

Kenn lurched forward as if to lunge at Justan and Gwyrtha instinctively moved back, but at the last moment Kenn lunged to the left instead and thrust his arm out sending a focused wave of heat right at Lenny. Gwyrtha's movement threw off Justan's aim and his shot went just wide.

The lance of air and fire magic struck the dwarf in the chest. Lenny flew from the saddle and Stanza's mane caught fire. The warhorse screamed and galloped off as Lenny struck the ground.

"Lenny!" Justan fired another arrow, this one catching Kenn in the neck. As the arrow left his bow, a sudden pain stabbed his chest. He looked down and saw frost clinging to his shirt, but he didn't have time to worry about his scar. Gwyrtha sped to Lenny's side.

The dwarf's clothes were smoldering and one side of his moustache was singed off, but by the string of curses that he was letting loose, Lenny seemed to be fine. The dwarf struggled to his feet and Gwyrtha stepped between him and the demon Kenn had become. Justan twisted in the saddle and focused his mage sight, preparing for the attack he knew would be coming.

The enormous beast snarled and thrust out his hand again. As Justan expected, another lance of heat shot towards them, this one aimed specifically at him. Justan could see the threads of magic coming, a blur of orange.

He thought back to his training, to the fireballs Professor Beehn had cast at him, to his time spent in the classroom at the Mage School snuffing out magic flames. He threw a wall of defensive magic up around Gwyrtha and himself, weaving together air and water in a tight grid, envisioning it as a pointed shield that would cut into Kenn's spell and direct the heat to either side.

Kenn's spell split down the center as it hit the shield and the red and yellow fibers of magic flowed by. Justan's plan had worked, but the damp ground on either side of them steamed and the few tufts of spring grass that sprouted between the rocks burst into flames.

Kenn's face twisted into a scowl. He gestured and the heat intensified. The rocks around them glowed red and Justan felt his shield start to crumple. A few of the larger rocks shattered. Gwyrtha grunted and Lenny swore as tiny shards of heated rock struck them.

Lenny patted wildly at the smoldering spots in his clothes where the rock had hit. "Dag-blasted-corn-flamin'-hoop-skirtin'-son-of-a-! Do somethin' quick, son, or we're stewed!"

Justan forced down panic and grabbed the hilt of his left sword. Calmness settled over him. This spell he was fighting was different from the ones he had faced in the past. Kenn wasn't a wizard. This wasn't a spell that he had woven together with his mind. This was instinctual magic. Somehow Kenn was able to control the magic contained within the body Ewzad Vriil had transformed with his will alone.

Justan reached out with his mage sight, as he was used to doing within the bond, but this time he plunged his thoughts into the heat. There at the very center of the spell, he found it, the cable of Kenn's will that held the spell together. If only he could attack Kenn's will directly. Unfortunately his lack of offensive magic once more crippled him.

Justan threw up another shield to reinforce the one that was failing, but knew that he wouldn't be able to keep it up. If Kenn continued the assault, sooner or later they were going to die. They needed help. Justan looked around for his friends, but Master Coal still hadn't come down the hill and Fist and Deathclaw were still busy with their own battle. Help was going to have to come from somewhere else.

The earth rumbled under their feet. Two great rocky spikes thrust up from the ground at Kenn's feet. They shot towards the beast like enormous spears, one of them piercing his thigh, the other, his lower abdomen. Molten blood squirted from the wounds, hissing and steaming. Kenn roared in pain.

Justan looked for the source of the attack and saw Qyxal kneeling on the riverbank, his hands thrust into the earth. The elf met his gaze and his smile was triumphant, but tired. Justan knew that such a powerful spell had exhausted most of his friend's magic.

Ken reared back and howled as he tore free from Qyxal's stone claws. He clutched at his wounds but Justan knew the damage wasn't severe enough. They had to think of another attack now before Kenn was able to counter.

A thought occurred to him. Qyxal's magic had worked. The magic of the dragonhair string hadn't worked but the elf's earth magic had. Justan thought back to the day the plant golem had attacked the Mage School and how Master Latva had enchanted the arrow he had used to kill the creature. Perhaps Qyxal could do the same, but with earth magic. An enchanted arrow might be enough to bring Kenn down.

Gwyrtha heard his thoughts and turned towards the elf, but so did Kenn. The great red beast spread his black wings and leapt into the air. He didn't get much elevation with his injured leg, but it was enough. He glided towards the elf, one claw-tipped hand outstretched, murder in his fiery eyes.

"Qyxal, run!" Justan called, and Gwyrtha darted forward. He let go of his sword hilt and picked up Ma'am.

The elf was on the move. He had re-mounted Albert and was headed for the trees, knowing it was his best chance of keeping away from the demon. But he wasn't fast enough. Kenn was airborne. The great red beast hit the ground at the forest's edge and snatched Qyxal up in one clawed hand. The elf screamed as his robes caught fire.

Chapter Thirty Eight

Kenn whirled to Justan in triumph, his burning prize held high in the air. "SEE, JUSTAN! THIS IS WHAT WILL HAPPEN TO ALL OF Y-!"

Justan's arrow struck true. Kenn's left eye burst into a fiery mess.

Kenn gasped in surprise, one hand reaching for his ruined eye. His face twisted with rage and pain and he threw the elf at Justan. His aim was off. Qyxal, engulfed in flame tumbled end over end. Justan watched helplessly as his friend arced overhead.

Fortunately Lenny was also watching. The dwarf dropped his hammer and ran, arms outstretched. The elf struck him and they tumbled to the rocky ground. Lenny rolled on top of his friend and frantically began patting out the flames. "Qyxal, blast it! Qyxal, you okay?"

Gwyrtha whirled towards their friends, but Justan turned in the saddle and looked back. Kenn stood enraged, one hand still clutching his face while he thrust his other arm out and sent another wave of heat.

Justan put up a shield as quickly as he could, but he didn't have time to shape it. The mass of red and gold magic struck his defenses head on. The force of it threw Justan from the saddle. He felt Gwyrtha hiss in pain just before he tumbled into a stretch of weeds and rocky ground.

Pain shot through Justan as he rolled, his lower back and knee striking jagged rocks. He struggled to his feet, preparing for the next attack.

Kenn lurched towards him, one leg still bleeding from Qyxal's spell, his abdomen leaking boiling ichor, and his maimed face a mask of rage. Justan backed away and grimaced with the sudden realization that he didn't have his bow. Ma'am had been thrown to the side when he fell. It lay on the ground several yards away. Gwyrtha, her hide seared by Kenn's last attack wanted to return to Justan's side, but at his urging, went for the bow.

Kenn sent a wave of heat rolling towards him and Justan put up another shield. As the heat struck, a lance of pain seared Justan's chest. *Not now*, Justan pleaded through the bond. A chill mist leeched from the frost-encrusted rune.

Kenn intensified the spell. Justan's shield began to crumple once more and he struggled to reinforce it. The great beast grinned and Justan realized that he wasn't going to be able to stop him.

Then the heat spell cut off unexpectedly. Kenn lurched forward as a boulder struck him in the back of the head. A familiar laugh rang out. Charz stepped out of the trees. With a wide grin on his face, the rock giant ran and leapt onto Kenn's back. Though he was only two thirds Kenn's size, his weight bore the red beast to the ground.

Before the orc could spit its acid, Deathclaw attacked. He leapt onto its back, wrapping his good arm around its throat. He pulled back and dug his rear claws into the tiny gap between the armored pates in its lower back. The flesh on his side still steamed and bubbled from the acid, but he ignored the pain and strained. His claws dug deeper, piercing through the fibrous crease in its armor until he felt warm blood seeping between his toes.

The orc screeched in real pain for the first time and stumbled. It thrust its head back, but Deathclaw moved his own head to the side, avoiding the blow. The orc began throwing punch after punch over its shoulder. Several of the blows landed in Deathclaw's face with stunning force, breaking skin and blurring his vision. He bit into its bony ear and didn't let go, digging in even further with his claws, widening the hole in its armored skin.

The ogre still sat on the ground, watching with a surprised look on his face. *Hurry*, Deathclaw hissed.

Fist rolled to his knees. Deathclaw had actually come to his rescue. The raptoid could have run, but it didn't. Fist stood. It was time to end this fight. He stumbled forward and raised his mace over his head.

The orc saw him coming and turned its back to him, putting Deathclaw in the way. Fist had thought it might do that. He swung the mace low. The head swept under Deathclaw's perch and struck the back of the orc's knee. The blow landed with such force that one spike punctured through the armor, tore through muscle and tendon, and scored the bone deep within.

The orc crumpled to the side. It screeched and rolled, trying to shake Deathclaw from its back. Deathclaw held firm, digging with his toes, and tore more of the fibrous skin around the armored plate.

Fist grasped the orc's wounded leg by the ankle and yanked, stopping its rolling long enough for him to swing his mace again, this time striking the side of its knee. The joint bent inward with a crunch. In a panic, the orc threw a series of elbows back into Deathclaw's sides.

Deathclaw felt the flesh on his left side give, felt ribs crack and knew he would not be able to hold on. He tightened his grip and with one last strain, tore the section of armored skin away. The creature rolled again and this time Deathclaw let it go. It skittered forward on its hands and one good leg until Fist caught up to it.

The ogre's strike hit the back of its head, stunning the creature. He swung again and again, knocking its armored head back and forth until a series of cracks appeared in its helmet-like skull. It slumped to the sand.

The ogre swayed, bleeding profusely from the knife wounds and tired from the mace's magic. He felt a pang of sorrow through the bond and turned just in time to see Qyxal and Lenny tumble to the ground.

Behind him, the orc stirred. It struggled to push itself up to one knee, but Deathclaw had retrieved his sword from the mud. He thrust Star through the gaping hole in its back. A wisp of steam rose from the wound and the orc shuddered one final time before collapsing to the ground. Its armored plates began to melt.

The giant had caught Kenn completely unawares. Charz straddled him and roared with mocking laughter, pounding away with his fists, elbowing, kneeing, gouging. Kenn turned and contorted. He tried to push the giant away, claw him, bite him, but the attacks were ineffectual against the veteran brawler.

The heat grew more and more intense as Kenn grew more desperate. The ground bubbled and smoked. Charz laughed it off at first, but his skin blackened and started to glow red and his laughter turned to curses. The heat grew until the giant finally stood and backed away, his arms thrown up to protect his face.

Kenn didn't let Charz escape. The great red beast tackled the giant to the ground. The temperature grew. Charz's curses turned into screams of pain. Kenn roared and threw punch after punch. The earth around them glowed. The giant's screams stopped.

The extreme heat drove the rest of them back. Master Coal arrived with his bonded and helped Lenny take Qyxal's still form further down the beach, while Gwyrtha backed to the treeline.

Justan felt the heat wash over him but he refused to move. Pitying both monsters, he reached up and unsheathed his swords. His emotions melted away and he could feel his right sword throb with restrained power.

Kenn continued to punch the giant's still, white-hot form until he was sure it was dead. He slowly stood and turned to see Justan standing on the riverbank alone, both swords in hand, mist rising around him in a small cloud. Kenn snarled and limped towards him.

Justan!

He sensed Fist's and Gwyrtha's fear, knew that they were approaching despite the heat. *Stop,* he said, *I have to be the one to do this*. He acknowledged their doubts, and exuded such calm that they obeyed.

Kenn, though he towered over Justan, no longer looked as imposing as before. His wings were bent and torn. One great horn had broken off near his head. His face was battered and bloodied, his empty eye socket spewed black smoke, and the snarl on his face pulled back his bruised lips to reveal several broken teeth. He limped and bled freely from multiple wounds, leaving steaming pools on the scorched earth. Still, his heat burned as fiercely as ever.

Justan felt movement under his shirt. Something was happening to his scar, but his sword leeched away the pain. He would worry about that later. If he survived. He stepped forward, vaguely aware that his friends were yelling at him. He was glad that the heat kept them away. No one else needed to die.

His left sword assured him that it would be okay. His right sword assured him that it had the power he needed. The heat swirled around him with the intensity of a kiln. He stepped forward again.

Kenn's remaining eye widened in surprise. "ARE YOU SO WILLING TO BURN?"

"I am sorry, Kenn," Justan said and continued to walk forward. Steam rose all around him. He supposed that it was his own flesh melting, but for some reason, he wasn't concerned.

Kenn limped forward and reached out. Justan didn't try to dodge. He felt the hot coals that were Kenn's fingers wrap around his waist and lift him in the air. Kenn grinned and focused his heat on Justan.

Justan's vision switched to mage sight. Kenn's magic was more deeply red than orange now, but oddly it wasn't touching him. His body was unhurt. His clothes weren't even singed. In fact, they were caked with frost. Justan looked down to see blue and gold magic flooding from his chest, blending together into a tide of green.

"BURN!" Kenn shouted. He strained and the rocks around them cracked. The water at the river's edge boiled. The trees at the forest's edge went up in flames. Justan's friends had to back further and further away.

The front of Justan's shirt shattered and a pasty white hand with long black-taloned fingers burst from his chest. The hand extended out on a long slender arm and clutched Kenn's forearm, its black talons digging into his red skin. Frost leeched from its touch as it pulled. A skeletal noseless head popped free from Justan's chest. It pulled again. A set of shoulders followed. The Scralag grasped with its other arm and completely pulled free of the rune, then released Kenn's arm and stepped onto the ground.

"WHAT IS THAT?" Kenn grimaced in terror at its razor grin and swung his other fist at the creature, but it raised one thin arm and caught the blow without so much as a quiver. Frost extended from its touch and caked Kenn's fist in ice. It gazed at him with its beady red eyes and a hiss escaped through its lipless mouth. It released his frozen hand and took a step forward.

The Scralag pulled its arm back, straightened its fingers and leaned forward, plunging its hand into Kenn's chest. Its arm sank in to the elbow and an explosive gout of steam shot from the wound. Justan watched with his mage sight as Kenn's orange glow weakened and faltered. Green flowed from the Scralag, entering the great red beast's body. Ice grew from the wound and expanded outward. Kenn's mouth opened in a soundless scream as ice crawled out of his throat and sprung from his empty eye socket. The ice grew over his body until he was completely encased.

Now, said a cold voice in Justan's mind.

He swung his right sword and struck Kenn's arm. There was a small click. All of the pain and emotion that had been siphoned away by his left sword was converted into an explosion of force that extended in a straight line away from the impact. Kenn's arm shattered, as did half of his frozen torso.

Justan fell to the ground and pieces of the great beast landed all around him. Kenn's enormous head crashed to the earth and cracked down the center.

Justan sat on the ground, bruised, weary and amazed. The Scralag walked up to him holding something large and steaming in its hand and Justan realized that it was Kenn's heart. The Scralag held it out to him. Justan cringed and shook his head.

The Scralag cocked its head at him, then raised the prize to its mouth. It opened its set of grinning razor teeth and bit down. The heart instantly froze and shattered. The Scralag chewed the icy shards.

I return, it sent, and reached out with one claw to touch Justan's chest.

"No! Wait!" Justan said, but it vanished, leaving only misty particles behind.

Chapter Thirty Nine

Justan reached up and felt his chest, almost expecting to find a gaping icy hole. Instead, beneath his ruined shirt, he found only the familiar frost encrusted rune. It had returned to normal almost as if nothing had happened. He looked around himself at the frozen chunks of Kenn's body and shivered. Something had definitely happened.

He felt oddly disturbed about Kenn's destruction. It wasn't just the fact that Kenn was dead. It was the way that he had found himself sitting there, unmoving, watching it all unfold, almost like he didn't have a choice in the matter. The Scralag had done everything.

Justan forced his body to stand and winced. His lower back and knee still hurt, and he was covered in bruises, but to his surprise, he was otherwise unharmed. All that heat and he had come away unscathed. Somehow the Scralag had protected him the whole time. The horrible visage of the Scralag as it bit into Kenn's heart came unbidden to his mind. Justan pushed the horrible memory away. He rubbed his chest. Somehow he didn't feel very protected.

Justan! Gwyrtha arrived at his side, looking him over and sniffing at him worriedly. Satisfied that he was okay, she gave him a lick and snorted in approval.

Are you okay? Fist asked.

Justan saw the ogre far away, standing alone at the river's edge. During the intensity of the fight with Kenn, he hadn't been able to monitor their battle with the orc. Fist was bruised and exhausted and cut in several places, but the wounds weren't severe. *I'm okay, Fist.*

Deathclaw was hurt, but he is gone.

He didn't go far, Justan replied. *But he seems-.*

What was that thing that came out of you? Fist asked.

I'm not sure. Justan briefly shared his memories of the day he had met the Scralag. *The wizards called it a frost elemental. Whatever it is, it is a part of us now.*

I see, Fist said, troubled.

Qyxal! Gwyrtha said, nudging Justan.

I will follow after you, Fist said in understanding.

Justan nodded and climbed onto her saddle. He could see his friends gathered around the elf's still form. Lenny and Master Coal knelt at his side, while Bettie and Samson watched somberly. Gwyrtha arrived and Justan slid down to join them. He walked to Master Coal, but Bettie grabbed his shoulder and shook her head.

"He's trying, Sir Edge. Give him some time."

Justan's guts wrenched as he looked down at Qyxal's blackened form. A great sense of frustration rose within him. What use was his magic, if he couldn't help heal his friend? Justan clenched his fists and fell into the bond.

He sent his thoughts through to Gwyrtha and inspected her injuries. They were relatively minor, just a few burns. He soothed the pain and reinforced her body's natural healing ability before moving on to Fist. With Gwyrtha's permission, he funneled some of her energy into the ogre's tired muscles and went to work on the lacerations he had received during his fight. When he had done all he could, he moved on to Deathclaw.

The raptoid was hiding in the trees once again. His wounds were more severe than any of the other bonded, but he did not want to let Justan inspect him closer. Justan didn't back off. At that moment it was more important to him than ever that Deathclaw let him heal him.

You can trust me, Justan pleaded.

Deathclaw hissed and Justan saw the visage of the Scralag pass through the raptoid's thoughts. Deathclaw had seen it burst free from his chest. Seeing the event from his bonded's perspective gave Justan shivers. The raptoid was wary, but there was something more, perhaps approval. *What was it?*

I still don't know. I've been trying to find out myself. I-. Justan felt a tug on his shoulder. He withdrew from the bond and opened his eyes. Bettie released his shoulder and gestured towards Master Coal. The wizard still knelt by Qyxal's head, his hands outstretched. Justan saw his magical energies pouring into the elf. Gwyrtha had laid down at Qyxal's side, her scaled head nestled against his.

A lump rose in Justan's throat. It didn't look good. Qyxal's body was blackened and twisted and his chest rose and fell erratically, as he struggled for each breath. Only the right side of his face was untouched. Somehow seeing his one perfect brow and cheekbone combined with one unfocused and pain-filled eye made it worse. Justan knelt by his master but the wizard said nothing. Samson spoke instead.

"Coal can't talk aloud right now. H-he is trying but the damage is too severe. He thinks he could perhaps save his major organs but the majority of his body is just too badly burnt to fix. Even if he could somehow save his life, the pain . . ." A tear fell from the centaur's eye and his breath caught. "The pain is the worst part now. He's trying to soothe it, but . . ."

Justan unsheathed his left sword. Gingerly, he placed its hilt in Qyxal's withered hand. The elf sighed and the pain left his face. His one good eye focused and glanced at the people gathered around him.

"I'm so sorry, Qyxal," Justan said and the lump in his throat turned into sobs. "It's a-all my fault . . . All my fault you are here. If not for me, you'd still be at the Mage School."

"Justan," Qyxal said, his voice little more than a hoarse whisper. "I . . . wanted to be here." He coughed and the sound was horrible, but the sword sucked away all his pain.

"But-," Justan started.

"Just listen, son." Lenny said quietly. "This ain't about guilt. This is about Qyxal. Listen to him."

"Justan . . . my books. The seeds . . ."

"Yes, Qyxal." They had been in his pack. They were on Albert. The warhorse was well trained. He wouldn't be too far away. "I will get them to your people."

"Antyni," Qyxal said. "Take them to Antyni . . . she is . . ." His eye looked to the side. A half grin hit his face. "Gwyrtha. Hi girl . . ." His eye unfocused and a final breath left his lungs.

Master Coal gasped and swore. He stood and ran a shaking hand through his hair. "I'm sorry." Bettie and Samson each clasped his shoulder.

Gwyrtha keened as Justan took his sword gently from the elf's hand and resheathed it. He stood and stared blankly at his friend. Fist walked up and wrapped him in a big hug and Gwyrtha's sorrow mixed with theirs. Together they mourned.

Lenny closed Qyxal's eye with one finger and stood. "Bettie."

The half orc didn't respond. She had her head laid against Master Coal's and was deep within the bond.

"Bettie!"

She looked at him and frowned. "What?"

"I'm sorry, girl, but it can't wait. We need somethin' to wrap him in."

The half-orc nodded and left Coal's side. "Leather okay?"

"Yeah, but it's gotta be clean. NO DIRT, understand?" Lenny looked down at Qyxal's still form. "Quickly now. We gots to get him back to his people in as whole a piece as we dag-gum can."

She dug through their packs and pulled out the leather tarp they had brought to sleep on. She dusted it off. "Why no dirt?"

"He's a dag-gum elf," Lenny said. "His body'll stay good forever, unless it's buried. If dirt's touchin' him he'd break down so fast, all we'd have when we got there'd be a pile of bones. His people're gonna want to plant him in their homeland."

The dwarf gently prodded the others from their mourning and explained what they needed to do. They walked to the river's edge and everyone worked in silence. Coal and Samson washed the leather tarp. Fist lifted Qyxal's body while Justan and Lenny meticulously cleaned the elf of any dirt. Coal cast a spell to dry the tarp and they laid Qyxal on top of it. Bettie retrieved a brush from her pack and gently combed the elf's remaining hair free of debris, then Lenny wrapped the tarp around the elf and tied the bundle with rope.

They gathered their things and Gwyrtha went to round up Albert and Stanza. As Justan had guessed, they hadn't wandered too far. Both had burns and Albert had lost a good portion of his mane to the fire, but Master Coal was able to heal them. Lenny tied Qyxal's bundled body to the back of Stanza's saddle.

Justan retrieved Qyxal's journals and the bag of honstule seeds and tucked them into the bundle. He choked back another flood of tears. He had seen far too much death lately, but this was the first time that someone he had been truly close to had been killed.

He walked over to the place where Charz had fought Kenn. A small crater had been left behind by Kenn's final assault on the giant. The heat had been so intense that the rock had melted and pooled. It was hardened now and veins of glass were scattered throughout.

Justan shook his head at what remained of the rock giant. His body in many places looked fused with the rock and glass around him. His face was a ruin, his features half melted away, his gaping mouth with its white teeth the only part of him that was recognizable.

Master Coal walked up to him. "I did what I could for Qyxal."

"I know," Justan said and they stood in silence for a moment.

"That creature that came out of you, was it-?"

"It was the Scralag." Justan said. He rubbed at the rune on his chest. "And its still here, inside me. I don't know what to do about it."

"It's bonded to you," Master Coal said. "You will have time to figure it out."

Justan nodded and thought he saw movement in the ground in front of him. Just to make sure, he switched to mage sight. His breath caught in his throat. "Master Coal . . ."

"Yes?"

"What is it?" Samson trotted over and joined them.

"I think Charz is still alive. L-look at the spirit magic." Justan could see a long whispy white cord connected to a spot deep within the giant's chest. "The bond would be gone if he was dead, wouldn't it?"

Coal sighed. "He would be the one to survive this, wouldn't he?"

"What do we do?"

"Leave him," Samson said.

"But he tried to help us," Justan said. "Shouldn't we help him?"

The wizard hesitated, but shook his head. "He's right, Sir Edge. We should just go. This far away from his cave, Charz will heal very slowly, but he will heal. If he wakes up, he may decide to attack."

"No," came a pained voice. Justan and the others backed away as Charz's twisted bulk stirred. His head strained free from the ground and the rock around his ruined face cracked and shattered, some stones and shards of glass still clinging to his rocky flesh. He moved his mouth and spat but the rest of his face remained an unrecognizable lump. "I can't see . . . Coal, is that you?"

"It's me, Charz." Coal said.

The giant let out a pained chuckle and tried to move again, but all he did was crack the ground around him. He grunted. "I . . . didn't see you when I came out of the forest. You must find it . . . really funny to see me like this."

"I find it sad, Charz." Coal said, and there was genuine sadness in his voice. "I always find your condition sad."

"Is that named warrior here?" the giant asked. "That, Sir Edge?"

"I'm here," Justan said in surprise.

"Good," there was relief in the giant's voice. "I have a favor to ask you."

"He owes you nothing, Charz," said Samson.

"It's okay, Samson," Justan said. "What do you want?"

"Kill me."

"Don't be ridiculous," Master Coal said. "He's not going to-."

Justan drew his right sword and laid it against Charz's throat. The sword pulsed with the need to expend the energy it had absorbed from Qyxal's pain and Justan knew that it would only take a thought to remove the giant's head from his body. "Why, Charz? Tell me why I should kill you."

"Cuz I'm done," Charz wheezed. "I'm tired, and you . . . you are a bonding wizard, aren't you?"

"N- . . . How do you know?"

"Thought about it after you left me here on the river ba-." The giant coughed hard, then spat out blood and black chunks. "I laid here for two days, you know that? Two days before I healed enough to drag myself back to my cave. You'd beat me. The first time ever . . . I thought about it over and over, played the fight over in my head."

"The rogue horse didn't give it away?" Samson snorted.

The giant hacked and spat and gave a pained smile. "Yeah, but I wasn't thinking about that. It was the way Sir Edge fought that second time when he came back. That's how I knew they were bonded."

"So why does that mean I should kill you?" Justan asked.

"Because you're the one that beat me, why else? And it's fitting that it's a bonding wizard," the giant said. He worked his head around, dislodging one rather large rock that was stuck to his forehead. "Hell, I'm beat twice now. That last fight was a great one though, wasn't it? I mean, look what it did to me. I never fought something like that." Charz sighed and coughed again. "Anyway, just do it."

Justan withdrew his blade. "Before I decide, I want to understand. So you've been defeated. Why do you want to die?"

"I'm not worthy to live." Charz said. "I've known it for decades now. All the people I hurt, all the people I killed . . . My master tried to show me, you know. For the longest time, he would track down the families of the people I hurt. He would show them to me. Show me how much pain they were in."

"He was trying to help them," Coal said. "He was trying to make amends."

"Yeah, I laughed in his face. 'They shouldn't have fought me,' I said. But I knew. I knew."

"Why didn't you stop, then?" Coal demanded. "He would have forgiven you."

"There was no stopping. I was damned. I knew it. What was the point of trying? I loved the fight. I loved the challenge. I knew that . . . no matter what, until I found someone better than me, I wouldn't be able to stop."

"But that's over now? You are ready to give up the fight?" Justan said.

"Yes. I'm ready for this to be over."

Justan shook his head and sheathed his sword. "I can't help you."

"Wh-why? Please?" The giant tried to sit up again and this time more glass and rock broke free before he gave up and lay back down. "You don't understand, there is nothing for me here anymore. I'm ready to pay for what I've done. Kill me."

"Sorry. This is not my decision. This is up to your bonding wizard."

"He's right, Charz," Coal said. "You go back to your cave. You talk to him. Tell him what you told us. He'll look inside of you and if what you are saying is true . . ."

"Let him be the one to kill you," Justan said. "Or set you free, so that you can rejoin him."

"Free?" Charz laughed and coughed again. "B-but we haven't spoken in years. What if he won't talk?"

"He will," Coal assured him. "He's just waiting for you to come to him."

"Ohh, I can't. I can't face him now. Not after everything."

"The only thing I am willing to do is help bust up that rock around you," Justan said. "We'll do that in thanks for you helping us out during the battle."

Justan and Coal called out. Fist and Bettie arrived moments later dragging a bewildered Lenny along with them.

"And why in the gall-durn, pitch-forkin' hell are we helpin' this rock-biter?"

Fist shrugged. "He says he is done fighting."

"Hello, dwarf." said Charz. "Is that you I hear?"

Lenny looked down at the giant's half-melted face and smirked. "Hoo, look at what that thing did to you. I thought you was dag-blamed ugly before."

Charz snorted. "Too bad I can't see to check your thieving face for improvements."

"Thievin'? That dag-blasted hammer was mine to begin with!"

"I won it in battle. By rights, it was mine," the giant argued.

"It weren't never yers. Yer the blasted thief that stole it from me!"

"Spoils of war, dwarf. It's a law as old as time," Charz argued.

"And I beat you Charz, so it became mine." Justan reminded him. "I gave it to Lenny, so now it's his."

"Dag-gum right," Lenny said. "I guess . . ."

"Now both of you stop it," Justan said. "Lenny, you don't have to help us, but I promised Charz that we would help him break free from the rock."

"I'll help, gall-durn it," Lenny said. "He's pretty well sealed in there. Maybe I'll get lucky and hit somethin' important."

Lenny, along with Bettie and Fist, broke the rock up around the giant. Despite the dwarf's threats to the contrary, they were careful and only a few times did they hurt the giant. Once freed from the ground, the extent of the giant's injuries was evident. One of his arms had been so badly melted he was unable to move it, and bits of rock and glass that remained fused to his skin jutted out of his frame at odd angles. With Fist's help, the giant was able to stand. Every move he made pained him. He was wobbly on his feet and walked with a pronounced limp, but still he was able to move.

"Can you make it back to your cave?" Coal asked.

The giant nodded his twisted head. "I can feel it pulling at me. Telling me to come back-." He started coughing and doubled over so hard, he nearly fell over. Fist grabbed his arm to help steady him. Charz spat out a gob of black blood. "Gah! Anyway, I've been stuck here so long, I could never get lost. I'll make it there and the stupid place will heal me up."

Charz stood for a moment in silence, hunched over, his head hanging low. "I'll get going then. Maybe I'll get lucky and he'll forgive me." The giant limped to the treeline and then, with one hand grasping a trunk, turned his head back to them. "I . . . well, thank you is all." With that, he entered the forest.

Coal stood by Justan and shook his head. "I can't believe it. I tried hard for years to help him, Edge. Years. I felt I owed it to his wizard. When I finally gave up, I never thought this would happen."

"He's been humbled," Justan said with a half smile. He had been humbled before. A vision of Jhonate swam before his eyes. "I know how powerful that can be."

"I hope you're right." Coal said.

"Now before we leave, I have my own bonded to deal with," Justan said. He called to Fist and Gwyrtha and made sure that they understood what he wanted to do. Then the three of them went to talk to Deathclaw.

Chapter Forty

The raptoid's pain reached out like a beacon. Without even looking inside his body, Justan knew that Deathclaw's side was in agony, as was his arm, and for some reason the raptoid's head was pounding harder than ever. They walked to the forest's edge and stood under the tree he hid in. To Deathclaw's irritation, Squirrel was sitting in the branch next to him calmly chewing a nut and ignoring his threatening hisses.

Justan left the bond wide open and linked all his bonded together. *Deathclaw, we are here. Let me heal you.*

The raptoid didn't immediately push them away this time. Justan sensed that Deathclaw felt their concern. He was stuck in a state of confusion. These were feelings he had never experienced before. He didn't understand why they had come back to the river for him. He didn't understand why they had fought for him.

They stood patiently until Deathclaw responded, *You . . . Why?*

You are part of our tribe, came Fist's thoughts.

Deathclaw. Tribe, echoed Gwyrtha.

We are your pack, said Justan.

Each statement was matter of fact. Despite his agony, a hint of understanding entered Deathclaw's mind. His heart beat faster. A new pack? Could this be true? *Human . . . Justan . . . you can fix this?*

Yes. I think so. But I'm still learning. I may need some help from Master Coal.

The wizard? Deathclaw recoiled at the thought of a wizard touching him again.

He will observe only, Justan assured him. He sent over soothing feelings regarding Master Coal, but he didn't push it. Justan wanted Deathclaw to know he could be trusted, but he also understood how intense the fear was. *I will not allow him to work his magic on you.*

Deathclaw's mind burned with uncertainty, but the pain was so great that he finally acquiesced. *I . . . allow it.*

Justan sent Gwyrtha to get Master Coal and dove into the bond. When he switched to mage sight, he was stunned. Deathclaw's body was alive with magic. Every cell was bound with the elements. His very blood was coursing with it. The magic seemed unstable yet at the same time it held together. The way the magic moved reminded him of Gwyrtha's body. He didn't have the same source of intense energy, but the flow of it was very similar.

Justan went to work. He looked at the biggest problem first. A great swath of skin and flesh on the left side of Deathclaw's body had been eaten away. Fist provided the memory of the acid that the modified orc had spit on him. The damage was deep. Most of his abdominal wall was eaten away in areas. Deathclaw was lucky that his climb into the tree hadn't caused his internal organs to burst out.

A human would have been crippled for life after such damage, but Deathclaw's body was already working on the problem. The flesh was being restored at a rapid rate. It was already doing more than Justan knew how to do, so he just pulled some energy from Gwyrtha to help speed it along. He discarded some of the ruined flesh and cleaned out some dirt and debris that had gotten into the wound and left it at that.

Justan looked at Deathclaw's arm. One of the bones in his forearm had been broken but was partially healed. From Deathclaw's thoughts, Justan knew that normally it would have healed by now if his magic hadn't been busy elsewhere. Justan soothed the swollen nerves around the break and stimulated the healing process further. He then moved on to the other minor cuts and bruises, but they had already mostly healed.

Finally he went to find the source of the raptoid's headache. It wasn't difficult. All he had to do was follow the pain. A tiny bulge in Deathclaw's brain was pressing against a major artery. Justan wasn't sure what could have caused it. Perhaps Ewzad Vriil had been messy when transforming him, or perhaps the additional changes brought about by their bonding had caused the problem. Either way, this wasn't something Justan knew how to handle. It was Deathclaw's brain. What if he made it worse?

Deathclaw, I have done what I can from here, but now I need Master Coal's help. I need you to come down from the tree. Please do it carefully. The wound in your side could get worse.

The raptoid didn't come down right away. The wizard and his beasts had arrived. How was he supposed to trust them? But Justan had been true to his word so far. The pain in his wounds had lessened and his body felt revitalized. Despite his instincts crying out against the decision, Deathclaw climbed down the tree.

He stood, watching them, his heart beating fiercely. He kept his back to the tree and made sure that he had an escape route available. If forced to, he was ready to fight.

It's okay, Deathclaw. There will be no need. Justan sent. "Would the rest of you back away though? He's not comfortable around everyone." Bettie and Lenny left and Samson backed away, leaving Justan and Coal standing in front of the Raptoid.

"Is he alright with me getting close?" Coal asked.

"I'll let you know if he has a problem," Justan said. "The thing is, he wants me to do the healing. I just need you to tell me what to do."

Master Coal stepped closer and put out his hands above the raptoid's head. "Please stay still," he said. Deathclaw watched the wizard's fingers, ready to run at the first sign of any unnatural movements.

A vision appeared in the air between the wizard's hands. Justan could see the pathway in Deathclaw's head where the tiny bulge was. Justan dove into the bond and listened intently to Coal's instructions. It only took a few minutes and they were finished. Justan immediately felt the relief in Deathclaw. For the first time in weeks, the pain was gone.

Justan turned and smiled at the wizard, but Coal was still staring at Deathclaw, his face wide-eyed with wonder.

"You see it, don't you?" he mumbled.

"What?" Justan asked.

Samson walked forward to stand by the wizard, his face etched in concern. "What is it?"

"I know how Ewzad Vriil has been creating these creatures." Coal turned to the centaur. "Samson, he has the Rings of Stardeon."

Samson's fists clenched. "I see."

"What are you talking about?" Justan asked.

Master Coal opened his mouth to answer but hesitated. "The rogue horses don't like to talk about it. Samson . . . I know this is a sensitive subject. Are you willing to tell them?"

Samson stood with brow furrowed, thinking about it. Gwyrtha walked over to him and nuzzled his hand. Finally he nodded. "Stardeon was the creator of the rogue horses," he said. "What Coal is saying is that somehow the same device our creator used to make us is being used by Ewzad Vriil to transform his creatures."

"It has happened before. In the past." Coal said. "One of the Dark Prophet's wizards used it, but the rings disappeared after the war."

"But how can you tell that just by looking at Deathclaw? I mean, I see that his body has some similar qualities as Gwyrtha, but he is still very different."

Deathclaw looked at Gwyrtha in confusion.

"He may not have all the other attributes she has but-." Coal shook his head. "Just look closer. Look at him with your spirit sight."

Justan did so, drawing a wisp of the bond over his eyes. The traces of magic in Deathclaw's every fiber were reinforced and held together by strands of spirit magic. "He's . . ."

"Yes! Exactly. He's not unstable like the creations of Ewzad Vriil we faced today. He is a rogue horse."

Justan stared at his master in stunned amazement. "He can't be. There's no horse in him. I've seen his memories. He was a raptoid living in the desert before Ewzad Vriil changed him."

"And that explains why he is different from Ewzad Vriil's other creations," Master Coal said. "Let me explain it another way and perhaps you'll understand. You see, no two rogue horses are the same. Most of them are mounts and most of them have some amount of horse in them, but each one is vastly different, as different as Samson is to Gwyrtha. There is only one common link to their make-up." He paused and looked back at Samson with an apologetic wince. "I'm sorry. I did not mean to . . . You tell them what you wish. This is your story." He took a step back and folded his arms.

The centaur frowned for a moment, but finally nodded. "When Stardeon first started creating the rogue horses, the results were disastrous. Every creature he made with his rings was unstable. The only way he could keep them from falling apart was if he continually charged them with his magic. He experimented for months trying to find something to stabilize the magic. He only found it by accident."

Justan listened to the centaur in rapt attention. He had always been curious about Gwyrtha's origins, but she held her old memories close. They were the only things she had been unwilling to share. Even now he sensed her unease with the subject of their conversation.

"What is it?" Fist asked. Squirrel sat on his shoulder, a nut half chewed, his head half cocked as if echoing the ogre's question.

"The heart of a dragon," Samson said. "That is the only part of the body that all rogue horses share in common. It's the only thing that keeps us from eventually falling apart, and unlike the other creations Ewzad Vrill made with Stardeon's rings, Deathclaw has it too. He was born with it."

"That's why his body stabilized after Ewzad Vriil changed him." Master Coal said. "Raptoids are a small species of dragon."

All eyes turned on Deathclaw. The raptoid hissed and ran into the forest. He didn't like the attention. He continued to listen, but preferred to ponder the revelations alone.

"We can't leave Vriil with those rings, Coal," Samson said. "Those are Stardeon's. They shouldn't be misused this way. We should get to them right away."

Coal looked into the centaur's eyes for a few moments and from the intensity of their gazes Justan could tell that they were arguing. The wizard cleared his throat and said, "Our first priority is to get to the Battle Academy and help Willum and Justan's family that are there. If

Ewzad Vriil is there, we will deal with him as well."

Gwyrtha let out a deep, angry growl and Justan felt her resolve stiffen. *Kill him for Stardeon.* Deathclaw hissed from deep in the trees. He wished the wizard dead as well.

"They are right," Justan said. "We can't stop at freeing the Battle Academy. He'll just build another army and attack again. Once we're done there, we will hunt Ewzad Vriil down and take those rings."

The Bowl of Souls series will continue in Book 4:

The WAR of STARDEON

In the meantime, you might want to read **HILT'S PRIDE: Book 1.5**
This Novella contains information critical to the series and introduces important characters.
A sample chapter follows:

I

The girl with the golden hair had come to die. It was the only answer that made sense. Hilt glanced back at the woman as the gorc's head hit the ground with a splash of dark blood.

She stood as if unafraid of the goblinoids that attacked. Her hair gleamed golden in the morning sunlight. Her eyes were fixed on him in curiosity, not in hope of rescue as he would expect.

Hilt stepped back from the dead creature as the next gorc attacked. He knocked aside its rusty iron blade. Stupid thing. It had to know it was outmatched. He had killed five of its comrades already. Hilt swept the tip of his left sword across its face, taking out an eye. It stumbled back with a howl, clutching at the wound. Hilt glared at the others, giving his swords a menacing twirl.

The two remaining gorcs grabbed their wounded comrade and retreated around a large nearby boulder, sending angry curses back at Hilt all the way. The fight seemed to be over, but Hilt knew that there were more gorcs nearby watching from the rocks.

Gorcs were little more than a nuisance to a trained warrior. They were a shade smaller than humans, larger and smarter than a lowly goblin, but smaller and stupider than an orc. Gorcs were in fact born from goblins, but gorcs despised their smaller brethren and formed tribes of their own.

Hilt didn't care where the creatures came from. They were mere rabble, unfit to stain his blade. He wouldn't have bothered if not for the girl.

He had first seen her earlier that morning climbing the steep incline of the mountainside alone. She had looked frail and vulnerable winding her way around the enormous boulders that littered the slope. Hilt had seen signs that the area was full of monsters and followed, intending to tell her to turn back. By the time he arrived, the gorcs had surrounded her.

Now that the immediate danger was over, Hilt turned to speak with her. But she was no longer standing there. The woman had turned back to the task of climbing the mountainside.

"Wait! Young lady!" Hilt caught up to her in moments. "Young lady, where are you going?"

"Young lady?"

She turned around and Hilt saw her up close for the first time. Now that she was out of the sunlight, her hair no longer gleamed golden. It was more of a dirtied blond. Her face was attractive, but weary. Her skin was tanned and wrinkled around piercing blue eyes. Her dress was long sleeved and woolen and quite dirty. This was a woman who spent most of her time outdoors, perhaps working the fields.

"I am surely no younger than you, swordsman." She turned back to climbing the steep slope. "Now leave me be. There are plenty more monsters for you to slay."

Hilt stared after her, blinking in disbelief. “Madam, I . . . I was not here to slay monsters. I was on a pressing mission when I saw the beasts surround you. I only followed you up here to keep you from getting killed!”

“Well you succeeded then. I am not dead.” she said, not looking back. “Now, if you’ll excuse me, I have my own ‘important duty’ to perform.”

He followed her up the slope a few moments more. “You truly aren’t going to thank me?”

“I never asked for your help, did I?” She took a few more labored strides up the mountainside, then paused and whirled around, her lips twisted into a scowl. “Just what were you expecting in thanks?”

“Expecting?” Hilt folded his arms across his chest. What an insolent woman. “When a man saves your life, isn’t thanks customary?”

“Oh! So you followed me up here seeking a reward? Hmph, you sound like nobility.” She eyed his clothing with suspicion. His garb was finely made but well worn and adjusted for easy movement. He wore leather boots, calf high with woolen breeches, and a white shirt covered by a chainmail vest and a fine overcoat. Sword sheathes hung at either hip and he had a small pack slung over his shoulders. “What did you want, a maiden’s kiss of gratitude? Well I ain’t no maiden!”

Hilt’s face wrinkled in confusion. “Madam I most definitely did not come seeking a kiss."

She misunderstood the look on his face and gasped, one hand raising to her mouth. "A kiss not good enough? You see me, a baseborn woman all alone and think to take advantage? I think not. I may not be a maiden, but I'm not street trash! Go look for your 'thanks' elsewhere. I'll take my chances with the monsters!"

Hilt's face went red and he sputtered in outrage as she turned and resumed her climb. "Foul!" he cried finally.

She snorted and resumed her climb.

"That was a most- . . ." he strode quickly up the steep slope and passed the woman before turning to face her. "That was a most foul accusation! I climb up here out of my way to save your life and I am rewarded with scowls and disparaging remarks?"

"There you are expecting rewards again," she accused, taking a step backward. Her foot caught in her dress and she stumbled. She would have taken a tumble down the slope if Hilt had not reached out and grasped her arm. She struggled and slapped his arm as he pulled her to her feet. "Unhand me!"

Hilt made sure she had regained her footing before letting go, then raised both hands and took a step back. "I am sorry for my choice of words. I seek no reward. Truly. I just expected common courtesy is all."

Her blue-eyed glare softened only slightly. "Alright then, you have your thanks. Now will you step aside, so I can get where I'm going?"

"I will not," Hilt said, arms folded, his voice firm.

Her fists clenched, but she forced a smile on her face. "Why thank you, kind sir. It was a privilege to be saved by a warrior such as yourself. There, is that better?"

Even though it was forced, Hilt had to admit her smile was pretty. He shrugged. "A bit better, yes."

"Then move it," she said, the smile still frozen on her face. She took a step forward, but Hilt did not move.

"I refuse," he said firmly.

Her eyes narrowed. "What do you want then?"

"Your safety," he replied. "No matter how mean tempered you

are, I cannot in good conscience allow you to continue any farther. The way ahead would mean your certain death."

"And what makes you so sure?" she asked as her forced smile faded.

"For one, the gorcs are still watching us from the boulders below. More will likely join them and the only reason they haven't attacked us again already is the fact that I left six of them dead down there. Secondly, do you see these signs, my lady?" Hilt gestured to a small pile of stones next to her feet. They were white and irregularly shaped, but stacked evenly to form a small pyramid.

She nodded. "Rocks. What of it?"

"Look around you," he said, pointing to his right. Another similar pile of stones stood several yards away and she could see another one even further away. They seemed to be spaced apart evenly. "We crossed over similar signs earlier when we entered the gorc's territory."

She looked down at the piles and back up at him. "So we walked past piles of stones."

"You don't understand. The first signs we passed were made of plain stones set in a circular pattern. They are used to tell goblinoids when they're at the border of another tribe's territory. The stones here, however, are stacked in a pyramid shape used by goblinoids to mark areas of danger. In other words, these stone represent a warning to their own tribe members to stay away."

"Good," she said. "That means they won't follow me up there. I hope you will follow their example."

Hilt grit his teeth in frustration. "Why are you so determined to die?"

"I won't die. At least I don't think so," she admitted, still seeming quite unconcerned. She tried to continue past him, but Hilt grabbed her shoulders with both hands, stopping her. She twisted and tore free from his grasp, nearly stumbling yet again. "Don't you touch me!"

"Then tell me."

"I will tell you nothing," she spat.

"I have half a mind to throw you over my shoulder and carry you down this mountain," Hilt said, his eyebrows raised at her ferocity.

"I would fight you the whole way!"

"You could not stop me. I could knock you unconscious if I had to. I would make sure you did not wake until I could take you to the nearest village and drop you off at an inn."

"I would have no choice in that case." Rage simmered behind her eyes, but she swallowed and gathered herself, then replied with complete calm. "However, if you did so, sir, I would only wait until you were gone and come back anyway."

"Be that as it may, I will do exactly as I threatened unless you tell me why you are so determined to ascend this mountain." Hilt said, jaw fixed in determination. "Tell me, woman, and do it fast because the gorcs are gathering in number."

Hilt pointed down the slope behind her. She turned to see that several more gorcs had joined the others and they were no longer bothering to hide. The one with the blinded eye was pointing up at them and snarling at the others. She looked back at Hilt and glared again.

"I can see that you are determined to continue, but do you really want to be caught and likely eaten by those creatures?" Hilt prodded. "I will make you this concession. Tell me the truth and if your answer is satisfactory, not only will I let you go on, I will go down and slay the beasts just to give you a better chance."

She looked at Hilt's unmoving stance and up at the long climb ahead, then down to the gorcs below. When she looked back at him her expression was resigned. "Fine. Since you must know . . . the prophet told me to come to this mountain and climb to the summit."

Hilt blinked, then his eyes narrowed in intensity. "The prophet? Tell me, what did he look like?"

"Well, he was . . . his face . . ." Her brow wrinkled in confusion and she paused for a moment to search her memories, "I-I don't know how to describe him, just his presence. He just . . . he just felt right. Like I was safe with him and that he would never lead me wrong."

Hilt stared at her for a few seconds before placing his face in his hands, "Oh blast it all. How did he know I would be coming this way? Blast!"

"Excuse me?" she said, wide eyed at his reaction.

He put up a conciliatory hand. "Forgive my language. It's just that he always does this. He makes people a promise and shoves them in my path." The next time he saw the prophet he would be sure to tell him about it too. Hilt shook his head and sighed. "I suppose my mission will have to be placed on hold."

Hilt reached for a leather strip that hung around his neck and pulled a slender tube made of a smooth gray wood out from under his chainmail vest. He lifted it to his lips and blew. There was no audible sound, but he felt it warm against his fingers and knew his message had been received. He nodded and tucked it back under his shirt.

"What are you doing?" she asked.

"I am telling my companion that I need his assistance." Hilt said. "He left Reneul before I did, but he has been taking his time. If I had not taken this detour I would have caught up to him by nightfall."

"But how-? Why . . .?" Her eyes widened in comprehension. "Wait. No-no. You're not coming with me."

"Oh, yes I am" Hilt said. He turned and strode parallel to the piles of rock that dotted the mountainside. "Come along. It would be best to stay out of the area the gorcs marked. They wouldn't warn their own people away without good reason."

"But-!" She hesitated, then hurried after him. "You didn't listen. I said 'You're *not* coming with me.'"

"And yet I am," Hilt replied. He paused and looked back at her. "You know, since we are to be taking this little journey together, I really should ask your name."

"Beth," she said. "But I still haven't agreed-."

He gave her a deep bow. "Beth, my lady, so nice to meet you. My name is Hilt. And don't worry, as soon as I get you to the top of this peak, I will take my leave and you will not have to see me again." He turned and continued along the slope, glad that the first winter snows had not come yet. The slope was steep and footing was hard enough as it was.

She followed behind him in silence for a while, which suited him just fine. The line of white stone markers eventually curved and turned up the steep slope of the mountainside and Hilt followed it, skirting the edge of the line they marked. The ground was a bit rocky and stubbled with tufts of grass for easy footing, but it was a strenuous hike nonetheless. Hilt fumed that the prophet had stuck him with such an arduous task.

He kept looking back at the woman to make sure she was holding up. She trudged along right behind him with her skirts held up in bunched fists to keep from entangling herself. Her face was red and she was breathing quite heavily, but to her credit she wasn't complaining. Luckily there was no sign that the gorcs had followed them.

They hiked to the top of the incline. The ground leveled off and the path was flat for a while before the next rise, so Hilt stopped so she could rest. He sat on a large rock and watched her stumble over and plop down on another rock a few feet away. She slumped over and rested her forearms on her knees.

Hilt eyed her curiously. "So Beth, my lady, the prophet tells you to climb a mountain, and you come wearing that?"

She gave him an irritated glance. "It's what I had on at the time."

"But where did you come from? There are no villages anywhere nearby and you aren't wearing a pack or anything. Do you have supplies? Food? Water?"

Her irritation turned into a glare. "He told me to go, and I went. What about you? You leave on an important mission from Reneul of all places going someplace urgently, and you throw it all away to climb a mountain with a woman that you obviously find quite crazy. All you have is that small pack on your back. Not exactly mountain climbing gear I would think."

"I am a named warrior. I can take care of myself," Hilt replied.

Beth snorted. "Pfft! Named warrior. Right!"

Hilt lifted his arm and showed her the rune on the back of his hand.

"Oh," she said. "I didn't-."

"It's usually the first thing people notice," he remarked.

"Well, it's not like I go around checking the back of people's hands all the time just to make sure they're not named."

"It covers the whole back of my hand. It's pretty hard to miss," Hilt pointed out. "Didn't you see me fighting?"

"I know a lot of good fighters and none of them are named," she said. Hilt rolled his eyes. "What? I'm supposed to see your fighting skill and say, 'oooh, he must be a named warrior'? Do I need to check your palms too just to make sure you're not a named wizard as well?"

"Don't be ridiculous." Hilt said. He shook his head and stood. "Let us start this over, shall we?" He cleared his throat. "Good morning, Madam. I am Sir Hilt, a named warrior come to take you down off this mountain before you get yourself killed."

He looked at her expectantly. She just stared back at him.

"Well," Hilt prompted. "Your turn. Come on."

A slight smile touched the corner of her mouth and she replied, "Why hello, Sir Hilt. I am Beth and I am climbing this mountain because the prophet told me to. I might let you tag along if you ask nicely."

Hilt smiled. "Very good then. Since we are to be travel companions, would you mind if I take stock of our situation?"

She laid back on the rock and stretched out her legs. "Sure, go ahead."

"The good news is that as far as I can tell, the gorcs haven't followed us," he said.

"Good," she yawned.

"The problem is that it is going to take us maybe two days to climb to the top if we can make good time. We haven't had any snow yet, but it is going to get cold especially at night." He paused and looked at her again. "Is that dress really all you brought?"

"Do I look like I'm hiding anything?" she said, resting back on her elbows.

Hilt frowned. "How did you get here?" She just stuck out her feet in response so he tried again. "Perhaps the better question is where did you come from? There are no villages for miles from here."

"Pinewood," she said.

"You walked all the way here from Pinewood? You would have had to travel all the way through the Tinny Woods!" He was impressed with the woman's ability to survive. The place was crawling with moonrats and the foul creatures would eat anything alive or dead.

"I was in the woods when the prophet found me. He told me to go and I went."

"But how did you survive?"

She sighed. "I don't know. I just walked east. When I was thirsty, there was a stream. When I was hungry, there were berries. At night I dug under the leaves and slept. I never saw a single moonrat. I heard them of course, but never saw a single glowing eye. Since then I haven't worried. The prophet said I could do it, so I know I can."

"So what did he tell you?" he asked.

"I told you," she said with a dull stare. "Climb the mountain."

"What were his instructions?" Hit prodded, growing tired of her obstinance. "What exactly did he say to you?"

"He said, 'Walk to the east. On the far side of the woods is a mountain. Climb to the top and you will find the answer you seek.' I said, 'When do I leave?' He said, 'Go now.' I said, 'Now? Wearing this?' He said, 'Yes.' I said, 'Shouldn't I prepare first? Pack supplies?' He said, 'If you go now, you will have everything you need.' I said, 'Okay.' Then I started walking."

Hilt looked at her askance. "You're fooling with me aren't you?"

Beth threw up her hands. "Fine. Believe me or not. That's what he said."

There was truth in her eyes and Hilt had to accept it. "Very well. It looks like the prophet has provided our course. Nothing specific as usual, just, 'go up the mountain.' Let us see what means he has provided us with. What do you have on you, besides your dress? Anything?"

"And my underclothes, but no," she said. "Thick wool socks on my feet, my shoes, and a needle and spool of thread that I had forgotten were in my pocket when I left. I had a hairpin but I broke it trying to pick the lock on the treasure chest I found back in the forest."

"You what?" Hilt said, eyebrows raised.

"Now that time I was fooling with you," she said, stone faced.

Hilt blinked at her, then laughed. "You did throw me off, there."

She was unable to suppress a smile in return, "So the named warrior laughs?"

"You don't know me. I am quick with a laugh," Hilt replied. "But still, a needle and thread are a commodity to take note of. As for me, I am carrying my swords, a waterskin, a dagger, a blanket, a coil of rope, my flame stick, some leather strips, some parchment, a quill and inkwell, some dried meat, and half a hard loaf of bread. It seems we shall have to find nourishment along the way."

"You carry all that in your little pack?" she asked, dubiously eyeing the bundle strapped behind his shoulders,.

"I am an efficient packer," he replied. Too much bulk or weight hampered his movements and he never knew when he might need to draw his swords for battle. "Now we should really keep moving. I would like to put a lot more distance between us and those gorcs by sundown."

She stood with a groan. "You worry about the gorcs? They didn't give you much trouble before."

Hilt snorted. "Gorcs are little trouble in the daylight. But at night, they could ambush us and with enough numbers I could have trouble protecting you. Come, let's continue."

He stood and resumed his route along the line of stone markers. They stretched along, small white dots in the mountainside as far as his eye could see, extending the length of the flat area and continuing up another steep slope. It was going to be a hard climb. Beth hurried up next to him, holding up her skirts as she kept pace. Her mouth was twisted like she wanted to say something, but they traversed the flat and rocky stretch of mountainside and nearly reached the next slope before she spoke.

"I still don't understand why you've decided to protect me," she said finally. "You said you were on a mission. Why the sudden change of heart? Why put the mission aside to help a woman past her prime on a hopeless quest?"

Hilt smiled. "My lady, you may not be a maiden, but you are hardly past your prime." She was probably near forty, but he gave a kind guess. "What are you, thirty?"

She wasn't fooled and gave him a knowing glare. "Thirty five."

Hilt shrugged. "Still younger than I, and I am most definitely not out of my prime, thank you."

"My age isn't the point," she said, letting go of her dress with one hand to waggle a finger at him. "You were all set to carry me down that mountain until I mentioned the prophet. What made you change your mind?"

"I am a named warrior. This happens from time to time."

"What hap-!" As she stepped over a rock, her foot caught in the frayed hem of her dress. She tripped forward and fell to the ground, banging one knee and skinning the palms of her hands as she tried to catch herself.

Hilt stopped to help her up. He bent to grasp her arm, but reared back as she let out a stream of curses. He stood stunned and watched while she rose to her feet on her own and stomped her feet, cussing all the while, ending with, "I hate this dress!"

She turned and directed her glare at Hilt, who stood with hands raised, his face not betraying his thoughts. "What?" Beth spat. "I told you I'm a base born woman!"

"If I might make a suggestion, my lady." Hilt began.

"Do you want a black eye?" she said, shaking a quivering fist at him.

Hilt paused. "No. But If I may-."

"Stop calling me 'My lady'. I am not your lady. I am a regular person who is having a very bad year! My name is Beth. Call me Beth!"

"I am sorry," Hilt said. He saw tears in her eyes and realized that there was much more to her story than she had told him. "Beth, I have a suggestion. Something that might help with your current difficulty."

"Wings? Can you sprout wings and fly me up this mountain?" She asked, wide eyed. A moment of silence stretched between them and a chuckle escaped her lips. She burst out laughing. She sat down on the ground and laughed until tears streamed down her face. "Gah! This is all so ridiculous! I'm sorry. I am sorry, Sir Hilt. I am crazy and I am sorry. Sorry for yelling at you. Sorry for dragging you up here after me. Sorry for everything."

"It's okay. It's okay." Hilt crouched beside her and offered her a hand. A note of sternness entered his voice. "Beth. Stand up."

She accepted his hand and allowed him to pull her to her feet.

While she dusted off her dress, he pulled his waterskin from its place at his side. He tossed it to her.

"Drink," he said and she did so gratefully. He took off his small pack and opened it up, pulling out several long strips of leather.

"Thank you," She said, wiping her mouth as she handed the waterskin back to him. He took it from her and replaced it at his side, then slung his pack back over his back.

"Now Beth, as I was trying to say, your dress is a nuisance. If you try to climb the mountain like this you are going to end up falling off a cliff or something. Now," He lifted the leather strips and drew his dagger. She eyed the dagger and took a step back. He held it out to her hilt first. "What I am suggesting, is that we turn that dress into bloomers."

"What?"

"Do you know what I am talking about? It may be more of a south-eastern style, but . . ."

"Oh! Of course!" Beth smiled and took the dagger and leather strips from him. She began cutting the skirts of her dress down the middle. "Oh, I wish I had thought of it before! Some times I am so stu-. Hey! Turn around."

"Sorry," Hilt said and turned his back to her as she continued her work, splitting the skirt and tying one half to each leg with the leather strips. When she had finished, she told him to turn back around.

"What do you think?" The leather strips looked like they were trying to contain a pair of ridiculously puffy trousers. She lifted one leg to show her freedom of movement.

"If I didn't know better, I would think you've done this before," Hilt replied, stifling a laugh.

She handed the dagger back to him. "It was a fabulous idea. I would do a cartwheel if not for my aching palms."

"Very good, shall we continue on?" Without waiting for a response he started up the slope, keeping an eye out for the path with the easiest footing.

He soon found a narrow trail worn into the mountainside that ran more or less parallel to the white stone markers. It seemed that the gorcs traversed this slope fairly often. This was fortunate, for it made the going easier, but it also meant that they could run into some of the creatures at any time. Hilt narrowed his senses, looking for signs of recent activity and listening for any sounds that could come from unwanted company. All he heard however was the scrape of their feet against the rocks and Beth humming a tune under her breath.

She was enjoying herself despite the steep climb. Being freed from the dress had put her in a good mood. Hilt was grateful for that, but at the same time, her humming was terribly out of tune. The worst part was that he recognized the song. It was one of his favorite tavern drinking songs and she was butchering it. She continued on, repeating the same verse over and over, each time just a little bit off. Finally he had had enough.

Hilt turned and said in what he hoped was a reasonable tone of voice, "No-no no. I believe you have that wrong. You see, the tune ends, '*and they all gave her a spaaankiiing.*'"

"What song did you think I was humming?" she asked.

"The Farmer's Drunken Daughter."

She laughed. "No. It was, The Dusty Dog's Last Laugh."

"No you weren't. That song goes, '*when the cobbler threw out the dry boooooones.*"

"Pff! Where did you learn the song?" She shook her head. "It goes, 'when the cobbler threw out the dryyyyyy bones!"

Her singing was even worse than her humming. Hilt grit his teeth. "I-. No-. Look that's not the point. It doesn't matter what the song is. Just-. Shh! New rule. No singing or humming."

"No humming?" she wrinkled her nose. "Why is that a rule?"

"Look, we are following a gorc trail. I am trying to listen for signs that they are close, so shh!"

She looked around at the barren rocky mountainside. "Where would they be hiding?"

"This is their land. Not ours. They know where to hide. Just-just be silent until I am sure," Hilt said.

"Fine," she said with a shrug and they continued on.

The trail was well used and free of debris. It meandered back and forth in a series of switchbacks that took them up the steepest part of the incline. They made good time, but as they neared the top, Hilt's concerns proved to be well founded. The sound of drums and gorc chanting began to echo down from the top of the ridge.

They crept up the last few switchbacks until they neared the top. Hilt motioned her to stay silent and left the trail, slowly climbing up the last stretch of the slope to peer over the top. Fifty feet ahead rose a sheer cliff thirty feet high. The trail they were on headed towards the cliff, then took a right and ran alongside it, leading to a wooded area bristling with pine trees. The sounds of the gorc camp came from that direction and he could see smoke wafting up from behind the trees. To his left, the line of white stone markers stretched on, ending at the cliff face. He swore under his breath.

Hilt slid back down to the trail and made sure to whisper to make sure his voice didn't carry to the gorcs. "I'm afraid we have three choices, none of them particularly good." He turned to see Beth lying on her side next to a large flat bounder, peering underneath. She reached one hand under the rock.

"Just a second, you sucker . . . there!" Beth rolled to her knees and stood, dragging out a long brown snake. She gave Hilt a triumphant smile and lifted it by the tail. It arched and hissed trying to reach her, but she kept it at arms length. "Got it!"

Hilt put a finger to his lips and raised a cautioning hand, then slowly drew one sword, and whispered, "Beth. Listen carefully. Drop it and back away. That is a Brown Viper. Very poisonous!"

She rolled her eyes and whispered back, "I'm not going to let it bite me!"

"Just put it down," Hilt said, ready to lop off its head as soon as she let go.

"Oh for goodness sake," Beth said and in one fluid motion, swung the snake up over her head in a wide arc and whipped it against the rock. Then as it lay stunned and motionless, she took one step and crushed its head with the heel of her boot. She smiled at him sweetly. "And that, Sir Hilt is how a Pinewood lady hunts for supper."

"I . . ." Hilt didn't know how to react. He was both confused and impressed by this woman in equal measure. He sheathed his sword.

"Very good then. Viper dead. So . . ."

She folded her arms. "Three bad choices?"

"Yes, three choices. At the top of the incline, we can either follow the trail to the right towards a gorc encampment, we can go straight and climb a sheer cliff, or we can go left and cross over the line of white markers."

She frowned. "Why are we so afraid of crossing those white rock piles again?"

Hilt closed his eyes, then took a deep breath and released it slowly. "It could be anything. Creatures, natural hazards . . . For the gorcs to mark a part of their own territory in this way means that they fear what ever is over that line."

"Ah, but I've got you with me, right? Nothing you can't handle." She smacked him on the shoulder, looped the dead snake over her arm and headed up the incline.

Hilt again considered knocking her unconscious and dragging her back down the mountain. Instead he joined her at the top, made sure that there were no gorcs in sight and led her to the left, crossing the white markers.

ABOUT THE AUTHOR

Trevor H. Cooley was born in South Carolina and has lived all around the United states, including Utah, New Mexico, Michigan and Tennessee.

His love of reading started in the second grade with Lloyd Alexander's Chronicles of Prydain series. He couldn't get enough and continued with David Eddings, Tolkein, Robert Jordan, Stephen King, and many others. Since then, all he wanted was to become a published writer.

The characters and concepts that eventually became the Bowl of Souls series started in his teens. He wrote short stories, kept notebooks full of ideas, and generally dreamed about the world constantly. There were several attempts at starting a novel over the years.

Not long after he was married, his wife told him to stop talking about the story and write it down. Many years and rewrites and submissions and rejection letters later, he finally put the first book on Amazon in May 2012. He currently lives in Tennessee with his wife and four children.

Website: trevorhcooley.com

Facebook: Trevor H. Cooley

Twitter: @edgewriter

CPSIA information can be obtained
at www.ICGtesting.com
Printed in the USA
LVOW01s0243230716
497463LV00011B/622/P

9 781479 357000